PRAISE FOR *SINS OF THE HIGHLANDER*

"Fast-paced, tense, and full of wicked desire...[this] novel attests to Mason's and Marlowe's skills and ability to collaborate on a taut, intriguing, and satisfying story."

—*Publishers Weekly*

"Another winner! Mason has outdone herself with this page-turning, emotional romance, rich in historical details and plot twists."

—*RT Book Reviews*

"A bewitching highland tale of revenge, betrayal, and romance...a terrific, spellbinding read!"

—*Fresh Fiction*

"A pure pleasure to read...Steamy, sultry."

—*The Romance Studio*

MORE PRAISE FOR CONNIE MASON

"You'll hardly have time to take a breath as you race through this action-packed, delightful tale...everything her fans expect—a rip-roaring adventure with sensual love scenes and three-dimensional characters you care about."

—*RT Book Reviews* on *Love Me with Fury*

"Mason delivers exactly what her fans expect by creating a world filled with adventure, sensuality, history, and characters whose biting verbal repartee keeps her fast-paced plot flying."

—*RT Book Reviews* on *Highland Warrior*

"Connie Mason never disappoints her readers...You'll love the exciting and sizzling adventure."

—*Fresh Fiction* on *Highland Warrior*

"Connie Mason gives us a fast-paced story that delivers exactly what romance readers are looking for—action, villains, and, of course, passion."

—*Joyfully Reviewed* on *Highland Warrior*

"A sizzling Highland romance...Sexy, smart, engaging."

—*The Romance Reviews* on *A Touch So Wicked*

"Filled with all the components of a great romance: likeable characters, an engaging plot, and sizzling passion."

—Examiner.com on *The Dragon Lord*

LORD OF FIRE AND ICE

CONNIE
MASON

WITH MIA MARLOWE

sourcebooks
casablanca

Published by Sourcebooks Casablanca, an imprint of Sourcebooks, Inc.
P.O. Box 4410, Naperville, Illinois 60567-4410
(630) 961-3900
Fax: (630) 961-2168
www.sourcebooks.com

Printed and bound in Canada.
WC 10 9 8 7 6 5 4 3 2 1

We'd like to thank our editor, Leah Hultenschmidt, and our agent, Natasha Kern, for putting us together to work on this collaborative effort. Leah's and Natasha's insight and encouragement have been invaluable.

And special thanks to you, dear reader. We appreciate you and hope you love the world of Lord of Fire and Ice. *Without you and your imagination to bring life to our words, it's just ink on a page. We dedicate this story to you!*

Chapter 1

"SO THAT'S THE GREAT AND MIGHTY BRANDR," a grumbling voice said from somewhere above him. The speaker snorted and loosed a bark of a laugh. "Doesn't look so great now, does he?"

Brandr tried to pry his eyes open, but they were crusted shut. His tongue was too thick for his mouth. Rough hands lifted and then dropped him into the back of a cart. The wood bit into his bare backside as they jostled over a plank road. He was vaguely aware that he was bound, hand and foot.

Odin's Lost Eye, what did they put in that mead?

His lids scraped across his eyeballs like wind-driven sand. Familiar northern stars wheeled overhead, brittle and cold. The stars of the South were hazy and soft, but he'd learned to track them across the sky in the faraway city where he'd served the Byzantine emperor. After a five-year sojourn, he'd been grateful to be nearly home. Brandr and his companions were only two-days' sail from his father's *jarlhof* when they tied up on one of the islands dotting the mouth of Hardanger Fjord. His chest had constricted in aching joy to see the Great Bear lumbering across the sky and the fixed Lodestar as high in the black heavens as it should be.

But Brandr had forgotten that while stars don't change, people do. Obviously, the folk of this island were no longer his father's allies.

A heavy weight pressed against his throat each time he swallowed. A thrall's collar burned shame into his neck. He was a warrior, the son of a respected *jarl* and a fire mage of no little power. The iron at his throat wiped all that away.

Brandr tried to focus his gift and call up enough fire to sizzle off the rope knotted at his wrists, but all he managed to do was singe the hair off the back of his hand. Whatever he'd been drugged with left his mind too disordered to attempt a fire mage's solution.

How could he have been so thick witted? True, that serving girl was fetching, but he should have been more wary. When she poured mead between her breasts and invited him to lick it off, he'd been happy to oblige.

"Let this be a lesson to you, brothers," one of his captors said. "Never follow your cock into more trouble than you can get out of."

Brandr's friend Harald always warned him about the same thing. Now he'd been proven right. Brandr would tell him so, if he ever saw his friend again.

Women were his weakness, and he'd known his share in the South. As a Northman, he towered over the populace of the Byzantine capital. With his fair hair and big-boned frame, Brandr was a novelty. The women of the great city were curious to learn if he was similarly proportioned beneath his scarlet uniform of the Varangian Guard.

None expressed disappointment.

But while the women of the South were inventive in the use of their tongues, none of them could speak his. He'd let his delight in hearing good Norse again lower his caution. When his friends returned to their longship, Brandr had stayed on at the mead house, drinking and dallying with the all-too-willing serving girl.

By the time he realized the euphoria and dizziness he felt wasn't the result of high spirits and mead, he was stumbling and slurring nonsensical words. The drink had been tainted with an opiate, but the realization came too late.

Now he was bare arsed and gagged with a leather strap. His beard and hair had been shorn off like a yearling lamb. If this were a skald's tale, he'd have laughed at his predicament, judging it fair recompense for stupidity.

But this was no tale.

The cart stopped, and his captors lifted him out. They carried him into a longhouse, through the common room where most of the inhabitants snored on broad benches lining the walls. Some had divided the space by hanging skins to enjoy a bit of privacy for their family. Most of the residents simply sprawled in the open, safe in their communal slumber.

The smoky central meal fire had subsided to glowing embers, but as Brandr passed by, the flame flared to life. He mentally ordered it down, but the blaze flickered a cheerful greeting. If he couldn't control his gift well enough to free himself, he couldn't chance letting his captors know he possessed it.

The aroma of a nourishing stew lingered in one of the pots. The smell of even wholesome food made Brandr swallow back rising bile. A burning acidic taste clung to the leather strap in his mouth.

Part of the longhouse had been walled off into a separate chamber with a stout wooden door. One of the men carrying Brandr rapped on it softly.

When there was no response, his captors loosed a collective sigh. The one bearing Brandr's feet dropped them and banged on the door with his fist.

The door flew open.

"What's the matter with you bunch of trolls?" a woman demanded in a hissing whisper. "It's the middle of the night. Some of us plan on working tomorrow. Why aren't you lackwits abed?"

Brandr strained to lift his head enough to snatch a look at the speaker. Backlit by the light of an oil lamp, her dark hair was as sleek as a selkie. She wore it unbound, shimmering over her shoulders and past her hips. She was younger than he expected, given her surly tone, and far more comely. Her cheekbones were high, with soft hollows beneath, a mark of bone-deep loveliness that never fades.

But a pair of frown lines marred her brow. Judging from her scowl, her temper was as black as her hair.

"We've brought you something, Katla." The speaker signaled for the other two to haul Brandr over the threshold and into the lamplit chamber.

One of them was a spotty-faced boy, Brandr realized with annoyance. He'd let himself be taken by a lad with no more than thirteen or fourteen winters to his credit. Once they cleared the doorway, the men dropped him without warning.

Brandr groaned. Instead of packed earth, this woman's chamber had hard slate flooring with no give to it at all.

Like the woman herself, he suspected.

She lifted her lamp and glared down at him. Her eyes slanted up at the corners, catlike. The light was too dim to determine their color as they swept over him in a quick, unflinching assessment.

"What do I want with this, Finn?"

"Consider him a peace offering, sister," Finn said. "It was wrong of us to try to force you into a match. But if you won't accept a husband, you need a strong thrall to do the heavy work for you."

"I keep an ox for the heavy work." Katla flicked a glance at Brandr's genitals.

"Want us to geld him for you?" Finn offered as he pulled out his belt knife. "Should make him more biddable."

Brandr swallowed hard against the gag. Trussed up as he was, he'd be hard pressed to fight off a gelding blade. He glared at the woman, sending her a silent threat. The flame of the oil lamp flared higher. Better she should have them kill him outright than unman him.

"No, don't," she said after a moment's consideration. "It would only make him eat more." Then she waved a dismissive hand. "No, no, he's not staying and neither are the rest of you. Take him away."

"All right, you heard her, brothers," Finn told the

others, who started to heft Brandr up again. "We'll sell him to the next bunch of traders who comes by from Birka then. Katla doesn't want the son of Ulf, after all."

"What?" She stopped Finn with a hand to his forearm.

"You heard me aright," Finn said with a satisfied grin. "This is Brandr Ulfson, back home from the South."

"Stay," she ordered. "I will have him."

A warning bell jangled in Brandr's brain. Most people never had a thrall offered to them freely. If they did, they'd never turn one down, especially one as obviously strong and healthy as he. But this woman hadn't wanted him until she heard his name. Her expression showed a mix of curiosity, grim satisfaction, and...fierce joy.

"*If* I give him to you," Finn said, clearly enjoying the upper hand with his sister, a situation Brandr suspected was as rare as a mild winter, "you must promise to take a husband. There wasn't a thing wrong with any of your last five suitors, and you know it."

"None of them was *my* choice."

"They would have brought wealth and cattle and lands to our family," Finn said. "You're too young not to marry again. You owe it to us, Katla, and you know it. You've got a tidy holding here, more than most widows receive from their husbands."

Brander realized Katla was responsible for this farmstead and all the souls sheltering in her longhouse. No wonder she was so surly. She was a woman alone with the weight of a man's responsibilities on her shoulders. She'd have to be tougher than a man too, in order to earn the same respect. And it didn't appear her brothers were helping her overmuch, except in schemes to line their own pockets. A comely widow like Katla with a prosperous farmstead could mean a windfall to the men in her family.

"But what about us?" Finn went on. "Would you deny your brothers the right to your bride-price? Say you'll accept the man of my choosing, and I'll give you the son of Ulf."

She frowned and worried her lower lip, weighing her options. "I suppose you'll never leave my hearth and make your own way if I don't marry again." She sighed. "Very well. Choose three men, and I'll pick one as a husband. But I won't tolerate a fool."

"Done!" Finn signaled for his brothers to drop Brandr.

He went down hard on the slate again with no way to protect himself. Fortunately, the opiate they'd given him also seemed to dull pain.

"I'll send the first man to you on the morrow," Finn promised.

"There's no rush," she said acerbically. "You get only three chances. Make them count."

Katla's brothers filed out, and she barred the door behind them. Then she walked around Brandr a couple times, giving him a more thorough examination. He followed her with his eyes, noticing that when she passed between him and the lamp, her night shift was thin enough for him to see the shadowy shape of her legs.

When she glanced at his genitals again, he couldn't help his body's response, swelling to his full state.

"Hmpf!"

It was not the reaction he was accustomed to.

Then she picked up a skinning knife from the top of a trunk in the corner. Had the bloodthirsty wench turned down her brother's offer to geld him so she could do it herself?

His erection softened.

"Get your eyes back in your head," she ordered. "You look like a demented owl."

She bent down and cut the leather strap that gagged him near the knot behind his ear. "I'm not going to maim you. Not unless you do something to irritate me."

He spat out the gag, grateful to be rid of its foul taste. "I'm glad to hear it. If you unbind my hands, I can take care of my feet myself."

"I am aware of that," she said dryly. "We have things to discuss first."

He failed to stifle a yawn. "Say what you have to say quickly. Whatever your brothers drugged me with is making me sleepy again."

She sat down on the end of her bed and studied him as if he were a type of fish in her net she couldn't identify. She seemed undecided on whether to keep him or throw him back. "You're taking that iron collar more calmly than one would expect."

"I'm alive...and whole." His head was starting to pound, but his thoughts were flowing clearer now. "A live man's luck can change. A dead one's never."

"My husband is dead." Her eyes narrowed to glittering slits. "Your father killed him."

So that's why she wanted him. Ulf the Ruthless was responsible for his predicament.

"Didn't he offer a *wergild*?" Brandr's father had a

wicked temper, but once the battle lust cleared, he was practical about his debts. He usually paid off those he'd offended in the required amounts to keep matters from escalating into a full-blown feud.

"I wouldn't dishonor my husband's memory by accepting blood money," she said.

"My father generally has a reason when he kills someone. Most of the time. It seems to me, your dispute is with him, not me. He'll not ransom me, if that's your plan. He won't believe I was stupid enough to let myself be enthralled. And if I did, he'll figure I deserve it."

"No, he won't." When she crossed her arms under her breasts, her nipples stood out stiffly beneath the thin linen of her night shift. She didn't seem aware of it.

"Then you don't know my father." Brandr bit the inside of his cheek to keep his body from rousing to her again. "The old bastard was winter hard when I left five years ago. I expect he hasn't thawed a bit."

"Probably not, since he now occupies a place of honor in the ninth circle of *Hel*'s cold hall."

Dead. All the air fled from Brandr's body in a whoosh. Ulf the Ruthless was a bull sea lion of a man. All Brandr's life, his father had ridden him mercilessly, never satisfied, never recognizing that Brandr would have given his left hand to please him just once. Never understood Brandr's strange affinity for the flames. Never trusted the gift of fire and refused to try to understand.

Now he was no more.

Just when Brandr had learned to control his unusual

gift and was bringing his father the most potent weapon the decadent South possessed, the secret of Greek fire.

"Ulf Skallagrimsson's ship was lost with all hands in a storm off the Orkney Islands last season." She cocked her head and eyed him as a robin eyes the worm she intends for breakfast. "So, you really didn't know your father is dead?"

He set his face into a grim mask. She certainly didn't deserve a peek into the maelstrom of his emotions about his father's death, especially since he didn't know how to name them yet himself.

"You won't have any better luck ransoming me with my brother. Our father taught us not to be burdened overmuch with family feelings."

She shrugged. "I hadn't thought of trying to get Arn the Leper to pay a ransom for you, but when I tire of you, it's a consideration."

"Arn the—"

"*Ja*, strange world, is it not? You sojourn all the way to Miklagaard and come back"—her gaze traveled over his length again—"perfectly healthy and sound. And your older brother stays home and is struck by a wasting sickness."

Brandr let this new horrific truth settle into his brain. The great city of the South sent its lepers away to eke out a living on scraps and thievery. In the North, while no one wanted to share a trencher with a leper, if a man had high enough rank to begin with, he'd not be outlawed for being unlucky. Brandr's brother, Arn, would still be *jarl* in Jondal as long as he was able to wield a sword.

Brandr would be expected to step in when Arn could no longer lead.

But not if he was a slave. Without a clear transfer of leadership, there'd be a scramble for power and a fight among the chieftains to determine who would succeed Arn. Brandr frowned, wondering how to avoid that disaster. When headmen fought, fields went unplanted, and the people of Jondal would suffer the next winter.

"Feeling for your brother, are you? Don't. A thrall is poor enough not to be able to afford pity for anyone." Katla leaned toward him. "I assume *my* brothers already took whatever wealth you brought back from the South."

Brandr snorted. He'd worn a gold chain about his neck, and a small pouch of silver weighed down one side of his belt. But the big chest of coin still rested in safety on the longship. That was to be divided evenly among him and his traveling companions.

Six were returning home to Jondal. Nine of them had started out for the great southern city, but one took a knife blade to the gut in a brawl the night after they set out. The wound went bad before they'd even cleared the wide mouth of Hardanger Fjord. Another was lost during a storm near Gibraltar. A third fell fighting the Saracens in the service of the Byzantine emperor. On an honorable field of battle, his flesh gave food to the eagles.

But Brandr and the other returning men from Jondal accomplished what they'd set out to do. Brandr had found a sorcerer in the South who schooled him in how to use his ability to call up flame, though he still hid his gift from all but his closest friends.

People feared those who were different, and inspiring fear wasn't Brandr's aim.

He and his friends had lived a praiseworthy adventure and returned North with enough silver to set up each of them in comfort for several lifetimes. Brandr's companions counted themselves lucky to come home without losing more of their number.

But they weren't home yet, and with Brandr enthralled, now they were only five. Even if his friends were able to track him from the mead house, they were too few to overpower the Tysnes islanders and free him without a bloody brawl. "*Ja*, your thieving brothers took everything of value," Brandr said. They couldn't take the wealth he carried in his head. If they had an inkling he bore the secret to Greek fire, they'd be trying to torture it out of him still. "You get only me in this bad bargain. What are your intentions?"

࿔

Katla wished he wouldn't keep turning those deep amber eyes on her. They made it hard for her to think.

"I'm not sure what you're fit for," she said, willing herself not betray how the sight of his hard body affected her. The son of Ulf had the frame of a warrior, honed to lean fitness. His muscles stood out beneath smooth skin marred by only a few battle scars.

Katla didn't mind not having a husband countermand her decisions, but she sorely missed the feel of a man between her legs. Brandr Ulfson made her remember that longing in exquisite detail.

She set her mouth in a tight line. It was a man's world. A woman had to be strong when dealing with one, even one wearing an iron collar, lest he run rough-shod over her. "Have you any skills besides wenching and drinking?"

"I'm a fighter by trade." His mouth turned up in a lazy, sensual smile. "Obviously, drinking isn't one of my strengths. At least, not when someone taints the mead. But don't discount wenching. I know how to please a woman. My bed skills are yours for the asking."

Her eyes flared with irritation that he'd divined the direction of her thoughts. Men took bed slaves all the time.

Why shouldn't a widow enjoy one, so long as she kept herself from bearing?

It wouldn't be a problem in her case. Katla suspected she was barren. Her husband Osvald's bastards littered several hearths, but she never showed signs of quickening during their year together.

She gave herself a slight shake. This new thrall was nothing but the son of her husband's murderer. She had to keep thinking of him as such. She'd sworn to avenge Osvald, and this was her first chance to make good on her vow.

"Keep your lewd suggestions to yourself."

Brandr Ulfson eyed her with boldness, so she felt obliged to return the favor. By shearing Brandr's locks, her brothers had accentuated his strong, even features. A man had to be breathtakingly handsome to still be so appealing after he'd endured the shame of being shorn.

She knelt beside him and ran her palm over his head, down his neck, and around his firm jawline.

"Since Ulf is already dead, I can't deliver justice to your father. Hiring someone to kill a leper might be considered an act of kindness, not retribution, so I've made no move against your brother," she said, jerking her hand away from his smooth cheek. She needed to keep her distance. "That leaves only you."

She wouldn't kill him. It wasn't as if he'd had a choice in who his father was, but short of visiting physical harm on the son of Ulf, she could still have justice of a sort. She'd humble him so abjectly his name would become a byword throughout the North, a warning to all men who fell into the hands of a vengeful woman.

But Brandr Ulfson wasn't an easy man to feel hard toward. There was a feral quality to his maleness that made her insides go soft, vulnerable. When he turned his penetrating gaze on her, she felt weak as water.

She straightened her spine.

"Letting you demonstrate your bed skills doesn't sound like revenge," she said. "It sounds like you're trying to trick me into pleasuring a thrall."

"If we shared a bed, it would be about *your* pleasure." His amber eyes darkened to sable. "Not mine."

"So bedding me wouldn't please you?"

"I didn't say that. I'm sure it would please me. Very much. But my aim would be your delight."

Her breath caught, and she couldn't move. He gave her a thorough look, starting with her mouth, lingering at her breasts, which tingled under his direct gaze, and traveling down her loins and limbs.

"You're a beautiful woman, Katla. And you've missed a man's touch."

"I haven't missed yours. And you will address me as 'mistress' or 'my lady.' You may not use my name, thrall."

She turned and rummaged through her clothes trunk for the oldest, most coarse tunic she could find. She hoped it would be big enough to fit him, but for now, she'd be satisfied with draping the undyed fabric across his groin.

"Varangians are supposed to value honor above all," she said. "Before I loose your bonds, will you swear upon your honor to obey me and not to run away?"

"I won't run. Your brothers took me by guile and womanish potions, but they took me. As long as your commands do not conflict with my honor, I so swear to obey you," he said. "May Thor strike me blind if I do not."

"If the god doesn't, I will," she promised as she cut the bindings on his wrists.

He worked the knot at his ankles as soon as his hands were free. Then he stood to pull the rough tunic over his head.

Upright, Brandr was even bigger than he appeared when lying on the floor. She took a step back from him. The tunic was snug across his broad chest and struck him mid-thigh, leaving his well-muscled legs exposed. At least his disturbing maleness was covered.

"Now what, princess?" He managed to make the title he gifted her with sound like a curse.

She had to show this man his place and quickly. "I saved you from the gelding knife this night. You will show your appreciation by kissing my foot."

She lifted her night shift to ankle height and presented one to him, toes pointed.

That should wipe the smug expression from his face.

He shrugged, bent over, and grabbed her ankle.

Then he yanked her upside down. Her bottom took a glancing blow on the floor before she found herself hanging precariously, her foot level with his mouth when he stood back upright.

It happened so quickly, surprise forced all the air from Katla's lungs. Her night shift billowed down to bunch at her armpits, exposing her to him. When she tried to kick free, he grasped her other ankle as well. Her fingertips splayed on the slate floor to steady herself.

She clamped her lips shut to keep from crying out. There were a dozen strong men snoring on the other side of the door. They'd all rush to her aid, but she'd die before she let anyone catch her in this undignified position.

He planted a wet kiss on her instep then lowered her to the floor. She managed not to land on her head, but her right shoulder took most of her weight before she rolled to lie flat on her back on the cold slate.

He glared down at her and bared his teeth in a wolf's smile. "Want me to kiss anything else, princess?"

Chapter 2

BRANDR EXTENDED A HAND TO HELP HER OFF THE FLOOR, but she pushed herself up and scrambled to her feet, keeping well out of his long reach. She gave him a scathing look. "That was not what I meant, and you know it."

He folded his arms across his chest. "Perhaps you'll be more specific in your instructions next time, princess."

Irritation fizzed up her spine. "Stop calling me that."

"You don't like 'princess'? Not high enough rank, I suppose. Perhaps you'd rather I call you 'empress.'" He gave her a mocking bow. "Thor be my witness, you don't lack the self-importance of one."

She narrowed her eyes at him. "I can have you whipped, you know."

He matched her glare for glare. "I'd like to see you try. If you wanted to do me harm, you should have done it when I was bound and helpless."

Katla snatched up the leather straps that had restrained him. "Then stand still while I tie your hands again."

"No."

"I gave you an order," she hissed. "And you swore to obey. Are you an oath breaker?"

Brandr shook his head. "I am not. I swore to obey so long as your commands don't conflict with my honor. I wouldn't suffer you to whip a dog. I won't allow you, or your gaggle of brothers, to beat me without a fight."

"So you're my thrall, but only when it suits you?" Katla wished for the thousandth time she'd been born a man. If she had a man's strength to match her will, she'd knock this Brandr Ulfson into his place so fast his teeth would rattle.

He yawned hugely. "If it's all the same to you, princess, could we continue this argument tomorrow? I need to sleep."

He started toward her bed.

"Oh, no, you don't," she said. "You will not sleep in my bed."

Brandr turned to her wearily. "Then where do you want me, O Great One?"

"Not there." She opened another trunk and pulled out a wolf skin and woolen blanket for him. "I want you on a pallet by the door."

One corner of his mouth turned up. "I knew you'd admit it sooner or later."

"Admit what?"

"You want me."

"Go to sleep, son of Ulf." Katla threw the pelt and blanket at him.

"Willingly." He'd spread the wolf skin and was already lying prone across the threshold before she climbed into her bed. "I live to serve, O Northern Moon of Beauty."

"Moon of Beauty?" She wouldn't have thought him much of a poet, but his words pleased her more than she wanted to admit. Her husband's tongue hadn't exactly dripped silver. "Why do you call me that?"

His eyes drifted closed. "In the South, servants habitually praise their masters with exalted titles. Of course, usually it's a backhanded swipe. A weakling will be named a 'Tower of Strength.' A portly matron will hear herself called 'Delicate Flower of Delights,' like as not. They don't seem to be clever enough to realize their servants are insulting them with ill-fitting praise names."

"So when you name me a moon of beauty, you're really saying—"

"Good night, Katla."

The infuriating man was asleep between one breath and the next. Her lamp guttered and went dark, as though an unseen hand had snuffed it out.

❧

The cock crowed from the peak of the longhouse directly over her bed. His raucous screech cut through the overhead thatch and jerked Katla awake. Pearly light filtered through the open smoke hole, dust motes swirling in the unseen currents.

And unseen beneath her bedclothes, her night shift was rucked up to her waist. She still throbbed with unrelieved passion and more than a little embarrassment. If she slipped a hand between her legs, she knew she'd find herself damp.

Katla had been dreaming of the son of Ulf and what might happen if she gave him a chance to prove his boast about his bed skills. Though her dream was rousing, it was far from satisfying. Given a little more time, her body might have reached a peak in her sleep, but she was frustrated that the act in her dream was so one-sided. It was as if Brandr were performing a menial task, not making love with her.

All her life, Katla had wished for *inn matki munr*, the mighty passion. More intense than any other emotion, deeper than the North Sea, stronger even than death, it was said that those who find it were bound so tightly, they even share the same thoughts.

Early in her marriage to Osvald, he'd shown her bed sport that made her skin riot in pleasure. But after the month of their honeymoon, Osvald hadn't spent much time on love play. His main goal was an heir. In truth, there were times when Katla felt more like a sexual receptacle than his wife.

Perhaps if Osvald had lived longer, or if she'd been able to conceive, they'd have discovered *inn matki munr*, but now she had little hope she'd experience the bonding that knit two souls together.

Clearly, taking a bed slave was not the path to the mighty passion. It wasn't even as good a choice as taking a lover, if her disappointing dream held any truth.

Katla gave herself a mental shake. Plenty of people lived full, productive lives without knowing that deep blending of spirits. She had too much to do and too many depending upon her to waste time mourning over what she didn't have.

And probably would never have.

She decided to ignore the hollow ache in her chest. It was a selfish wish anyway. Wanting to be loved would not feed her people. It wouldn't see them warm come winter.

Or fill the empty cradle in the corner.

She swiped away the weak tears that trembled on her lids, sat up, and peered over the end of her bed. Brandr Ulfson was still asleep on his pallet. If she was quick and quiet, she could dress for her busy day before he woke. She stole out of bed and opened her cedar-lined trunk.

∾

Brandr had always been a light sleeper. During his service in Byzantium, he further honed his ability to be instantly awake at the first audible change in his surroundings. It was a matter of survival. The skill was the difference between avoiding an assassin's blade or waking up in *Hel*.

So when the trunk lid creaked, he was aware Katla was up, but he didn't betray himself by opening his eyes. Instead he peered from under his lashes to take stock of his situation.

She was laying out her dress and tunic for the day. She bent over and, in one smooth motion, pulled her night shift over her head, baring her body completely.

The women of the South had come in a myriad of hues—dusky olive, warm cinnamon, black as jet, and milky white. The wellborn ones even used a concoction of alum to further lighten their skin and make it shine brightly. Regardless of color, they were all exotically lovely.

But none could match the glowing alabaster of Katla's skin for pure radiance. And without a single dollop of cosmetic enhancement.

Last night, he'd caught a glimpse of her delectable

curves when he held her upside down. That had been a fair treat. But right side up, she was magnificent. Her breasts were high and full. Her waist was pleasingly narrow compared to her hips. And her heart-shaped bottom was perfection.

Since Katla's hair was so dark, he guessed her mother must have been a Gaul. Northmen had been bringing dark-haired women back from the coasts of Europe for several generations. Brandr's father always said the women should be glad to come, since the men in their lands obviously weren't strong enough to protect them.

What a man has, he must hold. He must defend what's his; else he deserves to lose it.

Katla the Black. He wondered if anyone else had named her thus. It suited her. Surly and strong-minded, she was a veritable warrior and deserved a name fitting for one. She had no man to defend her, but the vixen didn't seem to need one.

Her breasts fell forward as she leaned down to pick up her linen underdress. Brandr ached to hold them, imagining those firm yet soft globes in his palms. He throbbed with need.

She slipped her dress over her head and down to cover herself, ending his torment. When he saw the ornate silver brooches she used to fasten the tabs of her tunic, he revised his estimate of her status upward. She obviously controlled the bulk of the wealth in her family, since her brothers didn't sport so much as a copper arm band between them. Her dead husband must have been a man of means.

Once she sat at the end of her bed to pull on her

stockings, Brandr felt it was safe for him to stir. So long as she didn't realize he watched, this morning's entertainment might become a regular occurrence.

"Oh! You're up." She eyed the bulge at his groin with suspicion. "How long have you been awake?"

Long enough. He yawned and stretched, then followed her gaze to where his cock tented the coarse tunic. He shrugged. "You've been a married woman. Surely you know men often wake in a happy mood."

"You're a thrall. You've no cause to be happy."

So you think. He smothered a grin behind his hand. "You're a free woman. You've no cause to be miserable."

She slipped the silver chain that bore the keys to all the locks in her household around her neck. "Who says I'm miserable?"

"The frown line between your brows."

She put a hand to the spot and tried to smooth the furrow out.

"That'll work only for so long, and then that line will become permanent," he predicted. "A person is as happy or unhappy as they decide to be."

"I'll be happy when you give me a fair day's work."

He rose and crossed over to her. "Let me start by giving you a reason to not to scowl so."

"What do you think you're doing?" she said when he closed the distance between them.

"Rest easy, princess. I mean you no harm." He touched her cheek, moving slowly, as if she were a spooked mare he was trying to gentle. "I want only to see if I can make you smile."

"This does not…" Her words trailed off as he glided a thumb over her bottom lip. Her eyes flared wide, but she didn't move away.

When she tipped her chin up, he detected a slight tremor of need in her. It called to him. He'd started this little gambit only to see if she'd allow him to kiss her. Now he ached to.

Before she could protest, he put his arms around her and claimed her mouth. She struggled a bit. He'd have been surprised if she hadn't, but she was so tiny it was no trouble to hold her still while he slanted his lips over hers. And she'd thank him later with a smile, he was sure.

Women of the South bathed in scent till their fragrance was overpowering. Katla smelled of clean wool and cedar shavings and warm woman. An earthy scent. The scent of home.

He dragged in a sweet lungful of her.

Then, as he'd hoped, he felt her unstiffen in his arms. Her lips parted softly, and his tongue swept in to explore the sweetness of her mouth. She began to kiss him back, nipping and playing with his tongue.

He moved a hand up from her waist to cup her breast.

She moaned softly, and he loosed his grip to allow more space between them. He wanted free rein to explore her body through the layers of her clothing. If he reached under her hem, he'd lay odds she'd be wet and welcoming.

For all her harsh words, Katla was ripe for the taking.

She rested her hands lightly on his shoulders, and then with no warning at all, she brought her knee up hard and sudden to his groin. He'd been a captain in the greatest corps of fighting men on earth, but he hadn't seen that ambush coming.

"Odin!" He released her and doubled over, fighting nausea while he cupped his throbbing balls. "Why in *Hel* did you do that?"

"Because it was the best way to get your attention. Fetch me some water, thrall." With a mocking smile, she dropped an empty bucket in front of him. Not at all the smile he was hoping to see.

"You had my attention." He forced himself upright to face her. "And you were enjoying that kiss as much as I."

"No, I wasn't."

Her lips might deny it, but her cheeks flamed, and her nipples stood out beneath her clothing. She trembled, either with rage or need. He couldn't be sure which.

"If you kiss me again without my permission, I'll reconsider my decision and let my brothers geld you."

"No, you won't, princess," he said as he stooped to pick up the bucket.

She glared at him. "A man's seed bag makes a fine coin purse, I'm told."

He laughed. She was bluffing. He hoped she was bluffing.

"I won't kiss you again without your permission," he said gruffly. "In fact, if you want me to kiss you, you'll have to order me to do it."

"Don't hold your breath," she muttered. "I'll never give that order."

He grasped her chin and forced her to look up at him. "*Ja*, you will. You need a man. You'll order me

to your bed before you and I part company, princess.
And we both know it."

Bucket in hand, he turned and strode from the
room without a backward glance.

Chapter 3

WHEN BRANDR BROUGHT BACK THE BUCKET OF WATER, Katla was seated near the meal fire, with a gaggle of children surrounding her. Heads bent, tongues clamped between their teeth in concentration, they were learning to sew straight, even stitches in pieces of worn fabric. Boys as well as girls huddled close as Katla gave them soft instructions.

"Of course, you must learn to sew, Darri," she said to one of the boys who'd protested that this was women's work. "A man must know how to mend sail on the open sea. On land, he must care for his own clothing if he doesn't have a wife to tend to it for him."

She bent and pressed a quick kiss on the boy's crown. "And if you make a habit of complaining, young man, you'll never have a wife."

The little girls giggled.

Brandr halted at the entrance to the longhouse, watching the woman who'd enslaved him. Surely this Katla wasn't the same one who'd ordered him to kiss her foot, the hard taskmistress who was set on humbling him.

She treated the children with gentleness, with doting fondness.

She smiled at the little girl by her side and gave her a quick hug along with a word of praise. When the boy called Darri lifted his swatch to show her, Katla's green eyes glinted with pride in his accomplishments.

"Excellent work," she told the child. "Stitches like that will stand up to a gale."

When the boy settled back, beaming under her praise, Brandr saw an expression pass over Katla face that surprised him to his toes. Her smile softened, became wistful and sad.

And yearning.

None of the children gathered around her was her own. He'd fallen into conversation with one of the men who worked in the tanning sheds near the mouth of the river that emptied into a sheltered cove. The man was ready to tell all he knew about Brandr's new owner.

"Katla's a fair mistress," the tanner had told him. "It was a kiss of luck that she was here to pick up the reins when her husband was killed. She's deep minded, that one. Better at managing things than Osvald ever was—meaning no disrespect to the dead."

The tanner cast a superstitious glance over his shoulder, but it didn't stop his blather. Brandr needed only to nod and look interested while his new acquaintance regaled him with the doings of the farmstead and the many folk who lived there and worked it.

No, there'd been no children in Katla's brief marriage, more's the pity, the tanner had said. But weren't her brothers trying to match her up with a new husband? The lady was young. There was still time.

Judging from Katla's expression of longing, she wasn't the sort to wait patiently. Brandr had heard that some women crave children as a man craves silver, but he'd never seen that hunger so clearly etched on a woman's face before.

Then he stepped into the longhouse, and his shadow falling over her made her lift her head. The soft, needy expression vanished in a blink.

"Help yourself to a bowl of porridge, thrall," she ordered and then turned back to the children, ignoring him completely.

The boiled oats were pasty and palatable only if laced with honey, but it would keep his stomach from knocking on his backbone. His mind was clear enough this morning to keep the flames of the fire from leaping up in greeting as he drew near.

"Son of Ulf," she said the moment he scraped the last bit of porridge from his bowl. Evidently, she was more aware of him than she seemed. "There are three dyeing vats in the side yard. Fill them with water."

"As you will, princess," he mumbled and rose to do her bidding. One bucket at a time, filling the vats would take most of the morning, but he supposed that was Katla's plan. Usually hauling water was considered women's work. She meant to humble him with the task, so he whistled a drinking song through his teeth each time he passed her. If he refused to let her see she could humiliate him, perhaps she'd tire of the game.

At midmorning, he noticed a group of men approaching the longhouse, making their way up the winding path from the wharf far below. Katla's land rose steeply from that sheltered cove. She possessed a private deep-water port in addition to being connected to the rest of the island with the serviceable plank road he'd been carted over last night. The plank road made cart travel possible over the spongy turf of the lowlands. The rest of her holding was a mix of small, arable fields, verdant meadows sloping on the island's soaring hills, and heavy timber.

Brandr heard the men's voices as they followed the switchbacks up the steep grade, but echoes off the hills and trees obscured their words. His hopes rose when the party of men drew near enough for him to recognize them as his traveling companions.

Harald was in the lead, a redheaded giant of a man. He was followed by Ragnar, a lanky fellow who was as quick with a joke as with a blade, and Orlin, the best tracker of the lot. Brandr often accused him of being part boarhound. The twins, Torvald and Torsten, brought up the rear, squabbling with each other as usual, as if they were lads of twelve instead of seasoned warriors with thirty winters to their credit. They strode past Brandr without a glance.

He realized with a start they hadn't recognized him with his beard and hair shaved off. Or perhaps the iron collar blinded them. No one looked twice at a thrall.

"Ho! The house," Harald boomed.

Katla appeared at the open doorway, seemingly unruffled by the intrusion. "Who seeks hospitality at the hearth of Katla Egilsdottir?"

No one would mistake this band of men for casual travelers. Everything about them bespoke "warrior." Brandr marveled at Katla's calm greeting. From the corner of his eye, he saw several of the men of the farmstead stop work and form up in a protective circle beyond earshot. Armed with pitchforks and spades, they'd be no match for Brandr's friends, but the loyalty Katla inspired in her people impressed him.

Her youngest brother, the one called Haukon, took a step toward Katla. She stopped him with a darting glance and a slightly raised palm. The youth scowled but stayed where he was.

Brandr's respect for Katla's grasp of the situation ticked up. She wouldn't allow her brother to start something he couldn't finish.

Harald introduced himself and the others. "We seek neither board nor bed. We were told we'd find our friend Brandr Ulfson among your household."

"There is no one here by that name." She snapped her fingers and motioned for Brandr to join them. "There is only my new thrall."

Surprise widened his friends' eyes when they recognized Brandr. Harald's cheeks went a florid red in sympathetic embarrassment for him.

"We'll buy him from you," Harald said. "Name your price."

"The son of Ulf is not for sale."

Harald offered a ridiculously high sum, trying to tempt her to change her mind, but Katla was adamant. Brandr was her property, and she would not release him. Not for all the silver in Byzantium.

"All right, woman! Keep him," Harald finally said in frustration. "But we've traveled to the earth's end with this man. Surely you will permit us a good-bye. Give us a moment with our friend."

"Very well, but be brief. He has much work to do

this day." With a swirl of her dress and tunic, Katla withdrew into the longhouse.

Once she was out of earshot, Ragnar shook his head and spat on the ground. "A demon in a dress, that one. Tell me what you did to deserve this, friend, so I can be sure to avoid it!"

"I followed my cock into trouble, as usual," Brandr admitted.

"By Thunder, she must be a handful in bed," Ragnar said with a laugh.

Brandr shook his head. "That's not what I meant. We're not...I mean we haven't—"

"Whether you bedded the woman isn't the issue. The trouble is that iron collar. Look around, men. Not a sword in sight," Harald whispered lest someone overhear him. "We can fight our way clear of here with Brandr in tow."

"No," Brandr said. "We've fought Saracens and Bulgars together, brothers. Noble enemies. Men whose valor we honored even as they died under our blades. There's nothing praiseworthy in slaughtering farmers and herdsmen."

"Then do that thing you...use your Gift." Harald's halting speech showed how uncomfortable he was speaking of Brandr's unusual ability. It smacked of magick, and men mistrusted those who trafficked in such things. "Set the thatch on the longhouse ablaze, and we'll escape in the confusion."

"No. There are children inside. Besides, Hardanger is our fjord. These are our people," Brandr said firmly. "I won't buy my freedom with their blood."

"Fair words." Orlin studied him for a moment

as intently as if Brandr were a broken twig or hoof mark or a steaming pile of fewmets, reading him for veracity. Then Orlin nudged Harald. "I'm thinking Ragnar was nearer the mark. My silver's on the demon in a dress. This Katla Egilsdottir has sunk her talons in him deep."

"You may be right." Harald folded his arms over his chest and looked down his long, straight nose at Brandr. "Your owner is far more comely than a woman with that much stubbornness has a right to be."

Brandr grinned at the memory of watching her wiggle out of her night shift that morning. "You don't know the half of it." His grin faded. "But that's not it. I gave my word not to run."

Harald shook his head in disgust, aware that Brandr's oath ended the discussion. "What shall we tell your father?"

"Nothing. He's dead." Even as he said them, the words sounded unreal to his ear. "My brother is *jarl* in Jondal now, and he'll need all your swords."

His friends scoffed.

"When did Arn ever want anything to do with us?" One of the twins demanded.

"Never, but he needs you now. He's…a leper. The chieftains will test his leadership."

Harald put a hand on Brandr's shoulder. "We'll hold Jondal then."

"I'd be grateful." Brandr covered Harald's hand with his in a quick clasp. These five men had each been more a brother to him than Arn had ever thought about being. "And so will Arn."

"No, he won't. It's not in him to be grateful,"

Harald said. "We'll try to hold Jondal for you, my friend, but you know as well as I that an iron crown won't wait. Plenty will rise to try to wrest it from Arn. We need you there to take it in peace. Get clear of this mess as quick as you can. What's your plan? I know you must have one."

Harald was always ready to pull out his ax, but Brandr was the strategist of the group. A well-executed plan often trumped superior numbers and strength.

"I don't know yet," Brandr admitted. "But I'll come up with something."

"I hope so," Harald said as they turned to go.

Brandr watched them till they disappeared around a bend in the path. "So do I, my friends. So do I."

～∽

Katla stretched and dug her fists into the small of her back, trying to work out the knots. The day's work had progressed nicely, even though the memory of Brandr Ulfson's kiss still made her lips tingle. She tried to banish thoughts of him as she walked past the barn where cows lowed, impatient for their evening milking. The ram's bell tinkled in the distance. Shepherds drove her flocks down from the upper pasture to the safety of the fold for the night. Between her herds of cattle, sheep, and goats, Katla owned more hooves than any other farmer on Tysnes Island.

She smiled as she surveyed the busy farmstead. She was happy. Certainly she was. Why had Brandr thought she was not?

Osvald's holding had been impressive when she first married him, but after his death, the farmstead prospered even more. She no longer had to answer to her husband for her decisions. Or have them overridden by him.

Whole families of women worked the big looms in her longhouse, producing linen and wool cloth for trade, while their men tilled the patchwork fields and tended stock. All told, thirty souls depended on Katla for each bite of food in their mouths and each coin in their belt pouches, including her three shiftless brothers. That would change if her prospective bridegroom could afford to set them up on their own farmsteads as Finn hoped.

Brandr Ulfson stomped past her with another armful of wood for the growing pile.

Make that thirty-one souls in her care.

She tamped down the flutter in her belly at the sight of him. The man was her thrall. It wouldn't do to start imagining the yearning hollowness in her chest had anything to do with Brandr Ulfson.

She'd experienced a moment of concern that morning when his friends turned up. She half expected the son of her enemy to take to his heels with his companions. They all had the battle-hardened look of warriors. If they were determined to take him, she'd have been powerless to stop them. But hidden in the shadows of the longhouse door, she watched as the men from Jondal left without Brandr.

He'd kept his vow not to run away. Brandr's worth rose several notches in her evaluation.

"Katla!" Waving one long arm, Finn loped up the hill from the wharf toward her.

"I see you managed to find your way home now

that night meal's not far off," she said, settling her arms across her chest. She wished her brothers would grow up. It wearied her to have to scold them as if she were their mother.

Finn shoved his sandy hair out of his face and eyed her up and down with a frown. "What are you doing? Your suitor's ship has docked. He's on his way to the longhouse, and here you are looking like a common drudge."

"Freya's cats!" Katla had forgotten they'd be bringing around a new suitor today.

She tucked an errant strand of hair back under her headdress. The linen kerchief that covered her braids had been starched and bright white when she donned it that morning, but it was probably limp and gray now.

"You promised, sister," Finn said. "I've lived up to my end of the bargain and brought you a man to consider, but you're not even trying."

"Well, if the man you're bringing doesn't like my looks," she said, "he'll have to look the other way."

"Don't fret. I expect he'll be too taken with this place to notice you overmuch, in any case."

Katla flinched. It was one thing to agree to a loveless match. It was another to be considered of no import whatsoever in the making of it. Was she really nothing more than the lands and stock she possessed?

The thwack of an ax splitting wood echoed off the stone barn. Finn glared in the direction of Brandr and the chopping block. He snorted.

"I'll bet the son of Ulf isn't taking much to that iron collar."

"No, but at least he isn't afraid of hard labor." Katla slanted her gaze at Finn. "Unlike some."

Since Brandr was a *jarl*'s son, Katla expected him to be demeaned by the tasks she assigned him. The gods knew her brothers couldn't be bothered to work, and they were only the sons of a *karl*, a simple landed farmer. But Brandr tackled each chore without complaint.

She was still amazed that he'd kept his word not to run away. It would have been a simple matter to escape with his friends that morning if his oath meant nothing to him. There was more character there than she'd suspected.

Against her better judgment, she watched his easy stride as he walked back across the barnyard. His bare arms rippled with strength, and that snug tunic showed far too much of his muscular thighs. Several women churning butter by the open barn door turned their heads to follow his progress. When he bent to stack the wood, his tunic rode up so high, the women were nearly treated to the sight of his bare buttocks.

"Better find a longer tunic for the man, or you'll get no work done from your women," Finn observed.

Katla couldn't blame them. Brandr Ulfson was extremely well made. She had to keep reminding herself he was son of her husband's murderer. Yet even knowing who he was, he was not an easy man to resist. Would it be so terrible if she stopped trying?

"Katla, the man's almost here."

Finn's voice pulled her out of her indecent thoughts. She turned to see her other brothers, Einar and Haukon, flanking a third man and coming up the hill toward her. Katla gave herself a silent scolding. It wouldn't do to be musing about her attraction to a thrall when she was about to meet the man she might marry.

"Who is he?" she asked Finn as the party approached.

"Albrikt Gormson. He owns a tidy property, three times the size of your farmstead, on the northwest corner of Stord Island," Finn said.

"Stord? That's a good day's sail, two if you meet rough seas. You must have made these arrangements before you brought me the son of Ulf. When did you intend to tell me you'd already set up another match?"

"At the last possible moment," Finn admitted.

Katla gave him a sisterly swat on the shoulder. If Finn would only show as much initiative in other things. "He hasn't another wife, has he? I'll be no man's second."

It wasn't unusual for a man to keep a concubine handy. Her husband, Osvald, had one, but he never turned to her unless Katla had been unable to welcome him. A few foolhardy men actually had more than one wife under the beam of their longhouses. While Katla had tolerated sharing her man with another woman on occasion, she'd never resign herself to sharing the running of a household.

"No, Albrikt has no wife. He's widowed."

"Any children?"

"A son, but he's gone to Iceland to manage Gormson's land there."

Katla nodded her approval. If the man had other land for his existing heirs, it would make it easier for her children to inherit this farm.

If she was blessed with children. She couldn't give up hope.

"If Gormson has come this far, you must have done some preliminary negotiating." When Katla married Osvald, he set up Finn and Einar on small farmsteads. Unfortunately, her brothers were indifferent farmers and ran their places into the ground with overgrazing and mismanagement. In the end, their holdings had been sold to pay their bills at the mead house. She hoped they'd do better next time. "What has he offered you?"

"Gormson will deed his property on Stord over to us in exchange for control of your land."

"And why is he willing to trade a larger holding for a smaller one?" Katla arched an eyebrow at her brother. She didn't like the idea of giving someone else control of her land. What would happen to the people who depended on her? "Does his steading have a source of fresh water? Timber? Stord is mountainous. Mayhap the land is all vertical."

Finn shrugged after each question.

"Have you even seen Gormson's land?"

"Well, no, but if the holding's that big, it should divide well three ways."

"*Hel*'s chambers are said to be spacious, but no one wishes to bide in that cold hall, do they?" Katla said waspishly. "Honestly, Finn, your head is supposed to be good for more than keeping your ears apart."

"You underestimate me, sister. This time, we'll get some ready coin from the arrangement too." Finn straightened to his full lanky height and gave her a withering glance. "But we're not likely to if he sees you like this. Go clean up. The bath house is already hot. I can smell the smoke from here. We'll give Gormson a long look around the place, and you can meet him at night meal, *ja*?"

A lovely hot bath sounded too delicious to pass up.

"All right." She snapped her fingers, and Brandr turned to look at her. "Son of Ulf, haul up a fresh barrel of water for the cooling room in the bath house."

"Oh, good. More water to haul. I live to serve, O Merciful and Clean One," he answered with a smirk and went to do her bidding.

"Insolent dog. I'd beat him if he were my thrall," Finn said. "Want me to do it for you?"

Katla lifted her skirt and started toward the already steamy bath. "I think he'd like you to try."

Chapter 4

HER HUSBAND HAD ALWAYS ARGUED MAINTAINING A bath for their people was an extravagance. It burned too much wood. It encouraged folk to rush through their labor so they could lounge in the communal bath. Osvald had it on good authority that steam weakened the structure of a bath house so much, it would have to be rebuilt every twelve years or so.

But Osvald no longer had a say in the matter, and if the bath house had to be rebuilt, Katla was sure her people would pitch in joyfully. Nothing soothed work-sore muscles, kept folk healthier or smelling sweeter than a regular bath. The bath house was a place to relax, to share a little gossip, to enjoy a respite from labor before the coming night meal.

Even though it was shared by both sexes, Katla allowed no dalliances or lewdness on the stair-stepped seating in the bath. Of course, if couples sized each other up there and then met elsewhere later, that was their own business, but the bath itself was almost as holy as the oak grove at Uppsala.

As they had since Osvald's death, when Katla

entered the bath, the other bathers found reason to
leave. She asked Gerte, one of the older women, to
bring up a fresh change of clothing for her and leave it
in the cooling room.

Gerte had told her once that vacating the bath for
the lady of the steading was a mark of respect. She
ought to be able to enjoy her bath in privacy.

It was good to be respected, but sometimes Katla
wished for a little time to talk with others without
having them behave as if she would turn them out
if they failed to please her all the time. It was Osvald
who banished those who didn't suit him.

Katla never did. Not even her three slug-a-bed
brothers. She didn't know why her people seemed to
fear her. She never worked anyone harder than she
worked herself.

Well, maybe Brandr Ulfson, she admitted as she
stripped off the last of her grimy work clothes and
folded them in a neat pile. *But the son of Ulf should
expect to work harder than others. He deserves it.*

She lifted a towel from the stack of clean ones and
spread it on the empty bench before she sat. Even with
the cloth, the hot seat warmed her bottom. Heat seared
her nostrils. The green scent of birch leaves lingered in
the air. A couple of bundles of switches were soaking
in a small barrel of scented water for later use.

Katla leaned back and closed her eyes, letting the
extreme heat loosen all her clenched muscles. Beads
of sweat formed on her forehead and upper lip. She
swiped them away.

The door to the cooling room creaked open. Someone
must have decided to come back for more heat.

The temperature ticked upward, and the sound of water sizzling on hot stones made her open her eyes. Steam engulfed a lone figure and released a fresh burst of fragrant birch. He poured a little more water on the rocks and then turned to face her.

It was Brandr.

"What are you doing here?" She resisted covering her breasts. Doing so would be an admission of her nakedness. It was no shame to be nude in a public bath, but her cheeks warmed in a way that had nothing to do with steam from the heated rocks.

"You ordered me here, princess."

She decided to ignore the sarcastic title. He was more likely to stop if she acted as if it didn't bother her. "I ordered you to fill a cooling barrel."

"Which I have done." He peeled off his tunic, baring his hard body. "I was told you kept a bath for the use of all your people. For better or worse, I'm one of your people now. Or do you prefer your thralls to stink up your hall?"

Brandr plunged his garment into the barrel of soapy water intended for washing clothes while the bather soaked up heat. At least the son of Ulf was a man of clean habits. She had to give him that.

"I have no other thralls but you," she said, studiously keeping her gaze glued to his face. "And I'd rather you didn't reek, so you may stay."

"Magnanimous as always, princess." He wrung the excess water from his tunic and hung it on an overhead beam. Then he strode over and sat down beside her.

"There are other places to sit," she said.

"If I sit across the room from you, I won't be able

to help looking at you the whole time." He flicked a glance at her and then looked straight ahead. "If we sit side by side, we can pretend we aren't sneaking peeks at each other."

He'd already seen more of her than he ought when he held her upside down to kiss her foot, but this was different. They weren't jostling for power. They were just bathing together. It erased the barrier of rank.

It was a perfectly ordinary thing to do. When she and Osvald came to the bath together, she'd bathed with any number of her crofters and retainers. There was never anything the least prurient about it.

But somehow, being here alone with this man felt…intimate. The thought of him glimpsing her breasts made them tingle. She crossed her legs to hide her sex from him, lest an ache start there.

She caught him in a sidelong glance. "You really don't know how to behave, do you?"

"Never saw the point. In the South, they called us barbarians." He shrugged. "I felt honor bound to live down to the name."

Curiosity tickled her imagination like the single bead of sweat that tickled down her spine. "What was that like? Living in the great city, I mean."

"Grander than you can imagine," he said. "In Constantinople—that's what the Christians call it, you know—the homes of the nobles have water running into them, piped in from the mountains far away. And the marble floors are heated so no one ever has to wear stockings unless they wish."

"It sounds wonderful," she said, curling her toes. On bitter winter nights, she never could keep them warm.

He regaled her with tales of the many races who lived and prospered in the southern city. In the vast market, a man might find goods from exotic Cathay and Hind and the Upper Nile. Her mind refused to imagine people by the hundreds of thousands attending the games in the gigantic hippodrome. Surely there weren't that many souls in all the nine worlds.

"Of course, the Christians there are half-mad," he said. "One faction is always out to declare the others heretics to their faith."

"We have had priests come here," she said. "A few of my people wear the cross, though most still seem to prefer Thor's hammer. Did you convert while you were in the city of the Christians?"

He shook his head. "No, but our gods seemed mighty far away. I fought beside men who wore the cross, but in the heat of battle, they cried out to Thor to save them. Who's to say who heard that prayer? God is God. It's foolish for us to argue over what to name him."

That sounded like sense to her.

Since Brandr had been assigned to lead the emperor's elite personal guard, much of his service had been in the imperial palace.

"No emperor rests easy once his sons are born," Brandr said.

"Why? Are they afraid enemies will attack their children?" Katla's protective nature rose up against any who would plot against a child.

"Hardly. The son isn't usually the one in danger," Brandr said. "The quickest path to the imperial crown is for a prince to kill his father."

"That's terrible."

Brandr leaned forward on his elbows. "The thought occurred to me a time or two."

"You would've killed your father?" Katla whispered. Norse law meted out the worst possible punishment for those convicted of patricide. One who murdered his father would meet Death on the wings of the Blood Eagle, his living lungs ripped through his ribs and spread across his back.

"No, probably not. But not because the old bastard didn't deserve it." Brandr stood suddenly and strode to the bucket of switches near the heated stones. "Ready for a birching?"

Katla wanted to ask him more about his father, but he'd abruptly changed the topic.

"I'll do you, and then you can do me." He retrieved a bundle of wet switches and tested them for softness against his own thigh.

Flicking herself with a bundle of birch switches was part of the bathing process. It made Katla's skin glow, and the smell of softened birch leaves filled the bath house with a fresh scent.

"I usually do myself," she said.

"That shouldn't be allowed," he said with a frown. "In Byzantium, a noblewoman has half-a-dozen body servants to tend her. She never has to lift a finger."

"So did you attend a noble woman at her bath?" she asked with a grin.

"No, but I've stood outside the bath house with my sword drawn for one. A royal princess can't be too careful when she's meeting her lover in a pool covered with rose petals." He held the bundle of birch out to her. "You can switch me first if you like."

Brandr didn't expect her to agree, but astonishingly enough, she took the switches from him. The offer had been the only thing he could think of to make sure the subject of conversation stayed changed.

He hadn't meant to let his murderous thoughts about his own sire slip out like that, so raw, so feral. He was in awe of his father. He hated his father. His feelings festered in a tight knot. It was such a jumbled tangle he resisted trying to untie the collection of mismatched threads.

He still hadn't wrapped his mind around the death of Ulf the Ruthless. There was so much unfinished business between them, it was more than he was ready to tackle.

So instead, he smiled at the naked woman before him.

"I thought your honor wouldn't allow you to let me beat you." A feline smile played about her lips as she smacked her own palm with the soft switches.

"This isn't a beating. Bear in mind I'm letting you go first so I'll know how hard you'd like me to switch you in return." He really tried to keep his gaze fixed on her face, but a bead of sweat trickled from her neck. He couldn't help but follow its progress till it balanced on a taut nipple. "Do you want to start on the front or the back?"

"Turn around."

He obeyed, spread his legs to shoulder width, and extended his arms out to the sides. The birch switches were so tender and supple and covered with wet, softened leaves, he barely felt the slaps on his calves. They stung pleasantly when she swatted his thighs and buttocks. His back tingled as she moved up to his shoulders and along each of his arms.

So long as he felt something, he didn't need to think about his dead father or his enthrallment or anything else.

"Face me, but close your eyes," she ordered.

He turned around and swept her form with a quick gaze. "Afraid I'll like what I see, princess?"

"No, I'm afraid I'll poke your eyes out," she said with poisoned sweetness as she brandished the birch bundle. "Accidentally, of course."

He clamped his eyelids shut.

The fresh scent of birch filled his nostrils as she slapped the bundle on each shoulder and across his chest. Blood surged in his veins, and his whole body thrummed with life as she moved down to his thighs.

When he opened his eyes, she was frowning at his cock, which had risen unbidden.

"I don't have any way to stop that from happening when a beautiful na—" He caught himself before he said "naked." It wouldn't do to point out the obvious, even if her bare body was the cause of his erect state. "When a beautiful woman is lavishing attention on me."

Color rose in her cheeks. Didn't she know she was beautiful?

"Most people wouldn't consider a switching lavish attention," she said dryly. "It's just part of your bath. Don't make it something else."

"I won't if you won't." He took the bundle of birch from her and dipped it in the aromatic water so it would be cool and refreshing. "Turn around."

She gave him her back and caught up her hair in

one hand to bare her neck. He ached to plant a kiss on her nape at the hairline. She'd be salty and sweet and unbearably soft, but he'd given his word not to kiss her again without permission. Instead, he lightly tapped her shoulders with the birch and dragged the leaves across her skin. Her flesh glowed as he moved along each of her slender arms with glancing taps.

Then he switched across her back, moving quickly from side to side, careful only to invigorate her skin, not hurt her. He birched her bum with a little more pressure, as she had his. He smiled at her sharp intake of breath and enjoyed the rosy blush creeping over her rounded buttocks.

He moved down her thighs and sweetly curved calves. When he told her to turn around, he was a little surprised by the raggedness of his tone. He was no stranger to passion, but he hadn't expected to want this woman so much. She was bossy and standoffish. And vulnerable beneath her hard outer shell. He'd seen glimpses of that softer Katla and ached to coax her out.

She closed her eyes. He wished she'd have left them open. He wanted her to watch him as he tried to delight her.

He flicked the birch across her breasts. Her nipples drew tight. He dragged the soft leaves around them in slow, teasing circles. Her lips parted. The slow rise and fall of her breasts with each deep breath was spellbinding. He forced himself to move on.

He feathered the leaves over her ribs and across her belly. He would have liked to tease the hairs on her sex with the supple switches. He'd trade a year in Valhalla to see this woman squirm. But she'd skipped over his groin, so he had to follow her lead if he wanted her to trust him. He stung her thighs till they pinked with glowing health, and worked his way down her shins.

Then he stood upright. Her eyes were still closed, so he drank her in from head to toe. He'd desired many women, but he'd never ached so for one. Perhaps it was the lure of the unobtainable. Katla was his owner, his mistress.

Well beyond his reach.

She opened her eyes.

He reached for her in spite of the difference in their stations. Naked in the bath house, they were only a man and a woman.

She put a hand to his chest to stop him.

"I think we've had enough heat."

Even though he was almost certain she desired him as much as he did her, she turned and headed toward the cooling room. Her pink bum cheeks undulated, a beckoning summons, as she walked away from him.

A wise man would listen when a woman turns him down, he could almost hear his friend Harald saying. *A wise man wouldn't follow his cock every time it took notion to lead.*

Brandr grinned as he trailed Katla into the cooling room.

He never claimed to be a wise man.

Chapter 5

BY THE TIME BRANDR PUSHED THE DOOR AROUND AND entered the cooling room, Katla had already climbed into one of the barrels of water and settled into it up to her chin. Water sloshed over the sides and pattered onto the stone flags.

"You need not have followed me," she said before she ducked completely under the surface.

Brandr stood over the barrel, waiting for her to come back up. She finally did, sputtering and shaking her head. Her long hair sprayed droplets all around.

"What makes you think I followed you?" he asked. "This is the only place for the cooling barrels, and I found I agreed with you."

She smirked up at him. "That makes once. What did you agree with?"

"We've had enough heat from the bath."

It was time they made some of their own. But he still wore the iron collar, so he couldn't approach seducing her as he might any other woman.

He climbed into the adjacent barrel, sucking in his breath at the bracing difference in temperature between the meltingly hot bath and the cool water. Brandr had grown to enjoy the languid baths of the decadent South, so he hopped out as quickly as he'd gone in. Then he took one of the drying cloths and rubbed his body with vigor.

He was conscious of Katla's eyes on him, fleeting as the soft flicks of the birch branches. Never staying in one spot, never lingering long, her inquisitive gaze licked him from head to toe. His skin sparked under the invasion of her eyes as if she'd actually touched him. The cold water that had invigorated the rest of him had relaxed his arousal, but her glances whipped him back into a stone-hard stand.

She still didn't offer to climb from her barrel.

"Better come out, princess," he said as he walked toward her with a dry towel. "Your lips are turning blue."

"My lips are none of your business."

He grinned. Not yet, but they would be. All of her would be his business if he had his way about it. Brandr snapped the towel open and held it before him.

"Come, mistress. Let me dry you off."

"I can dry myself." She reached for the towel, but he pulled it back.

"That is not in question."

"Neither is the fact that you're my thrall and you must do as I wish."

For a moment, naked desire flashed in her eyes, then she looked away. Her dark lashes were soft, wet crescents on her cheeks. If he didn't know better, he'd say a blush was creeping up her neck. He'd trade a year in Valhalla to know what it was this woman wished.

"A lady of your status shouldn't have to tend herself."

If she wasn't his mistress, he'd have lifted her out of the barrel already, whether she wanted him to or no. As her thrall, he could only coax her into allowing such intimacies. "I'd think you'd jump at the chance of making the son of Ulf your body slave."

Her head snapped up at that, and she considered him coolly, weighing his words for sarcasm. Then without a word, she rose from the water, lifting a slim leg over the wooden sides.

He tried very hard to keep his eyes on hers, but it was a losing battle. His gaze drifted down to her perked nipples. His mouth watered to take one of those taut berries between his lips. He ached to suckle her till she wept with longing.

She turned and gave him her back, fisting her hands at her waist.

Her wet skin glistened. He buffed the towel over her shoulders and down her spine. His hands slid to the curve of her waist and flare of hips, with only the thin layer of cloth separating his palms from her skin. He wished he could feel the satiny smoothness directly.

For a moment, he imagined bending her over. Her slim fingers would splay on the moist flagstone. In that vulnerable position, her sex would be exposed in a yawning pink crevice. His engorged cock twitched at the thought of grasping her hips with both hands and ramming into her, slamming with need, thrusting deep, unable to restrain—

"Do you intend for me to air dry?" she asked, turning her head to shoot a quick glare at him over one shoulder.

He draped the cloth over her and massaged her flesh.

Warmth radiated through the thin linen, and he felt Katla's muscles tense under her smooth skin. She wanted him, but she resisted her own body's urges.

He'd have to see about that.

Brandr ran a couple cloth-covered fingers down her spine, not stopping when he reached the crevice of her bottom. She stiffened, so he covered her buttocks with the towel. He massaged her through it, lifting and spreading, teasing her tender flesh.

"Oh." The sigh was so soft he almost missed it.

"Is something wrong?" he asked with a grin.

"No, you're just terribly slow." A serrated edge of irritation crept into her tone. He hoped it meant she was fighting growing arousal.

"Not slow. Thorough." He knelt to dry the backs of her thighs and the sensitive crevices behind her knees. His grip tightened on one of her calves. Her skin was warm, almost feverish. Then he loosened his grip and moved his hand, drifting up to her buttocks and back down.

Her skin rippled with gooseflesh, and he knew his touch sent pleasure dancing over her.

"I don't think this is a very good idea." She turned and snatched at the towel.

"Why?" He whipped the cloth behind his back, out of her reach. "Haven't I obeyed your every command? Nothing will pass between us you don't wish."

Her brows drew together, and he wished he could kiss away those lines between them.

"I don't trust you."

"You should," he said simply. "I gave you my word."

He stood and looked down at her, every fiber of

his body straining toward her. It was more than animal attraction, though there was plenty of that. Even though she'd enslaved him, he admired this woman who shouldered the responsibility for so many. Plenty of men would have failed where she'd succeeded.

And yet, there was a fragility beneath her outward toughness. She was careful to keep it hidden, but he'd heard vulnerability in that sigh. Here was a woman worthy of more than his lust. She deserved his protection.

Whether she wanted it or not.

But first, he had to win her trust.

"I won't lie to you. I want you," Brandr said. His cock throbbed at her nearness, but he fought the urge to pull her closer. "Believe me, I want you *very* badly, but I won't force you."

She swallowed hard.

"I wear your iron collar. My purpose is to serve you," he said. "Let me."

❧

Brandr stood stock still. His chest didn't even rise and fall to show he breathed. His eyes darkened as he looked down at her.

Then, though his lips barely moved, she heard one word.

"Please."

Katla drew a sharp breath. It was rare enough for a man to use that word with another man. It dented a body's pride to plead, and Brandr was intensely prideful. After all, he was arrogant enough to turn her upside down to kiss her foot. She knew it cost him something to say "please." For that slice of a moment, she realized how badly he wanted to continue touching her, even if it was only as her body slave.

A muscle ticked in his cheek. He was struggling to control himself.

Why should she mind if he continued to towel her off? Hadn't she accepted him as thrall with the express purpose of debasing him in mind? What was lower than a bath slave?

Except this didn't seem like the sullen service of a thrall. His touch was deft, sure. A lover's touch. When he asked to serve her, his voice was rumbling and masculine, imbued with simmering arousal, not the resigned tone of a slave who serves because he must.

Brandr made her ache. He wakened longings no mistress should feel for a servant. Yet, she was still in control. As he said, nothing would happen she didn't want.

"All right. You may continue."

He exhaled, and Katla almost recalled her words. This meant something to him.

And, she realized with uneasiness, to her.

He fetched a fresh cloth and started by raising the towel to her face, gently pressing the cloth to her forehead, her temples, her closed eyelids and cheeks. His touch was feather light, as if he were trying to imprint the memory of her features on his fingertips.

The fresh cloth smelled of a snow-washed mountain breeze along with his sharp masculine scent. The towel moved down, patting her neck dry, tracing the narrow shelf of her collarbone from the hollow spot at the base of her throat to her shoulders.

When she sneaked a glance up at him, his attention was totally riveted on the bit of her he was drying at that moment. She'd never been scrutinized so minutely. He was completely absorbed by each of her parts, as if he were learning every piece of her.

Her skin warmed with a rosy glow.

His gaze drifted lower and stopped at her breasts. The towel hung limp and unused. She held her breath as he stared, his gaze hungry and straining.

"You're so beautiful, so perfect," he said huskily. "If you were made of marble, you'd grace the emperor's great hall. He displays the work from a thousand lands, but I swear he has no piece of art to match you."

Her heart glowed at his words, but if she was going to remain in control of this little adventure, she couldn't let him think her moved. "A thrall shouldn't speak to his mistress with the tongue of a skald."

His gaze jerked back to her face. "Your pardon, princess. But even a man with no poet in his soul finds one when he's properly inspired. It's hard to keep my thoughts to myself around you."

His hands found her breasts. Through the linen cloth, she felt his heat as he ran his fingertips along the crease beneath each one. Then he hefted their weight in his palms and dragged his thumbs across her taut nipples. He was still ostensibly drying her off, but his touch was increasingly charged with sensual power.

She bit her lip to keep from thrusting her breasts toward him. She ached to feel his touch directly on her skin, but she couldn't order him to do it. Not and remain in control.

He let the towel curl down to bare her breasts. The

naked hunger on his face made a throb start between her legs. Her breath shuddered over her teeth.

Brandr dropped to one knee before her, drying her ribs. She suppressed a giggle when he brushed over the last one. She'd always been ticklish on her left side. Osvald had avoided that spot because he couldn't abide laughter in bed.

But Osvald wasn't here. So when Brandr raked the tender place with the linen again, she allowed an unrestrained laugh to slip out.

He smiled up at her. "I like that. You should do it more often."

He circled her navel and inserted a cloth-covered fingertip into the indentation. He gently patted down her hips. His warm breath coursed over her belly. The small hairs covering her sex swayed with each exhalation.

Her womb clenched. His lips were so near. She could order him to pleasure her, to use his mouth on her to relieve the ache, but then her dream rushed back into her.

The servicing of a slave was no substitute for a lovingly offered act.

"Spread your feet." His voice was rough with longing.

Teeth clenched to keep from crying out with need, she did as he asked. He cupped her sex with his whole hand, and she throbbed into it.

His fingers alone would probably do, she thought as her head lolled back.

He teased the cloth between her legs, into her sensitive folds. She was wetter when he moved on down to her thighs than when he first began to gently blot her dry.

This is foolishness, Katla told herself. She was playing

a dangerous game with a man who was the son of her enemy. She ought not be seeping moist warmth over his touch.

Or wondering if his cock or fingers or tongue would best end her torment.

When he bent to dry her ankles and lifted one of her feet, she caught a whiff of her own arousal, sweet and musky. He'd used a slave's task to make her respond to him with a deep, throbbing ache.

"You smell wonderful." Brandr stood and dropped the cloth, just staring at her for a moment. He leaned toward her slightly, and she thought he was about to kiss her, but he caught himself and straightened.

"Order me to kiss you," he said.

"What?"

"I promised I wouldn't do it unless you ordered me, and I want to kiss you."

Brandr slid a hand along her neck and around to cradle the back of her head. Then he stepped closer so their bodies were touching, grazing each other at sensitive points, her nipples raking his chest, his erection rubbing against her belly.

"I burn to kiss you," he whispered. "Everywhere."

She sucked in a quick breath. He threatened to set her ablaze. Her whole body sizzled when he pulled her closer, lifting her with an arm around her waist so their parts meshed more fully.

Skin on skin. Heart to heart and groin to groin.

He pressed his cheek against hers. The stubble of his regrowing beard scraped her skin. Then he drew his open mouth over her sensitized flesh. He stopped shy of her lips, nostrils flared, a wild light in his eyes.

Katla swayed on her feet.

"You want my kiss," he said, his voice liquid seduction, a low purring sound that went straight to her womb and made her throb in time with the slow rock of his hips against her pelvis. "Admit it. You want my touch on your skin. You want my cock between your legs."

He was right, damn the man to the ninth circle of *Hel.* She was nearly incoherent with need. If she told him to kiss her, it wouldn't stop there. Brandr Ulfson was ready to mount her. And she was ready to let him.

Almost.

If she did, it would mean he'd won. He'd seduced his mistress into letting him take her. She'd lose all control over this man if that happened.

That was no way to avenge her husband's death.

She tamped down her longing and straightened her spine. She would be strong. She always had to be strong. A woman without a man had to be.

"You forget yourself, thrall. Step away from me."

He didn't move for the space of several heartbeats. Then a cold light burned in his eyes, and he released her. Anger and lust warred on his features, but he said nothing as he stepped back.

"Your tunic is still in the other room. It should be dry enough by now," she said, trying to keep her tone even and failing miserably. "Go put it on."

"*Ja*, princess. As you will." He stomped toward the door to the main bath but stopped before putting his hand to the latch. His thick cock was still engorged, and the muscles beneath his skin twitched, ready for action; however the expression on his face was anything but a lover's summons. The oil lamps seemed to flare brighter for a moment, but Katla dismissed it as a trick of light. "This is not over, you know."

She lifted her chin. "It is if I say it is. Step lively, thrall. You will attend me at table this night."

Brandr made a low growling noise in the back of his throat and left, slamming the door behind him. The lamps flickered hotly and then dimmed.

Must have been the blast of air from when he opened the door, she reasoned, though she didn't remember ever seeing them vary so wildly before.

Katla sank onto the bench near the cooling barrels, afraid her legs wouldn't hold her up any longer. She crossed her arms over her breasts, her body throbbing for the release Brandr would've given her.

But she couldn't have done otherwise.

She would control him. Not the other way around. She still had to avenge Osvald.

She drew a ragged breath and tried to clear her head of the heart-stopping things he'd done to her. The things he'd made her wish he'd do. Her belly turned a slow backflip at the thought of his mouth on her.

His kiss. Everywhere.

No, Katla told herself sternly. She had no time for such dallying. Her brothers had brought another suitor for her to consider. Albrikt Gormson of Stord Island was no doubt waiting in her longhouse that very moment, wondering what was keeping her.

She didn't need a lover. She might well have a husband before long. A man who wouldn't play games, who wouldn't have to be ordered to kiss her, and who most especially wouldn't be the son of her enemy.

Katla stood and dressed in the tunic and overdress old Gerte had delivered to the bath house for her. She fastened her best brooches at her shoulders. After plaiting her hair, she twined the braid around her head and fitted the elaborate headdress over her wet hair.

Dressed in her best ensemble, she was the perfect picture of a high-ranking Norse matron. She had to be. If she was to give Gormson's suit a fair hearing, she must present herself in a way that brought credit to her house.

Her body still craved Brandr, but the worst of the madness was passing. She sniffed the air, hoping she no longer smelled like a wanton. The stiff brocade overdress had been laid by with cedar chips, so the fresh scent of wood followed her out the bath house door. But before she reached the longhouse, she had to admit Brandr was right.

This was not over.

Chapter 6

KATLA'S LONGHOUSE MIGHT NOT HAVE BEEN THE largest structure in the islands, but it was undoubtedly the cleanest. She demanded her people respect their living space and one another by keeping their home spotless and sweet smelling.

Therefore, when she pushed through the big double doors, she was aghast to find the floor was slick with spilled food and slopped drink. Swirling scents of a rich feast combined with ale, beer, and mead fumes. They coalesced into a smoky fug that hovered in the high peak of the longhouse.

A grease fire sputtered on the central hearth, and Inga, the girl whose job it was to turn the spit, was trying to beat it out with one of the sheepskins. With another determined slap of the rug, Inga quelled the blaze, turning the air gray and hazy with even more smoke now that the flames had died.

The girl had been Osvald's bed slave, but Katla had freed her when he was killed. Inga asked to be allowed to stay on as a freed servant, and she'd become one of Katla's best workers. Right now, Inga was the only one who seemed to be trying to keep some semblance of order.

Katla bit her lip to avoid shouting for quiet. Shouting was unbecoming.

No one had waited for her arrival before being served. As she walked down the long room, she saw trenchers piled high with glistening chicken cooked in beer, root vegetables glazed with honey, and barley bread slathered with butter.

Her people raised their horns to her, drinking to her health as she passed, but her brothers were the founders of this feast. Finn obviously wanted to impress her suitor with a lavish display, not mindful the bounty she'd laid by with such care would have to last till harvest. When the last carrot was gone and the last barrel of barley meal was spent long before the new crop could be harvested, what would her brothers do then?

She shot Finn a glare that should have lit him aflame. Perhaps later, she'd have Inga beat *him* with a rug.

There was a stranger in the seat of honor next to her empty place. Katla knew without being told this was Albrikt Gormson of Stord Island. He had the solitary look of a man who commanded other men and demanded their unquestioning allegiance.

In that, they were cut from the same cloth. She, too, was alone and firmly in charge.

Most of the time.

Katla could tell Albrikt was a formidable man among a race of formidable men. His russet hair gleamed with oil, and his beard was neatly braided. A wicked scar snaked across one of his cheekbones, turning a corner of his mouth up in a habitual sneer. It demolished any chance Albrikt would be considered handsome, but that was low on the list of masculine attributes she needed in a husband.

A warrior, this one.

Osvald had been a farmer. She'd tread warily till she learned if Albrikt was the sort who wore his power lightly or if he felt the need to grind others down with it.

His eyes were so pale, they glinted like a wolf's, feral in the dimness. A silver armband bound the thick muscle of his bared sword arm, and his tunic was trimmed with ermine. He was a man of wealth, if the richness of his garments were any indication, and obvious physical power.

How on earth had her chuckleheaded brothers ever managed to reach even a tentative agreement with this man? Especially such a lopsided bargain that had him giving up his much-larger estate for her?

"Glad you could join us, sister," Finn said. "You certainly made us wait long e—"

"A wait well worth it." Albrikt cut him off without apology, rising to his full, impressive height. "Katla the Black, your brothers told me you are a good steward of your late husband's wealth. I respect wisdom and industry in a woman, but they failed to mention that you are also exceedingly comely."

She dipped in a low curtsey. Albrikt Gormson's words were fair enough, but they didn't make her belly flutter like Brandr's rousing confession.

I burn to kiss you. Everywhere.

She forced herself to focus on the man who'd

presented himself to court her, instead of the one who was trying to seduce her.

"Welcome, Albrikt, son of Gorm." Katla swept around the table to take her place at his side, careful to face forward, but she watched him from the corner of her eye as a mouse would give heed to the cat lolling by the fire. "I trust the food is to your liking."

"*Everything* is to my liking." Now that the formal introductions were over, he obviously felt he could address her with more intimacy. He imbued the word with unmistakable meaning, and in case she had any doubt, he followed it up with a slow perusal of her profile, not stopping at her chin.

Since her brothers didn't seem to mind the man ogling her in public, she'd have to ignore it. The man was her guest. She couldn't make a scene.

"I'm sure my brothers showed you the extent of my possession. My husband left me a snug holding," she said, taking a small sip of her ale.

"Your brothers couldn't show me that." Albrikt barked a short laugh. "Just what every man wants in a wife—a snug holding. I'll look forward to that tour."

She bit her tongue.

Her nape prickled, and she lifted her gaze as the doe raises her head when she senses an arrow is on the string, aimed for her heart. Brandr Ulfson was leaning against one of the longhouse's massive support posts midpoint along one wall.

His deep brown eyes were riveted on her.

She jerked her gaze away.

"You have missed my meaning, sir," she said to her guest, her tone clipped and icy.

"Mayhap." Albrikt leaned toward her. "And mayhap you wanted to distract me with wondering just how snug your *holding* is. You're a cagey one, Katla. No one without a level head between her ears could make a small farm like this one support so many mouths."

She allowed herself a small smile at this acknowledgment of her accomplishments. It pleased her even more than when he called her comely. Her appearance was none of her doing, so she could hardly take pleasure in an accident of nature. But the success of her steading was due to her hard work and management. And Gormson had noticed. Her cheeks warmed at his praise.

"So I expect you're clever enough to know finalizing the contract is the last time a woman has real power in a marriage," Albrikt said.

"When you put it like that, there's very little incentive for me to take another husband."

"I didn't make the world, but that's the way of it. Besides, your brothers have told me you've sworn to marry. So you want to negotiate the best possible terms from me. I understand that." He clinked the rim of his drinking horn with hers. "And respect it."

"We are far from finalizing terms or anything else."

Albrikt speared a plump sausage with his knife. "Your brothers have already admitted they want my land on Stord. What is it *you* want from me?"

"I don't know you well enough to know if you have anything I want," she said tartly.

A trencher groaning under the weight of food was plopped down before her.

"Surely from among all that, you'll find something you want, my lady," Brandr said.

"That's enough from you for this evening," she warned.

He bent in a mocking bow before he came around the table and took his station behind her.

Gormson turned and shot Brandr a glare. "When thralls speak out of turn on Stord, we remove their tongues."

Katla would never allow such a cruel thing, but she hoped Brandr was eavesdropping from his place of subservience. It would serve him right to stew a bit.

"This one is new to the iron collar," Katla said. "He hasn't been thoroughly schooled in his duties yet."

Albrikt grunted and shoveled in a large bite of chicken. "A sound whipping would teach him quick enough."

"The son of Ulf is the first thrall I've ever owned, so if he offended you, the fault is mine." Katla picked at her own trencher, unsure where to begin so as not to topple the mound of food onto the table. "Obviously, his training is far from complete."

"The son of Ulf?" Albrikt turned around to give Brandr a more thorough inspection. "Ulf of Jondal?"

"That's the one. Ulf the Ruthless. The man who killed my husband." Katla took a long draught of ale. She rarely drank to excess, but she suspected this night might call for it. "But Ulf is dead, so I took his son as my thrall to avenge the death of my husband."

Albrikt stared at her for moment, his pale eyes darkening as his pupils widened. Then he chuckled.

"Katla the Black. And here I thought you were named for your raven hair." He slammed his palm on the table and loosed a full-throated guffaw. "Now I see they meant your heart. Enslaving the son for the deeds of his dead father! That's an idea I'll remember and use as the occasion calls for it." He laughed again. "I like you, woman. We're well suited, you and I. You remind me of me."

She arched a brow at him. "I think it should remind you not to anger me."

"Noted," Albrikt said with a gruff nod. Then he turned to Brandr. "A friend of mine was on the Orkney coast when Ulf Skallagrimsson's ship went down in that storm. He told me your father wailed like a little maid before he sank for the last time."

Then Albrikt fell to his meal with renewed relish and an occasional chuckle.

Katla sensed Brandr stiffening behind her and hoped he'd control himself. If he insulted or, Odin help her, attacked a guest, she'd be honor bound to punish him, despite the provocation. To distract him, she lifted her horn for him to refill and was glad to see him tight-lipped but struggling to bridle himself.

"Pay him no heed," she whispered to Brandr.

"I will if you will." He shot a glare at Albrikt but stepped back when Katla waved him away.

An insult to a thrall was not uncommon, but Albrikt's other words seared her mind.

Enslaving the son for the deeds of his dead father.

She'd thought it the logical course when her brothers first dropped Brandr across her threshold. When it was put so baldly, enthralling the son of Ulf did smack more of cold vindictiveness than honorable vengeance.

She reminded Albrikt of himself. The last thing she wanted was to be like this warrior from Stord. Not that he was a bad sort, even though he did take an unnecessary swipe at Brandr, knowing a thrall had no recourse. He was no different than many other men she knew—shrewd, strong, and ruthless.

Still, there was something about the man that made her hackles rise. He was not here because he wished to court her for herself, however much he might appreciate her appearance, and he'd already dismissed her property as small.

So what did he really want?

Chapter 7

ALBRIKT GORMSON IS NAUGHT BUT A VIOLATOR OF *sheep and wants only to add you to the flock, Katla,* Brandr would have told her if the princess would deign to let him speak. He'd always been a steady judge of character, and in short order, he'd decided Gormson had none.

Desiring a woman was one thing. He completely understood Gormson's lascivious glances at Katla, even though they made his fingers ball into fists.

But the urge to subjugate, to dominate and control her, was quite another thing. He saw that need flare in Gormson's eyes more often than raw lust.

This man meant Katla, and the people she cared for, no good.

Brandr stood by, refilling Katla's drinking horn, and Gormson's as well, when the man thrust it toward him. In his mind, he gutted and quartered Albrikt several times, but he guarded his expression with care. Only the discipline he'd learned in the Varangian Guard allowed him to stand by in silence.

But that didn't mean there'd never be a time to

act. No matter how frustrated he was with Katla, he wouldn't let Gormson bring her to grief.

"Have you made preparations for the defense of this farmstead?" Gormson asked.

"We have," Katla said circumspectly. "But we've had peace on Tysnes for so long, there's been little need."

"There's every need," Albrikt said. "I'm a fair hand with a blade. Mayhap you'd like a demonstration. Who's your best fighter?"

"There's too much work to be done to chance injuring someone in a mock battle. I won't risk any of my people."

Gormson turned and eyed Brandr. "Then risk one who isn't part of your household."

"That's not necessary. I'll take your word for it. No doubt you're very skilled with a sword."

"The ear may hear, but the eye believes." Albrikt leaped up and plowed into Brandr, shouldering past him with enough force to spin him around, nearly knocking him off his feet.

Brandr clutched at the back wall to remain upright, but he bit back a snarl. He was less successful about keeping the torches from flaring brightly around the long room. When he tamped down his anger, they returned to normal.

Katla gaped after Albrikt as he continued to walk another few paces.

Then Albrikt stopped and turned to look back at Brandr. "No challenge? Not a word of rebuke? Do you not care that I just insulted you, thrall?"

Brandr's eyes blazed. "'Tis not the first time you've done me insult, but my collar protects you. A slave cannot issue a challenge."

He hadn't forgotten Gormson's slanderous words about his father.

"And it won't be the last time you're insulted, so long as you wear that iron collar," Albrikt said as he walked back to stand nose to nose with Brandr. "You may as well get used to insults."

"That's enough," Katla said. "Both of you."

Albrikt didn't even glance her way. He put both hands on Brandr's chest and shoved. Brandr stumbled backward a few paces but didn't fall.

"Aren't you going to defend yourself?" the big Stordman demanded.

"If I strike you, I strike off my own head."

"Oh, that's right. Pity." Then Albrikt delivered a blow to Brandr's jaw that sent him sprawling into the dirt.

Katla shrieked but quickly clamped a hand to her mouth when Brandr glanced toward her with mayhem in his eye.

"I have tried to serve you with honor, princess." Brandr rose to his feet, his jaw rigid. "Will you give me leave to defend myself?"

Katla shook her head. "Albrikt, I insist—"

"Never mind, Katla," Albrikt said. "He's as gutless as his father."

"Why are you trying to anger me?" Brandr asked through clenched teeth.

"To see if it is still possible. Or did they put an iron ring around your ballocks as well?" Albrikt shook his head, curled his lip at Brandr, and spat in the dirt. "You pathetic excuse for a half man."

The roar that spewed from Brandr's throat made everyone jump back a pace. He lunged toward Albrikt, tackling his midsection and sending both of them clattering across the long table in a flurry of flailing arms and legs. Brandr pounded Albrikt, landing several punches that would leave marks on Gormson's ribs. Albrikt returned the blows, sending a ringing cuff that blacked Brandr's eye.

When they separated enough to rise to their feet, Albrikt drew his dirk.

Katla sucked in a sharp breath. "Stop! This is still my table, and we will have order here."

"Your thrall attacked me," Gormson said, swiping the blood that gushed from the broken skin on his brow. "I have a right to demand his blood."

"So you do," Katla said, tight-lipped. "But he was provoked, and he's unarmed."

Albrikt straightened and shoved the dirk back into its sheath at his waist. "You're right. Never let it be said the son of Gorm fought an unfair fight. Call it a moment's truce while this waste of skin finds a weapon suited to him."

Katla turned to Finn. "He was armed when you enthralled him, I assume."

"I was," Brandr answered for him. "A broadsword in a shoulder baldric, and a dagger."

"Then fetch his weapons, and be quick," Katla said. "We'll move this dispute outside."

Residents of the longhouse spilled into the inky night, bearing torches and forming a circle.

Brandr followed Katla out. The set of her shoulders was rigid and high. She was obviously furious, but she reined in her emotions with admirable control.

He wondered if she was angry with him or with

Albrikt. Both, if the scowl she shot in each of their directions was any measure.

"This is my home. My word is second only to the Law, and these are the rules for this *holmgang*," she announced in a ringing tone. "This fight is for first blood only."

"He struck me," Albrikt said. "I have a right to a kill."

"Not if you still wish me to consider your suit," Katla said. "Son of Ulf, if you kill Albrikt Gormson, you will be dealt with according to the Law."

Even though the penalty for a thrall who killed a freeman was horrific, Brandr was tempted. "Gormson still gets to court you. What do I get if I don't kill him?"

"If you prove you can show restraint, you'll be allowed to go armed hereafter," Katla said. "Do we have an accord?"

Gormson growled his consent.

Brandr nodded. "We have an accord."

Finn came loping up, bearing Brandr's weapons. He handed the baldric to him and stepped back into the ring around the combatants.

Brandr drew his sword and made a few practice cuts in the air, testing the blade for weight and balance, in case Finn had ill-used it. He ran his thumb along the edge. A bead of red welled up on the pad of his thumb. Brandr gave a satisfied grunt. Then he settled into a fighting stance and bared his teeth at Gormson in a wolfish grin.

"Now we're even," Gormson said, determination glinting in his pale eyes. "Though some might still call this an unfair fight, thrall."

"I'll take my chances." Brandr nodded in satisfaction

as he circled Gormson, looking for an opening in the Stordman's defenses.

"You know a woman's word is worthless once the *holmgang* begins, don't you?" Gormson hissed. "If I gut you from balls to breastbone in one stroke, that still counts as first blood, doesn't it?"

"That's how I see it." Brandr feinted left and then struck from the right.

Gormson parried the blow with ease. "Now we have an accord."

Albrikt was older than Brandr, but he was still a warrior in his fighting prime, with a wealth of experience to aid him. Brandr, however, was blessed with the nimbleness and strength of his younger years and a soul still smarting from Gormson's insults.

He'd have borne the insults to himself, but he wouldn't let his father be slandered. The day Brandr's father wailed like a little maid hadn't dawned.

They exchanged several ringing blows, but when Gormson pulled his dirk from its sheath, arming both hands, Brandr's chances dimmed significantly.

Brandr lunged, and Gormson leaped out of the way. But not before his dirk sliced through Brandr's tunic. Gormson feinted and ran into Brandr's waiting blade, but he neatly deflected the sharp edge with his own dirk, whirling away unhurt.

There had been a time when combatants in the *holmgang* would stand toe-to-toe, whacking away at each other with no finesse at all, trusting brute strength to win the day. Now fighting was more like a macabre dance, full of leaps and quick turns. They both came close to drawing blood, but Brandr only nicked

Gormson's leather breastplate, and Gormson had only shredded more of Brandr's disreputable tunic.

Brandr was vaguely aware of the chants of encouragement from the crowd. Einar was taking wagers, shouting out the odds in a loud voice.

He wanted to glance at Katla, but Gormson launched a fresh assault, and his world spiraled down to the next parry, the next thrust.

Keep your feet. Don't stop moving.

Neither gave quarter nor expected it to be given. Their eyes burned feral. Black *berserkr* rage stole over them, setting their blood aflame.

It seemed both were tiring, when Brandr changed tactics and let Gormson get close to him. When Albrikt swiped at him, he used his sword hilt to catch the older man's blade. With a quick flick of his wrist, he wrenched the sword from Gormson's hand.

Brandr buried his fist in Albrikt's belly, and the dirk dropped from Gormson's grip. With his opponent doubled over, Brandr swept Gormson's legs from under him in a swift kick.

Albrikt landed flat on his back, sucking wind. With a final roar, Brandr brought his blade down suddenly on Gormson's neck, stopping a hair's breadth from the older man's pulsing life vein. Brandr's chest heaved, and every bit of his blood screamed out at him for stopping short of the actual kill.

The crowd fell into stunned silence. A thrall had bested a freeman, a landed *karl*. It would take a moment for their world to right itself.

"Do you yield?" Brandr asked between gasping breaths.

"No," Gormson said between clenched teeth.

"Then I guess I'll have to blood you." Brandr pressed down enough to pink Gormson's neck with a thin mark. He straightened and looked down at Gormson. "Be sure to thank Katla the Black. She's the only reason you're still breathing."

Chapter 8

FINN AND EINAR TRIED TO HELP GORMSON UP, BUT HE waved them away angrily. Brandr hoped he'd stomp off and abandon his pursuit of Katla, but he allowed himself to be persuaded to reenter the longhouse.

Brandr was forced to listen as Katla commended him for his fighting abilities.

"Not many would relish facing a captain of the Varangian Guard, even if he does wear a thrall collar," she said. "You fought with honor, son of Gorm."

After a few more horns of mead, Albrikt was his blustering self again.

Brandr was relieved when she made her excuses and retired for the night once the singing and drinking games began. After a few moments, everyone's attention was riveted on her brother Einar near the central fire. He was trying to drain a horn of mead as long as his arm in one gulp and had failed in his second attempt. He called for the horn to be topped off.

Brandr used the raucous chanting while the horn was being refilled to cover his exit. As silent as a wraith, he slipped into her chamber.

The noise of the crowd faded, but Katla evidently wasn't aware he'd entered. She was humming the same drinking tune the gathering was singing in the next room. He moved farther into the chamber with stealth, not daring to breathe too deeply lest she hear him.

Katla faced away from him on the far side of her bed. Her starched headdress was propped on one of her trunks, and she'd unbraided her hair. The long tresses glistened in the lamplight, still damp, as if she'd plaited it when it was wet. It cascaded in waves down the length of her spine, the wispy ends teasing her hips.

Her fingers worked the catch on the brooch above each breast. Once the tabs at her shoulders came free, she stepped out of the stiff brocade overdress. The lighter tunic beneath clung to her form. Brandr clearly discerned all her curves under the thin fabric, and the shadow of her legs through the thin cloth teased him.

Marriages were ever made with an eye to increased wealth, Brandr knew, but Gormson should happily give up his Stord property for a woman like this. Even if all she brought to the union was herself.

Then she bent double, grasped the hem, and pulled her tunic off over her head. She moved slowly, as if her mind were otherwise occupied.

That was fine with him. Desire roared in him, and he was hot and ready in only a few heartbeats. He ached to bury himself in her softness, to feel her velvet heat wrapped around him.

Unfortunately, she wasted no time slipping on her thin night shift.

She slid her hands under her heavy hair and gave it

a shake, spreading the dark mantle across her shoulders to dry. When she turned to climb into bed, she saw Brandr in the shadows and startled.

"What are you doing in here?" she whispered furiously.

"Watching you undress," he said honestly.

She narrowed her eyes at him.

"But that wasn't my main purpose."

A dark brow arched in suspicion.

"You aren't going to marry that louse-bitten toad, are you?"

"That is none of your business." Her frown eased into a sly smile. "Oh, I see. If I wed Albrikt, you're afraid for your tongue. Don't worry. If I decide to accept him, I'll make sure the marriage contract stipulates that you remain my exclusive property."

"You're not seriously considering it." Brandr barely resisted the urge to grasp her shoulders and give her a shake. "If you are, you should know it's not you he's interested in here."

"Oh, really? Well, that's flattering."

"You're too bright a woman to need flattery. Oh, *ja*, I'm not saying he won't use you." The thought of Gormson in her bed made Brandr's eyes burn. "He'll rut you every time he takes a notion, but that's not the main reason he's considering this match. There's something else he's after."

To his surprise, she didn't argue. She sank down on the bed, tucking one foot under her.

"What do you think that might be?"

So she'd felt it too, the sense of strategic measurement in Gormson's gaze, not just when he looked at her, but also when he surveyed the long hall. When he silently counted the number of sword arms ringing the fire.

Brandr knew Albrikt did it, because he'd done it himself.

"He's no farmer," Brandr said, "else he'd not trade for a smaller steading."

"Even if I came with it?"

Was she angling for a compliment from him? Wasn't his cock tenting his tunic every time he looked her way enough?

Or maybe she simply wanted another stick to bash him with. She'd have it if he admitted she was a powerful inducement to an otherwise uneven trade.

"Even if you came with it," he said firmly. She winced at the slight. "There's something else that draws him to your property."

"I sensed the same," she said thoughtfully. Then she looked up at him sharply. "But how would *you* know that?"

It wasn't unusual for a woman to have unwarranted knowledge of the hearts of others, but that was because they were naturally endowed with a measure of magic from the cradle. Everyone knew that.

Men typically shied away from dabbling in *seid* craft. There was a saying in the North, old as the rocks and trees: *If action is needed, turn to a man. For understanding, seek a woman.*

But Brandr had always had a knack for discerning the hidden thoughts of others. He read it in the set of their shoulders, the twitch of a muscle under the skin. He could smell out a lie like an elkhound on the hunt. If a game of chance required him to sense the other man's next play, he won every time.

"Just trust me on this," Brandr said, running a hand over his shorn head. "Gormson isn't the man for you. Stay away from him."

"That almost sounds as if you're trying to give me an order." She cocked her head at him. "I am your mistress. I seek neither your counsel nor your consent for what I choose to do."

"But you asked—"

"Enough." She stood to give more weight to her words. "Go to sleep, thrall."

"As you will," he said and prepared to bed down across her threshold again.

"No, not in here. It's not…seemly. On the other side of the door."

Shoulders slumped, he put his hand on the latch.

"Brandr."

His head snapped up. Even though she was sending him away, he liked the sound of his name on her tongue. It was the first time she'd used it.

"I'm glad you weren't harmed this night."

"Me too."

She studied him for a long moment and opened her mouth to say something, but seemed to think better of it. She waved him away. "See to it no one passes by you during the dark watches."

"You think someone will try?"

She shook her head, her lips curving in a reluctant smile. "No, I suppose you're right. After that display of swordsmanship, I'm safer with you by my door than if I had a dozen guards."

He nodded, suppressing a smile. She wouldn't have to fight Gormson from her bed so long as Brandr served her. He meant to see she didn't welcome Albrikt there either. "As you will…"

He closed the door softly behind him before he finished his thought. "Katla."

❧

Brandr had no trouble falling asleep across Katla's threshold in the large common room. The steady breathing, even the rhythmic snoring of others, helped him into a state of relaxation so deep he didn't miss having a proper bed.

But a stealthy step was all it took to jerk him to alert wakefulness.

Brandr slitted his eyes and peered into the dark. Someone was moving down the center of the long room toward Katla's chamber.

At first he thought it must be Gormson. He struck Brandr as the sort to drive a dagger between a sleeping guard's ribs, then resort to rape in order to clinch the marriage. But the dark shape wasn't broad shouldered or tall enough to be the man from Stord.

Every muscle in Brandr's body tensed as the form drew nearer. Then when the figure leaned over him, Brandr's hand shot up and caught him by the throat.

Brandr was on his feet in a heartbeat and smacking the would-be intruder against the wall.

"*Huff da!*" The fellow's voice squeaked, and Brandr recognized him.

"What are you doing, Haukon?" he whispered as he released his hold on the boy. "Your sister doesn't wish to be disturbed."

"I don't want to see Katla. I want to see you."

Brandr sank down with his back to the door he guarded. "Why?"

Haukon hunkered beside him. "I want you to teach me something."

"What?"

"I've heard tales of the Varangians. You're the fiercest fighters in the world," Haukon said. "Teach me to handle a sword."

"Why? As long as you and your cowardly brothers have a pot of poison, you can handle your enemies right enough."

The boy bristled. "It wasn't my idea to taint your mead, Ulfson. That was Einar's doing."

"So you and Finn just went along with it?"

"Mayhap we shouldn't have, but what's done is done," Haukon said. "Now is all we can claim."

"*Ja*, and now you're stealing the only time I'm like to get for sleep." Brandr lay back down again and closed his eyes. "Thralls don't set their own pace, you know. I'm sure your sister has a full day planned for me."

"Come, Ulfson," Haukon urged. "Teach me, and I'll see you get extra food."

Trust a stripling to think of his stomach first.

"No," Brandr said.

"But I'm very quick. Everyone says so. It won't take long for you to show me what I need to know."

"Only five or six years."

The boy sighed.

"But what if a gang of men like those friends of yours turns up again?" Haukon whispered urgently. "I want to be able to defend what's mine."

Haukon's heart was in the right place, but his request was laughable. "If men like my friends ever make landfall here with mayhem in mind, your best bet is to hide in a hole till they leave."

"I won't do that."

Brandr opened his eyes. It was still too dark to make out the lad's face, but the determination in Haukon's tone tugged at him. He remembered his father schooling him and his brother in the way of a blade. Ulf was a hard taskmaster, demanding to the point of viciousness, but he saw to it his sons could defend themselves.

No one had done that for Haukon. Even though the boy would have no hope of success against a blooded warrior, he wouldn't show an enemy his back. Grudging respect made Brandr sit up.

"Whether it was your idea or no, you helped put the iron collar on my neck," Brandr said. "Give me one good reason why I should help you."

"Because...Katla wouldn't like it."

Brandr snorted. "Good enough."

Chapter 9

"MAY I RECLAIM FOR ALL TIME MY RIGHTFUL INHERITANCE, the Iron Crown of kingship."

Malvar Bloodaxe leaned a hand on slabbed stonework as he whispered his prayer. The man-made hill rose starkly from the plain, a tribute to the defiant will of its ancient makers and in honor of the gods of the Orkney Islands.

"May Gormson's arm be strengthened, and may all my ally's plans succeed."

Power tingled through Malvar's palm and up his arm. There were places in the world where the primeval forces still thrived, where gods even older than the pantheon of the North yet walked unseen. This remote mound of earth on the largest island in the Orkney chain was one of them.

"May my prisoner's tongue be loosened and the path to victory made plain."

Malvar closed his eyes, letting the spirits of the place speak to him in half-heard sibilance, whispers from the disembodied souls of woad-painted warriors and fallen heroes. They reached out to him from the tall, waving grass, from the red sandstone bones of the island beneath its thin skin of dirt, from the artfully worked slabs that were used to build this sacred place in the deep past.

This is our land, they cried. *Our water and earth and sky. Our blood sacrifices and feasts. Let not the Carpenter God push us from it.*

Malvar opened his eyes, anger hazing his vision red. Not a handful of winters ago, the self-styled Norwegian king, Olav Tryggvason, had landed on the islands and forced the inhabitants to convert to Christianity at sword point. The Norse deities of the islands, Odin and Thor and that lot, were too weak to help the people resist then.

But there were Others hovering about the island. Forgotten Ones, whose time was both long past and yet to come. They waited with the patient stillness of a spider for their chance.

Once the Norse king left, Malvar heard their bloodless voices in the night. Hisses of hate woke him from a sound sleep and drenched him in a cold sweat. Then the more he listened, the more he understood.

Might was the only truth, blood the only currency that mattered.

Shoved underground, belief in the Old Ones was growing stronger now. Men who craved violence and bloodshed as much as the ancient gods did were drawn to worship them.

In Orkney, the Hebrides, in deceptively quiet fjords along the Norse coast and barrier islands, Malvar Bloodaxe was amassing allies. He appealed to those who had a score to settle. They were second sons who didn't stand to inherit their fathers' lands, men who longed for a return to the way of the warrior. They wanted to resume the Viking raids, when a man might increase his wealth with a sword stroke instead of by trade or tilling.

The Old Ones would see it done. Those ancient spirits delighted in mayhem and murder and atrocities that turned men's bowels to water. With the army Malvar was gathering, the Old Ways would return.

There's not a farmer or a merchant in the lot, Malvar thought with a contented smile.

Satisfied the spirits had heard his prayer and supported his intent, Bloodaxe stooped to enter the cairn. He was forced to crawl along the passageway burrowing into the heart of the man-made hill.

Even the most powerful leader must be humble before the specters of Old Ones, he supposed.

For he was born to be a powerful leader. His grand-sire had been Eric Bloodaxe, exiled king of Norway, the man who'd earned the chilling name Malvar was proud to bear. Which meant Olav Tryggvason was a pretender, and Malvar Bloodaxe was the rightful Norse king.

With the men whose allegiance he'd claimed and the power of the Old Ones behind him, he'd take back his grandfather's crown.

But first, he needed the right information, the right fjord to target for his initial incursion. Once he'd subjugated an entire fjord, he'd be able to move on to the next. As terror of his might heralded his approach, the subsequent fjords would fall into his hand like ripe plums.

Dragonships would sail the Northern seas once more, bringing death on the wind.

Malvar reached the end of the tunnel and stood upright in the open chamber where the ceiling vaulted to twice a man's height. Torches blackened the walls, and the place was ripe with the stench of burning pitch. A thin ribbon of smoke found its way out the shaft at the apex of the vault, but the air was still unwholesome if one had no relief from it for extended periods of time.

Especially when the air currents sent a whiff of human feces and misery wafting along the subterranean corridors to mingle with the smoke.

The guard at the interior opening of the tunnel snapped to attention when he recognized his leader, both spiritual and temporal.

"How is our prisoner this day?" Malvar Bloodaxe asked.

"Not very talkative."

"Well, that is something we shall have to remedy, isn't it?" Malvar said as he strolled over to survey the available whips and knives laid out on a table. "Has his back healed?"

"Not yet."

"Good. We'll concentrate on the front then," Bloodaxe said, picking up a cat-o'-nine-tails and cracking it. The sound echoed through the subterranean vaults, and a muffled wail came in response from one of the other tunnels leading off the main chamber. Anticipation of pain was almost as effective as pain itself. "We'll start with this. Bring him."

The guard disappeared down one of the short

corridors and came back, half-dragging his charge. The prisoner was naked, his beard and hair so matted with filth only shearing him like a sheep would render him human once more. His ribs stood out in stark relief. He stooped as he shuffled along, because he was unable to stretch out to his full height in the tiny cell in which he was kept.

"Greetings, Ulf, *Jarl* of Jondal," Bloodaxe said courteously as the guard bound the prisoner's unresisting hands spread eagle between two posts.

It was a stroke of luck the man's vessel foundered off the Orkney coast and he'd been reported lost with the rest of his crew. As far as anyone else knew, Ulf Skallagrimsson was freezing in *Hel*. No one would ever think to look for him in the bowels of the earth.

"I trust you're enjoying your stay with us," Malvar said with a laugh.

The man peered from under his shock of rapidly graying hair, the mad glint in his eyes the only evidence of a living soul in the soon-to-be-broken body. Ulf worked his mouth for a moment and then spat a gob of phlegm on the packed dirt at Bloodaxe's feet.

Malvar smiled. Naked loathing was such a deliciously powerful emotion. It shimmered in the foul air, and Malvar's arms strengthened with the force of his captive's hate. He'd send his own venom right back to the *jarl*.

The cat flicked over Ulf's chest, leaving an artful cluster of red weals. The man gritted his teeth to keep his agony silent, but Malvar knew that restraint wouldn't last long.

"Now, then what shall we talk about?" Malvar sent the whip singing again. This time it drew bright beads of blood and a grunt of pain. "How about...the defenses of Hardanger Fjord?"

Chapter 10

ALBRIKT GORMSON STAYED AS KATLA'S GUEST FOR three more days. During that time, there was no more water carrying or wood chopping for Brandr, though he did still wait on her at table. She seemed to want him to hear all of Gormson's conversations, for each night after slipping away from the drunken feast, she asked Brandr's opinion of what was said.

Whether she'd act upon Brandr's thoughts was another question. She held herself aloof from everyone.

When she disappeared into the bath house each evening, he drilled Haukon in swordplay. They met in a secluded clearing a little apart from the longhouse, where the clack of the wooden swords he'd insisted upon wouldn't be heard by others. The lad was quick, but Brandr refused to let him practice with a real weapon until he mastered the basics.

At Katla's command, Brandr followed at a discreet distance when Gormson insisted on walking the boundaries of her land with her. And one afternoon when Albrikt wasn't with Katla, Brandr kept a watchful eye on the Stordman as he inspected the private wharf and considered the sheltered bay that brought traders almost to her doorstep.

It was such a well-hidden cove, a man might sail past its narrow inlet without realizing two dozen ships could ride at anchor unseen beyond the curtain of rocks and trees. Being a sailing man, Brandr understood the bay's value.

And Gormson's interest in it.

Albrikt insisted upon a daylong hike through the forest to the highest peak on Katla's property. Brandr dogged them, ostensibly to bear the food and drink for Katla and her suitor, but he suspected he'd been ordered along because she didn't feel safe with the man so far from the rest of her people.

Gormson was the sort to take what he wanted if he thought he could get away with it. Brandr was glad Katla seemed to know it.

From the most elevated point on Katla's steading, a man could view the island's edges, north and south. To the East, the mouth of Hardanger Fjord opened invitingly. It was also the place where a signal fire was laid and ready to be set in the event Katla's people came under attack. If the rectangular stack of wood, which stood as tall as a man, was ablaze, it would be visible for miles.

"Who will come if the fire is lit?" Gormson wanted to know.

"We have alliances with several other farmsteads on Tysnes, but have no fear. We've been at peace for so long, the wood for the signal fire is like to rot before it's burned," Katla said with satisfaction.

On the last evening at night meal, Albrikt pressed his suit with fervor.

Brandr smiled broadly when Katla refused to give him an answer beyond thanking him for his offer. Her brothers had promised her a choice from three suitors, she said, and she would not give any a yea or nay until she'd had proper time to consider all her possibilities.

Brandr could have kissed her on the spot. If he hadn't given his word not to, of course.

Honor was a damnably difficult thing to live with sometimes.

෨ඏ

"Katla, I don't know what you're playing at, putting him off that way," Finn said as they stood side by side on the wharf to see Gormson off. "You'll never do better than Albrikt."

"Send for the next two suitors, and let me be the judge of that," she said as Albrikt's broad-breasted *knorr* cleared the bay, its red-and-white striped sail swaying from the single mast in the choppier open water. "Son of Ulf!"

"I'm right here." Brandr stepped forward, adding through gritted teeth, "And I'm not deaf."

She knew he was nearby. Hadn't he been her shadow the whole time Gormson was in residence? Even if she hadn't ordered him to keep watch over her, he'd have found a way to do it on his own. Now that the Stord Islander was gone, Brandr breathed easier, but the iron collar chafed his soul no less. And the need to find a way to free himself so he could return home was no less on his mind.

She pursed her lips at his grumbling. It bordered on

disrespect, but she let it pass. Katla evidently had other things on her mind besides humbling him.

"I'll be gone the rest of the day," she told her brother.

"Where are you off to?" Finn asked.

"I need to gather gull eggs, because *someone* butchered too many of my laying hens for his huge feasts." She shot a glance toward Finn, curling her lip. "So we need to let the next several batches of eggs hatch."

"Can't even entertain a guest to suit you." Finn shook his head in disgust. "Since there's no pleasing you, Katla, why are you surprised when I don't try?"

Katla flinched as her brother stomped away. Brandr wondered why no one else could see she wasn't as immune to hurt as she tried to seem.

While the rest of her people headed back up the hill to the longhouse and their day's labor, Katla started walking down the wharf toward a trim little coracle. Brandr fell into step with her from force of habit.

It had nothing to do with she being his mistress and he being her thrall. It was the swing of her skirts that drew him this time.

"The bird cliffs are on the far side of the island," she said. "How good a sailor are you?"

His mouth twitched. "I sailed to the Great Inland Sea and back without getting lost. I think I can manage a trip around Tysnes."

"*Ja*, well, then you'll have no trouble readying the coracle while I fetch food and water," she said brusquely as she turned to follow her people up the hill. She glanced over her shoulder at him and, amazingly enough, shot him a quick smile. "I'll be right back."

Brandr stepped into the small craft. His chest

swelled with pleasure when the shallow hull swayed under his feet.

A man needed the wind in his face and the salt spray on his cheeks from time to time. He'd been landlocked only a short time, but even so, he missed the sea.

The climbing tackle and ropes they'd need to gather the gull eggs were in a tangled pile near the prow. By the time he recoiled the ropes, checked all the coracle's lines, and made sure the sail was in good repair, Katla was making her way around the last bend in the path leading back down to the wharf. She carried a couple water gourds and a basket.

And her smile was still intact.

A whole day on the sea.

And in the company of a comely, smiling woman. His heart hadn't been this light since before the iron collar was bolted around his neck.

He scrambled back onto the wharf to hand her into the coracle. Once she was settled on the seat near the prow, he loosed the mooring lines and gave the little boat a shove. Brandr leaped into the craft before it bobbed too far from the dock. The hull dipped under his weight but then righted itself so the waves didn't wash over the sides.

He unfurled the sail and caught a breath of wind. Once out of the sheltered cove, the wind picked up, billowing the sail. The coracle lifted above the curling whitecaps, skimming along with eye-watering speed. Katla turned sideways on the front seat to watch the island's coastline whip by them in a green blur where the heavy pine forests rushed down to meet the sea.

Brandr was content to watch her.

Sunlight danced on the water, and the wind loosened her hair from its kerchief. She trailed a hand in the spray, with a laugh full of joy in the wind-whipped, sunny morning. It was a musical sound, a sound to bind a man's heart. And if that weren't enough, her smile was blinding.

Brandr realized he was finally catching a glimpse of the real Katla.

She played the dour matron with conviction. She oversaw her people and stock with grim efficiency, husbanding her resources against the unknown. She was as ruthless as a general strategizing how best to make use of his forces for an upcoming battle.

But Katla's foes weren't armed with axes and arrows. She struggled against want and hunger and cold. No one in her household would suffer from them while she drew breath. She fought them away from her people with dogged relentlessness, land bound and thoroughly wedded to her duty to care for those in her charge.

But she really wasn't so tied to the land as she first appeared. She obviously loved the ocean far too much.

In her heart of hearts, she was a sea nymph. A laughing, beguiling water sprite who'd somehow washed ashore on Tysnes Island. Without a man at her side, she'd been forced to act the part of the severe leader and provider for her people. She did it well, but seeing her now, breathless with joy as they bounded over the swells, Brandr knew she was out of her true element most of the time and shouldering a far heavier burden than she ought.

He wished he could lighten it for her. If for no other reason than being able to see her mouth lift in a genuine smile. Mayhap there was even a way to make those frown lines between her brows disappear completely.

He shook his head at himself. A sea nymph? He wasn't usually so fanciful, but Katla seemed to bring out the hidden skald in his soul.

"You really do know how to sail," she said as they skirted the coastline, tacking and reefing when needed to keep their forward momentum going.

"And you really love being on the water," he said. "Did your husband take you sailing often?"

"Osvald?" She rolled her eyes. "No, he never sailed if he could avoid it. He'd rather have taken a couple days and tramped across the island on the plank road than take the coracle, even though the boat is much faster." She patted her belly. "Weak stomach."

Brandr laughed and nodded. His brother, Arn, had been the same way as a boy, but their father forced him to stay on a longship until he stopped puking and learned to roll with the ocean. It had seemed cruel at the time, since Arn couldn't help his weakness, but once he found his sea legs, he never heaved his guts over the gunwale again.

Brandr had to admit it was one time when their father's harshness hadn't been the wrong course.

"I used to sail to the bird cliffs with my father," Katla said, her tone suddenly wistful. "My mother used to go with him, but she died when Haukon was born. I'm the eldest, so Father spent more time with me than he might have otherwise. He taught me to handle this coracle."

"Really?" It was an odd thing for a man to teach his daughter. Work was fairly well divided among the sexes, with the women toiling inside, cooking and weaving, the men out in the elements, farming and hunting.

And Viking, in the not-so-distant past.

"My brothers didn't care for the sea or fishing or even traveling for trade. Of course, Finn and the others don't care for anything that resembles work, but I loved sailing. How can you even call it work if you can feel the sun on your face and the wind lifting your spirits along with the sails?" Her smile faded a bit. "My father used to say I should have been born a man."

"I'm glad you weren't," Brandr said as they glided into the deep shadow of the land.

Briny spray misted around them from the waves dashing against the rocks, and the coracle heaved more wildly as they drew closer to their destination.

Her smile returned. "Well, I'm glad not to be a man. Now especially," she said as they tied up the coracle at the base of the cliff where a huge flock of gulls nested in the craggy granite.

The sheer rock face rose over six times Brandr's height. Beneath the waves, jagged rocks lurked. A tumble from the cliff into the water was to be avoided at all costs.

Katla handed the climbing tackle to him, her grin turning wicked. "I'm very happy to be a woman. After all, the man gets to climb to the top of the cliff first."

Never should have given the man trousers, Katla lamented in silence as she watched him scramble up the rock face from the bobbing coracle. The morning after Gormson had arrived, she'd found a baggy pair that covered Brandr decently yet weren't fine enough to elevate him from his lowly status as her thrall.

She sighed. This climb would have made for a spectacular view if she hadn't. She'd be treated to the sight of his well-muscled thighs and tight buttocks as he worked his way up the cliff.

But he needed the protection of his trousers. The sharp rocks might cut his knees and other more important parts to shreds otherwise.

Brandr was about halfway up, the climbing tackle coiled over his broad shoulders. He flattened himself against the granite and stretched to reach the next fingerhold.

A chunk of stone broke off in his hand. It tumbled from his grasp, splashing into the sea next to the coracle. Katla was drenched by the spray but couldn't tear her gaze from the rock face.

Brandr's feet slipped, and he dangled by one arm.

Katla gasped.

"Are you hit?" he called.

She shook her head, not trusting her voice.

Then he grinned down at her, obviously unaware her heart had skipped several beats. He swung himself back around, found a toehold, and clutched a different bit of rock. This one held his weight as he lifted himself with just his arms to a narrow ledge. The rest of the climb passed without incident, but several times, Katla had to remind herself to breathe.

Once he disappeared over the top of the cliff, she cupped her hands around her mouth. "Tie the line off on a boulder or tree and toss the tackle seat back to me."

"I understand how this works, you know. You're not the only one who's ever gathered gull eggs." His face appeared over the ledge, his features set in a hard grimace. "You may tell me what to do or how to do it, but not both."

"You warned me to be specific. I don't want a repeat of the way you kissed my foot," she called back testily.

"No danger of that, princess." The leather seat came hurtling toward her, stopping an arm's reach above the coracle. "There'll be no kissing today—on your foot or anywhere else—unless you order it."

"Unless I order it," she muttered. "It's a wonder the man continues to breathe without my say-so."

Didn't he *want* to kiss her?

"What's that?" he shouted down.

"Nothing."

Absolutely nothing. Why had she even brought the matter up? There was no way she was going to order him to kiss her, and that was final.

Katla stood, balancing in the rocking coracle as he lowered the seat the rest of the way. She slipped the triangular seat over her head and slid it down her body to fit the wide leather strap under her bottom. Then she lashed the upper part of the harness around her waist to give herself a secure ride. She tied the basket holding their food and drink to the harness and pulled on some work gloves.

"All right," she shouted. "You can—oof!"

She rose, legs kicking, into the air. Then she dipped suddenly, enough to trail her skirts into the water for a heartbeat before rising again. Masculine laughter washed down to her as he swung her toward the cliff face. She kept herself from bashing into the rock with her feet and palms. She bounced a couple times against the sheer face. Once she came to a complete stop, she glared up at him.

"I wasn't ready."

He leaned over the edge and cocked his head at her. "But I was."

Brandr looped the slack in the rope around one arm and over his massive shoulder, not straining under her weight a bit. Then he straightened and disappeared from her view.

"Let me know if you need more or less line," he called down.

She snorted. Everything was always a struggle with this man. He challenged her at every step. No matter how long Brandr Ulfson wore the iron collar, he'd probably never think of himself as her thrall.

Katla worked her way along the rock face, swinging out in long jumps from one clump of twigs and dried vegetation to the next. Gulls usually laid three or four eggs, but she never took more than two from any one nest. Birds screamed and dived at her, but none came close, since they never knew when she might kick out from the cliff face and become as airborne as they.

Katla supposed they must think her a much larger bird and wouldn't chance a fight.

Each time she called out, Brandr hauled her up higher on the cliff face. She supposed she ought to feel some trepidation, both for her precarious perch above the surf and for the man who literally held her life in his hands.

But despite their wrangling for control, she trusted him. He'd given her his oath to obey her and not to try to escape his fate. In the few days she'd known him, he'd proved his honor was important to him. She felt safer when he dogged her steps. Her life was spent caring for others. For the first time in a long while, someone was looking after her.

And it felt wonderful.

She reveled in the sense of lightness, in the ease with which she danced along the rock face. When she pushed away from the cliff and swooped to a new spot, it was almost as if she sprouted wings.

She was nearing the top, only another few spans of a man's arm, when her rigging began to loosen. The knot on the upper part of the harness unraveled, and the piece at her waist gave way. With the next leap, her bottom slipped forward off the thick leather strap.

Katla screamed and grasped at the rigging, catching it with one hand. She spun in midair. Her body slammed against the rocks, but she clutched the leather strap in a death grip.

Every muscle in her body clenched tight. She was dimly aware that the basket with their provisions tipped and all her carefully harvested eggs had fallen into the sea below. But she didn't dare look down.

If she fell, she'd be dashed to pieces on the rocks. Panic froze her. She could only cling to the rigging, unable to even think what to do to help herself.

"Katla! Grab on with your other hand!" Brandr

shouted down to her, leaning so far over the ledge she feared he might topple off.

His words cut through her stunned rigor. She sucked in a quick breath and heaved her other arm up. She managed to wrap her fingers around the rope and gripped it with all her might.

"Hang on."

She didn't think she could release her grip even if she wanted to.

Brandr pulled her up, hand over hand. When she was near enough for him to reach her wrists, he dropped to his knees and then flat on his belly. He grasped her so hard his nails bit into her flesh.

She found a toehold and pushed herself up. Brandr's eyes were wide, his mouth drawn into a hard line. She saw herself mirrored in his darkening pupils, her face a mask of terror. He gave a mighty heave and tugged her over the rugged lip of the cliff.

He rocked on his knees and fell backward, dragging her body on top of his. His arms clamped tight around her, as if he'd never let go, and together, they rolled away from the cliff's edge onto a bed of spongy moss and salt grass.

Both of them panted for breath. Katla could feel his heart galloping beneath hers. She tried to control the shiver of delayed terror that wracked her body but couldn't quite manage it. Brandr stroked her hair and down her back, his touch gentle and full of comfort.

"Oh gods, Katla," he said, when the worst of her trembling stopped. He cradled the back of her head in his palm, pressing her cheek to his. "I thought I'd lost you."

She'd thought so too, for a moment.

While she dangled over the precipice, the Great Dark had loomed before her, a daunting and unknown place. She knew all the stories of Valhalla. She'd heard skalds weave the tales of Freya's hall for unhappy lovers, and how they lived in the land beyond death, reveling in the bliss Fate had denied them here. She'd even listened politely while visiting priests described the Christians' blissful heaven and their fiery hell.

Who was to say what really bided on the other side of that dark portal?

Her body hummed with life. And a new awareness of just how close Brandr was pressed against her.

Katla looked down at the man who had saved her life. She'd enthralled him, and yet he hadn't let her drop to her death. Then she said the two words she'd promised herself she'd never say.

"Kiss me."

Chapter 11

HE DIDN'T NEED TO BE TOLD TWICE.

Brandr captured her face, palms on her cheeks, and slowly brought her mouth to his. Her soft lips molded to his, fitting together so perfectly there was no space, no break in the seal between them.

He ran his tongue along the seam of her lips, tasting her. She was sweet, a sip of nectar. Succulent, juicy, and moist as the exotic pomegranate he'd tried in the South. Salty, a chilling reminder of the sea and the jagged rocks she had narrowly escaped.

When her lips parted, he drank more deeply of her, determined to push aside all thought of those horrible things that might have been. His tongue sought hers with feverish desperation.

Without breaking their kiss, he rolled so they lay side by side. He hitched a leg over hers, keeping her close, claiming her. Her eyes were shut, but Brandr kept his open so he could watch her.

So he wouldn't lose her.

Her dark lashes were silky crescents on her cheeks. Her brows drew together in longing.

Her lips parted wider, and she sucked the breath from his body. Then she refilled him with her own. Brandr was used to taking the lead with a woman, but Katla seemed to want to wrestle him for control, even now.

He wasn't the least surprised. She wouldn't be Katla otherwise.

She kissed him fiercely, as if it were the last thing she'd ever do.

Or maybe the first thing.

A brush with death made a body feel reborn. He'd stared down that cold specter a few times himself and recognized the vibrant rush of lust that followed. He heard his own heartbeat pounding in his ears, felt Katla's throbbing against his chest. The echoing rhythm of blood surged in his stiff cock.

Katla pressed herself against him, rocking her pelvis. She felt it too—the drumbeat of life pulsing between them. She groaned into his mouth.

She was no longer the acknowledged head of her people, bowed by her burden and stiff under the mantle of leadership. She was only herself. Unfettered, passionate, free of all constraints.

Alive.

He abandoned her mouth to press hot kisses down her neck to the open collar of her thin underdress. Her skin was tender, and he barely restrained himself from sucking a bit between his teeth and giving her a love bite. He didn't want to chance anything that might cause her to stop him.

She smelled of cedar and warm woman. Her scent made him ache so badly, the line between pleasure and pain started to blur. He couldn't find enough bare skin to ease his throbbing need.

Her hands roamed over him, pulling up the hem of his tunic and slipping beneath it to smooth her palms over his abdomen and chest. His nipple tightened when she raked a nail around one. He almost sat up and yanked off the garment to give her unimpeded access, but he feared she'd come to her senses and call a halt if he stopped kissing her.

In a one-handed feat of dexterity, he unhooked her left brooch and pulled down that side of her overtunic. He cupped her breast through the linen underdress and thrummed her nipple. It strained toward him beneath the thin layer of fabric. He covered it with his mouth and sucked, linen and all.

She murmured something. He couldn't make out the words, but they sounded earthy, needy, full of deep hunger. When he nipped the tender flesh, she cried out his name.

It was a surrender.

He released her nipple. It showed clearly through the damp underdress, the wet fabric nearly transparent. He pressed another kiss to the fabric, and she arched into his mouth.

Her bare skin would be sweeter, but he didn't dare try to undress her completely. Not here. Not if it might lead her to start thinking again instead of feeling.

He kissed back up her neck and captured her mouth again. This time, she didn't fight him for control of the kiss. He rolled her onto her back and ravaged her lips. He made love to her mouth, plunging his tongue in and out.

Would her body receive him as warmly and with as much luxuriant wetness?

It was time to find out.

❧

Brandr's hand was on her breast again, teasing her through the wet linen. She ached when he rolled the taut bud between his thumb and forefinger.

She wanted to climb inside his tunic and feel the heat of rock-solid chest against her damp breast.

And his kiss! Skalds sang of the nine worlds of creation. Of all of them, only smoldering *Muspel* was said to be a place full of fire. Brandr's kiss was a molten world of its own.

He consumed her. Every place his mouth touched, he branded her. He turned her insides all warm and liquid with nothing more than his lips, teeth, and tongue.

His beard and mustache stubble had grown enough to be soft, yet it was still short enough to prickle her cheeks and chin. She ran her hand over his sleek head. It was like stroking a selkie.

She gave in to the downward pull in her groin. A heaviness gathered between her legs, a throbbing, aching mass. When she felt the breeze slip up under her skirts, she knew he was rucking up her hem, sliding his fingertips from her calf, over her knee, and up her thigh. She propped up one knee to give him easier access to the tender skin of her inner thigh.

He skimmed over her, brushing the small hairs over her sex and then trailing down her other leg. She moaned into his mouth in frustration.

His hand stroked her again, and this time she lifted herself into his questing fingers, but he moved on once more, teasing and circling.

She longed for his intimate touch. She was near to begging for it.

She reached for him, rubbing his hard shaft through his trousers, and this time, *he* groaned.

The next time his hand passed over her, his skillful fingers slipped into her soft folds. He massaged the lips of her sex and circled her opening until she squirmed for him to slip a finger into her.

Two fingers.

The yawning emptiness was still there. She wanted more. Needed more.

Slick with her own wetness, Brandr's fingers glided with ease to her most sensitive spot, but she didn't break off their kiss. She couldn't get enough of the man's mouth. Tendrils of bliss radiated through her.

The world started spinning. She tore her mouth from his kiss to catch her breath, hoping for a slice of sanity. But she fell into Brandr's amber eyes instead.

She gasped a lungful of sweet air. The musky perfume of her arousal mingled with the crisp sea air and thick pine. She swallowed hard but couldn't look away from him as he continued to drive her to aching fury.

He made soft sounds of encouragement. She knew he was speaking to her, but her mind refused to make sense of his words. Her whole world spiraled down to the heat, the friction, the aching need between her legs.

And the throbbing emptiness of her womb.

"Please," she whispered as a single tear slid into her

hairline and down to her ear. The man had reduced her to pleading, but she could feel no shame over it. Want knew no shame. "I need…"

"What do you need, Katla?" His voice rumbled over her, a wave of masculine sound. All that was feminine in her shivered in its wake.

"You."

She groped for him again, and this time, her fingers found the drawstring at his waist. He helped her pull down his trousers.

Then he moved into position between her legs.

He braced himself on his elbows to spare her from the full brunt of his weight. He needn't have bothered. She wanted to feel him.

All of him.

He leaned down to kiss her again. The tip of him teased her entrance.

She gasped at the contact, longing to be filled. Ached for his thick, long length inside her.

He slid into her in one slow stroke, penetrating her so deeply her breath caught in her throat. The emptiness retreated, but the ache remained.

Then he began to move.

She rocked with him, rising to meet his slow thrusts with an undulating roll of her hips. When he fully sheathed himself in her, his lips parted, and she recognized bliss on his face. Each time he pulled out, his brows drew together, as if he were bereft at nearly severing their deep connection.

Her insides tightened, coiled. A knot with no end, no way to untangle itself.

Brandr picked up speed, and each time he drove

into her, the pressure on her sensitive spot made her cry out a little, sobbing for more.

Then when she thought she couldn't be tied in any tighter a cluster of frayed ends, it was as if someone tugged the right thread, and she unraveled like a spool of yarn bounding across the longhouse floor. Her inner walls clenched.

He stopped moving, sheathed to his balls, while she spasmed around him. Her limbs shook, and her body bucked with the force of her release. She drew a shuddering breath as her womb constricted once more.

When she subsided, he gave one more slow thrust. A low growl sounded from the back of his throat, and she felt him erupt in hot pulses inside her.

He rocked his hips a couple times as he finished, and then his full weight settled on her. He laid his forehead on the mossy ground beside her head, close enough that his stubbled cheek tickled her ear.

Brandr lay there panting for a few heartbeats while Katla tried to recover her breath as well.

Then he started to rise.

"No, don't," she said, wrapping her arms and legs around him. It felt so wonderful to hold him inside her. She couldn't bear to be empty again so soon.

He laid his head back down, obviously content to remain where he was, still joined with her.

Katla stroked his head and neck, reveling in their deep connection. She smoothed her hands down the rough tunic covering his back. It would have been lovely to have touched his bare skin, glorious to feel it against hers, but the act had been so instinctive, so spontaneous, they were both still almost fully clothed.

"I wish you had taken this off," she said. Now that her mind was functioning again, she could actually form intelligible sentences. Osvald had ridden her hard on occasion, but he never reduced her to such incoherent need.

He turned his head to nuzzle her ear. "I didn't want to do anything that might give you a chance to change your mind." She could hear his grin.

It was hard not to smile a bit in return. How could he know her so well already? She'd never felt so sated, never had such a shattering release. If Brandr took advantage of a momentary weakness, she realized she didn't care a whit.

Then with the benefit of a clear head, she thought about it for a moment.

She'd taken pleasure with her thrall. He'd reduced her to senseless, blind need. This had the potential to change matters between them, to tilt the balance of power in his favor.

But perhaps not as much as if he were a freeman. She was still his mistress, after all. Still in control.

And she needed to be seen to be in control.

He rose up on his elbows and grinned down at her. "I'd like you a good deal less dressed too. Mayhap next time we'll pick a place where that's possible."

"Next time?" she said as he slipped out of her. "What makes you think there'll be a next time?"

He arched a brow at her. "Because you and I both liked that. A lot."

"You presume too much." She pressed against his chest, but he didn't budge. "Let me up."

His smile faded. "Did I hurt you? What's wrong?"

"I'm fine," she said. "But we've been gone too long with naught to show for the time wasted. We need to get back."

With a dark frown, he rolled off her.

She quickly smoothed down her skirts to cover her legs. Her silver brooch was partially hidden in the grass, but she leaned over to retrieve it now. She lifted up the corner of her overtunic to cover the damp spot on her breast and refastened the brooch. Her nipple was still perked and tingling under the thin linen.

"Did we lose everything in the basket?" she asked, studiously not looking at him.

He didn't answer. His silence forced her to meet his gaze. He regarded her through narrowed eyes, as if she were a type of beast he didn't quite recognize, and he wasn't sure whether she was a threat or not.

"Did that mean nothing to you?" he finally said.

She swallowed hard. It meant worlds. She'd never felt the like, but it wouldn't do to let him know it. A woman had to be strong, lest a man run roughshod over her. How could she remain his mistress if he knew how adroitly he'd controlled her, how weak she was in his hands?

"It was a pleasant diversion," she said simply. "And that is all."

She rose to her feet and was chagrined to find her legs wobbly. The basket was upended near the cliff's edge, and all the gull eggs were either lost or ruined. The meat pasties she'd packed must have tumbled into the sea, but one of the drinking gourds was still intact. Katla took quick gulp and held it out to Brandr.

"The sun is near setting," she said, "and we have work to do at home."

He waved the gourd away and stood to pull on his trousers. "As you will, princess," he said with a scowl. "As you will."

Chapter 12

THE SUN SANK INTO THE WESTERN SEA, AND THE coracle skimmed over shadow-dark waters as they skirted the island. The basket that should have been filled with gull eggs was empty, but the air around them was overflowing with frustration and bewilderment and unspoken rage. Katla's stiff posture and deliberate failure to even glance his way signaled she wasn't inclined to talk about it.

It was just as well. Brandr was still so dumbfounded by her abrupt change toward him, he didn't know what to say.

She'd been so passionate, so unabashedly needy, so soul naked and hungry. In satisfying her needs, his own had been met beyond his wildest imaginings. He'd never experienced anything like her.

Then in a few blinks, she was as ice bound as a frost maiden. As if she hadn't just melted under him. As if they hadn't held each other's souls inside their joined bodies.

The woman took her pleasure like the worst of men, who used their partners and moved on without the least acknowledgment that, if for only a moment, they'd taken part in something special.

Something precious.

He'd had his share of lovers, mostly married women, so there could be no mistaking the relationship for anything other than an arrangement to satisfy mutual needs. But he'd never run so flaming hot and then so suddenly cold with any of them. When the physical relationship burned out, the association ended with genuine affection and usually abiding friendship.

Katla's glossy hair still shined in the rosy light of the dying sun. Her skin still glowed. No man worthy of the name would deny she was a beautiful woman.

But if Brandr wasn't careful, she'd eat his heart for night meal and serve up his balls for breakfast.

By the time the coracle sidled next to the wharf, Finn was there to meet them. He held out a hand to help his sister from the craft. While Brandr leaped out and secured the coracle, he wondered how Katla would explain coming home empty-handed after being gone all day.

A skald could turn her near-plummet to the surf into a tale that would earn many a night meal, but Katla didn't strike him as the type to dramatize her own exploits. The real tale of how they tumbled into each other's arms after her scare was ripe enough for the makings of a maidensong—a forbidden love story.

Though love had little to do with their passionate tryst, he'd learned in the end.

As it turned out, Brandr needn't have worried

about how Katla would account for their time away. Finn was too full of his own news to ask after theirs.

"We've found another suitor for you, sister."

Brandr made himself busy, coiling the rope and stowing the climbing tackle. His ears pricked with interest though his head warned him not to care about what he heard.

"Oh, Finn, what nonsense is this? I thought you were going to mend the fence around the cattle byre today." Katla shook her head in disappointment. "You promised you would."

"And so I did. That fence is better than new. You can see for yourself when you get there," he said with an injured sniff. "I didn't have anything to do with this new suitor. Finding another fellow for you was Einar's and Haukon's doing."

"You really mended the fence? I'm surpri—" She caught herself before she insulted her brother. "That's good, Finn. I'm...pleased," she finished primly. "But where did Einar and Haukon find another suitor in such short order? At the mead house?"

"Well..."

"Oh, Finn!"

"You didn't say anything about where we had to find the men to court you," her brother complained. "You only said they mustn't be fools."

"How can Einar and Haukon tell the man isn't a fool, if they've got their noses in a mead pot?"

Brandr had to admit she had a point. He'd certainly been a fool the last time he was in a mead house. And he was still paying for that folly.

Finn rubbed the back of his neck in obvious

frustration. "Katla, we had an agreement. The son of Ulf as your thrall in exchange for your acceptance of another husband. Will you give this new man a fair hearing?"

"Fine." She crossed her arms over her chest. "When?"

"On the morrow."

She rolled her eyes. "Well, at least it will give him time to sober up."

Then she stomped away from both of them. Brandr and Finn watched her determined stride up the steep path.

"Has she always been like this?" Brandr asked.

"No," Finn said absently. It didn't seem to occur to him it wasn't proper for a thrall to ask such a thing about his mistress. "Only since our mother died. She's the eldest of us. When Haukon was born and we lost Mother, Katla had seen only eight winters or so herself. But she took it into her head that she had to stand in our mother's stead, and she never got over the notion."

So the mantle of responsibility had fallen on Katla early and heavily. Brandr began to understand a little of how that weight had shaped her.

"I suppose she'll always think we can't wipe our own backsides," Finn said. "Nothing will get done unless she's there to supervise. I blame Osvald."

"Why? A man can't help dying." Especially in a world where men like Brandr's father were happy to help them do it.

"No, but he might have had the decency to give her a child before he picked that fight with Ulf Skallagrimsson," Finn said. "If she had a bairn of her own to tend, mayhap she wouldn't need to mother the rest of us all the time."

Brandr raised his brows in surprise. So his father hadn't murdered Katla's husband. It might even have been self-defense. He wondered if she knew Osvald had started the row that ended his life.

Finn was probably on the mark about the bairn too. Brandr recalled the look of yearning he'd caught on her face when she was surrounded by children that first morning of his enthrallment. She was warm and nurturing with the offspring of others, but a woman who was hungry for a child of her own wouldn't be satisfied with anything less.

Having her own bairn would have changed matters for Katla.

Her burdens had made her hard. Had she also become so brittle she'd break?

Brandr wondered what would happen if he shouldered some of her duties and let her breathe. Would the smiling, laughing Katla he'd seen in the coracle return to stay?

Would the heart-stopping vixen on the cliff top welcome him to her bed again? She was young enough for childbearing yet. Perhaps he could give her a child where her husband failed.

He damn sure wouldn't mind trying.

Despite his firm conviction that he was probably on a fool's errand, that Katla was as much a man-eater as the black-maned lion he'd seen in the emperor's menagerie, Brandr decided it would be worth taking a chance. He'd glimpsed Katla's softer self, the one he hoped was her true self. If there was a chance he could coax that Katla to stay, he might also convince her to free him so he could see to the trouble brewing in his brother's *jarlhof*. Either way, he was willing to brave her claws should he fail.

He also decided Finn wasn't the do-nothing slacker and general lackwit Katla took him for.

At least, not all the time.

"That fence you mended," Brandr said. "Was it wrought in timber or stonework?"

"Timber," Finn said. "I prefer to work with wood. I'm no farmer."

Brandr frowned, perplexed. "Then why do you need Katla to wed so you can have your own land?"

"In truth, coin would mean more to me than land right now," Finn admitted.

Brandr had been wearing a heavy gold chain when Finn and his brothers enthralled him. The pouch of silver at his waist had been full. It was more wealth than many fjord-bound men would see all their lives.

"What did you do with the coin you took from me?"

Finn shrugged. "We had debts. Einar's partial to playing *tawl-bwrdd*, but the die is not partial to him, more's the pity. Your silver saved him from his creditors."

Brandr had seen men squander a fortune over dice games in Byzantium. Gambling had never been his weakness, but he couldn't fault a man for having one. His failing was always a pretty face and the flip of a skirt. The iron collar chafed his neck. Chasing a beddable maid had certainly cost him more than a fortune this time.

"What will you do with your portion once Katla weds?" Brandr asked.

"I'll learn shipbuilding," Finn said quickly. "If I see enough coin as a result of Katla's match, I'll hie myself to Osberg, where I can hire out to a master who'll teach me the craft."

"Katla said you didn't like sailing."

"I don't," Finn said with a sheepish grin. "But I do like wood."

"I know a shipwright in Jondal," Brandr said. "He's always looking for more hands. At least he was five years ago. Things may have changed. But if they haven't, I could recommend you to him."

Finn cast him a sidelong glance. "Come take a look at my fence before you offer that, or I'll suspect you're trying to get on my good side. I can't free you, you know."

"I know." Only Katla could do that.

And even if she did, he wondered if he'd ever truly be free.

❧

The night meal was a much simpler affair now that her brothers weren't trying to impress a potential suitor with the richness of her steading. The ale flowed less freely, and no stronger spirits had been offered. Inga and the other cooks served up a thick stew with fresh barley bread. Nourishing and filling, assuredly, but not designed to awe.

Katla had never felt less like eating, but she knew her people expected her to share in the communal meal that night. So she chased her turnips around her trencher and forced herself to join in conversations with others, to laugh at Finn's jokes and scold Einar for idleness and Haukon for wolfing down his food. The gangly youth was still growing and ate like it. He shoveled his food in as if it might escape should he be too slow.

But her mind was back on the top of the bird cliff.

She relived those stolen moments with Brandr in such throbbing detail, a soft ache started in her belly. When he leaned over her to refill her drinking horn, his masculine scent crowded her senses and set all the small hairs on her body at full attention.

Katla was acutely aware of his presence behind her, though she wouldn't allow herself to turn to look at him. She couldn't help seeing his strong forearms and long-fingered hands as he served her.

Square-nailed. Beautiful. Strong hands.

They were the hands of a warrior, a sailing man, a lover.

Brandr's hands had driven her to such madness, she was helpless before him. He'd seen her as no one in her whole life had.

Needy. Weak. Vulnerable.

Osvald hadn't wakened that deep hunger in her, never made her lose her calm reserve.

She dared not allow it to happen again.

Katla raised her horn to her lips and tried to swallow back the lump forming in her throat.

"Inga!" Finn called across the long room. "Give us a song, girl."

The quiet serving woman nodded and drew out a pan flute from her bag of possessions. When she put it to her lips, the entire company fell silent, leaning forward in hushed expectancy.

Katla's hall boasted no skald, but they were gifted with music on a regular basis. Inga played as well as any piper she'd ever heard. The first tune was a ripping good jig that set everyone's toes tapping.

Katla considered her freewoman as she played. Inga was comely enough, she supposed. Her facial features were pleasing but unremarkable. Her cornflower blue eyes were no bluer than many others seated in the hall. Inga's form was curvy enough, but to Katla's eye, she didn't seem blessed with attributes beyond the ordinary. Her honey-blond braids were thick and fell to her waist, but many women boasted the same. Katla's dark tresses were more unusual.

She had often wondered if Inga's musical ability was why Osvald took her for his bed slave each month when Katla's moon sickness appeared. When the girl played her pan flute, her whole being seemed to light from within. There was a liveliness, a sensuality, a soul deepness on display in her music that Inga kept carefully hidden the rest of the time.

Had she sparked to life in Osvald's bed, as well?

Katla gave herself a mental shake. No good could come from wandering down that road. Besides, Inga had never given her cause to resent her by flaunting her special relationship with Osvald. A good wife shouldn't trouble herself over her husband's concubine.

Especially her *dead* husband's concubine.

Would she have felt differently if she and Osvald had shared the same kind of fire she and Brandr discovered in each other's arms?

As if he'd heard her think of him, Brandr leaned

over to refill her drinking horn. Her insides tightened and tingled.

When Inga finished playing the jig, everyone pounded their fists on the table in appreciation. She smiled shyly and ducked her head.

"This next one is a new tune," she said, her voice barely reaching the far ends of the longhouse. "I learned it from a Danish trader a month gone by and have been practicing it since. It's finally ready to play for you. He said it was called 'I Dreamed a Dream.'"

Inga raised the pan flute, and a yearning tune curled from her instrument. The tone was pure and sweet, wrapped about with her breath, as if she were sending bits of her soul out with it. The wistfulness of the song stole around Katla's heart and squeezed.

She, too, had dreamed a dream.

She longed for children and a man to help her raise them. Someone to bear half her load. She imagined what it would be like to be desired for herself alone, not for her land or for any other gain.

She ached for love, not just for a joining, even one as breath stealing as the one with Brandr Ulfson's had been. She yearned for it, straining like Inga's bitter-sweet melody, stretched almost to the breaking point.

She dreamed of *inn matki munr*, the mighty passion. This love of legend was said to be so strong, so intimate a bond, lovers could actually hear each other's thoughts.

Instead, she'd had a husband who left her bed for a week every month to join his body to this pretty musician's. A husband who couldn't give her a son, though he claimed to have sired plenty at other farm-steads all over the island before they wed.

The song went on and on, plucking at Katla's soul, piercing her weakest point.

A tear trembled on her lashes. She tried to blink it back, but it escaped and raced down her cheek. She swiped it away angrily before anyone could see.

The sweet, sad melody sang the hidden desires of Katla's heart as surely as if it were being pulled from her chest instead of coaxed from Inga's flute.

At this point in her life, she expected she'd have so much more. Someone to love her despite her faults, someone whose soul fitted neatly with the bends and crooks in hers.

How could the unknown creator of Inga's tune possibly know the despair she felt?

By the time the song reached its end, Katla had to cover her mouth to keep from sobbing. There was suddenly not enough air in the great hall, and she struggled for her next breath. While the rest of the company pounded their approval, Katla rose and fled to her chamber.

Not bothering to light her lamp, she threw herself on the bed and buried her face in the linens, where it was safe to give vent to her grief. She wept into the feather tick as she hadn't wept at Osvald's graveside.

She'd never know the mighty passion, never hear her beloved's voice in her head, whispering a secret language only the two of them shared. No one would ever love her merely for herself.

The death of a dream was even harder to bear than the loss of a husband. She drenched the Frankish linens with her tears.

Every person in the longhouse needed her. Her days blurred with one task after another.

What did any of it matter?

She was always surrounded by a crowd of people, but Katla was so alone it made her chest ache.

She heard the click of the latch but didn't look up. She knew who it was. No one else would be so bold as to enter her chamber without permission.

Lamplight flickered to life, sending his long shadow wavering against the back wall.

"What do you want, son of Ulf?"

"You."

Katla swiped her eyes with her forearm and sat up. She blew her nose loudly into a small square of cloth and crumpled it in her hand. She turned to face him. He looked at her with an intensity that should have scared her. Instead, it made her breath catch and her nipples perk to aching hardness.

"I won't free you simply because you bed me," she warned.

"I'm not asking to be freed," he said, his voice husky with desire. "But I do intend to bed you."

Chapter 13

HER NOSE WAS RED FROM WEEPING. HER EYES GLITTERED with tears that still threatened to spill over her lower lids. Her lips were puffy.

She wasn't even pretty at the moment.

But she was the real Katla. Not the smiling, laughing Katla he'd warmed to that morning, but real nonetheless. Her carefully crafted mask of dutiful leadership had been stripped away and replaced by a vulnerable honesty.

Her deep unhappiness tugged at his heart, though he had no idea why it should claw at him so. She was his owner, the one who kept the iron collar on his throat, but despite everything, Brandr ached to make things right for her.

If he didn't know better, he'd suspect she'd witched him. Whatever the reason, his soul was drawn to hers, and he'd never wanted a woman more than he wanted the one before him now.

He approached the bed but made no move to touch her.

"I saw your shoulders tremble in the great hall, and

I knew you wept," he said softly, finally lifting a hand to graze a knuckle over her still-damp cheek. "And…I couldn't help but come to you."

Her moss-green eyes fluttered closed for a moment, and she worried her lower lip, clearly unsure what to do.

"You'll have to call for help if you try to send me away. I won't leave willingly," he finished, hoping the threat of a brawl would make her decide in his favor.

She opened her eyes and met his steady gaze. Her chest heaved twice, and her lips parted softly. Her chin began to quiver again.

"I won't send you away."

She extended a hand to him. He bent over it and brushed his lips across her knuckles as he'd seen the courtiers in Byzantium do to their empress. Then he turned her hand palm up and pressed a kiss on the soft center.

He heard her shuddering breath, but he was in no hurry. She wasn't going to send him away. He had all the time in the world. He was determined to love this woman with toe-curling slowness.

"Will you tell me why you were crying?"

She shook her head.

"Later, mayhap," he suggested.

"No."

"We'll see." He cupped her cheeks and kissed her forehead. Then he raised her to her feet. "Let's get you ready for bed, then."

She blinked at him in surprise. After their desperate, hurried joining on the cliff top, she obviously wasn't expecting restraint from him.

That was all right. He was wise in the way of women.

At least, when it came to bed play. There were a hundred ways he could surprise her.

He unfastened her shoulder brooches and laid the silver ornaments on the trunk nearest her bed. Then he unclasped the chain around her neck that bore all the keys to every lock in her household.

He knew the load those keys represented, the responsibility for the lives of so many, was far heavier on her than their actual weight.

"Raise your arms," he ordered.

She lifted them in surrender, and he pulled her tunic over her head. Her underdress clung to every curve. It would have peeled off the same way as her tunic, but he wasn't ready for that yet.

He wanted to savor her. To put his stamp on every finger-width of her skin.

"Sit."

"Don't get used to giving me orders, Ulfson," she said, some of the usual vinegar creeping into her tone, but she plopped her bottom on the bed's foot all the same.

He knelt before her and pulled off her leather shoes. Then his hands slipped beneath her hem to untie the bindings that wound around her calves and held up her stockings.

She really did have lovely feet. They were delicate and well formed, with high arches. Her small toes were topped with neat, square nails, smoothly filed.

He raised first her right foot, then the left, to his lips for a kiss on the joint between her big toe and its nearest neighbor. Each time, he was treated to a glimpse up her leg to the shadowy realm beneath her linen underdress.

His cock urged him to more than a stolen glance. If he'd listened to his member, he'd have plunged a hand under her skirt and claimed her sex, then and there. He knew how to drive her to helpless need that way. To tease her with glancing touches and circle her sensitive spot till she writhed and wept, but he held back.

He wanted to hear her beg for his touch. So he consoled his cock with another peek at her soft curls as he kissed her right foot once more, this time slipping her big toe into his mouth and giving it a hard suck.

She all but purred.

"Took you long enough to get around to obeying my first command," she said, her lips twitching in a suppressed feline smile.

"Figure I've owed you those. And I always pay my debts." He shot her an answering grin and flipped her hem up to bare her knees. "Besides, the view's well worth the trouble."

Her eyes flared with feigned indignation, but her lips fought a smile. "Swine."

"I haven't done anything to deserve that." He lifted a brow at her. "Yet."

She fell back on the bed and loosed a deep, fruity laugh. "Then by all means, get to work."

"You peeked into my mind, princess," he said as he eased his shoulders between her knees to spread her wide. He delivered a string of kisses up the inside of her leg. "Now keep still. I dare you."

The skin of her inner thigh was soft and sweet, and he hitched the linen to bare more of her legs as he moved up them. She smelled wonderful, her warm, musky scent blooming afresh each time his lips drew nearer to her sex. He pressed open-mouthed kisses on her, running his tongue into her intimate cleft.

She made a helpless little sound of need.

He drew back to look at her. Katla's dark hair was spread out over the bed in a fan. She'd draped a forearm over her eyes, trying to shield herself from him, he supposed. Before this night was through, he promised himself he'd break through every barrier she erected between them.

Her breaths came short and quick. Her hem was rucked up around her waist in front, exposing her flat belly. Her legs were splayed in abandon.

He parted the soft lips of her sex. When his warm breath passed over her, she quivered.

He ached in response.

He tongued her once, and she raised herself into his mouth. He suckled the little nub, swirling his tongue over the spot.

The sounds of longing she made went straight to his cock, and he felt the pressure of his seed rising in the shaft. If he kept at this, he'd end up spilling in his trousers.

He pushed the underdress up more, baring just the undersides of her breasts, leaving the pert tips still covered. He moved up her body, ignoring her sigh of frustration, leaving a trail of nibbling kisses along her ribs.

He ran his tongue along the crease beneath each breast. She rocked her pelvis against him, and his cock throbbed almost painfully.

He laid his head between her breasts and drew a deep breath. The goal was to make *her* beg for him, not for him to succumb to the need to rut her blind in greedy, uncontrollable lust.

Once he reduced her to helpless pleading, then he could rut her blind in greedy, uncontrollable lust.

For now, he forced himself to run through the ingredients for Greek fire in his head—anything to delay his body's inexorable reactions to Katla.

Quicklime, sulphur, bitumen…He felt steady enough to lift her dress the rest of the way to completely bare her breasts. He nuzzled them, running his open mouth around her areola, teasing her with his nearness. *Pitch, resin, nipples—damn, I mean naptha.*

"Brandr, please," she moaned, arching her back and thrusting her breasts upward.

He forgot all about Greek fire and closed his lips over one while he massaged the other with his thumb and forefinger.

Her hands ran over his shorn head and down his back. She rocked her hips against him.

He rose up to look at her. "I thought you were supposed to lie still."

She shrugged. "I thought you dared me to try. Besides, that tunic of yours is rough. We need to get you out of it."

His face stretched in a wide smile. "You only had to ask."

❧

She sat up so she could remove his tunic over his head. It was so tight across his shoulders, there was a moment or two when she thought the seams might rip. Finally, she worked it free.

"That's far too small for you."

"I'll have to take the matter up with my mistress," he said with a lopsided grin as she smoothed her palms over his chest. Muscles tensed and flexed under his warm skin. "Or mayhap her brothers. I don't know what they did with my clothes, but I wasn't bare arsed when they first drugged me at the mead house, you know."

He bent his head and claimed her mouth in a deep kiss.

He'd certainly been naked when Finn and the others dropped him on her floor. She already knew he was magnificent, from that time when he lay bound and helpless before her and then later in the bath house. Perfectly proportioned, endowed by nature with every masculine beauty. She could hardly wait to see him that way again.

"What were you wearing the night you were taken?" she asked when he stopped kissing her long enough to peel off her underdress. The linen slid over her skin with a soft rustle, and she was suddenly naked before him.

His eyes glowed with appreciation as he moved closer. The tips of her breasts grazed his hard chest.

"I asked you a question," she reminded him.

"Oh!" he said, not stopping his leisurely perusal of her. "I was dressed for travel. Leather breaches, woolen cloak, a tunic with tablet-woven trim, and—as a matter of fact, now that I think on it, seems to me Finn was wearing that tunic at table this night."

"Don't count on him returning it."

"Right now, princess," he said as he gathered her hair in his fist and tipped her face up to his, "my old tunic is the last thing on my mind."

As he bent to her, everything else fled from Katla's mind as well. The world seared away in his fiery kiss, and her whole life sizzled down to the wonder of his mouth on hers and his skin gliding smoothly against her skin.

Her hands found the drawstring at his waist and plunged in to stroke his hard shaft and fondle his balls. He growled with pleasure, and a thrill of power surged over her. There might be a way to reduce him to pleading as easily as he seemed to bring her to her knees.

But the need between her legs was back and throbbing with a vengeance. Mayhap she'd play at tormenting the man after her own desires were satisfied.

They tumbled together into the bed, a tangle of arms and legs. Once they finished rolling, Katla found herself on top of Brandr's long, strong body.

"Now, princess," he said, folding his hands beneath his head. "Mount your stallion at your pleasure and ride him as you will."

She sat up abruptly, surprised. Osvald had never allowed her to straddle atop him like this. It wasn't fitting for a woman to so dominate a man.

"Besides, woman, if it's a child you want," her husband had always said, "why force a man's seed to swim upstream?"

She blinked back the tears Osvald's remembered words called forth. If she was barren, it wasn't his fault. Hadn't he done his duty by her, giving her a quick swive almost every night? If no child quickened in her body, Osvald was not to blame.

"What's wrong?" Brandr sat up and wrapped his arms around her.

She was ashamed to realize she was shaking.

"Nothing," she said quickly.

He kissed her temples, her closed eyelids, the tip of her nose. "You're sure?"

She nodded. This wasn't about getting with child, even if such a thing were possible. This was merely about scratching an itch. About making the empty ache go away, if for only a little while.

"Lie down, Ulfson," she said fiercely as she forced her hands between them to push against his chest. "I'm going for a ride."

Chapter 14

DARKNESS CLUNG TO THE CORNERS OF THE CHAMBER, but the woman astraddle his groin glowed in the light of the lamp like a being aflame. Lust boiled through his veins. For a moment, he imagined tossing her off, dragging her to her knees, and mounting her from behind, rutting like a stallion claiming his mate.

But Brandr had given her the reins. He couldn't jerk them away from her now without losing whatever small amount of trust he'd gained.

Her green eyes met his as she rubbed herself along his shaft. He writhed beneath her, desperate for her to take him in, equally as desperate not to beg for her to.

"Now?" The word escaped his lips without his conscious volition.

She leaned down and kissed him, strafing his chest with her taut nipples. "Not yet."

She slid down onto his thighs. He half sat up and reached for her, but she straight-armed him.

"Not yet, I said." She pushed his hand away gently. "You promised to lie still until I say different. Remember? Shall it be said your oath is no good?"

"No, Katla," he said through clenched teeth as he settled back into the mattress. She'd not corrected him once, even though he'd used her name several times. It was a small victory. "My word is all I have, all any man has. You know I'll keep it."

"I'm very glad to hear it," she said as she moved up and settled her naked rump on his groin.

His balls tightened. The tip of him protruded between her legs, and she massaged the bit of rough skin just beneath the head with her thumb. He broke out in a cold sweat, biting his lip to keep from spilling his seed onto his own belly. She leaned forward and kissed his lips hard.

The agony of needing to be inside her pushed coherent thought from his mind.

"What will you do if I give you permission to move?"

"I'll...ah...I..." He couldn't make his tongue form words. "I'll..."

Wet and slick, she slid over the length of him, luxuriating in her own arousal. "Move, Brandr."

His hips rose to meet her. His breath hissed over his teeth when she teased him with her soft, wet entrance, but she didn't let him slip in.

She cupped her breasts, arched her back, and let her head fall back. He'd never seen anything more beautiful.

He ran his hands up her thighs and spread the lips of her sex, then thumbed her most sensitive spot.

She groaned.

He grimaced in satisfaction. His aching erection made a true smile impossible.

"Now?"

"*Ja*, now."

She took him in hand and guided him in. Katla

moved slowly, obviously reveling in the power of engulfing him, consuming him. Her velvet insides molded around him, conforming to his length and girth as if she'd been fashioned especially to fit him.

He touched her as she moved, pushing her toward the pinnacle.

Her first spasm began.

Brandr went off like an arrowshot inside her, their releases in tandem.

She milked him with her contractions until he was spent.

Her inner walls clenched once more, and then she collapsed bonelessly on his chest.

He stroked her hair, glad she'd made no move to sever their joining before it was unavoidable. Her breathing slowly returned to normal. He felt her cheek lift in a smile against his breastbone.

He'd made her happy. Warmth flooded his chest. As far as accomplishments went, pleasing Katla the Black was as fine a thing as a commendation for conspicuous valor from the Byzantine emperor himself.

Then very softly, there came a small, ladylike snore.

"You're welcome, princess," he said as he pressed a kiss on her tousled crown. He waved a hand to snuff out the lamp without disturbing her.

Then he closed his eyes. He needed to take his rest when he could. With any luck at all, she'd wake in a couple hours, ready for another ride.

&

"Sister, a word in your ear."

Katla stopped and waited for Finn on the path leading

to the barn. Her best milk cow was calving. The black, small-horned beast had added three heifers and a bull calf to Katla's herd over the years, all of them healthy and sound.

Since a person's wealth was measured in stock as often as in coin, it was a happy occasion whenever a calf was birthed. While this particular cow had never had a difficult delivery before, Katla always tried to be near in case she had to tie a rope around the calf's legs and help it out.

"What do you want, Finn?"

"Well, I wanted to talk to you about…that is…I see you've given Ulfson new clothes."

"Hardly new."

In the distance, a cow lowed in distress. She turned and set off toward the barn at a quick pace. Finn fell into step with her.

"The tunic and trousers belonged to Father—no, don't give me that look," she said, not slowing her determined stride. "They're so old no one else would want them."

"But how could you give a thrall Father's things?"

"He'd want them used. You know how he was. He never let anything go to waste," Katla said with conviction. "Besides, weren't you the one who told me I needed to find clothes that fit Brandr? It's a stroke of luck that Father was a large fellow too."

"Brandr," Finn repeated. "You call him Brandr now."

Katla rounded on him, fists at her waist. "That's the man's name, isn't it? What's really bothering you, Finn?"

He pressed his lips together as if now that he had her full attention, he wasn't sure how to proceed. He seemed preoccupied with his own boot tips.

"Speak your mind, or I'll go on about my business."

He looked at her directly then, his pale blue eyes filled with concern. "One suitor just left us. Another is due here this evening. Do you think it's wise for you to take a thrall to your bed while you're being courted?"

"You have no right to ask me that," she said, stalking away in a huff.

Finn followed.

"Was your bed cold last night?" she demanded.

"No, but that's not the point." Finn raked a hand through his hair. "I'm not the one looking to marry."

Neither was she, but she'd made the bargain with her brothers. One way or another, she'd have to see it through.

"I'm of age. I'm no man's wife at present. What passes in my bedchamber is my business." She stopped long enough to poke the center of her brother's chest to emphasize her point. "Mine alone."

"But, Katla, he's a thrall."

"Wasn't Inga a thrall when Osvald took her to his bed?" she asked.

Even though Inga had been freed later, the taint of the iron collar would follow her throughout her life.

"That's different."

"No, it's not." Katla kicked a rock down the path ahead of them in frustration. "Why should a woman's pleasure be any different than a man's?"

She knew what he was really trying to get at. A thrall was a pariah in their world. An iron collar was cause for derision and scorn. While no one would question a man's right to make use of a female one for bed sport, a woman who submitted to a male thrall might be seen to be demeaning herself.

Of course, Brandr probably would argue that Katla hadn't been all that submissive. They came together like a pair of wolves last night.

Three times.

Her lips quirked in a private smile.

"Have you considered that in your bed, Ulfson might forget his place?" Finn asked, stopping as they neared the growing woodpile. "He might think himself your equal. Or even your superior."

"Don't trouble yourself on that score," Katla said, waving away his objections. She'd reduced the man to quivering need. Of course, Brandr had returned the favor, but she'd definitely had the upper hand as she rode him. "I make sure he knows who's the slave and who is master."

"Good," Finn said. Then he chuckled. "You intended to humble the man. I guess there's no better place for that than the bedchamber, come to think of it. I just wanted to make sure you weren't doing something foolish."

"Like what?"

"Like imagining you had—oh, I don't know, tender feelings for the man."

Katla sighed. Tender feelings. If having her insides coil in knots that defied untangling every time she saw the man counted, then yes, she was having *very* tender feelings. It fair stole her breath away just to think on Brandr Ulfson.

But that didn't mean she must be ruled by her feelings. Sentiment didn't fill the granary or milk the cows. It wouldn't see her people in warm cloaks come winter.

Still, she couldn't let Finn know how closely he'd struck to the mark.

"In all my life, brother, have you ever known me to have a tender feeling?"

Finn's shoulders lifted in a quick shrug. "You have me there, sister."

"Then stop fretting like an old woman," she said, fisting her hands at her waist. "Brandr Ulfson is my thrall. Nothing more. I may do what I wish with my own, and no one dares gainsay me. That's all there is to it."

Finn breathed a sigh of relief. "I'm glad to hear it, but I can't imagine your next husband will allow you to keep him. What will you do with Ulfson once you marry?"

"I'm not even betrothed yet. I've met only one possible suitor, and you promised me a choice from three." Katla's head snapped around in the direction of the barn. The cow was bawling loudly, in obvious agony. She sprinted off in that direction, calling over her shoulder to Finn. "As far as what I'll do with Brandr Ulfson once I marry…we'll take that ship when it sails."

"I'll give you a hand with that cow." Finn loped after her. "You need to be ready for Otto Sturlson this evening. We can't have you greeting him with dung on your shoes."

⚓

Brandr straightened on the other side of the woodpile. Cold rage burned in his chest. Katla's words skewered him as deeply as a Saracen's blade.

Have you ever known me to have a tender feeling?

After all the things he and Katla had done with each other, he still meant nothing to her. She was as heartless as one of the great white bears that roamed the far North. Ferocious and pitiless, the predators fed on anything that moved.

As Katla had fed on him.

Brandr Ulfson is my thrall. Nothing more.

She had that right. There'd certainly be no more.

A man could stand only so much, and he'd reached his limit. He'd bridled himself. He'd let her take the lead, something he'd never even remotely considered doing with a woman before. He'd sought to peel away her protective layers to find the vulnerable soul beneath.

Now he knew there was nothing there.

Thrall or not, he'd be damned if he'd ever come to her bed again.

Chapter 15

KATLA AND FINN LABORED TOGETHER FOR SEVERAL hours. In the end, they saved the calf but lost the cow. She bled out as soon as the bull calf slipped wetly from her tortured body.

He was a hardy little thing, despite his difficult entry into the world, and was fighting to rise on wobbly legs before Katla could even clean him properly. She put him in a stall with another cow, and fortunately, the surrogate seemed willing to accept him.

Katla leaned on the top rail of the stall and, bone weary, laid her forehead on her arms. The bull calf sucked greedily on the cow's distended teat. His vigorous slurps eased Katla's fears for him.

Katla breathed deeply, but the fresh newness of the calf and the smell of clean straw wasn't strong enough to mask the stench of blood and offal left in the next stall.

"I'm sorry about the cow," Finn said. "I'll fetch some fellows to butcher her."

It was a great misfortune to lose her at this time of year. Of course, Katla's people would be happy to have fresh meat, and since Finn still intended to impress Katla's prospective husbands with lavish banquets, part of the cow would serve for those feasts in the coming days. But the majority of the beef would have to be salted and smoked for later use. If winter had been on the wind, they could have hung the carcass and left it to freeze, sawing joints off as needed. When the meat thawed, it would have been as good as fresh.

At least the tanners would have a fresh hide to work into shoes and belts, bridles and harness. From horn to hoof, every bit of the animal would be used for something. Someone would probably even fashion a fly whisk from the cow's tail.

Katla sighed. She felt every bit of her was being used up too. The burden of caring for the welfare of so many seemed heavier than usual when she was tired. Perhaps she'd feel better after a bath.

"While you're at the house, ask Gerte to bring some fresh clothes to the bath house for me, please," Katla called after Finn as he headed toward the long-house. "You'll want a bath too, I expect, since we've a guest for night meal."

"*Ja*, I'll have her pick something appropriate for meeting a suitor. We want you at your best, you know," Finn said with a dismissive wave.

"Finn."

Shoulders slumped, he stopped and turned back to her, expecting a rebuke.

She closed the distance between them. "It wasn't your fault we lost the cow. You did everything you could. And you helped me save the calf. Thank you."

He nodded curtly, but his face brightened under her rare bit of praise. His step was jaunty as he continued to the longhouse.

Mayhap Finn is finally growing into himself.

Katla trudged toward the bath house, mulling over his words from that morning. Like it or not, her brother had raised a valid question.

What *would* she do with Brandr once she married?

A hard lump settled in her chest. He hadn't been part of her life long, but as she went about her days, she found herself watching for him. When she chanced upon him at his work, she couldn't help but stand apart and admire the line of his long legs and the breadth of his shoulders. He had an easy way about him, and she smiled when she overheard him talking and laughing with others. Even though he was a thrall, her people responded to him with acceptance.

She'd caught the occasional look of pity for him, but that was to be expected for one who wore iron about his neck.

Strange she hadn't seen him this day, but then she'd been in the barn for most of it.

While she and Finn had worked together over the cow, her brother admitted he wasn't much interested in farming, no matter how much land he received as part of Katla's marriage contract. He confided in her about his hope to learn shipbuilding and how Brandr had offered to help him.

It was an extraordinary thing for a man to do for one who'd tricked and enthralled him.

But then, Brandr was extraordinary.

Last night was ample proof of that. If Katla were a

skald, she'd compose a poetic *edda* about his inspired bed skills that would make him the stuff of legend. He'd untied her every knot. Even now, her body glowed with the contentment of having been well loved. All her joints felt pleasantly loose.

After being with Brandr, the idea of taking another man into her chamber left her slightly queasy.

She shoved the thought from her mind as she pushed open the bath house door.

There, standing with his back to the door in the fragrant steam, was Brandr Ulfson. Wearing nothing but an iron collar and his glorious skin. He turned when she entered, but she couldn't make out his expression. Without a word, he started for the door to the cooling room.

"Brandr, stay," she said, wishing she wasn't covered in muck and grime. She'd have run to him and wrapped her arms around him otherwise. "I haven't seen you all day."

"I haven't been slacking, if that's your worry." His voice was drawn as tight as a bowstring.

Usually he didn't sound that strained unless she was naked as well.

"No, of course not." She unfastened her brooches and peeled out of her overtunic, mildly surprised when he didn't come help her undress. It had seemed to be one of his favorite pastimes. "You work circles around most of my people."

"That's why I wear your collar, isn't it, princess? A thrall is made for work, and that's all."

"After last night, I beg to differ," she said with a smile. "You're made for many other things as well."

"How satisfying to be useful." He turned and continued toward the door.

"Where are you going?"

"To the cooling barrels," he said gruffly. "I've had enough."

The door banged shut behind him. Katla stared after him for a moment. Was he angry with her for some reason? Then the steam of the bath house curled around her, and she realized he was probably just overheated from being in the bath.

Who knew how long he'd been sweating on the hot benches, waiting for her there in the birch-scented steam?

She hoped he'd wait in the cooling room for her and offer to dry her off again. Her body tingled at the prospect of his rubbing a towel over every bit of her clean skin. The last time he did that, she was sure he'd have taken her right there on the cool, smooth floor if she'd only have let him.

This time, she would.

⁂

Brandr didn't waste any time in the barrels of tepid water. He didn't want to chance still being there when Katla emerged from her bath, all sweat slick and rosy. Even though he was determined not to bed her again, Katla naked and drenching wet might be more than he could resist.

His clothes were still slightly damp when he stepped out of the bath house. The evening breeze that swept down from the high peaks was brisk. He followed his nose back to the longhouse where the night meal was nearly ready.

Katla's youngest brother, Haukon, had slaughtered a pig that morning, and Inga had roasted it all day in a pit outside the longhouse. Brandr still managed to sneak in a lesson in sword work with Haukon each day. The lad was willing but not especially gifted. Nevertheless, the discipline of regular drill had made him a better worker in other respects as well. Katla hadn't scolded him for idleness in several days.

Unlike Einar, who still disappeared whenever the threat of physical labor reared its head.

The savory smell of roast pork set Brandr's mouth watering. He made himself useful hauling large wooden trenchers piled high with meat from the outside pit to the warming stones by the interior meal fire. Inga would keep it ready to serve till the guest of honor arrived.

Brandr managed not to cross paths with Katla as the household gathered to welcome her newest suitor, but he couldn't keep from watching her walk back to the longhouse from the bath house. She was dressed like a fine lady in a fjord-blue overtunic that complemented her fair skin. The brooches at her shoulders this evening sparkled with precious glowing amber embedded in the worked silver.

"Freya's tears," he muttered and shook his head. It made sense she'd favor gems connected with the lascivious Norse goddess. Freya was frankly calculating about her bedmates. After overhearing her conversation with Finn, Brandr knew Katla was as coldly strategic about who shared her bed, and for how long, as the love goddess ever thought about being.

Did she really think a husband would give her a

choice about using a thrall as a bed slave once she wed? Did she think Brandr would allow himself to be used now that he knew he was nothing to her? His brother's iron crown waited for him in Jondal if he could only find a way to have the iron collar removed here. It was high time he focused on earning his freedom.

Instead of following Katla into the longhouse, Brandr hung back on the edge of the crowd, watching Einar and Haukon escort her newest suitor up from the wharf.

Otto Sturlson was a flamboyant figure, swathed in exotic silks and ermine. A Spanish blade encased in a heavily embossed shoulder baldric bumped against his back. His neck was ringed with a dozen gold chains, and jewels glinted from each of his fingers.

Brandr recognized the breed.

The man was a trader. There were plenty of his sort plying the waters between here and faraway Byzantium. Shrewd, gifted with languages, and dangerous when they needed to be, Norse traders could be found in every European port.

But as fine as the man's clothing and weapons were, he was clearly past his prime. Flesh hung from his wiry biceps where muscle used to be. Brandr wondered if he had the strength to wield the magnificent sword he carried. His hair was iron gray, and when he flashed a horse-toothed smile, Brandr's stomach curdled.

Clearly Sturlson was done trading and wanted a snug fire to curl up beside while he waited for old age to claim him.

Katla had already buried one husband. What were her brothers thinking, trying to match her with such an old man?

The last ray of sunshine glinted on the gold at Sturlson's throat. Well, there was his answer.

Brandr kept out of Katla's way until she was situated at table. Then there was no escape. He still had to see to her trencher and keep her drinking horn filled.

In some respects, it wasn't an onerous job. Sturlson was a natural storyteller. If the old man hadn't itched to see more of the world, he might have remained in the North and been a skald. Brandr always welcomed news of strange, unexplored lands, and from his position behind Katla, he heard it all.

Otto wove tales of Rus towns on the Dnieper River. He claimed to have seen jackals prowling the ruins of a once-great city called Rome. He and his crew had portaged over rough roads to sail down the Volga into the Caspian Sea. From there he rode on the great humped back of a beast known as a camel to a place named Baghdad between two rivers.

"In that rich land," Sturlson said expansively, "the women are said to be the most beautiful in all the world."

"You were there," Katla said, "and yet you speak as if you don't know whether they were or not. Is there a man alive who doesn't fancy himself a fair judge of women?"

Despite his determination not to find anything praiseworthy in his mistress, Brandr's lips twitched with suppressed amusement. Otto Sturlson had expressed an opinion on everything under the sun.

Leave it to Katla to catch him without one.

"That's because I never actually saw the women. They are kept hidden away from the eyes of all but their husbands. Assuredly," Otto said, leaning toward Katla, "if you lived in Baghdad, your jealous husband would never let you see the light of day."

"Then I must be glad twice," she said before she took a long sip of her ale.

Sturlson cocked a wiry gray brow at her. "How is that?"

"Glad that I do not live in this Baghdad and glad not have a jealous husband."

Otto smiled. "And yet I promise you, fair lady, any man who becomes your husband will be jealous. He could not help it." He lifted a gnarled knuckle and grazed her cheek with it. "Beauty does that to a man. I'd hoard your loveliness with more care than I lavish on my gold."

"I don't think I'd fit around your neck."

"It would be great fun to find out," the old man said with a wink.

Brandr's fingers balled into fists, but he forced himself to unclench them. What did he care if the old goat played the besotted fool over her? Otto Sturlson didn't know her as Brandr did.

She used men, as she used everything under her control, with no more tender feelings than if they were one of her sheep or oxen.

"Have you ever heard the tale of Freya and the Brisingamen necklace?" Otto asked.

"Who has not?"

"I asked only because I see that you wear amber, the goddess's tears," Otto said. "Are you a devotee of the love goddess?"

"Not especially, though I've never disrespected her," Katla said with the caution any sensible person would show. It was never wise to be dismissive about any of the gods. "Freya had plenty to weep about."

True words. But women who intend to wed for wealth, bed for sport, and toss men away like used rags should stick to lies. Freya would have been better served by a lie when her husband wanted to know how she acquired her new necklace.

"*Ja*, but Freya was so sorely tempted by the Brisingamen necklace, we cannot blame her," Otto said.

According to legend, Freya wanted the fabulous jewelry so badly she was willing to submit to the four hideously ugly dwarves in four nights of unholy passion to possess the gem-studded finery.

"The old stories tell us she never removes the necklace to this day. She must have thought it worth the cost at the time," Otto said.

"But the cost was higher than she expected, once her husband discovered the bargain she struck to acquire it," Katla reminded him. Freya's husband abandoned her forever. Amber was said to be evidence of her sorrow, and wearing it honored her grief over the loss of her mate. Katla touched the amber drops embedded in one of her brooches. "Freya will never stop weeping for her lost love."

Otto seemed to consider this for a moment. "I don't suppose your brothers told you, but I possess far more wealth than I'm wearing. I've a couple caches of silver secreted about, each of them big as a head of cabbage. I will not be able to spend it all in the years left to me. That's why I'm looking for a young wife."

The hair on Brandr's neck bristled. Did Katla want a pile of silver so badly she'd take Otto Sturlson to her bed?

If coin was all Katla was interested in, Brandr was certain his share of the chest of silver his friends had sailed on to Jondal with would weigh out to be more than Sturlson's worth. Brandr was a wealthy man too.

Unfortunately, he wore iron around his neck instead of gold, so he was unable to claim his share of the wealth at the moment. Her words echoed in his ear.

Brandr Ulfson is my thrall. Nothing more.

"Since you brought up the matter of the wealth you wear, I have to admit it seems a bit excessive," Katla said between dainty bites of pork and barley bread. "More than most men might dare."

"*Ja*, I ring my neck with gold to tempt some young fellow to try to take it from me."

"Why would you want to do that?"

Sturlson shrugged. "I'm an old man, Katla. You think I do not know it? I don't want to end my days wallowing in my own piss. Why should I wait for a straw death?"

The prospect of dying in bed of extreme age or disease was an end any man worth the name would shrink from. Inviting a fight was an ingenious way to avoid it.

Otto Sturlson's cleverness ticked up a notch in Brandr's estimation.

"Has anyone ever tried to take your gold?" Katla asked.

"*Ja*, but so far, I have kept my head and my wealth." He fingered one of the gold chains at his throat. "It does me good to know I still deserve them."

She laughed lightly at his wit.

"Of course, a beautiful young wife can be the death of an old man too." Otto leaned toward Katla with a leer. "That kind of a straw death I wouldn't mind at all."

Even though Brandr knew he was nothing to Katla but a means to scratch an itch, he narrowly resisted offering to help Sturlson avoid dying in bed.

He knew Katla wouldn't appreciate it. Thralls should be seen but not heard.

Chapter 16

MALVAR BLOODAXE SNIFFED THE WIND THAT WAS blowing clear and briny from the narrow sea. The voices of the Old Ones muttered in lugubrious whispers, but he pushed them to a small corner of his mind.

The time wasn't quite right yet.

He would have one chance, one cast of the die to make his plan work. If he lost patience and threw too soon, he might wreck all.

He climbed to the top of the grassy howe and faced East. From Orkney, it wasn't so far a sail to his ultimate goal. With half-closed eyes, he fancied he could see the broad, gaping entrance to Hardanger Fjord. Like a whore with her legs wide spread, the rich land beckoned him to come and claim it.

A flash of the vision he'd had last night seared his mind once more. He could smell the blood and smoke of carnage, hear the screams of the dying.

The Old Ones whimpered softly, their sighs half-covered by the waving sibilance of the tall grass. It had been so long since freshly spilled blood had nourished the earth, since fire had darkened the sky, since death had ridden on the water with the cold breath of *Hel* in its sails.

The world has become too civilized, Malvar thought with a curl of his lip. The ancient spirits were starving for lack of a proper sacrifice.

"Soon," he promised the whisperers.

At least the Old Ones there on Orkney had been given a taste of fresh blood, albeit in droplets instead of the rivers of gore they craved. They'd been praised in daily shrieks of pain, but Malvar knew it was never enough for them. They were like a ram in rut who can't find a ewe. An empty belly with no meal in sight. A barren womb.

The Old Ones' need was never completely filled.

But Malvar's work was about to bring forth fruit. Ulf Skallagrimsson was near to cracking. Malvar had enjoyed toying with him. The *jarl*'s resistance to pain was impressive but not perfect. Ulf wailed like a woman when properly motivated.

Now it was time to raise the stakes.

This morning Malvar would threaten to take his manhood. A man will say anything to save that bit of skin. Malvar had avoided resorting to it, because the real trick would be in assuring himself that what Ulf said to save his balls was true.

Each day he hoped for a message from Gormson. He desperately needed that staging area on Tysnes to launch his campaign of cleansing death into the fjord.

If his ally couldn't marry into that sweet, sheltered cove, then by the ancient powers, he'd damn well better find another way to claim it.

Chapter 17

OTTO STURLSON STAYED ON FOR ANOTHER TWO DAYS. Unlike Gormson, he expressed little interest in the running of Katla's steading. He didn't even ask about the extent of her holding, much less demand a thorough tour.

He seemed more intent on Katla herself.

When he saw she wasn't about to abandon her duties to entertain him exclusively, he made himself marginally useful by directing the work of a group of men who were laboring to remove stones from an arable field. It seemed the ground sprouted a fresh crop each spring, and had to be cleared before Katla would risk the sharp edge of her plow. Otto showed the men how to stake out the field in sections and work methodically together instead of each trying to cull his own little portion. They finished the work in record time.

But when Sturlson took his leave, Katla refused to give him an answer to his suit. Her brothers had promised her a choice from three possible husbands, and she wasn't about to shorten the process. Otto thanked her for considering him in a flowery, poetic speech and declared he'd wait at the nearest mead house for her decision.

During the time Otto Sturlson was in residence, Brandr once again slept on the outside of her threshold without being asked. Katla hadn't sensed Otto was likely to force himself on her, but it pleased her that Brandr set himself to guard her, in any case.

What didn't please her was how distant he seemed. Brandr was smiling and affable as always with everyone else. He joked with the men, and while they'd normally ignore a thrall, the workers on her farm seemed to forget Brandr wore the iron collar. Katla had smiled when he tugged the braids of the little goose girl till she colored with delighted embarrassment. Brandr was helpful and well-spoken with the women, thoroughly ignoring the longing looks that followed him as he moved about his chores.

Discretion was all well and good, but she'd have thought the man might spare her at least one secret smile or telling glance over the past few days.

On the night Otto Sturlson took his leave, Katla retired to her chamber early and dressed in her finest night shift. It had a row of cording at the neck shot through with silver thread. She brushed out her braids and let her dark hair fall in shining waves past her waist.

Brandr should like that.

Her insides frisked about like a spring lamb in anticipation. Any moment he'd come, and then she'd fall into that delicious dream with him again. That place where everything else faded away and only the beating of their hearts marked the passage of time.

She settled into her bed to wait for him to slip out of the main room and join her. Brandr was being cautious, waiting for a time when he wouldn't be missed.

Finn ought to appreciate the man's newly developed sense of propriety.

The singing and laughing after night meal died away as the household settled for sleep. No one touched her door latch. Her lamp guttered and went out. The moon appeared in the smoke hole overhead, and still Brandr didn't come.

Her chest ached.

She closed her eyes and tried to find sleep, but that warm blanket of forgetfulness fled from her.

Finally, she climbed from her bed and padded to the door. She opened it a pinch and saw Brandr's form across the threshold as always.

But he wasn't asleep either. He raised himself on his elbow and glared up at her through the crack in the door.

She opened the door farther and motioned for him to come in.

His face set like granite, he rose to do her bidding.

Once the door was latched behind him, he crossed his arms over his chest. "What do you want, princess?"

"Keep your voice down," she hissed. "Someone will hear you."

"You actually care if someone does? I'm impressed." His hard glare said otherwise.

"Of course I do. I'm being courted, after all. Finn has me thinking I should behave a bit more primly about having you in my chamber by night."

He merely looked at her, making no move to come to

her as she'd hoped. She fished about for a reason to have called him in other than the dull ache between her legs.

"You had plenty to say about Albrikt Gormson," she said, "so let's hear it."

"Hear what?"

"Don't you have an opinion about Otto Sturlson?"

"I wasn't aware the opinion of a thrall was of much value to you," he said stonily.

"Let us pretend that it is." She crossed her arms over her chest in an echo of his posture.

He shrugged. "The man can talk the stars from the sky and can evidently still handle a blade. I'd fight by his side in a pinch."

She rolled her eyes. "I mean about his qualities as a possible husband for me."

"How would I know about that? I never visited the bath house when he was there. I can't tell you a thing about the length of his cock."

Her jaw dropped. "What's wrong with you?"

"I was wondering the same thing about you."

"Me?"

"*Ja*, why are you doing this? You play at being available to wed. Yet you call me in here hoping I'll rut you."

He took a step toward her, and her heart rate hitched up several notches. That was exactly what she'd hoped.

"Isn't that why you came?" she asked.

He cast his eyes down. "I came because you commanded. I'm your thrall. Your property. Your…thing."

"Every time we've been alone, all you've tried to do is bed me," she said.

This time when he raised his gaze to her, he looked at her with the hard eyes of a stranger.

"Why are you acting now as if it's not something you want?" she asked.

"Because I've realized something about you, princess," Brandr said through clenched teeth. "You don't give a damn about anyone."

"That's not true." Everything she did was for the good of her people. Her whole life was dedicated to the well-being of others.

And she cared about Brandr, even though her heart condemned her as a weak-willed, light-skirt for it. She'd accepted him as her thrall to wreak vengeance for Osvald.

She didn't feel the least vengeful now.

Fast as thought, he closed the distance between them, wrapping his arms around her. He fisted a handful of her hair and forced her to look up at him.

"Then tell me you need me, Katla. Tell me it means something to you when I join my body to yours."

She needed him like she needed her next breath. The admission danced on her tongue, but she held back. If he knew she needed him, he'd have the power to hurt her.

Instead, she'd let her body speak for her. She pressed herself against his hard length and raised herself on tiptoe to kiss him. His lips twitched under her mouth, but he didn't respond.

"Kiss me, Brandr."

His tongue dove between her teeth almost before the words passed her lips. His kiss seared her with its heat, with the promise of unbridled passion. She was taken by surprise at the suddenness and intensity of the longing he woke in her.

Then just as suddenly, he stopped kissing her and stepped back, arms at his sides.

She frowned at him in puzzlement. "What's wrong?"

"Nothing, princess. You ordered me to kiss you, and I have done so."

"And that's all?"

"If you wanted a different sort of kiss, or a longer one, you should have told me."

His eyes were so cold they froze her heart. "Don't you want to kiss me?"

"A thrall has no wants but his owner's wishes," he said icily. "I kissed you because you told me to. But be warned. If you order me to bed you, be very specific about your preferences."

She flinched as if he'd slapped her. "Why are you being so hateful all of a sudden?"

"What do you care if I am? A thrall is of no consequence," he said with a snarl in his tone. "You may do what you wish with your own, and no one may gainsay you. Least of all, the thrall himself."

Alarm bells jangled in her mind. His words sounded familiar.

Because they were hers.

"If I were in this chamber as a free man, I'd bear you to bed and lavish every finger-width of your skin with a lover's touch."

For the first time since he entered her room, she saw hunger on his features. But the longing was quickly replaced by a hard mask of disdain.

"But since you always make sure I know who's the slave and who's the master, I'll wait for your direction."

Somehow he'd overheard her conversation with

Finn. She hadn't meant those things. Not really. She just wanted to quiet her brother's needling.

"So tell me what you want, mistress." He took a step closer. "What would you have me do? Bend you over and rut you like a whore?"

She slapped him.

Cold fury burned in his eyes. If he weren't her thrall and sworn to obey her, she'd fear him.

"Get out."

"As you will, mistress." He gave her the shallowest of bows. "As you will."

Chapter 18

"KATLA!"

She looked up from the rows of peas she was planting to see Einar and another fellow carrying a litter down the sheep track from the upper pasture. A body lay on the evergreen boughs that formed part of the litter. She held a hand to shield her eyes from the sun's glare and squinted to try to make out who they were carting down the steep slope.

Haukon's red hair blazed against the green pine. Katla lifted her skirt and ran.

Brandr came from out of nowhere to fall into step beside her. They hadn't had a private moment since she threw him out of her chamber, and their public interaction had been limited to orders and curt nods. She was surprised to see him now.

"What's wrong?" he asked as he loped beside her.

"It's Haukon," she said between gasping breaths. "He must be hurt."

When they drew near the conveyance, Katla ordered Einar and the other man to stop. The lad was conscious but white lipped with pain. Haukon cradled one arm, but even so, it was bent at an odd angle.

The bones of his forearm were obviously broken.

"How did this happen?" Katla knelt beside him and fingered the injured limb. His skin was swollen and hot under her touch. Haukon bit his lower lip, but otherwise he fought not to show his agony.

"The idiot was trying to teach me what he'd learned about swordplay," Einar said. "He thought he'd show me how to attack from above. He leaped down from the top of a boulder and missed me."

"You moved," Haukon said through clenched teeth. "You said you wouldn't."

"Why should I let you fall on me?" Einar asked.

"We've been at peace on Tysnes for years. What were you doing playing at fighting in the first place?" Katla's stomach balled in knots. Haukon could lose the use of his arm over this foolishness. If the injury went bad, she might even have to amputate. "Who put such notions into your head?"

"I did," Brandr said. "Haukon asked me to teach him what I knew about handling a blade." He put a hand on her brother's shoulder. "You were doing well and showed promise."

Quivering with rage, Katla turned on Brandr. If he wanted to hurt her, he should stick to insulting her in her bedchamber, not filling her little brother's head with nonsense. "Why did you do this?"

"The lad wanted to defend what's his," Brandr said. "That's a man's right."

"Ulfson didn't tell me to leap from a boulder," Haukon said, shooting a quick glare at his brother. "That was Einar's idea."

"Take him to the bath house," Katla said, and she

turned back down the hillside to fetch her medicinal supplies. As lady of the house, it was her place to doctor her people, to nurse them through sickness and ease suffering when she could. She knew she'd have to hurt her brother badly to reset the bones.

Her chest ached. When their mother died, a wet nurse was found for Haukon, but eight-year-old Katla did everything else for him. She soothed him when his teeth came in and taught him to take his first stumbling steps. His little fingers had curled so tightly around hers.

She'd have fought off a wolf pack for him.

The thought of what she might have to do to save him now made her want to retch.

She hurried to the bath house with her pouch of medicines and herbs. When she pushed open the door, she saw Haukon lying insensible on one of the wooden benches. Einar and Brandr stood over him.

"What happened?" She scurried to them. A leather strap was tied firmly to Haukon's wrist, biting into his flesh.

"I reset the bones," Brandr said. "He fainted while I pulled the ends into position, but he'll come around. He didn't cry out once. You'd have been proud." He bent and untied the strap around Haukon's wrist. "You'll need to bind the arm to keep it still till the bones knit."

"I know what I need to do," she said in a clipped tone. Then she cocked her head at him. "How did you know?"

"*Ja*, Ulfson, doctoring is the province of women," Einar chimed in. "Or priests of Odin."

"We had an Egyptian physician attached to the Varangian Guard. He needed extra hands sometimes after a fierce battle." Brandr shrugged. "I helped when I could. I watched and learned."

Katla nodded. Haukon was starting to stir, and the worst of his treatment was done. She didn't have to torture her brother after all. She flicked a glance at Brandr. "Thank you."

He nodded gruffly and knelt beside her brother. He held him still while Katla started to bind up his arm. "If you have anything in that medicine pouch for pain, I suspect he'd be grateful. Bone pain is the worst sort, they say."

Katla's chest constricted. Being so near to Brandr made her ache afresh over the cruel things they'd said to each other in her chamber. And over the way she'd slapped him for it.

He's wrong. Pains of the heart are far worse.

❧

"Katla, you have to make a decision," Finn said over his bowl of porridge a week later. "Gormson has sent me three messengers, all demanding to know your answer."

She looked up from the bowls she was filling. Heads nodding and still yawning, a row of children huddled near the central meal fire against the early morning chill. Their parents were already hard at work. Katla enjoyed seeing to the morning meal for the youngest members of her household.

Haukon sprawled on the end of the bench, drawing out his own breakfast with a second bowl of porridge. The broken arm certainly hadn't damaged his appetite.

Brandr sat in the shadows, eating in sullen silence.

"I can't give Gormson an answer yet. You know that," she said as she ladled a generous dollop of honey onto each portion. "I haven't met my third suitor yet."

She distributed the bowls, ruffling the children's tousled heads, trying to tamp down the surge of longing their round-cheeked faces roused in her chest. The desire for a child of her own was fast becoming a guilty ache that couldn't be assuaged. The children fell to their meal like starving puppies.

"Einar ran into Otto Sturlson at the mead house last night." Finn scraped his bone spoon around the soapstone bowl to eke out the last dregs of his breakfast. "Otto is anxious to know your choice as well, though he's being less insistent than Albrikt."

"Same answer." Katla held up three fingers. "Two is not three."

Brandr finished his bowl of boiled oats and honey and stomped out of the longhouse to begin the long list of chores she'd already assigned him. Katla tried not to watch him go, but the corner of her eye always seemed to find him.

She thought working together to heal Haukon might have eased matters between them, but it hadn't. They still hadn't spoken to each other privately since that night in her bedchamber when she'd slapped him. It had been a serious insult—some couples had divorced over such treatment—enough to thoroughly distance him from her.

Once during the past week, he'd stumbled upon her in the bath house while she was birching herself. She was dripping with sweat, and she'd applied the birch branches hard enough to raise little red weals on her thighs. She hadn't meant to. Frustration made her strike harder as she slapped her legs with the birch switches.

Brandr stood and looked at her for the space of several heartbeats, the tendons in his neck strained and tight. But then he backed out the door without a word.

Katla had no idea what to do. One didn't apologize to a thrall.

And yet when she woke in the night, she wished he'd slip into her chamber unannounced as he used to do. She hugged her pillow and longed for his solid presence in the bed with her. For his warmth.

For his touch.

"But surely you must have an idea which of them you prefer," Finn was saying.

Katla wiped down the low bench and handed the big kettle with the remnants of the porridge to Inga. "I haven't given the matter any thought."

"You must." Finn handed his bowl to Inga as well.

"Not until I meet the third man."

"About that…" Finn stood and pressed his mouth into a tight line. Something seemed ready to burst out of him, but he changed his mind at the last moment and swallowed the words back. "I need to see how that bull calf is doing this morning. Walk with me, sister."

Katla followed her brother into the sunshine and strolled beside him on the path leading to the big stone barn.

"What's wrong, Finn?"

"I didn't want to say this before anyone else, but…we can't find a third suitor for you."

Katla laughed.

Finn didn't.

Her eyes flared with surprise. "You're serious?"

Finn spread his hands before him. "You're not the most amiable person, you know. And your reputation for...strong-mindedness has spread throughout the islands. No one wants to marry a storm cloud, Katla. Not even if she comes with a fair holding."

"Well, this is a stroke of luck. I didn't want to marry again, in any case," Katla said, tight-lipped. It stung to be rejected so roundly, but she couldn't let Finn see that it hurt her.

The thwack of an ax biting into pine split the air. Brandr was chopping wood again. He'd already laid by enough to keep them all warm for the next two winters, but he finished his other work so quickly, she had to keep wood splitting on the list to keep him busy.

"But not having a third suitor is no cause for concern. You can still marry. There are two good men who'll have you, and that's more choice than most women get," Finn said. "All you need do is choose."

"I need do nothing." She picked up her pace as Brandr and the woodpile came into view. Pity they had to pass him by on their way to the barn. "I agreed to pick from three suitors, not two."

"But Katla—"

"No, Finn. You and I struck a bargain. I intend to hold you to it." She stomped by Brandr without a sidelong glance. "And there's an end."

"All right," her brother called after her. "Brandr Ulfson is your third choice."

She whirled around. "You're not serious." If he thought to force her hand by offering Brandr, when he must know a thrall wouldn't be considered, Finn was sadly mistaken.

"I am," Finn said with stubbornness. "You must choose between Albrikt Gormson, Otto Sturlson, or Brandr the Thrall."

Brandr stopped chopping in mid-swing and turned toward them. He'd removed his tunic for work. Sweat ran down his bare chest in runnels, accentuating the smooth mounds of muscles beneath his taut skin.

"But he's a slave," Katla said. "He can't marry."

"Actually, princess, I can." Brandr leaned on the ax handle, his expression as carefully bland as if they were discussing the weather. "You'd simply have to order me to marry you."

If she'd been a cat, her back would have been arched, and she'd be spitting mad. Order him to marry her, indeed.

"There, you see. Problem solved," her brother said. "Unlike the other men we've tried to interest, he can't say no."

"Finn!" Katla scurried back to him and whispered furiously, "Brandr Ulfson is not a valid choice. I cannot marry him, and you know it. You're still giving me only two choices."

She was the lady of the house. It would destroy her standing to wed a thrall. Not to mention the embarrassment of having to order him to do it.

"If memory serves, all you required was that none of your prospective suitors be fools," Finn said. "You agreed to choose from three men in exchange for the son of Ulf as your thrall. You were there, Ulfson. Isn't that right?"

"I wasn't at my best that night, but that's how I remember it," Brandr supplied unhelpfully.

"Then take him back," Katla said. "I don't want him any longer."

Finn shook his head. "You've made your play. Ulfson is yours. And now I've given you your pick from three men. A bargain's a bargain, sister," he said with a wide smile. "I intend to hold you to it. I expect your decision by nightfall. Both Gormson and Sturlson are on their way here."

"You didn't give me any warning, Finn," she complained. She longed to smack the smug grin from her brother's face, but she'd suffered so from self-recrimination over the last time she slapped someone, she laced her fingers together before her to keep them still. "And just when did you plan on telling me this?"

"At the last possible moment. The time has come, sister. You'll have your choice, and then we'll have a wedding." He folded his arms across his chest, clearly satisfied with his own cleverness. "And there's an end!"

Katla made a low growl in the back of her throat and turned to stride away from them.

Finn chuckled and then cast a chagrined glance at Brandr. "Sorry about that, Ulfson."

"Don't be." Brandr joined his laughter. "It was worth it just to see her hackles rise."

When their laughter ran its course, Brandr spoke to Finn in a low tone. "If she chooses me, I want you to know I'm not without means. I'm still a *jarl*'s son, despite this collar. I'll see you receive a fair marriage settlement."

Finn clapped a hand on his shoulder. "Don't fret. She won't choose you. And she won't shackle herself to that old man either. I just needed a bit of leverage to get her to commit to Albrikt Gormson. He's the one who's offering the most. He's our choice. Has been all along. We needed to give Katla a nudge toward him so he'll be hers too."

❧

All day, Katla's insides were wound tighter than a spool of new yarn. When she made her bargain with Finn, she hadn't really thought the matter through. At the time, finding a way to keep her vow to avenge Osvald seemed the most important matter.

In truth, she hadn't thought of her late husband in days.

Her plan to humble Brandr Ulfson was a failure on all counts. He didn't seem at all troubled by the labor she set him to. Wearing the iron collar didn't chafe his spirit as much as she'd hoped. He seemed to ignore the fact that he was her property most of the time. Even though she'd shamed him by slapping him, she suffered more pangs over the incident than he seemed to.

The more she thought about it, the more wrong it seemed to hold Brandr to account for the misdeeds of his father. Osvald and Ulf were both dead. Perhaps they'd already resolved their differences in *Hel*'s cold hall.

But she was still trapped by her bargain, and now she'd have to make a choice. After she finished her chores, she hiked into the woods to be alone to think.

Katla climbed through the thick pine forest to the highest point on her property and settled herself beside the stack of unused signal firewood. Clouds threatened rain, but Katla was unconcerned. A light misting would cool her off after the exertion of the climb.

Three men. Three possible outcomes. She weighed the attributes and failings of each of them.

Albrikt Gormson was a strong fellow, a man in his prime. There was something of the warrior about him, a throwback to a few generations ago when might triumphed over industry and raiding was preferred over trading. If she was worried about the security of her people, he'd be a good choice, and her brothers would each receive a portion of land of their own. Maybe this time they'd make something of the opportunity.

But Gormson demanded control of her steading as part of the marriage settlement. He'd put his own stamp on the place. Katla's burden would be lightened, but she wasn't sure she was ready to give up the reins so completely. She knew what it was like to have a husband who countermanded her orders. She remembered Osvald's heavy-handedness well enough to know she preferred being in charge.

Otto Sturlson was affable enough. He'd not interfere with the way she ran her household. He'd even been some measure of help in clearing their land. An infusion of his coin would benefit her people. She'd be able to buy another plow and a second team of oxen. If they cleared another field, they'd be able to feed that many more mouths.

But her brothers would receive only coin in the

settlement, something they'd shown a propensity to waste like water. They'd be looking to her to fill their gullets again in no time.

That Otto was elderly couldn't be dismissed. Though an old man might be able to give her children, if she were capable of bearing them, he likely wouldn't be there to help her raise them to adulthood.

Besides, she'd already buried a husband. She wasn't anxious to be made a widow twice over.

Lastly, there was Brandr Ulfson.

Her mind went blank. There was no advantage to wedding him. Even if she freed him, the taint of having worn a thrall's collar would follow him the rest of his days.

Her own high status as the lady of the house would be tarred by it as well. Even any children that resulted from the marriage would be marked by Brandr's past thralldom.

Katla had seen the way folk looked sideways at Inga when she wasn't aware of it. There was always a curl of the lip, a hint of disdain for Osvald's former bed slave. If not for Inga's musical gift and quiet, unassuming ways, Katla probably would have run the girl off for her own good. Perhaps her life would be easier some place where her status as a former slave wouldn't be the first thing to cross folk's minds each time they looked at her.

While Katla's people seemed to accept Brandr readily enough now, what would they make of such a sudden elevation in rank? Perhaps a person could work hard and scramble up a class or two within their strictly measured society, but from thrall to master of a prosperous steading? The gap between the two was broad as the North Sea. An unprecedented rise like that would upset the order of things.

To say nothing of the way Brandr would upset her.

The man made her weak. Not just physically, though she'd be hard put to discount that. Knowing a man like Brandr waited in her bed each evening was beyond the hope of most women.

But Brandr exposed her deepest need, the desire to be loved, to find that mystical *inn matki munr*, to hear her lover call her name without voice, his love resounding in her head and heart. She ached for that soul bonding.

While Brandr Ulfson had offered to ease her body's complaints, he'd never offered a word of affection to her.

And she would want his affection.

Katla wasn't ready to be so needy, so in another's power. It would almost be a reversal if she chose Brandr. She could easily become his thrall in all but name.

She lay back in the long grass and folded her hands over her abdomen. If she couldn't think her way out of this tangle, at least she'd find some rest.

But the sun popped from behind a cloud and wouldn't let her keep her eyes closed. In the sudden warmth of the shaft of sunlight, the high meadow came alive with the drowsy hum of bees.

Katla enjoyed watching the busy little insects as they flitted from one patch of sweet clover to the next, their dangling hind legs yellow with pollen. They were so orderly and industrious, but their short lives were preordained by the will of their queen. They seemed to have no thought for themselves, often laboring to the point of starvation. They lived for the good of the hive and their queen's plan that—

Katla leaped to her feet. Of course!

Finn had planned this all from the beginning. He'd laid the groundwork with Gormson's match long before he wangled a way to force Katla into another marriage. When Brandr Ulfson fell into his lap, he'd been able to set his scheme in motion. Even when she demanded a choice from three possible suitors, he'd manipulated everything to assure the choice that benefited him most would be hers as well.

"That two-faced troll," she said with vehemence. How could he call himself her brother if he used her thus?

Finn had arranged for her to pick from a strapping fellow in his prime, a man nearing his dotage, or a thrall. He'd neatly arranged matters for her to have no choice at all, really.

Finn was far cleverer than she'd credited him.

She'd blundered right into his trap, like a bear lured by the smell of honey.

She wasn't sure whether to be proud of her brother for his meticulous planning or furious with him for having outmaneuvered her.

Katla scrambled to her feet and headed back down the long hill. Either way, she was determined to have the last word.

Chapter 19

WORD THAT KATLA WOULD ANNOUNCE HER CHOICE AT the night meal spread through the household, and soon all tongues were wagging about only one thing.

Who would be their new lord?

Brandr sensed the restive anticipation in the crowd that gathered that evening. They milled and shuffled like a herd of cattle on the verge of stampede, wondering which way to jump.

Though he tried to deny it to himself, his gut was jumping too. He experienced a bit of the same increase in sensory acuity a man feels before a battle. The smells in the crowded longhouse were sharper. Wool, leather, roast meat and spices, and the whiff of too many bodies enclosed in a limited space blended into a single pungent scent. The colors of the tunics were brighter. Even the grain in the wood of the tables leaped out with stark definition.

Every muscle in his body was tensed and ready, as if he were about to engage in the fight of his life.

When Katla arrived, he was acutely aware of her, down to the last dark hair that had escaped her starched headdress. When he leaned over her to serve her, her unique scent—warm woman and cedar—crowded his senses. The curve of her breasts heated his blood, but he kept his face unreadable, the stony, battle-hardened look that had been the last sight on earth for countless Saracens and Bulgars.

Finn had the good sense to place Albrikt Gormson and Otto Sturlson at opposite ends of the head table, neither of them enjoying a favored place at Katla's side.

It irritated Brandr that the seating arrangement pleased him. Why should he care if she did marry? If she had a husband, perhaps she'd tire of bedeviling him and free him.

For a moment, he wondered what would happen if she should choose him as her husband. The idea was ludicrous, and he was angry with himself for entertaining the thought. The woman had enslaved him. She'd used him. Then she'd slapped him, the worst of all possible insults.

But she still made his belly clench each time he heard her voice, and his chest ached at the sight of her.

After most of the meal was finished, Finn stood and shouted for quiet. "As you know, my sister has promised to choose her next husband this night. Since this is a decision that touches all our lives, there's no point in waiting longer. Tell us, Katla. Who will you have?"

Katla stood. Brandr was behind her, so he couldn't see her face, but he thought she trembled a bit. That wasn't the least like her.

"I had hoped to do this privately," she said softly to Finn.

"Nonsense," Otto Sturlson bellowed from his end

of the table. "You may as well announce your decision in public. 'Tis not as if everyone wouldn't know your choice within a few heartbeats, in any case. Even the trees have ears here."

Good-natured laughter from everyone in the hall greeted this. Brandr had to agree with him. Nothing passed in Katla's household without examination by the whole lot.

He was sure no one was ignorant that he'd shared the mistress's chamber on more than one occasion. He'd stumbled over several whispered conversations that ended abruptly when the gossipers realized he was near.

"I have given the matter much thought, and I thank each of my three suitors for the honor of their favor. Or rather, I thank two of them. Brandr Ulfson has had no choice in this, so his favor is in question."

Finn winced, so Brandr knew she'd shot him a withering glare.

"Albrikt Gormson," she said with a ringing tone, and something inside Brandr shriveled. "You are a fine man, and any woman would count herself fortunate to be your bride, but regretfully, I must decline your offer."

Gormson rose to his feet with a horrible scowl at Finn. "I thought you had your sister in hand."

Then he shifted his glare to Katla, and Brandr's fingers balled into fists without his conscious volition.

"You will rue this insult, Katla the Black," he promised and strode from the hall without a backward glance.

Brandr hadn't thought Gormson's heart was engaged in the match, but his reaction to her refusal made him reconsider. From the hard set of Albrikt's shoulders, Brandr knew Katla had made a grave enemy.

Katla turned to look at Otto Sturlson. Gut sinking, Brandr realized one of the advantages for Katla in this match. The woman craved her independence. If she married Otto, she'd probably be a widow again in a handful of years.

"Otto Sturlson," she said. "You, too, are a fine man, and your stories and good humor would be welcome in my hall each night. But I cannot marry you."

Otto shrugged and smiled. "I'm not surprised, girl. Given the difference in our ages, our marriage would have been a short one. But maybe all the more pleasant for its brevity!"

Laughter greeted this pronouncement.

"Mayhap I'll stay with your household, in any case," Otto said. "If you've room for a sometime skald."

Katla nodded. "You will be a most welcome addition to my home."

Brandr forgot to draw breath. Did that mean she'd chosen him? A thrall, an outcast?

"Sister," Finn rose and whispered furiously into her ear. "What are you doing?"

"I'm announcing my choice."

"Don't do this. You can't marry a thrall."

"Then why did you name him as one of my suitors? Do you wish to change your mind and end this charade?"

A hard lump formed in Brandr's chest. She wasn't claiming him as her choice. She was playing a game of strategy with her brother. Brandr was merely a pawn to be sacrificed so she could win.

Finn met Brandr's gaze for a moment then looked back at Katla. Resolve stiffened his jaw.

"No, Katla," Finn said. "The son of Ulf offered a fair marriage settlement for you."

"He what?"

"You didn't think I'd name him if he could not, did you? Einar and Haukon and I will see a decent settlement from this union. But you'll be wed to a thrall." Finn folded his arms calmly across his chest. "If you wish to join yourself to an iron collar, we won't stop you."

A red flush crept up Katla's neck and stained her cheeks. Her bluff had been well and truly called. The entire company leaned forward to get a better view. This little drama was better than a skald's tale.

"Of course I won't wed a thrall."

"It's too late to call Gormson back. He was so angry, he wouldn't have you now if you went on your knees," Finn said. "Then I guess it's to be Otto Sturlson."

"No, it won't be."

"Katla, we had an agreement. You must wed."

"But I won't wed a thrall," Katla said. "I'll free Brandr Ulfson as a wedding gift. In fact, I'll free him this very moment. Call for the smith to strike off the collar."

"A word in private before you do that, princess," Brandr said.

"Are you trying to give me advice, thrall?"

He nodded. "And I think you'd rather hear it away from so many other ears."

Without waiting for her word, he opened the door to her chamber and strode through the portal. She followed.

"What is it?"

"If you intend to strike off my iron collar, you'd better give me that order first," Brandr said gruffly.

She frowned at him in puzzlement.

"The order to wed you," Brandr supplied. "I didn't court you. I didn't ask to be included as one of your choices. The gods know once I'm free I'll be gone."

For a blink, her mouth turned down, and her eyes glittered with more moisture than necessary.

"You intend to leave once you're freed?"

"My father is dead. My brother's ill. I'm needed at home," he said simply. "You don't need or want me here."

Ask me to stay. He willed her to hear the words he wouldn't give voice. *Need me, Katla. Want me.*

She gazed at him so intently he wondered for a moment if she were trying to witch him so she could divine his secret thoughts. But if she did, they didn't seem to mean a thing to her.

"If that's how you want matters, so be it," she finally said with same crisp efficiency with which she did everything. Simple. Straightforward. Cold. "We'll strike the collar after the wedding, then. And I'll shove the coracle off for you myself."

❧

Preparing for a wedding usually took a good deal more time. There were final agreements to be hammered out, preparations for a bridal feast, and invitations sent to neighboring farmsteads. A bridal crown of dried straw and wheat needed to be woven. A circle of earth was cleared and ringed with smooth stones to serve as the place for the ceremony. Ale and mead were brewed in abundance.

It should have taken weeks. Katla rallied her people and got it all done in five days. Katla the Black and Brandr Ulfson would wed on Friday, the most auspicious day of the week for marriages to begin. Katla didn't care whether their union would be blessed by the goddess Frig or not. Friday was just the soonest she could arrange. The sooner this was done and her life back to normal, the better.

Everyone in the household pitched in, even Katla's brothers. Finn wouldn't tell her what he and Brandr agreed to for a bridal price, but it must have been more than satisfactory, since none of her brothers complained to her.

But occasionally, Katla stumbled upon the last bits of conversation, which instantly dried up when the speakers realized she was there. It was an open secret that her people thought her daft to marry a thrall, even one as well favored and evidently as well born as Brandr Ulfson. The fact that he was the son of a *jarl* resurfaced as grist for the gossip mill, but it didn't expunge the taint of iron around his neck.

"And besides, she took him as her thrall in the first place to avenge Osvald," one man said. "How does making Ulfson her husband satisfy the need for vengeance?"

"You've never been married, have you, Snorri?" came one wag's reply.

Their ringing laughter died when Katla showed herself. She steeled herself not to care what anyone thought. She would wed Brandr and he would leave and life would go on.

And that was exactly as she'd have it.

The nagging emptiness in her chest damned her as a liar, but she wasn't about to show her true feelings. Especially when she resisted naming them, even to herself.

The morning of the ceremony, she was led to the bath house by a group of women for her ritual purification. It was the first time she'd had company in the bath since that day she'd shared it with Brandr. Surrounded by her women, Katla felt less alone than she had in years.

They gave her giggling advice about how to keep a happy home, and secret ways to please a man.

"Sometimes, a man can't seem to finish his business, if you catch my meaning. If you want to bring the matter to an end, just you stick your tongue in his ear, dearie," Gerte said. "That'll do, see if it don't."

"But why would you want it to end?" one of the younger women asked, clearly mystified.

"Wait till you've a whole gaggle of children and a load of work waiting for you the next day," Gerte said. "Sleep is every bit as fine as a man's big thing between your legs. Even better sometimes."

"But if the man's as well favored as Brandr Ulfson, who wouldn't give up a little sleep?"

The younger women chuckled in agreement, and Katla laughed along with them. For once, Brandr's slave collar wasn't even mentioned. His universally appreciated maleness was the only issue.

Her body tingled with the awareness until she

remembered Brandr wouldn't share her bed again that night. He'd leave as soon as she struck off the iron.

She willed herself not to care. This was the only way to best Finn at his own game.

But since she had all her women together and out of earshot of any man, she couldn't resist asking, "Have any of you ever known *inn matki munr*?"

"The mighty passion?" Gerte said. "What's mightier than a fine man's thing?"

Giggles burst out again, but once they subsided, Gerte began speaking again.

"I never had the pleasure of *inn matki munr* myself, but I knew one who did. Once," the old woman said. "'Tis a rare thing, you see, that kind of soul bonding. Scarce as hen's teeth."

"Could they really speak to each other without voice?" Katla wondered.

"*Ja*, they could. It was my grandmother and grandfather. That's how I know of it," Gerte said, enjoying the rapt attention of the other women. "And it mattered not how distant they were from each other. She could hear him, and he her."

"Truly?"

Gerte nodded sagely. "But I think she'd have wished not to be blessed with it at the end. His ship capsized, and she had to listen to him drown, though he was half a world away. She was never the same after that. I think she died a bit with him."

The silence that followed was broken only by the moisture condensing on the ceiling, pattering down on the slate floor. Then Gerte clapped her gnarled hands together.

"But we've a bride to prepare, so let us be merry," she said.

Katla's women hustled her back into the longhouse and gathered in her chamber to put the finishing touches on her finery. She was draped with her best amber and silver jewelry. Gerte brushed her dark hair till it shone.

Last of all, Katla selected the key that opened the largest of her trunks, the one that held her most prized possessions. From this, she drew out her father's sword.

It was crafted from Spanish steel, and the hilt was crusted with amber and carbuncle. Katla drew the sword from its ornate baldric and tested the edge against her thumb. A bead of bright blood appeared. The blade was still sharp.

She'd not seen the sword since she gave it to Osvald during their wedding. By rights, it should have accompanied him in his soul-boat burial mound, but she couldn't bear to part with her last link to her father. Instead, she'd returned the short sword Osvald had given her during the ceremony. If he thought that stunted blade adequate for a bridal gift, Katla reasoned it should be sufficient for his needs wherever his spirit wandered in the other worlds.

Gerte took her father's sword from her and balanced it across a tablet-woven cushion. The old woman would carry it for her to the place prepared for the ceremony.

There was no way to avoid offering the blade to Brandr. It was tradition. Her first duty as a wife was to present her husband with a sword. Offering her father's sword was ripe with meaning for a couple truly committing to each other. Since she still had her father's weapon, it would be considered a grave insult to withhold it. Katla wondered if she'd be able to barter for her father's blade back after this sham of a ceremony was ended.

If the blade had rested with Osvald, at least she'd have known where it was. Brandr wasn't called "the Far-Traveled" for nothing. He might take her father's sword to Jondal or Novgorod or Iceland. She'd never see it again. Or him.

"'Tis time, my lady," Gerte said gently. "Your bridegroom awaits."

Chapter 20

KATLA LED THE WAY OUT OF THE LONGHOUSE. FINN was waiting to escort her to her wedding. He cast her a lopsided grin that seemed vaguely apologetic.

"I see you're wearing your best tunic and newest trousers," she said as she took his arm. "Have a care, or people will think you're turning into a terrible peacock."

Finn wasn't usually vain, but he'd taken special pains with his appearance this day, combing and braiding his hair in ornate plaits. He smelled of Katla's lavender-scented soap, and his cheeks above his beard had been scrubbed so hard they were still ruddy. But Finn didn't appreciate Katla's drawing attention to his clean habits, lest others considered him effeminate. Norse men feared very little, but being thought less a man was at the very top of that short list.

"It's tradition. I must be seen to do you honor, sister," Finn said gruffly. Then he covered her hand with his and squeezed as they walked toward the circle of smooth stones. He leaned toward her and softened his tone. "I know you don't think so, but I truly do want to see you happy."

"Ha," she said softly, conscious the eyes of all were upon them. "You're more concerned about the bridal price than anything, and we both know it."

"*Ja*, when I started this, that was true. Einar and Haukon have made some bad choices. All right, me too, come to that," Finn admitted. "I needed to figure a way for us to get a fresh start. When Gormson first approached me, I thought I'd found it, but I didn't know how I'd be able to convince you to take his offer. You never seem to need anybody."

Katla blinked hard at that. If he only knew the times she felt lost and alone. So many people depended upon her that she didn't have the luxury of wallowing in her own needs.

A large contingent followed Katla up the gentle slope, but most of the guests, her neighbors as well as members of the household, had gathered around the circle of stones, jostling for the best view. After all, it wasn't every day a well-born lady wed a thrall. This was a wonderment worth an elbow or two to the ribs to secure the best vantage point.

The crowd parted before them, revealing the sacred space and Brandr Ulfson waiting for her in the center of it.

"I think you'll find, if you give this a chance, that you've made a good bargain, sister," Finn said.

Katla barely heard him. She caught sight of Brandr, flanked by Einar and Haukon with his arm still in a sling.

Probably making sure he doesn't bolt until the deed is done.

No man had ever looked less like a slave. There was nothing subservient in his squared shoulders. His hands were fisted on his hips. He might have been a Norse nobleman from a previous generation when Viking was an honored occupation that brought wealth back to the fjords. She imagined him standing defiantly by the dragon head of his ship, sailing into the unknown with an uncowed spirit.

Brandr wasn't dressed in finery, but she suspected he'd talked Finn into giving him back the clothes he'd been wearing when he was taken as a thrall. The tunic was of good quality, and the clothes fit his lean form well. His beard and hair had grown back considerably, the dark blond curling around his ears and framing his sensual mouth with gold. He still bore the hateful iron collar, but there was no deference in his eyes. A glint of something dark and hot sparked in them when his gaze caught Katla's.

Her vision tunneled briefly, and she realized she was holding her breath. Tamping down the way her belly tingled, she stepped into the smooth circle with him, followed by Gerte, who flashed a toothy smile to all. The old woman relished her role as keeper of the ceremonial sword and was determined to make the most of it.

Once everyone quieted, Finn announced their intent to wed and stepped aside, signaling his consent to the union. Brandr recited the required vow of a husband in a strong, clear tone. Katla followed his lead as they exchanged rings. As she voiced the time-hallowed promises, part of her wished this was a marriage in truth, that Brandr wasn't leaving as soon as the collar was struck from his neck.

Not that she expected to be embarrassed by her

bridegroom's sudden departure. She'd explain that the marriage was only to fulfill her bargain with Finn. Then she'd invite the assembled guests to feast in honor of her wiliness, lest any be disappointed after traveling for the sham wedding.

No new lord would change matters in her household. Life as they knew it would continue without disruption. She'd be seen as a woman who honored her word and yet managed to arrange matters to her own liking.

But when she looked up at Brandr, she wasn't so sure a marriage in name only *was* to her liking. She was forced to avert her gaze lest he read the sudden longing in her. Then she turned and took the sword from Gerte.

"My father's sword," she said as she laid the naked blade across his upturned palms. "It belonged to a worthy man. Bear it with honor and strength. May it see you safe through many battles."

Brandr brought the steel to his lips and pressed a quick kiss to the flat of the blade, as was customary. Then he handed the sword to Haukon, bypassing Einar, who was supposed to be his main attendant. Haukon beamed at being chosen to keep the bridal sword for him until the ceremony was completed.

Brandr reached over his shoulder and pulled out a long blade from its baldric. The steel had been repeatedly folded and fired, forged in faraway Damascus Finn had told her when he described the sword Brandr had worn when they captured him. Finn had returned it now, and it shimmered in the dying sunlight, hammered into brilliance by a master of the craft. The waves of its creation left an undulating pattern on the blade, glittering like living flame.

He dropped to one knee before her, point of the sword buried in the smooth dirt, both hands on the ornate hilt.

"I give you the edge of my sword, the strength of my body, the breath my life," Brandr said, his gaze glued on the tips of her slippers peeping from beneath her hem. "If you have need of any of them, they are yours for the asking. And even if you don't ask, they are still yours. From this day forward, you are my wife. I'll defend what's mine as long as there is a beating heart in my body."

He looked up at her, something unexpected in his eyes. She'd seen that mad glint in a man's gaze only when there was a cache of treasure to be had.

Katla swallowed hard. This wasn't part of the rite. His words weren't a declaration of love exactly, but it was a pledge of protection worthy of a mighty passion. She accepted the sword from him and laid it with reverence across Gerte's cushion.

Brandr had promised her the protection of his body. The word of a man of valor was worth even more to her than the fabulous sword he pledged it on.

He hadn't been required to offer such a pledge. Even though he was going to leave her, he'd come to her aid if she needed him. Her heart was strangely comforted by the thought.

Katla lifted her hand, surprised to find it unsteady, and signaled for the smith to step forward.

Brandr was led to a block of wood at the edge of the circle, where he knelt and presented his neck to the smith as if he were submitting to a headsman with an ax. After three ringing strikes of hammer and chisel, the iron collar's bolt gave way, and Brandr rose a free man.

No one spoke. Seeing a thrall freed was a rare enough occurrence. Seeing him elevated to the status of lord of the household was almost unthinkable.

"Bet you feel lighter," Finn said, obviously wanting to break the tension.

Brandr rubbed his neck, still staring at the collar that lay in pieces. "*Ja*, I do. Such a little thing, but it's weightier on a man's spirit than it looks."

Then he strode with purpose over to Katla and scooped her up in his arms.

She yelped in surprise. This, too, wasn't part of the rite. They were supposed to share a ritual kiss on the cheek, and then she and Brandr were to lead the procession back to the longhouse for the bridal feast.

Instead, Brandr twirled her around once, her long skirt flaring out like a sail seeking the wind. He kissed her right on the mouth. His lips were firm and sure, and when hers parted slightly, he was quick to invade her with his tongue, a beguiling summons. A stab of longing sliced through her when he finally released her mouth.

"The iron collar was a heavy burden, but Thor strike me blind if my new burden isn't even heavier!" He tossed Katla up and caught her again while the crowd laughed and applauded his wit.

Then, still carrying her, he started back down the slope to the longhouse. All the guests fell in behind them, repeating the joke to those who'd been too far away to hear Brandr's words. Someone started singing a familiar bawdy song, and the chant was picked up by the others.

"I'm supposed to walk," Katla hissed in his ear.

"And yet it pleases me to carry you, wife."

If he still meant to leave, this display would only muddy matters. "Brandr, put me down. You're confusing everyone."

Especially her.

"How so?"

"You're acting like…like…"

"Like a newly married man? What a coincidence. That's exactly what I am. Besides," he said as he stopped before the big door to the longhouse, "it's bad luck for a bride to trip over the threshold. If I hadn't carried you down the hill, I'd just have to pick you up again now to carry you over."

A few servants had remained behind to see to cooking of the feast. Inga looked up from her place by the central meal fire and nodded a greeting.

"All is in readiness, my lord," she said softly.

Katla bristled and stiffened in Brandr's arms. This was her household, not his.

"What's wrong?" he asked, sensing her reaction. "Am I not master here now?"

Tradition proclaimed he was. A married woman didn't retain control of anything unless the contract stipulated as much, and Finn had been willing to barter away all of her rights to her holding. Her only hope at maintaining an even keel for her people was for him to leave.

"You're a master who doesn't intend to stay," she whispered as he set her lightly on her feet.

"I might if you asked me to," he said as he led to her to the main table.

His promise was tempting, but she resisted the urge to beg him not to leave. When she married Osvald, she'd given him her whole heart, but he hadn't returned the favor.

Need someone, and you only give them an invitation to hurt you, she reminded herself. She couldn't need Brandr Ulfson.

Or at least she couldn't let him know if she did.

Then the longhouse flooded with guests, and there was no more opportunity for private speech. Everyone cheered when Katla presented the bridal ale to Brandr and he proclaimed it the best he'd ever tasted. So many toasts were offered, she felt slightly light headed from too much drink. Katla was prone to moderation, but there were no limits to the merry-making this night.

Inga played her pan flute. Otto Sturlson had the entire company complaining of pain in their sides over his hilarious recounting of the tale of Thor and Loki in the land of the Frost Giants. Otto even slipped a kerchief over his head to act out the part of the thunder god in woman's guise.

Katla wiped away tears of mirth at the image of the virile god's vain attempt at disguising himself as female.

She slanted a quick glance at Brandr. He seemed to be enjoying himself, as a bridegroom should.

Finally, men began banging their drinking horns on the tables and started a low chant, calling for the bedding to take place.

Gerte hustled Katla into her chamber. The old

woman lit the lamp with her tinder and flint and then started stripping Katla for bed.

"No, Gerte, there's no need." She was certain Brandr would announce his plans to leave, voiding the marriage, and that would be that.

"There's every need, mistress," the old woman said as she removed Katla's slightly wilted crown of woven wheat. "If we don't get you naked and under the covers, the men will take it upon themselves to help your new husband do it."

"They didn't behave so when I wed Osvald."

"They didn't drink so free at that wedding either," Gerte said. "Besides, Osvald was a hard man. He would've ordered a man whipped till he passed out if he laid a finger on you."

"And you think the son of Ulf the Ruthless wouldn't do the same?" She considered it more likely Brandr would punish the offender himself rather than ordering it done, but Katla felt obligated to defend the principle.

"Oh, *ja*, he'd try, but folk don't respect him the same. Meaning no offense, I'm sure, but I don't expect he'd be obeyed if he ordered more than a refill of his mead bowl." Gerte's bony fingers worked the catches on Katla's brooches and pulled the tunic over her head. "Wasn't he naught but a thrall till this night?"

Gerte's words grated Katla's soul. "Brandr is the son of a *jarl* and a captain of the Varangian Guard. He wasn't born a thrall, you know."

"*Ja*, so he says, but we've all seen the iron on his neck. We've naught but his word for the rest."

Gerte pulled back the bedding and waved her over. "Quick, my lady, the men will be here soon. Then once they see the pair of you settled, you and your man will have the whole night together," Gerte said. "Of course, in my day, the men stayed to see the bride deflowered, just to make sure the knot was tied good and proper."

Katla's brows arched in surprise.

"It wasn't as bad as it sounds. My husband kept me covered up while he did the deed. But don't you worry your head. Those days are past, and it's not as if you're a green maid. They'll leave as soon as your husband orders them out." Gerte frowned, obviously recalling her previous comment about whether the word of a former thrall would be obeyed. "I hope."

Then she lifted her bony hands in a gesture that consigned the coming events to the lap of the gods, and slipped out of Katla's chamber.

Bridal night or not, Katla wasn't about to face a drunken mob bare as a peeled twig. She hopped out of bed, donned a thin night shift, and scrambled back under the covers as the door to her chamber opened.

Brandr's broad-shouldered form was framed by the doorway for a moment as he accepted some lewd advice with a good-natured laugh. Then he firmly closed the door on the crowd gathered on the other side, not even allowing them a peek at Katla in the bed. He slid the latch home with a loud click.

He turned toward Katla. Brandr's face was fixed with a look of intense concentration as he met her gaze, the raw-boned lines of his features divided into light and dark planes in the flickering flame of the lamp. Then he pulled his tunic over his head and stripped off his undergarment, baring his chest and arms.

"I thought we had an agreement," Katla said. "You said you were leaving as soon as the iron collar was struck."

He shrugged. "I'm a free man, am I not? I'll leave when it suits me."

He toed off his boots and pulled off his socks. Then he turned his back to her, untied the drawstring at his waist, and peeled out of his trousers. The smooth skin of his tight buttocks was kissed by the lamplight. Corded muscles stood out in stark relief beneath the skin of his thighs and calves. When he turned back to face her, his cock rose.

If he'd had to claim her before witnesses, he was certainly equipped to do it.

Katla drew a ragged breath. He was even more beguilingly male than she remembered. Or maybe the punishing pace of work she'd set for him had burned away the last traces of softness, leaving him even more hard bodied and deeply sculpted. She cleared her throat loudly. If she didn't speak now, she'd lose the will to.

"What if I want you to leave?" she asked.

Brandr narrowed his eyes at her. "If you want me to leave, I will. But you'll have to convince me that's truly your desire."

She sat up straighter. "That's truly my desire."

"I don't believe you."

"How can I convince you?"

"Only your body can do that. If you don't want me to stay, I'll know." He took a step closer to the bed. "If you're lying when you say you want me gone, I'll know that too."

Chapter 21

HE DOVE ONTO THE BED WITH HER. THE ROPES beneath the straw tick creaked in protest. The sheets smelled of her, cedar and warm woman and just a hint of musk. He slid under the linen and hitched a possessive leg over hers.

"Brandr, I don't think—"

"Good." He nuzzled her neck and nipped an earlobe. "You do too much of that as a general rule."

"But we need to talk about—"

He silenced her with a hard kiss. Once her body unstiffened and her lips softened and parted in welcome, he suckled her bottom lip for a moment and then drew back. "No more talk. And nothing else can stand between us either."

He hooked a finger over the neckline of her night shift and traced along the edge, teasing her bare skin. Then he gave the bow between her breasts a hard yank. The thin fabric parted, baring her to the navel.

Her lips parted softly, but she didn't protest.

She wants me to look at her, he thought, almost giddy with lust.

Her skin was a wonder, warm and smooth. Gooseflesh rose in the wake of his fingers. Her nipples became taut as he teased around them. Her breath hitched, and she made a small, needy noise in the back of her throat when he bent to taste them.

She arched herself into his mouth.

Sucking one, gently pinching the other, he worshipped her nipples until she moaned. Then he ran his hand over her ribs, past her belly, and pulled up the night shift to invade the dark curls at the apex of her thighs.

She was slick and wet. When he slid into her soft folds, she tilted into his hand.

He drew a bit of her moisture out with his fingertip. Then he put the finger in his mouth and sucked off her salty sweetness. Her breath came in short pants as he traced her lips with the same finger and then sealed her mouth with a soft kiss. The taste of her made his cock twitch.

"You see," he whispered. "You don't want me to leave, do you?"

She shook her head. "I don't want you to leave."

Katla reached behind his neck and pulled his head down into a blistering kiss.

∽

She couldn't get enough of him. It was as if a gaping maw had opened inside her, ravenous and needy. She had to have this man or die.

The ache, oh gods, he'd made her ache before but not like this. She never dreamed she could ache so. The emptiness overwhelmed her. If she didn't feel him between her legs soon, she'd fly apart in all directions.

She rocked herself against his hip, grinding against his pelvis. She throbbed to feel him inside her. What was the man waiting for? Did he want her to beg?

Probably.

Katla pressed her lips together in a hard line as he kissed his way down her body. His tongue found her sex, and he traced all her little folds with the tip. Her wanting grew more desperate, pounding in tandem with her heart.

His mouth was soft and wet on her. If she hadn't fisted the linens, her nails would have cut into the heels of her palms.

He growled with pleasure as he suckled her and she whimpered.

Damn the man for making her need him so.

The heaviness in her groin weighed her down. She thrashed on her pillow. Incoherent sounds escaped her lips.

Her mind wandered between the worlds. She was the earth, a cavern, a secret, deep place only the bravest ever dare.

Then when she thought she could sink no lower, the tight heaviness inside her burst forth into vibrant light. Her body shuddered with the force of her release.

Before the last spasm faded, Brandr had moved up and filled her so she convulsed around his thick length. Once she finished pulsing, he began to move. He reached down and hitched her legs up over his shoulders, so he could plunge into her without the least gentleness.

Good. She couldn't bear gentleness from him now. Gentleness might give her space to think.

She needed him hard and male and demanding. She needed the slap of his balls against her. She needed his hoarse cry of triumph when he emptied himself into her, his body strained and as taut as a bowstring while his seed pulsed hotly.

The ache was stilled. The emptiness fled away. For a moment, the cares of the steading, the coldness of the cradle in the corner, the fact that her new husband wasn't really the sort of man she should have chosen at all—none of those concerns signified a thing.

All that mattered was the thud of Brandr's heart on her chest and his breath on her neck.

He slid her legs off his shoulders and settled down on her, his breath coming in short gasps. When Brandr looked down at her and smiled, her chest flooded with warmth.

She still had no idea if she and Brandr could make a marriage. But by the gods, they could make love.

❦

"Brandr, whether you will it or no, you and I must talk. Now," she said another coupling later.

"Katla, I—" He meant to plead exhaustion, but his throat closed up. She'd let the sheet drop, and her nipples peeped through the open slit in her night shift. He could still taste them, sweet and responsive in his mouth. His cock rallied for a third time.

Her lips were moving. She was undoubtedly saying something, but all the blood in his brain seemed to have fled, taking his understanding with it. He was fully engorged.

"Don't stand there gaping at me like a codfish." Her tone turned strident, demanding his attention. "I asked you a question."

Had she asked something? He hadn't caught a word. All he could do was grit his teeth as his erection grew so intense the aching pleasure was a knife's edge from pain.

"Aren't you going to answer me?"

"*Ja*," he stammered, shaken by the lust that lanced him. The punishing pace she'd set for him had kept desire at bay of late. Now, even though he'd already slaked his need not once but twice this night, it rushed back into him with the force of a cataract plummeting into a fjord.

"Give me a moment," he said as he plumped up his pillows and laced his fingers behind his head beside her, hoping she'd repeat her question without his having to admit he hadn't been listening when she asked the first time.

By the time he'd decided it was safe to look on her again, her wide eyes glistened with unshed tears.

"So you care for me not at all, then," she said in a small voice. The hurt, the desolation he felt emanating from her slight form squeezed his heart.

"Not care for you?" Where had that come from?

Love talk had never passed her lips before this night. He hadn't imagined her capable of it, let alone craving it. He expected a ripe and randy bedding, not talk of something as murky and changeable as a person's feelings.

His chest ached at the hurt on her face, and this time he recognized the cause. It made no logical sense. It simply was.

Not care for her? He'd sooner not breathe.

"How can you say that?" he asked, mystified. He

leaned toward her, stopping with his lips mere finger widths from hers, fighting to bridle himself. If his cock had any say in the matter, he'd be on her like a stag in rut yet again. He wanted so much more for her this time.

For both of them.

A tear trembled on her lower lid then tumbled to slide down her cheek. He lifted a hand to caress it away from her pale skin.

"Katla, how can you say I don't care for you?" Brandr said softly.

Her night shift neckline fell forward, revealing the shadowed hollow between her breasts. He forced himself to meet and hold her gaze.

"I wouldn't blame you. After all, I enthralled you," she said.

"I might have done the same if our situations were reversed." In the interests of peace, he decided it might be wise to appease her a bit by being agreeable. "I know I'm not the most amiable person."

He chuckled. "No, you're not."

She shot a wounded glare at him. Obviously, he wasn't supposed to agree with her all the time.

"I don't know why it should be so. Maybe why isn't important, but there's something about you that fits me." He tucked a strand of her hair behind the pink shell of her ear. "We may not always have smooth sailing weather, but I'd rather fight with you than live in quiet, stagnant peace with anyone else."

"Truly?"

"Truly."

"How can I believe that?" Her chin quivered, and

her night shift slid off one shoulder to bare a breast completely. "You've not said more than a handful of words to me for days. You didn't seem to even see me anymore."

Loki's Hairy Backside, he was certainly seeing her now. He ran a hand over her head, willing himself to focus on just her emerald eyes.

"I see you. And I see what you want." Brandr inhaled her scent. She smelled as fresh as new-cut grass. "Every soul longs for love, for *inn matki munr*." Her long hair curled around his fingers as he stroked it, running his hand over its silken length. "'Tis the stuff of maidensongs and skald's tales, not at all the kind of life a man clapped into thralldom can aspire to."

"And you don't want to settle for less now. I understand," she finished for him. "Don't let me trouble you a moment longer. My body is telling you to go."

She threw back the covers and would have bolted, but he grasped her arm and held her fast.

He lifted her chin with his other hand and forced her to meet his gaze.

"I don't pretend to understand the mighty passion, but I know love is not something that comes in half measures. Either it is or it isn't," he said, refusing to release his hold on her even though she attempted to wrest herself from him. "For me, it is. I do care for you, Katla."

She ceased struggling. "How can you?"

"I don't know," he said. "I've puzzled over it for weeks, and I've come to the conclusion that it doesn't matter if it doesn't make sense. All I know is while I draw breath, all I am is yours."

She froze, as still as a carved rune stone, just looking at him with those enormous green eyes of hers. She was clearly weighing his declaration for truth.

It seemed strange, even to him, who felt it firsthand, but there was such a lump of caring in his chest for this woman, he thought he might choke on it, gods help him.

"If that's the way of it, then, I take you at your word," she said with a trembling smile. "And just so you know, I care for you too."

He placed a hand around her waist and drew her close. Then he caught one of her hands and pressed it against his chest, letting her feel the pounding of his heart.

"You consume me, Katla, and I don't care a whit. Let the fire burn."

Brandr had meant to hold back, to wait for her to respond, but something primal surged in his blood, singing the chaos of lust. He had to obey the savage call or burst out of his own skin.

He plundered her mouth, nearly overcome by her sweetness. Her scent surrounded him, intoxicating him, his senses dazed and reeling. When she answered his kiss and leaned toward him, brushing her taut nipples against his chest, blood pounded so loudly in his ears he thought she must be able to hear it.

Then the drumbeat moved much lower, to his swollen cock, throbbing with the rhythm of his life's blood in ever-quickening pulses.

Brandr pressed her body against his, knowing he should be more gentle with her. She was so small, so fragile seeming, he was afraid if he didn't hold back, she might shatter to pieces in his arms.

Katla didn't seem to think she was that breakable, though. When he started to release her, she pulled his head down with a soft groan, urging him to stay.

They took each other's mouths, vying for supremacy with their entwined tongues. Katla nipped at his lower lip in a tiny love bite, and it made his groin ache all the more. The desperate little noises she made at the back of her throat nearly drove him mad.

His hands roamed over her, finding and exploring each dip and valley, the exquisite curve of her back, the plump lushness of her bottom. He worked her night shift up, hearing the seam part at her hip, but unable to stop till he dragged the flimsy garment over her head.

When Katla lay back on the sheets, he paused for a moment, drinking in the sight of her. Her pale skin was gilded with light from the guttering lamp, setting her aglow like some ethereal being.

That's it. She was an elf-maiden who'd strayed far from the delights of Aelfham, the elfin home world. She graced his life with beauty beyond a mortal's capacity to comprehend.

"You're not stopping?" she asked, her voice dusky.

"Not for all the nine worlds," he promised. "Guess you don't want me to leave, after all."

She shook her head, and her breasts shuddered with a sigh. "Now what?"

"Now, princess, I show you what caring feels like."

Chapter 22

SLOWLY, HE REACHED OUT A HAND. STARTING AT THE base of her throat where her pulse fluttered, he began tracing a lover's journey over her flawless skin.

Oh, the feel of her, all warm and soft and willing!

He paused to dally in every crevice, the crease beneath her slender arm, the delicate skin at the bend of her elbow. He passed over the hot, erotic places he'd normally have focused on to find something as simple and uniquely Katla as the dimple on her knee. Defying the urgency of his rioting cock, he took his time, learning her by heart.

All of her.

He ran his fingertip around the outline of her hands, to the deep base of each finger, and threading his way around her knuckles. He taunted the hidden crease beneath each breast. He drew circles around the shallow indentation of her navel.

His touch dropped lower, and he teased her legs apart. His fingers launched a gentle invasion. All the while, his gaze never left her face.

Brandr delighted in watching as pleasure and need parted her lips and made her eyes go languid.

When she reached out to touch him, he stopped her. "Not yet, princess. You first."

"No." She pressed her fingertips against his lips. "Most of the time with Osvald, only one of us took pleasure, and it brought no ease to either of us. You and I will go into this madness together or not at all."

Then to his joy, she feathered her fingertips over his chest. A slight breeze found its way through the overhead smoke hole, cooling the fever heating his skin.

"This caring you speak of," she said, her voice sultry, "surely it must go both ways. If one is not pleased, how can the other take pleasure?"

He dared not even draw breath as her clever hands danced over him, tickling along his ribs, teasing his nipples into hard knots. Then she reached down and cupped his ballocks, her gentle massage only sending his groin into a deeper ache. She explored his thighs, scooting close enough to reach around and run a thumb along the crevice of his buttocks.

His breath hissed over his teeth. "You little minx."

She laughed, deep and throaty. Her breasts teased him with glancing brushes as she moved closer.

But she carefully avoided the throbbing shaft that yearned for her touch more than any other finger width of his skin.

Instead, she raked his ribs with her nails and splayed her hands across his flat belly. When she finally grasped him, the pressure inside him had risen, so it was all he could do not to come in her hands.

"Katla, I can't—"

She surprised him into silence by wrapping her hands behind his neck and hooking a leg over his hip.

"Can't what?" she asked with feigned innocence as she pressed herself against him, her hot moistness tormenting the tip of his cock.

"Can't stand not swiving you for one more beat of my heart." He covered her mouth with his. All his longing and hope poured into her. Lust and caring surged through him, twin cascades plunging into a rain-swollen river.

He loved her, he realized with a jolt.

Katla, his one-time mistress and owner. From the dark crown of her head to the soles of her delicately arched feet, he loved her.

And the greatest wonder of all was his ice princess seemed to care for him a bit too.

But if he didn't take her right now, he'd die on the spot.

He rolled to pull her on top of him and pushed her hips down, gently impaling her on his rock-hard erection. He groaned, awash in the pleasure of her slick, hot flesh.

She cried out, but not with pain. The gasp that tore from her throat was the feral sound of feminine triumph as she engulfed him completely.

He moved inside her, reveling in her softness. Heart on heart, their bodies joined in perfect concert, seeking the deepest bonding possible.

Before, they'd strained against each other. Now they moved as one. Their hands, mouths, bodies, and hearts clasped tightly, and when they interrupted their kiss, it was only to tumble into each other's eyes.

There is surrender in bliss. It's a kind of dying the body welcomes, not unlike the wounded warrior who

longs for the Valkyries to bear him to Valhalla. Brandr
and Katla teetered for just a moment on the brink of
that death then plummeted over the edge together.
He felt her contract around him in spasms of joy as his
seed pulsed into her.

Unwilling to part from her, he wrapped his arms
around her. Gradually, the fever of lust subsided.
When their bodies separated, she shifted to settle
by his side. He looked up into the thatch overhead,
utterly spent. A single star winked in the center of the
smoke hole.

There was no need for words. Their bodies had
said it all. A mantle of caring enveloped them, sending
delayed shivers over their skin. Love sparked and
crackled in the very air they breathed.

Their other couplings had been feral and hot, like
a pair of wild creatures mating. But this joining had
touched a part of him he hadn't even been aware
was there.

They were well and truly bonded.

She kissed his neck and snuggled close, relaxing
against his body with the same lethargy that was stealing
over him. In a few moments, her even breathing told
him she'd escaped into the land of dreams and shadows.

Just before he followed her in sleep, Brandr decided
he'd never ask the gods for another thing for the rest
of his life. After this night, he'd already received more
than the full measure of happiness usually meted out to
mortals. Another drop of joy might tempt Loki beyond
bearing, and everything Brandr cared for might be
snatched from him by that envious trickster godling.

No, better to be safe than sorry.

Katla was his. It was more than he had a right to ask. More than he'd likely ever see again, especially once the morrow came and he put his plans in motion.

The ones he was sure Katla wouldn't like one bit.

❦

A shaft of sunlight broke through the smoke hole and stabbed Katla in the eye. It was rare that she slept past the cockcrow or missed hearing the clank of the bell around the ram's neck as her flocks were being driven into the high pasture.

But this day she'd slept till midmorning, judging from the position of the sun. Somehow, she couldn't bring herself to care. Katla extended her arms over her head in a leisurely stretch.

Then she jerked upright in a sudden motion.

Brandr wasn't beside her.

She ran a palm over the linens. The indentation in the tick where he'd been was still warm. His scent lingered in the bedclothes. He hadn't been gone long.

Katla rose and dressed quickly. She usually stirred at the slightest sound. She must have been sleeping like the dead for him to sneak out of bed, dress, and leave the chamber without her knowledge.

That's what comes of being loved to exhaustion, she thought as she tugged on her stockings and wrapped the binding strips of cloth about her calves.

Loved.

They hadn't used the word, but she felt it. In the deep relaxation of her long sleep, in every loose-jointed limb, she reveled in the afterglow of well-being that follows a bone-jarring coupling.

Each time. Her mind was a little fuzzy. She'd actually lost count.

Inga was working at the central meal fire when Katla emerged from her chamber.

"Pack a pot of meat and bread for us, would you please, Inga?" Katla said as she moved toward the open door.

Sunlight caught the bright red fabric on one of the looms propped in the entry, making the color even more vibrant. Or mayhap it only seemed so. The breeze blowing through the longhouse was fresher, the scent of sausages frying more spicy and pungent. Even the soft drape of her underdress swishing against her skin as she moved was tinged with pleasure. Katla could find no cause for complaint about anything this fine day.

"My husband and I will go for a long walk and break our fast in the woods."

Inga's face crumpled in confusion. "But Br—your... husband already broke his fast and ordered food packed for the journey. A keg of water also to be brought to the wharf, which Finn said he'd see about. I still need to—"

"What journey?"

"I...he did not...I assumed you knew."

Oh gods, he was leaving. After last night. After everything.

Katla ran out of the longhouse and down the winding path to the wharf. Brandr was setting the rigging on the coracle and arranging bundles of cargo to distribute the weight evenly. Finn's water keg rode in the center of the craft.

"What do you think you're doing?" she asked when she reached the spot where the small vessel was tied up.

"What's it look like?" Brandr shielded his eyes against the glare of sunlight to look up at her for a moment then resumed his work. "I'm preparing for a voyage."

Her heart sank to the soles of her feet. Why had she let herself need him? He was still leaving.

He'd said he would, she reminded herself sternly. She shouldn't have been surprised. She swallowed hard and steeled herself not to show her bleeding soul.

"Where are you bound?"

"Where are *we* bound, you mean?"

"We?" For a moment, her heart leaped up in gladness. He hadn't intended on leaving her after all, but it didn't mean she could go with him. "No. I'm not going anywhere. There's too much for me to—"

"Don't worry, sister." Finn's voice came from behind her. "You won't be gone long."

"That's right. I won't be gone long, because I won't be going at all." She fisted her hands at her waist. "Where is it I'm not going?"

"To Jondal," Brandr said calmly as he accepted and stowed the bundles Finn had brought down for him.

Katla recognized the vibrant blue of one of her dresses peeping from the top of a rucksack. Someone had taken her key, gotten into her trunk, and packed clothes for the voyage without her knowledge.

"I'm taking you home," Brandr said as if that ended the matter.

"This is our home."

"No, it's not," Brandr said. "It'll always be your place. And no matter how long I bide here, I'll always be Brandr the Thrall when folk think I'm out of earshot."

She started to protest, but he silenced her with a piercing look.

"You know it to be true," he said quietly.

Inga padded softly up and handed Brandr the basket of food he'd requested.

"Ask Inga," he said. "She'll tell you it's so. Even once the iron collar's gone, there's a shadow about our necks no amount of scrubbing can clean."

"I would travel with you as your servant, mistress." Inga cast a darting glance in Katla's direction then averted her gaze to the rough wood of the wharf. Her submissive demeanor spoke volumes. She felt the weight of her past keenly.

There were times when Katla had struggled with jealousy, but now she felt nothing but pity for her late husband's bed slave.

Surely things would be different for a man. Brandr was well liked. She'd seen it herself. With time, her people would come to accept him as master here.

"Perhaps when we return, Inga, we'll take you on the next trip. We won't be gone long," Brandr said. "Three or four weeks—five at most."

Brandr strapped an oilskin over the cargo to protect it from the elements.

"Finn and your other brothers have agreed to wait till I can collect your bride price from my share of the bounty my friends and I brought back from Byzantium. We'll return to Tysnes Isle before the weather turns and can stay for a bit, if you like," he said. "Then we'll sail back to Jondal to winter in my brother's hall."

Katla's jaw gaped. "But it's my duty to care for the people here. I can't leave them."

He climbed out of the boat and walked toward her. "I didn't think I could be a thrall either, but a person can get used to anything. You might be surprised what your people can do on their own. Besides, your brother will see to the folk of this holding, won't you, Finn?"

"*Ja*, of course I will." Her brother drew himself up to his full, lanky height.

"Oh, Finn, you can't even see to yourself, much less run a farmstead."

Even though Finn wilted a bit as she said it, she stood by her assessment. He'd shown his quality of late, but she couldn't trust him to carry on without her. Katla turned back to her husband.

If this was the first battle of wills between them, she was determined to win it.

"Brandr, I understand you feel you have to leave. My bride price has been agreed upon, and you must honor your debts," she said primly. "I wish you safe travels, and will see you when you return."

"Our honeymoon isn't near done," Brandr reminded her.

A month of loving and feasting and sipping the special bridal ale and mead was usual for the newly married. It wasn't her fault they wouldn't be enjoying their time together.

"It'll be an odd honeymoon with you gone, but I'll manage," she said stiffly.

One corner of his mouth turned up. "And you think that ends the matter."

"There's no other way to see it."

He shook his head and sighed. Then he grabbed her and slung her over his shoulder so her head hung down behind his back and her bottom smiled at the sky.

"What about now, wife?" he asked. "Do you see things differently from that angle?"

"Brandr, put me down!" She tried to squirm away, but he held her fast.

"Stop wiggling, or you'll feel my hand on your backside," he warned.

Her bottom heated at the thought. "Lay a hand on me, Brandr Ulfson, and you'll have to sleep with one eye open for the rest of your life."

He laughed and gave her buttocks a love pat. "You didn't complain of my hands last night."

Since it was within reach, she gave *his* bum a sharp smack. He ignored her.

"Farewell, Finn." Brandr clapped his free hand on his brother-in-law's shoulder. "I'll be back with the bride price before you know it."

"And you'll be welcome, so long as you don't try to return the bride," Finn said with a laugh.

"Don't just stand there." Katla pressed against Brandr's back to raise herself up so she could glare at Finn, but she couldn't break free from her husband as he stepped into the swaying coracle. "Help me."

"Sorry, sister. I can't even see to myself, you know." Finn slipped the chain that held her all-important keys off her neck and secreted them in the pouch at his belt. Then he loosed the mooring lines of the coracle. "Doubt I'd be any help to you."

"I didn't mean that."

"Did you not?" Her brother gave the vessel a shove into the deep water of the cove as Brandr deposited her on a small trunk. "I never can tell when you're joking, Katla. No matter. Safe travels."

She stood, and the coracle bobbled dangerously. Brandr unfurled the sail.

"Can you swim, Katla?" he asked with maddening calm.

"No."

The water temperature was so cold, few in the North bothered to learn, since the ability to swim would only prolong dying if a boat capsized. Better a clean, quick drowning than a miserable, desperate struggle against an end that would come in either case.

"Then I suggest you sit down," Brandr said as the wind freshened and the coracle lifted in the water, quickening in the breeze.

She turned around on the trunk, facing forward so she didn't have to look at his smug face for another heartbeat.

Chapter 23

"I DON'T KNOW WHAT TO TELL YOU, MALVAR. WOMEN are more fickle and changeable than the sea. She ought to have been ordered to accept the match." Albrikt Gormson curled his lip in disdain. "Why her ball-less brothers even gave her a choice I'll never know."

Malvar Bloodaxe poured wine into two precious goblets of Frankish glass. He usually reserved these special vessels for celebrations. They'd have to do to console his ally in an especially ignominious defeat.

To be turned down in favor of a thrall.

It must gall Albrikt more than liquor on an open wound. If a woman used Malvar so sore, he'd have her tongue cut out and fried up with onions for his night meal.

He handed one of the goblets to Gormson.

"You wouldn't have sailed across the North Sea to bring me this ill news unless you had a plan to counter it," Bloodaxe said.

Gormson shrugged. "I had thought to attack the farmstead and so claim the harbor we need, but there's a signal fire system among the islanders. Katla the Black would receive help in short order."

Albrikt drained the wine and slammed the goblet down with far more force than the fragile glass would bear. A tiny fracture in the delicate stem bloomed near the bottom of the cup.

A muscle in Malvar's cheek ticked, but he knew the value of controlling his ire. He simply marked down the ruined goblet to Albrikt's account and knew, someday, the man would pay for this mistake as well.

"It seems fairly straightforward to me," Malvar said. "You must send a small party ahead, advancing from the opposite side of the island, to disrupt the signal fire, and then you sail into the cove with three or four longships and overwhelm the residents."

Gormson shook his head. "It's not as simple as that. That cursed thrall she married used to be a captain in the Varangian guard," the Stordman said. "He's a fierce fighter."

"One man among a couple dozen sheep."

"You didn't see him," Albrikt said. "He's is the sort who can rally others, and he has a military man's eye. There were a number of goodly sized men in the household. I wouldn't doubt Brandr Ulfson has started training them for defense."

"Ulfson?" Malvar's ears pricked at the name.

"*Ja*, Brandr the Far-Traveled has come home."

"And recently wed. Don't forget that," Malvar said, rubbing salt into Gormson's wounded pride. "Ulfson will be too interested in what's under his new wife's skirt to be wary. He'll not be looking for an attack."

Albrikt nodded slowly, seething resentment making his eyes narrow for a moment. "You're right. The timing might make all the difference. We'll take that cove by the end of next week."

"Of course you will. The Old Ones have told me it will be so."

Malvar smiled when Albrikt surreptitiously made the sign against evil. Fearful people were always more easy to control, and it amused him to think that Albrikt believed he could protect himself from the Old Ones with a mere gesture.

So Brandr Ulfson has returned. Interesting.

There was bound to be a way for Malvar to use that information against the traveler's father. It might be the last stone needed to crack Ulf Skallagrimsson's flagging will. If nothing else, it would please him to inform the *jarl* that both his sons were about to fall into a trap from which there was no escape.

One their father's weakness had made possible.

Chapter 24

KATLA'S BACK WAS AS STRAIGHT AS A RED PINE AS THEY continued to cut through the dark blue water of Hardanger Fjord. She turned her head to follow the flight of a pair of eagles headed for their aerie, and gripped the gunwale when the waves grew rough, but she never said a word.

The old proverb is right. "It's the still and silent sea that drowns a man," Brandr thought ruefully.

Whenever Brandr tried talking to her, she pretended not to hear him. He'd expected her to sulk for a while, but the whole day was spent, and the dim purple smell of nightfall was on the brisk wind.

Even now she wouldn't speak to him.

"Might as well talk to a tree," he muttered as a light shower of rain pattered over them. He raised his voice. "There are a couple oilskin cloaks in that trunk, princess. Perhaps Your Highness would deign to fetch them out for us."

That made her shoot him a glare over her shoulder that ought to have turned him to stone. But to his surprise, she seemed to acquiesce. She rose and opened the trunk.

And pulled out one cloak for herself.

She spread the oilskin over her shoulders and sat back down, still facing away from him.

Brandr tied off the tiller to keep the boat in trim and stomped to the center of the craft. He stood over her as the rain fell in stinging needles, but she gave no sign she was aware of his presence.

"Move," he ordered when she continued to ignore him.

She drew her hood tighter around her face, snug and dry under the pelting rain.

Brandr bent over and yanked the trunk out from under her. A finger's width of water had accumulated in the bottom of the hull. She gave a little yelp when her backside landed in it with a wet plop.

"Don't expect an apology."

Brandr opened the trunk and pulled out the remaining cloak. He flipped the oversized gear that could double as a tent around himself and made his way back to the tiller. Ordinarily, he enjoyed a bobbing vessel. Dancing with the sea to keep his balance was part of the fun of sailing, but his mood was too surly now to enjoy anything about this trip.

Especially since Katla had made it plain *she* wasn't enjoying anything.

"You've no one to blame but yourself," he growled.

"Really?" She moved back up to perch on the trunk, facing him this time. "Did I force my way onto this boat? No. Did you ask me if I wanted to come with you? No. I had no say in the matter at all."

He untied the tiller and brought the heading of the prow around a point or two so they'd clear the rocky shoulder of mountain jutting into the fjord.

"Would you have come with me if I'd asked?"

"No."

"Which explains why I didn't."

Now that she was faced toward him, he almost wished she wasn't. Her eyes were filled with recrimination.

"What will happen if one of the children comes down with a fever? Suppose Haukon's arm takes a turn for the worse. Will Finn know what to do?" she demanded. "Did it occur to you that there are people on Tysnes who need me?"

Did it occur to her that *he* needed her?

"I suspect you've taught a few of the women a thing or two about herbs and cures. Inga, for one, is more capable than you credit her." A tightness about her mouth appeared and disappeared in flash. He wished he'd chosen a different example, but the point was valid. "The people of your household will be fine."

Which was more than he could promise about their marriage at the moment.

"Brandr, this is not going to work," she said with a heavy sigh. "You can't settle all our disagreements by picking me up and carrying me off."

"Want to bet?"

A man had to run with his strengths, and Katla made him weak in several ways. It was only fair he should use whatever advantages nature had given him.

"Oh, you're bigger and stronger than me, I'll grant you," she admitted.

At least on the outside. If Katla was sized to match her will, she'd be a giantess.

"Our marriage is but a sapling. It'll never make a tree if we continue like this. We'll have no peace if you treat me so." She rose and glared at him. "And that's a promise."

The conversation obviously over, she turned around and plopped on the trunk, faced away from him.

Brandr stared at her back. Where was the soft, pliant woman from last night who'd admitted she cared for him?

The rain shower passed as quickly as it had come. They glided deeper into the fjord, the sides of the mountains enfolding the water in a snug green embrace.

Brandr inhaled deeply. The air smelled of pine and dark earth and the brisk tang of the sea.

The smell of home.

He sighed. If only he was bringing a willing bride home with him.

❧

Twilight didn't linger in the North. By the time Brandr maneuvered the coracle close to the steep bank, stars peeped though the scudding clouds. He leaned over the prow to loop a line around a tall boulder, then dropped the anchor stone off the stern.

"There are a few lights in the hills," Katla said, pointing in the direction of one. "Will we venture out to see if the crofters can give us shelter?"

Brandr was mildly surprised she initiated a conversation, but he wasn't about to complain.

"No. I want to speak to my brother about relations with the other families in the fjord before we stray far from the water," he said. "You'll allow that things may have changed over five years."

"We're asking only for a roof for a single night."

"Last time I abandoned caution in a port, I ended up with an iron collar."

She grimaced. "About that. I'm...sorry."

His brows shot up. The woman constantly surprised him. An apology was the last thing he expected from her.

"Your brothers are the ones who clapped it on me."

"But my stubbornness kept the collar there," she admitted. "I shouldn't have."

He shrugged. "You wanted revenge for your husband. I understand that. It was a little misplaced, but your motives were sound. Besides, it's a comfort to me now."

"A comfort?"

"If something happens to me, it means you'll feel bound to make someone else's life miserable in my honor," he said with a laugh.

She sank back down on the chest and covered her mouth with her hand. Her shoulders shook. He thought she was laughing with him for a moment, but then the starlight struck her glistening cheeks.

Loki's sweaty balls, she's crying.

Against a woman's tears, there was no defense known to man. If Katla ever learned that little nugget of wisdom, he was done for.

"That's what I've done, isn't it?" she said with a sob. "I've made your life miserable."

"Not completely."

She sobbed louder.

She wouldn't want him to lie, would she? The taint of thralldom was no light matter. It would be foolishness to pretend otherwise.

She made little whimpering sounds, obviously trying to stop crying and failing utterly at it.

"Katla, please. You don't have to cry so." He felt as useless as tits on a boar. "I promise I'll never pick you up and carry you off again."

Even as he said it, he feared that would be a difficult promise to keep. She vexed him so, he had a hard time imagining not carting her off again if the occasional called for it.

She shook her head. "That's not why I'm crying."

What else have I done wrong? he thought, but wisely refrained from saying.

"You'll always bear the mark of iron because of me," she said. "I want you to take your place as my husband in our household, but you're right. The people will always see you as a thrall." She loosed a moist hiccup. "A thrall I had to order to marry me."

"No one put a knife to my throat."

"No one had to," she said with a sniff. "You already had an iron collar there."

He cupped her chin and forced her to look up at him. "Even with a thrall's collar, do you really think you could make me do something I didn't want to do?"

"I made you kiss my foot."

A smile tugged at his lips. "And you weren't pleased with how I did it, were you?"

"Not the first time," she admitted with a shy grin that faded quickly. "Are you saying I won't be pleased with how you intend to be my husband?"

"No." He hoped not. "I'm saying I went into this marriage freely."

"Not because I gave you an order?"

He leaned down to kiss her softly. "No. And I didn't drag you onto this boat because I want to ill-treat you either."

"Why did you do it then?"

"Because I had to leave. There was no avoiding that. And I want you with me, Katla." He hunkered down before her so he could look her eye to eye. "Life will separate us often enough, like as not. I didn't see why we should be apart by choice so soon."

"But I've done nothing but upend your life from the moment I laid eyes on you," she admitted. "Why do you want me with you?"

Brandr was no coward, but he'd rather face a charge of Saracen cavalry than this one woman and her unending questions.

Especially when the answers involved love.

Love opened a heart for pain, for risk, for loss. But even though he'd never felt the like before, he'd recognized its stirring for a while now. It was time he named the swirling in his gut. He drew a deep breath.

"I want you with me because I love you, Katla."

She inhaled sharply. "Why?"

He kissed her forehead with a resounding smack. "Because you ask too many questions. Now why don't you see what Inga packed for us to eat while I set up a lean-to."

Surprisingly enough, she swiped her eyes and obeyed him for once.

Could that be the secret to peace with a difficult woman? Was love the way of taming the she wolf?

I could admit to loving Katla all day, he thought as he

strung a rope from the mast to the prow and draped his cloak and hers over it, tacking the corners to the gunwale on either side of the narrow craft. As shelters went, it wasn't much, but it would turn the rain.

They made a thrifty meal of potted beef and cold barley buns, and washed it down with some of the mead he'd packed with the cargo. After a few rounds, all traces of Katla's tears were gone, and she laughed at his tales of the oddities in distant Byzantium.

Finally, he pulled the *hudfat* from the trunk and spread it beneath the tent of cloaks. The supple leather sleeping bag was roomy enough for two to share body heat through the chill of a night on the water.

With any luck at all, he and his bride would share much more than that.

When he turned around, Katla was climbing over the stowed cargo and stepping across the narrow distance from the long-necked prow to the steep land.

"Where are you going?"

"To find a little privacy." She alighted on a goat track and turned to face him from solid land. "You may have a bladder the size of a head of cabbage, but some of us aren't so blessed." She began climbing the switchbacked path up the slope. "There are bushes on the crest of the rise. I'll be right back."

"Don't stray far." Brandr watched until she disappeared over the rise, and then dropped the front of his trousers and aimed off the port bow. He'd never considered the inequity of it before, but now that he gave the matter thought, it seemed to him nature had made some fairly simply things unnecessarily difficult for women.

Yet another time, he thought as he relieved himself, *when it's good to be a man.*

My princess is used to a lime-washed privy, not a bush. He chuckled at the thought of her living rough for the short duration of their journey. Once they reached Jondal, he'd be able to offer her his private chamber and its thick bed of furs and a latrine built right onto the *jarlhof*, so she wouldn't have to brave the bitter wind come winter.

After the discomforts of travel, she'd enjoy life in his brother's hall.

He, on the other hand, could be just as satisfied with a *hudfat* in a rocking coracle.

Ja, it was good to be a man.

Then he imagined Katla in glorious nakedness in that *hudfat*.

It was *very* good to be a man.

He thought about disrobing and waiting for her in the sleeping bag. Body heat was best shared with skin-on-skin contact. Then he decided he ought to watch for her descent on the starlit slope.

When she didn't come, he cupped his mouth and called her name. His voice echoed against the sides of the fjord.

There was no answer.

Chapter 25

KATLA DIDN'T HEAR THEM APPROACH UNTIL THEY WERE upon her. A sudden blow to her temple sent shards of light careening across her vision. Then she perceived the terrifying strangers in only random flashes and snippets as she drifted in and out of sucking blackness.

A flurry of hands. Biting rope around her neck. No air.

A growling voice gave terse orders.

A gag with a rancid smell and even worse taste was thrust between her teeth.

Rough hands lifted her under the armpits and bore her along with her feet floating over the uneven ground. The way her head reeled, she felt as if she were flying, her booted feet hovering a few hand spans from earth, like a pair of gulls skimming the waves.

Someone called her name. The voice echoed against the mountainside until it faded in receding sibilance.

Brandr.

Her captors lengthened their jolting strides. She forced her eyes open. If she somehow won free, she'd need to be able to retrace her steps back to the ridge and the coracle in the fjord below.

She couldn't let herself think about how worried Brandr would be. How long would he wait before he came after her?

The dark terrain rushed past her in shades of gray with no discernible landmarks. She pointed her toes and kicked, trying to leave an impression in the track to show she'd passed that way. She managed to scuff the tip of her boot in the dirt in a couple places.

"Stop that, wench," one of the men growled. "Or I'll knock out your teeth."

"Probably be for the best, considering the work she's got ahead of her this night," another said, laughing at his own wit. "I hate when a woman scrapes a tooth on my prick."

Her night meal threatened to come back up.

A faint light showed over the next hillock, the dim shaft of illumination from a smoke hole in the roof of a hovel. One of the men ran ahead and threw open the door. Katla and the ones bearing her hustled through the opening, and the portal banged shut behind them.

They dropped Katla on one of the earthen benches lining the walls. She yanked the gag from between her teeth and spat on the floor to clear the taste from her mouth.

One of the men backhanded her, sending her sprawling into the dirt.

"Good blow, Tryggr," one of the others exclaimed. "Show her who's headman."

"Don't be spitting on my floor, wench."

The floor was packed earth, like the floor in the main section of Katla's longhouse, but unlike her tidy home, no one had bothered to sweep out the bones and refuse from past meals for several months. A gob of spittle would do this filthy place no harm, but Katla restrained herself from saying so.

"Let's see what we got here." Tryggr grasped her hair and lifted her to her feet.

It was easy to see why he was the leader of this ragtag group. He was the only one who looked as if he'd recently been fed. Hard and unfeeling, he was a vicious hawk of a man, his eyes as cold as a bird of prey's.

"Not bad," Tryggr admitted as he stroked her cheek with the back of his knuckles. She tried to jerk her face away, but his grip on her hair was firm. "The slavers from Birka will pay a pretty price for the likes of you."

He shoved her to her knees.

"More if she's a virgin," another said. "Shall we find out?"

"I'm a married woman." Katla was shocked at the reedy sound of her voice. She fumbled at the rope around her neck, but her captor jerked it tight.

All her wind was shut off, and she gasped like a cod flopping on the bottom of a boat's hull. She clutched at her throat, trying to pry the rope loose, but it was so tight she couldn't wedge so much as a fingertip under it.

Just as her vision started to tunnel, the headman loosened the rope. She dragged in a lungful of smoky air, grateful for every murky bit of it.

"You'll wear the rope till we can fit you with iron. Cross me again, and I'll crush your throat. You'll get no second warning. I've no time for unbiddable thralls," Tryggr said with a snarl. "Obey or die. Do we understand each other?"

She nodded slowly.

A babe wailed from a dark corner of the fetid hovel.

"Shut that brat up or I will," the headman growled.

A terrified young mother sat bolt upright on her bed of badly cured furs. She bared her breast and gave the child suck, crooning urgent endearments. The woman cast a darting glance in Katla's direction and clutched the babe closer to her, turning to shield the child from the headman's malevolent gaze with her emaciated body.

"So she admits it. She's not a virgin, she says," one of the men said. His pinched face reminded Katla of a weasel. "Then there's no reason she can't entertain us till the Birkamen come, is there?"

"No reason at all," Katla agreed with what she hoped was a confident laugh. The men laughed with her, thinking her receptive to a debauch with them. Then she glared at them. "Except my husband might not appreciate it, and I imagine he'll arrive long before the slave traders. When he gets here, he'll show you the color of your insides."

She hadn't actually seen Brandr kill someone, but she'd watched him vanquish Albrikt Gormson and knew his reputation as a warrior.

"And who's this husband of yours that we should shake in our boots?" Tryggr asked, toying with his end of the rope as if considering whether to draw it taut around her neck again.

"Brandr, son of Ulf, Captain of the Varangian Guard," she said defiantly.

The rope tightened a bit, and a muscle under Tryggr's left eye ticked. "You lie. The son of Ulf was enthralled. We heard the tale only last week."

Katla's conscience lanced her. She wished with all her heart she'd never enthralled Brandr, but for now, she held Tryggr's gaze.

"Then you heard wrong. He'll be coming," she promised evenly. "When he gets here, you'll see there's no iron on his neck. And the only thing that will save you from his wrath is if I can tell him that you haven't harmed me."

"Sigurd, go stand the watch," Tryggr ordered. "Sing out if you see this son of Ulf."

Sigurd swore and rose halfheartedly, while his smaller, weasel-faced companion smirked at him.

"But what good is having a new woman if we don't make sport of her?" Weasel-man said, his hand fingering his own genitals through stained trousers. "I claim first time with her." His gaze darted first to Sigurd and then cautiously to the head man. "After Tryggr, o' course."

"You'll get all the fresh woman you could wish for once the Bloodaxe comes," Tryggr said.

"How do you figure?"

"The men'll all be dead, simpleton. Once the Bloodaxe sweeps through this fjord, even you'll have your pick of women." Tryggr turned his attention to his other friend. "Get going, Sigurd. I'll not tell you again. And don't let me catch you buggering the ewe. If you don't keep watch for Ulfson, you'll get no woman at all this night."

Weasel-man laughed uproariously as Sigurd stomped out.

Tryggr raked his gaze over Katla and licked his lips. Lust oozed from him like sour sweat.

"I don't know who this Bloodaxe you speak of may

be, but if you touch me, my husband will feed you your own balls. On all the gods, I swear it." She willed herself not to show fear, though her insides roiled like a bucketful of eels.

Tryggr's lip curled. Then he pulled a small object from his belt and fondled it for a moment. It was a talisman of sorts, fashioned in the likeness of the headless torso of a woman, her belly distended in late pregnancy. Tryggr ran his thumbs over her full breasts and around her belly.

"What do the Old Ones say?" his friend asked.

"They say for you to shut up so I can concentrate," Tryggr said. He consulted the figure once more with an intense stare. Then he looked at Katla and jerked his head toward the dark corner.

"Get over with the rest of the women. We'll wait and see if your husband comes, but I wouldn't count on it if I were you. It would take a wolf's nose to track us in the dark." He bared his teeth in an oily smile. "If he does come, it's still three to one. Once we're done with him, we'll do for you."

Katla didn't need to be told twice to put some distance between herself and the headman. The woman with the babe, who was now sucking its own bottom lip in fitful slumber, slid over to make room for Katla on the fur.

Katla noticed an iron collar on the thin, lank-haired woman. On the wide earthen bench across the narrow space, three other females snored softly, their bodies entwined like a litter of puppies.

She sank down, her insides shaking, but outwardly, she was as stiff as the rank wolf pelt. She propped her spine against the back wall. There was no way she'd lie down among these miserable women.

She ached to snatch up the helpless babe to protect it from the lice and other vermin that must lurk in the communal bedding, but its mother held it close.

A nightmare. That's all this is. In another heartbeat, I'll wake.

But she didn't.

Katla hadn't traveled beyond sight of the coastline of Tysnes Island since she was a very little girl, when her father took her and her brothers to see the great temple at Uppsala. The people of the North were a rough lot, and the nine days of festival before the *Blot* were as wild as she could imagine, but there were clearly defined limits to people's behavior, even during the *Blot*.

The Norse peoples were bound by the Law.

Her chest had swelled with pride as the whole assembly listened to the Law Speaker recite the ordinances and requirements. It took two days for him to intone the complex system of rights and responsibilities for civilized men.

Then the priests of Odin began their rituals. The animal sacrifices were bloody, but nothing worse than what she'd seen growing up on a farm.

Katla didn't retch until nine men were hung on the sacred oaks alongside the carcasses of roosters and horses and dogs. Her father promised she'd understand when she was older.

She still didn't.

But thanks to the Law, her father had told her, a man could take his family on a voyage of many weeks and expect to return home in safety.

Then while she married and buried and ran her household on quiet Tysnes, the world beyond those narrow confines had changed. If Tryggr and his lot were any guide, men of the North had cast off the constraints of the Law and gone wild on the inside. She'd seen household gods before, but never that crude female figure. Whomever these men venerated, it wasn't the Norse deities.

There was honor among the court of Asgard.

Anyone who took somebody against their will was no more than a beast that walked upright.

Her conscience pricked her. There was a balance ingrained in the fabric of the world, and she wondered if her own misdeeds had tipped the scales against her.

She'd been taken by Tryggr and his pack of ruffians because her brothers had taken Brandr.

But Finn and the others hadn't abused him. They didn't crush his spirit as the poor woman next to her was obviously crushed.

Katla's chin sank to her chest.

Whom was she fooling? Finn had offered to geld Brandr and would have done it if Katla had given him the nod. She threatened to whip him the very first night.

She was no better than Tryggr.

It would serve her right if Brandr sailed on without her. She swallowed back a sob but couldn't keep a tear from seeping from the corner of her eye.

"Will your man really come for you?" the woman beside her whispered.

Katla hoped so. It was her only chance. She swiped her wet cheek. "*Ja.* He will. He promised to protect me."

"Mine didn't," she said. "After a couple weeks, Tryggr offered to sell me back to my husband, but he refused to take me. Said he didn't want someone else's leavings." The woman's mouth barely moved as she spoke.

"Didn't he know you carried his babe?"

She shook her head. "Linnea isn't his. She's mine. Only mine."

A hard knot formed in Katla's throat. The woman had been held in these deplorable conditions for many months, and she clearly had no idea which of her captors fathered her child.

The woman was silent for such a long time, Katla assumed she'd fallen into exhausted slumber. Then her soft whisper came again.

"Can…can your man kill Tryggr?"

Katla nodded. Brandr would have to.

"If he does, I will work for you till my fingers bleed." The woman sat up and turned haunted eyes on her. "I see kindness in you. Please, I beg you. Take us with you when you go."

⁂

Tracking in the dark was no mean feat, but Brandr pressed on, going slowly lest he overrun a turn in the trail left by Katla and her abductors. Bent grass and broken twigs told their story. The indentations in soft earth showed there were three men, one of goodly size. After the initial scuffle at the top of the rise, he saw no more trace of Katla except in the deepening of the tracks left by the others.

They were carrying her.

Brandr hoped that meant she was only bound, not

injured. Fury made his eyes burn, but he shoved the feeling down. Katla would not be helped by the out-of-control rage of a *berserkr*. He had to keep his head.

As he knelt to examine the snapped-off tips of a gorse bush, Brandr wished for his friend Orlin. Of all the men who'd gone with him to Byzantium, Orlin was the best tracker. Quiet but lethal, the hunter had been free with his knowledge of signs in the earth. Brandr had learned all the wood lore he could from his taciturn companion.

Then Brandr came across a long, indented ridge in the dirt between the tracks left by the men. There. Another.

She was struggling. She'd managed to drag her toe along the ground.

A grim smile lifted his lips.

Trust my Katla not to make things easy for them.

The sky was lighter over the next rise. A fire meant habitation.

He sank down and scrambled up the hill on all fours. Pressing himself flat on his belly, he peered over the crest, lest he present a void in the starry sky behind him and so warn a watcher of his presence.

A slovenly croft spread below him. Movement drew his eye. A watchman.

The man walked from one outbuilding to the next, stopping from time to time to scan the surrounding hills. Finally, he stopped to relieve himself against a sagging cattle byre.

Brandr had run his quarry to ground. But as he crept closer, Orlin's advice rang in his head.

"No animal is more dangerous than the one you hunt in its own den."

Chapter 26

"KATLA."

Even though she was still sitting up, she'd been feigning sleep, hoping it would lull her captors into forgetting about her for a while. When she heard her name, her chin jerked up, and her gaze swept the common room.

The other women were still asleep. Tryggr and one of his companions were tossing knucklebones against the low bench. When his underling threw well, Tryggr scowled so fiercely Katla suspected his pinch-faced friend began to hope for ill luck.

She bit back her disappointment. She must have skimmed the surface of sleep and only dreamed she'd heard Brandr call her name.

"Courage, love."

There. She hadn't imagined it. She was wide awake, and his voice sounded as clearly as if he'd spoken directly into her ear.

Except he wasn't anywhere near. She glanced up at the smoke hole, half expecting to see Brandr peering down at her. Only sluggish fumes escaped into the black night.

"I'm coming."

The voice was so close she flinched. The woman beside her on the wolf pelt didn't stir. Tryggr didn't stop the dice game mid-toss to leap up and grab his sword.

No one else heard Brandr speak.

Either Katla teetered on lunacy or...

Old Gerte's words about her grandparents and the special bonding of *inn matki munr* resurfaced in her mind.

"It mattered not how distant they were from each other," Gerte had said. "She could hear him, and he her."

Was it possible? It was worth a try.

I heard you, Brandr. Now hear me. She scrunched her eyes shut and thought, clasping her hands so tightly her knuckles went numb. Everything in her wanted to shoot a plea for him to hurry and come for her, but if the arrow of thought was limited, she tried to concentrate on something more practical. *There are three of them, one outside, two in. Have a care.*

She swallowed hard, straining her ears for a reply.

There was only the click of dice, the occasional crackle of the smoky central fire, and a rustle of skin and fabric as the women on the other bench shifted in their sleep.

No reply came to her from the dark.

❧

Brandr smacked the man's cheeks, trying to bring him around. He'd held him in a choke hold only long enough to render him insensible for a short while. Now the fellow's eyes were rolling around, and his head lolled back, but he was aware enough to respond to questions.

"Blink once for yes, twice for no," Brandr said to the man who was trussed up and gagged before him.

It had been a simple thing to sneak up on him, since the man had lowered his trousers and started to mount one of the sheep. Brandr could have killed him with a quick jab of his dagger under the man's ribs, but he might have raised an alarm with his dying breath, and Brandr judged the information he might glean from the sheep molester was more valuable than a corpse.

Besides, Brandr wanted to be sure he deserved killing for more than buggering livestock.

"Did you and your scurvy friends take a woman captive this night?"

The man's lips pulled back from the leather gag, revealing teeth that had been filed down till there were vertical ridges on each of his upper choppers. The indentations were stained with permanent blue dye in an attempt to give him a fierce appearance. The gag rendered the effect more comic than terrifying.

The man blinked once.

"How many men in the house? Blink the number." When he didn't respond immediately, Brandr laid the flat of his blade across the man's windpipe to encourage honesty. "Two, eh? You're sure."

The man blinked once emphatically.

"Is there anyone else in the house?"

Another blink.

"The woman you took?"

He blinked once then twice more.

"More women?"

The man started to nod but thought better of it with Brandr's dagger at his throat. He settled for blinking once more.

"How many?"

The man's eyelids fluttered several times.

"Lots of women. Maybe children too," Brandr surmised. He brought the butt of his dagger down hard on the man's temple, sending him either to dark oblivion and a three-day headache or a more merciful death than he deserved.

Brandr didn't much care which.

He couldn't break into the *sethus* and engage Katla's captors in that tight space with so many innocents within range of a sword stroke.

He needed to draw the other men out.

In case the man at his feet was only unconscious, Brandr picked up his feet and dragged him a few paces away from the byre. Then he opened the gate and quietly drove out all the mangy-looking stock.

He needed a diversion, and a burning outbuilding would do admirably.

Controlling an existing flame wasn't so hard a trick, so long as Brandr was able to concentrate on it. He could usually make a blaze burn hot and fiery or subside to smoldering ash with a mere thought.

But calling up fire from nothing...that was another matter entirely. It required a clear head and an untroubled heart, neither of which Brandr possessed at the moment. He was so worried for Katla he wondered if the flames would appear when he conjured them.

"The fire of creation is all around us, bound in the air, hidden between one breath and the next," the sorcerer who trained him in Byzantium had told him. "If the flames hear your summons, they will come to you, and you can bend them to do your bidding. If they hear you not…"

The old master had shrugged with his palms turned up, a purely Eastern gesture, and cast his gaze skyward. Fire was too volatile an element ever to be wholly under a mage's control, especially if the mage wasn't of calm mind.

Brandr extended a splay-fingered hand to the night sky then held it before his chest, sheltering his hand against the breeze. He closed his eyes and drew a deep breath, trying to empty his mind of everything but the dance of all-consuming light. Then he blew softly on his palm, letting the god who'd made him a fire mage work, if He willed.

When Brandr opened his eyes, a small blue flame flickered in the center of his palm, hovering a breath above his skin. There was no heat, but the fire cast a circle of yellow light around him, shooting beams as if Brandr held a tiny sun in his grasp.

With the speed of thought, the flame arced from his hand to the rotting thatch on the cattle byre. It caught in a heartbeat and sprinted along the sagging ridgeline, standing at attention like a row of fiery warriors waiting the command to charge. He ordered it to work.

He'd give the blaze a few moments to take firm hold, and then he'd sound the warning.

❧

"Fire!"
Brandr was in her mind again.

"Fire," Katla repeated softly then louder. "Fire."

Tryggr turned to glare toward her corner. "What did you say, wench?"

"Fire!" A voice bellowed from outside the *sethus*. It was Brandr again, and this time everyone heard him. The whoosh of flames outside made the smoke hole in the roof stop drawing correctly, and a fug of black hovered along the dwelling's ridgeline.

Tryggr and his companion drew their swords and headed for the door. Before he ducked into the night, he turned and glared at the women, all of whom were awake now and cowering. Then he glowered at Katla while he surreptitiously made the sign against evil with one hand.

"I don't know how you knew there was a fire, but don't try any more *seid*-craft tricks. If any of you tries to leave this *sethus*, when I catch you, I'll cut you up and feed you to the pigs. And two of the others with you."

After he slammed the door behind him, Katla heard the dull thud of a beam being dropped into brackets, locking them in from the outside.

&co;

Brandr waited in the shadows, sizing up his adversaries while they spilled out of the *sethus*. One was considerably smaller than he, but he'd learned never to discount a wiry, quick fighter, and this man moved with the slippery grace of a ferret. Such a one might have more tricks up his sleeve than a man who relied on brute strength alone.

The other fellow was easily Brandr's match for weight and height, but he moved swiftly to the flaming cattle byre, swearing the air blue at his loss. He found his unconscious friend, still tied up, but instead of coming to his aid, he gave him a vicious kick.

Fighting two at once was always a dicey bargain. If one of them was a madman, all bets were off.

"Where are you, son of Ulf?" the big fellow shouted, doing a slow turn. "Show yourself, traveler, and we'll kill you quickly."

Brandr narrowed his eyes, trying to strategize the best approach.

"Come for your woman, have you? Too late. She won't want you after I've had her," the man taunted, grasping his crotch.

Brandr's eyes burned. That one he'd kill last. Slowly.

"There's nothing for you here in Hardanger. Son of the *jarl*, you call yourself. Not for long," the man said, his eyes flashing feral in the dark. "There's change on the wind, and death to your kind is riding with it."

"*Ja*, once the Bloodaxe comes, he'll—" the little one began.

"Shut up, fool," he snarled at his friend. "What are you waiting for, coward?" the big one shouted to Brandr. "Ah, I know. You need a little more encouragement. Bet you thought this is my *sethus*. No, we're just borrowing it from the farmer who used to live here. He was nice enough to let us use it when he and his family died...sudden-like."

The little one laughed at his friend's wit.

"Who'd want to live his whole life in a hovel like this?" He snatched a burning brand from the cattle byre and tossed it onto the roof of the *sethus*. "Come and fight us, or watch your woman burn, Ulfson."

Brandr tried to squelch the blaze on the *sethus* roof with his mind, but the blood in his veins was the blood of warriors, and its battle song was too loud for him to think over. He couldn't find the calm center he needed to use his gift.

Fire spread over the dry thatch running along the ridgeline like lemmings headed for a cliff.

Brandr's lineage was filled with men who'd lived and died by their swords. The urge to brutish violence went clear to his bones. Now the *berserkr* lust he usually kept under tight control burst into full passion.

A feral cry burst from his lips and head down, he charged.

❧

"Katla, get out of there!"

Brandr's voice sounded in her head again. She leaped to her feet and ran to the barred door.

The other girls clawed at her, pulling her back.

"No," they shouted. The tallest one continued: "You heard him. If you escape, Tryggr will kill two of us with you."

"But I'll take you with me," Katla said. "We can't give up. We have to try."

"Look at Aldis there." The tall one pointed to the woman with the babe. She sat rocking herself in the corner with her knees tucked under her chin. "There's no try left in her. If we leave her, she'll die."

"Then we must take her too," Katla said, struggling to shake free of the others' grasps. "Or we'll all die."

A contemptuous snarl lifted one corner of the girl's mouth. "You shouldn't cross Tryggr. I'm his favorite.

He'll listen to me. I'll tell him you tried to run, but we stopped you, and then it'll be only you who'll die."

Then there was a loud, whooshing sound, and when Katla looked up, flames licked at the thatch over their heads.

That settled the argument. The girls turned as one, shrieking and pounding on the barred door.

Katla stripped off her outer tunic and plunged it into the bucket of scummy water by the smoldering central fire pit. Then she ran back to Aldis and her child and covered them with the wet fabric.

"Come," Katla urged, holding a hand over her nose and mouth against the billowing smoke. "We must find a way out. Is there a bolt hole? A root cellar?"

"There is only the one door, and he's barred it." Aldis clutched her babe to her chest, and the child wailed, sensing its mother's anguish. "One way in. One way out."

Burning ash began to fall around them.

"Katla, hold on." Brandr's voice had a serrated edge of panic.

Aldis was wrong, Katla realized, her whole being dead calm as her fate scrolled before her. There was another way out. Once the burning thatch collapsed on them, their souls would fly to the stars through the open roof.

Good-bye, Brandr, she thought with fervor, hoping he could hear her. *At least I'll leave this world knowing a good man loved me with a mighty passion.*

She wished she'd returned it with more grace.

Chapter 27

IN A MELEE, A MAN DARE NOT LOOK FURTHER THAN THE tip of his own blade. Brandr's attention was divided between three adversaries, the little wiry fellow, the big man, and the fire quickly engulfing the *sethus*.

Any one of them, he was sure he could best.

All together, he had his doubts. The other men took turns fighting, snatching bits of rest Brandr was denied. His sword arm grew heavier with each pass.

The women's screams from the burning house pierced his chest sharper than a blade. He pivoted, slashing with his broadsword, trying to get close enough to lift the bar on the door and free Katla.

The little man sneaked in under his guard while he whacked away at the big fellow. Pain screamed up his leg. He twirled and caught the wiry man across the throat. Blood spurted like a red fountain as he sank to his knees in the dirt.

"Guess he won't be here when the Bloodaxe comes," Brandr said as he sliced the other fellow across the chest. The man's hardened leather breastplate took the brunt of the blow and left him unscathed. "What's your friend going to miss?"

A wicked smile stretched unpleasantly across the big man's face. "The return of the Old Ones and the Old Ways. And death to those who think to stop us."

The man shrieked a battle cry and launched a flurry of blows.

Brandr could think only as far as the next parry. The coppery scent of blood filled the air, mingling with the reek of smoke and his unwashed enemy. Sticky warmth streamed down Brandr's thigh, but he couldn't let it slow him down. His wound was a small matter now.

Keep moving. Only the dead deserve rest.

Part of the *sethus* roof collapsed near the back wall. A fresh chorus of wails pierced the night. The women's screams were joined by a baby's cry. Brandr tried to send an order to still the flames, but he was too distracted by his remaining combatant to focus his thoughts adequately. The big man began circling again, thrusting and jabbing.

The fire roared in triumph.

"Don't be thinking you've done anything praiseworthy, Ulfson. You've killed only a pus-filled worm," the big man said, kicking his friend's body out of the way. He crouched into a defensive posture and beckoned with one upraised hand. "Come now and try to kill a man."

"I would if there was one to hand," Brandr said through clenched teeth. "I'll settle for killing you instead."

He sucked in a deep breath then loosed his rage in a fierce *berserkr* howl before he charged. His blade sang a death song as it flashed in glittering arcs. His strength waned. This blistering attack would be his last.

Only death would stop him.

Katla pried Aldis and her child from the corner mere heartbeats before that part of the roof would have caved in on them. Sparks filled the air, and the woman collapsed in a coughing fit as the black smoke grew thicker.

"Come," Katla urged, crouching down. "Stay low. The air is better here. We must get to the door."

The other women were obscured by dense smoke, but she could hear them still clawing at the locked portal. Perhaps there was a way to dislodge the hinges.

"It makes no difference," Aldis wailed. "Here or there. We die anyway."

"Do you want the child to die too?"

The woman's face crumpled, and she thrust the babe into Katla's arms. "Take Linnea. Take her. I can't bear to watch when death comes for her."

Katla clutched the squirming babe to her chest and crawled one-handed toward the door. Aldis keened behind her but didn't follow.

"Keep moving. Only the dead deserve rest."

Brandr's last message jerked her from hopeless stupor and filled her with determination. Katla wouldn't give up. Not so long as she could draw breath.

A fiery beam crashed to earth behind her, burying Aldis behind a wall of flame. The keening stopped abruptly, the sound snipped off mid-wail.

Katla kept moving.

The child stopped struggling and went limp in her arms. She passed the bucket by the central fire pit and splashed a handful of water over the babe's face. Linnea sputtered, gave a weak cry, and began rooting against Katla's breast. Katla swallowed back a sob and poured the last of the water over both of them to protect them from burning ash. Then she continued to crawl toward the door.

As she neared it, the smoke parted, swept away as if by an invisible hand. Overhead, there was a loud whoosh, and the fire was suddenly snuffed out. The opening to the *sethus* swung wide, and a man was framed in the doorway, his face in shadow.

The other women pushed past him, squealing with relief.

He strode into the *sethus* and knelt beside Katla long enough to scoop her into his arms.

"Brandr."

With a grunt, he rose, carrying her and the baby out into the night. Once they cleared the doorway, Brandr set her down a safe distance away. She sank onto the stubbled grass, dragging in breaths and coughing out the smoky air trapped in her lungs. The sickly sweet scent of roasting meat made Katla want to retch.

There was no sign of the other women. Katla assumed they'd taken to their heels without stopping to see who'd won the fight.

"Is there anyone else inside?" Brandr asked.

The child's mother was dead. She shook her head and clutched the snuffling baby tighter.

"It's dangerous to leave the *sethus* like this then," Brandr said, "Only half-destroyed. It might fall down on someone."

Then as Katla watched in amazement, a blue flame bloomed in the center of Brandr's palm. He tossed the ball of fire to the charred roof and rib cage of beams, where it caught and blazed up into an inferno almost instantly.

Katla gasped. "What did you…what *are* you?"

Her vision wavered for a moment, then darkness gathered at the edges. Finally she winked out as completely as a pinched-off candle.

❧

Brandr lifted the baby from Katla's arms and set the squalling mass off to the side.

As long as the brat's making enough noise to wake the dead, there's nothing truly wrong with it, Brandr reasoned.

Katla, on the other hand, was pale and drawn, her eyes open and unseeing. He checked her for injury and found none. He laid his head between her breasts and was relieved to hear her heart beating, though it was thready and rapid.

"Princess." He gave her shoulders a slight shake and tried to wipe the black soot from her face with his sleeve. Panic clawed at his gut like a cornered badger. "Katla. Love. Come back."

Her eyelids fluttered closed, and she coughed twice.

She sat up, her body racked by another bout of hacking. He wished he had a water gourd to offer her. She lifted her arms to him, and he gathered her close, rocking her slightly.

"You're alive," she whispered. "We're both alive." Then she pulled away and cocked her head at him. "Why is the baby crying?"

"Because it's a baby, I expect," Brandr said with a grin. Always looking out for someone else, his princess was back.

"She. Not it. And her name is Linnea. She's not hurt, is she?" Katla snatched her up and examined her down to counting her toes. The child quieted and tucked its tiny thumb between a pair of rosebud lips.

Brandr sank down beside her. Of the three of them, only he was bleeding, but that's how he'd have ordered matters if he'd been given a choice. He'd already decided the wound on his leg wasn't serious. Blood had matted his trousers to his flesh, and it would bleed again when the wound was cleaned, but there was no major damage.

"What did you...before I..." Katla began. "I saw you and...there was..."

"What did you see?" He'd known this was coming, but he'd hoped to break the truth to her in a gentler way. Of course, there was nothing gentle about what he was.

"You were holding fire," she whispered.

"*Ja.*" He blew on his palm. "Like this?"

The blue flame sparked to cheerful life. He'd almost forgotten how good it felt to summon fire. As if his life had turned a perfect circle. Complete.

Katla scooted away from him, her eyes round as an owlet's. "Are you a...*seid*-man?"

Brandr snorted. "What do you take me for? I dabble not in magick. You've been in my bed, and you've seen me fight. Do I seem the weak-wristed type who takes power by dark methods?"

"No, but...how else could you do that?"

One shoulder lifted in a shrug. "I don't know. I've always been able to call the fire. I set any number of accidental ones when I was a boy, and was whipped for it more often than I like to remember. Mayhap if

I'd told my father the truth of how the fires happened, he'd have seen the matter differently, but I doubt it."

She leaned forward to peer at the tiny flames licking his palm but not raising so much as a blister.

"Some are gifted with prodigious memory. Others can sing the stars from the sky. I was given control of the fire." He snuffed out the flame between his palms. "At least, that's how it's supposed to work."

"What does that mean?"

"I didn't understand it myself until I met a sorcerer in Byzantium and sat under his tutelage. According to him, there are four elements—earth, air, water, and fire. Once in a great age, someone is born with the ability to call a particular element to them, to shape and control it."

"And you're one of them?"

He grimaced at her. "I'm a fire mage, Katla. I don't know how I do it, any more than I know everything involved in drawing a breath. It's just part of who I am."

"I see." She stared at the burning *sethus* as the back wall collapsed in a shower of sparks.

"To control flame takes concentration," he said as he rose and retrieved his sword. It was still implanted deeply in the big man's chest. "I wasn't able to stop the fire right away because…well, I was a little distracted."

He pulled out the sword and cleaned the blade on the grass. "Did that worthless piece of shite harm you?" He shot her a piercing gaze.

"No, once I told him you'd be coming, he decided to wait until he'd dealt with you," she said with a sigh. "Thank the gods."

"It wouldn't have been your fault."

"Nothing happened." She shook with delayed tremors but managed to settle herself. Then she asked in a small voice, "Did you start that fire?"

"No, not on the house, at any rate." He shoved his sword back into the shoulder baldric. He pointed to the mound of cooling meat that used to be a man splayed on the ground. "That was his doing."

"Oh."

"I'm very careful about how and when I use my... ability."

Brandr noticed a bulge beneath his slain enemy's belt. He bent and fished it out. It was a small figurine of a pregnant female. He'd never seen its like, but the way his palm tingled, he sensed it was a thing of power.

"The return of the Old Ones and the Old Ways," the man he'd killed had said.

Could this image have anything to do with that?

He secreted it away in the leather pouch at his waist. When he reached home, he'd ask someone with a much wiser head about the figurine and the power he felt emanating from it.

Silence drew out between him and Katla, a wall of separation growing higher as the moments slipped by. He turned and looked back at the *sethus*. The last of the roof had collapsed into the main room, and the charred walls began to sag inward.

Say something.

"What do you want me to say?" she asked.

He turned back to her. Had she heard his thoughts? No, that was fanciful in the extreme. Katla was many things, but fanciful was not one of them. She was the practical sort. If she had an ability to hear another's thoughts, she'd have used it on him long before now.

"Say you understand," he suggested.

"How can I? You don't even understand it."

He had to give her that one.

His leg was starting to throb. He swallowed back a foul curse.

"There's no need to be vulgar," she said primly.

"Wait. Are you telling me you heard that?" He hurried back to her and settled by her side.

"I'm not deaf. Of course I did."

"But I didn't say anything," Brandr said. "I only thought it."

A smile burst over her face. "Oh, then I didn't imagine it. I heard you, your thoughts, in my mind when I was trapped in that awful place."

"You did? What did I say?"

"Encouraging things mostly," she said. "Things to give me hope."

"Can you hear my thoughts now?" he asked, imagining her on his bed of furs in Jondal with a whole night of loving before them and nothing of this sorry night in their heads.

She studied him for a moment then shook her head.

"Pity," he said with a waggle of his brows. "You'd have enjoyed it."

She gave his chest a playful swat.

"Maybe it works only under duress." Katla frowned, tapping her front teeth with her fingernail. "While I was in the house, I tried to send my thoughts to you as well. I told you how many men were in the house and to be careful. Did you hear my voice in your mind?"

She looked so hopeful he wished he could say yes. If she had a special gift, perhaps she'd be more inclined to accept his.

But truth would serve him better than hope at present.

"No, I didn't hear your voice," he admitted, "but as I said, I was distracted at the time."

"But not too distracted to make fire out of thin air."

"No, I set the cattle byre ablaze before those two came out of the house."

That was how his gift worked. He needed to be able to empty himself of all fury, all feeling. A double-minded mage is mute to his element. The fire wouldn't be able to hear him. If he'd been able to control his emotions, he'd have put the fire out before he engaged in swordplay. But with Katla in danger and armed men between them, there was no use seeking that dispassionate, calm center he needed to draw the flames out or make them dance to his will.

And he certainly didn't need to go into a long, drawn-out explanation of how his gift meshed with the secret of Greek fire.

"So," she said with a sigh, "I'm married to a fire mage."

"*Ja*, you are. Any regrets?"

She shook her head and gave him a quick kiss. "At least it's a useful oddity. We'll never have to worry about having tinder and flint."

Chapter 28

"YOU SHOULD HAVE TOLD ME YOU WERE INJURED," Katla scolded once they were back aboard the coracle and she discovered Brandr's trouser leg was stiff with blood. She settled the sleeping baby into the center of a coil of rope and tended to her husband's wounds. The short Scandinavian night ended, and the sun peeped over the mountaintops.

Brandr submitted to her nursing with grumbles and complaints, but she suspected he enjoyed the attention.

"I wouldn't have made you catch that stray nanny so I could milk her if I'd known you were bleeding," she said.

"*Ja*, you would, and we both know it," he said with a laugh. "I didn't mind. The last thing I want is to listen to a hungry babe crying all the way to Jondal."

He hadn't complained when she insisted they bring the baby with them. He'd been concerned only about how she'd feed it. Once they rounded up the goat, Katla was able to fill a skin with its milk. Then she dipped her sleeve into the rich liquid and let Linnea suck the linen. It was a slow process, but it seemed to work for now.

When the babe curled her tiny fingers around Katla's, she thought her heart would burst with the tender sweetness of it. She decided then and there. Linnea was hers as surely as if she'd borne her inside her body for nine months.

Brandr had carried the baby down the steep goat track to the coracle. He actually seemed to like her a little.

Of course, Katla hadn't told him she intended to keep the child yet. That was a talk best saved for smoother waters and a full night's sleep.

"There," she said as she tied off the bandage on his thigh. He had such beautiful thighs; it was a great pity one would be marred with a slashing scar now. She ran her hands up and down his legs, reveling in the light dusting of hair and corded muscle beneath his skin. His tunic rose, and she knew his cock had come to life beneath it. After all they'd been through during the night, his body still roused to her.

Men were so delightfully simple sometimes.

He pulled her down for a long, deep kiss. Desire stirred in her belly, but she tamped it down.

"I can't," she said as she broke off their kiss. "I mean I want to…" Judging from the raging ache that leaped to life in her groin, she wanted to desperately. Evidently her body was just as delightfully simple as his. "But I'm filthy. Covered with soot and reeking. And on a boat? How can you even think it?"

Brandr laughed. "You're alive and here, and I want you. You'd be surprised how little that part of me cares about such niceties as cleanliness or a steady foundation. But if you feel that strongly about it, then we should at least have a bath."

"Where?"

"In the fjord, of course," he said with a shrug as he stood to pull his tunic over his head, leaving him gloriously naked.

But she didn't have long to admire him. He dove off the port bow, drenching Katla with spray. The water was so cold her throat closed off, and she gasped for breath. Brandr's sleek head emerged from the dark blue water.

"Oof! I'd forgotten how cold this water is." He shook his head, and droplets scattered around him, sparkling like silver. Then he windmilled his arms and cut across the surface back toward the coracle and climbed aboard. The small craft dipped to one side, but he was quick enough that no water washed over the gunwale except the rivulets that streamed down his body and puddled along the bottom of the hull.

"With water that cold, that's enough. Your turn," he said with a grin as he settled back on the seat by the tiller to let the rising sun dry him. The quick dip had melted his erection, but he was still so beautiful to look upon, Katla's eyes hurt.

"I can't swim, remember? And I don't much care for a salty bath."

"The water's brackish this far into the fjord. Enough fresh water pours in from rivers and streams to cut the seawater."

Sure enough, no briny crystals clung to Brandr's skin.

"I still can't swim, but I think I could make do with a sponge bath," Katla said cautiously. "Turn around."

"Why?"

"It's not like the *laug* at home," she said. "I'll be naked."

"I've seen you naked," he said, his body obviously warming to the idea again. "And not just in the bath house."

"Not in broad daylight."

"Katla, I'm your husband. Did you not promise to please me in our wedding vows?" He folded his arms across his chest. "It pleases me to look at you. All of you. Besides, if you dally much longer, there may be more ship traffic, and I won't be the only one who gets a peek."

He leaned back and stretched out his long legs, clearly enjoying the sun's kiss on his skin. His clean skin.

Katla couldn't bear the smoky reek of her underdress for another heartbeat. She wiggled out of it and leaned over the side of the boat to dunk her long hair into the water.

༄

Brandr's breath hissed over his teeth.

There was his wife, bare arse to the sky, breasts falling forward. She grasped the gunwale with one hand and rinsed her hair out with the other, setting the boat rocking. He was treated to quick peeks of her pink slit that appeared and disappeared as the angle of the deck changed.

Either she had no idea how erotically alluring that position was, or she was trying to kill him.

Then she washed off her sooty face and rose up, tossing her head, her long hair slapping her back wetly. "Oh, that's cold!"

Nipples perked, gooseflesh rippling, she settled on the trunk. Muscles shivered under her smooth skin.

Brandr dipped a leather bucket into the waves and set it down by her feet. "Mayhap that'll be easier than leaning over the side."

It'd be easier on him. He was trying control himself after the horrific things she'd been through in the night. It wasn't every day a woman who was so used to being in control was abducted and powerless. But when she presented herself to him like that, glistening and vulnerable, it was all he could do not to grasp her hips and rut her blind.

After the night she's had, the last thing she needs is a hard swive.

Her gaze darted sharply to him, pinning him with a direct stare. Then she reached down and dipped a square of clean cloth that was left over from his bandage and began rubbing her skin with it, starting with an upraised arm. Water trickled down in rivulets, past her armpit and down her side.

When Katla swirled the cloth around each breast, he stifled a groan. He longed to lick the droplets of water from her pert nipples.

She washed her belly and down her legs to her curled toes. Then she spread her knees, parted her intimate folds and squeezed the cloth so water ran down her inner thighs.

He gritted his teeth so hard, he half expected one to crack.

Every fiber of his being longed to take her, to mount her like a ram mounts a ewe, to drive into her with abandon, his balls slapping against her thighs.

"Has it ever occurred to you, husband," she said with a feline smile, "that sometimes a good, hard swive is exactly what a woman needs?"

She stood up and gave him her back. Then she bent over and splayed her hands on the deck.

A growl escaped his throat, because no coherent words would form in his mind. He was on her in a heartbeat, grasping her hips and sliding his full length home.

His whole world went suddenly warm and deliciously wet. Her tight inner walls snugged around him. She was more than ready. She wanted this with the same ferocity he did.

There was no finesse. No lover's skill on display. He gave himself up to the animal joy of rutting.

Rough. Fast. Deep.

They fell into rhythm with the steady rocking of the coracle, one with the cadence of the waves.

Then just when he thought it couldn't be better, he heard Katla urging him on in panting tones.

"Harder."

Odin on Yggdrasil, I love you, woman.

෴

He loves me.

More intimate than his cock penetrating deep inside her, Brandr's words curled around her mind. The sound reverberated to her core. His voice caressed her soul.

It must be *inn matki munr.*

The link was potent but one-sided. He still couldn't seem to hear her. She'd tried to send him any number of intimate messages, but he gave no sign he received them.

Surely that couldn't be right.

But Katla had no more time to puzzle over the mystery. Her senses were so crowded by Brandr's fierce strokes, she couldn't think. She could only feel.

She didn't need gentleness. She needed him hard and demanding. It was a reminder she was still alive and her body was still hers, and only her husband had a right to it.

He exercised his rights with such mastery, filling her, pushing so deep, she'd never feel empty again. She strained back against him to engulf him even more deeply.

Then he reached around and cupped her mound, stroking her aching place while he took and took and took.

She unraveled under him, her legs going rubbery. He lowered her to her knees on the curved hull, never breaking their connection, while her insides rioted around his hard shaft. When she stopped convulsing, he pushed into her once more, a long, slow thrust. She felt him pulse inside her, his seed spurting hot and deep.

Her breath came in short gasps. When he finished, she seemed to melt, go boneless. He rose and gathered her in his arms. Then he carried her to the waiting *hudfat* and tucked her in.

"If you were any sweeter, I'd die of wanting you," he whispered before he kissed her cheek. Then he opened his trunk and pulled out a fresh pair of trousers and tunic.

"Aren't you going to sleep too?"

He cast a glance at the sun creeping higher in the sky. "No, if we sail now, we'll reach Jondal by tonight, and after last night, I'd rather take my ease in my own bed. A man sleeps better behind a stout door, knowing his friends are nearby."

Katla started to rise from the makeshift pallet. "Then I'll stay up too."

"No, rest you now," Brandr said as he adjusted a bit of one of the cloaks to serve as shade for the sleeping baby. "I don't know much about bairns, but I do know when they sleep, you should too."

Katla lay back down, closing her eyes and listening to Brandr slip the mooring line and haul up the anchor stone. She was aware of the moment of quickening when the coracle's sail billowed with wind and the craft lifted in the water, surging on the waves.

Her senses were pricked to hear his voice in her mind again, but the deep timbre never came. Obviously she couldn't hear him think whenever she wished. And just as obviously, he wasn't sending his thoughts to her consciously.

Why could she hear him only sometimes? And more importantly, why did he never hear her?

∽

Brandr ran a hand over his face, trying to wipe off the tiredness. He glanced at Katla's still form, wishing he could lie down beside her and follow her into the land of walking shadows.

But it was more important to get her and the babe she'd somehow acquired to safety.

Of course, if his brother, Arn, had lost control of

his chieftains, Jondal would be in turmoil. His service in the Imperial Palace had taught him that infighting between rival factions could be fiercer than single combat with a total stranger.

The *jarlhof* in Jondal would offer no safe haven if the Iron Crown didn't rest steadily on his brother's brow.

Chapter 29

"TIME TO WAKE, PRINCESS," BRANDR CALLED. "UNLESS you want to greet the folk of Jondal naked as a new-hatched chick."

Katla pried open her eyes. She'd roused every couple hours as they traveled through the day, to feed and change the baby. She'd moved the child close so she could remain in the *hudfat* while she tended her. Fortunately, Linnea was an undemanding babe who didn't fret and let the coracle's motion lull her into deep sleep once her needs were met.

Brandr had ripped up an old tunic to use for the babe's fresh swaddling, and he'd strung the skin filled with goat's milk over the gunwale so the cold water of the fjord kept it from going sour. Each time little Linnea dropped off, Brandr ordered Katla back to sleep as well.

For once, she didn't feel the need to argue with him.

As tired as Katla was after her interrupted sleep, she knew Brandr was even more exhausted. Dark smudges showed under his eyes, but excitement sparked in them despite his fatigue.

"You're nearly home," Katla said as she dressed inside the capacious sleeping sack.

"*We're* nearly home," he corrected.

The coracle sliced smoothly through the untroubled water. The mountains rose steeply on all sides, and the setting sun threw half the narrow fjord into deep shadow and gilded the other with its dying light. A male tern swooped past the boat and scolded them as they glided by a small rocky beach.

"There's the female," Katla said, pointing toward the slight movement that drew her eye. The drab bird blended into its surroundings as it hunkered on the shallow indentation that probably held a couple eggs. "She's on the nest."

"My uncle used to say terns mate for life," Brandr said. "He watched the same pair nest near his long-house for nearly twenty years."

Mate for life. She and Brandr were pledged to do the same. Divorce was not unheard of. The grounds for severing a marriage were laid out in the Law, but as warmly as she felt toward him now, she couldn't imagine denouncing him at the door to her longhouse before witnesses.

And after the way they joined their bodies together earlier, denouncing him beside their bed seemed an even more remote possibility. He'd loved her body just as she needed him to, now rough, now gentle.

Love. She felt it. Why was she so hesitant to say it? Something inside her resisted letting him know she was beginning to need him more than her next breath.

"The tide and wind are with us," Brandr said once she emerged from the *hudfat* fully dressed. "Just around the next point, you'll see my brother's *jarlhof* on the right."

The pine forest was so thick, and it raced down almost to the water's edge. Katla wondered how she'd see anything. Especially since they were quickly losing the light. An endless expanse of trees rushed up to where the mountains poked out their craggy bald heads. The rocky tips were still sun kissed, but the shadow of evening crept steadily upward. A third of the way up the slope, just where the shadow stopped, a high, steep roof of thatch rose above the treetops.

She stole a glance at Brandr, and her heart swelled at the look of fierce joy on his face. Five years was a long time to be so far from all the things he obviously loved.

Time enough for those things to change.

"When I was trapped in that *sethus*, the men talked of someone coming to this fjord. Someone named Bloodaxe," she said. "Do you know whom they meant?"

Brandr shook his head, some of the pleasure of his homecoming draining from his features. "No, but I know they meant no good. There's someone in Jondal who might know who this Bloodaxe is."

"If she's still alive."

Katla heard his thought but kept quiet about it as they approached the wharf, so Brandr could concentrate. Besides, until she untangled the mystery of why she seemed able to hear his thoughts while hers were mute to him, she didn't want to broach the subject.

He muscled the coracle to the wharf, where several *drakkars* rode at anchor. Their long-necked prows were topped with carved dragon heads, fearsome images designed to frighten the land spirits into allowing the sailors to make landfall without any interference from their shadowy realm.

Brandr frowned at the ships. "Looks like Arn already has company."

"Not friendly company?" Katla picked up little Linnea and held her close, reveling in the moist, sweet breath of the sleeping babe. So innocent. So trusting. The world was filled with danger for one so help-less and weak. Katla tightened her grip till the child squirmed fitfully.

"I don't know yet if they're friend or foe," he admitted as he climbed out of the boat and made it fast. "I recognize a few of the ships. They belong to chieftains who're supposed to be loyal to my brother."

"Supposed to be? You don't sound very sure."

"Time has a way of changing things. Jondal is stra-tegically placed in the center of Hardanger Fjord. It's two-days' sail to the mouth or the headwaters. Its very location is a temptation to those who seek to expand their influence. But we hope for the best," he said, strapping on his shoulder baldric before he handed Katla and the child onto the wharf beside him. "Plan for the worst. Stay behind me."

Ordinarily, Katla followed no one, but she felt no inclination to argue as she and the babe trailed him into the woods. The smell of moss and rot and green growing things tickled her nostrils. They hadn't gone a dozen paces into the deep shadow when they heard a low voice order them to halt.

Brandr froze, hands upraised to show he meant no ill. "Harald, is that you? You're getting close sighted as an old woman."

His friend stepped from behind a thick-trunked pine, with an arrow knocked on the string. The red-haired giant grinned sheepishly. "Sorry, Brandr. I didn't recognize you with your hair and beard cropped so short. See you managed to lose the iron collar."

Katla stepped from behind Brandr on the narrow path.

"I think you already know my wife," he said to his friend.

"The thrall collar wasn't enough. You had to go and find a new slave ring," Harald muttered. "A child too? Didn't think you'd been gone long enough for that."

"We need to find a wet nurse for her as soon as possible," Katla interrupted before Brandr could say the child wasn't theirs. Whether he was willing to claim the babe or not, Linnea was hers, and that was all there was to it. "Do you know if there's a nursing mother at the *jarlhof*?"

Harald shrugged his massive shoulders. "Ask once you get there. Well, you're here at least, Brandr. That's as good as we can expect."

"What's happened? I can't remember a time a guard was posted on the wharf." Brandr asked as he fell into step with his friend. Katla and the babe brought up the rear, her ears pricked to their conversation.

"Arn's failing. We've tried to prop him up, but the chieftains are set to challenge him. We thought we could hold his *jarlship* a while longer, provided none of the others joined in. So we watch the harbor in case someone decides to take a stab at the Iron Crown." Harald clapped him on the back. "But you're here now. Let's drain a horn together to celebrate your homecoming."

"It's still a good idea to watch the harbor," Katla said, thinking of the enigmatic Bloodaxe Tryggr and his cohorts were expecting.

"She's right," Brandr said. "Stay here, and when I get to the *jarlhof*, I'll send someone to relieve you."

Harald scowled at Katla, clearly blaming her for interrupting his reunion with his friend and the drinking that by rights ought to ensue. "What else am I watching for besides disloyal chieftains?"

"I don't know yet," Brandr said. "But I mean to find out."

⤜⤐

Long before they reached the great hall, the folk of Jondal discovered the second son of Ulf had returned. People lit torches and poured from their homes and shops to welcome Brandr back. Obviously his friends had neglected to mention his unfortunate stint as a thrall on Tysnes Island, because every face was etched with welcome.

And more than a little relief.

When the mighty quarreled, the folk who did the farming and smithing and building and wedding and birthing were the ones who lost the most. By the time Brandr and Katla reached the tall, carved doors of the *jarlhof*, the villagers had stirred up the atmosphere of a fair. Brandr and his bride collected nearly the entire population in their wake.

The massive doors swung open, and Hilde, his brother's wife, was there to greet them.

"Brother," the tall woman said as she nodded gravely to him. "We bid you welcome. You and yours."

She'd always been spindly, but now she was gaunt. Instead of honey-blond hair escaping her starched headdress, Brandr was surprised to see Hilde's hair was white. Her eyes were like a hunted doe's, wild and terrified, but so tired of running, the arrow that found her heart would be a blessing.

Like any good Norse matron, she gave her first attention to their immediate needs. Hilde gave orders for their accommodations to be aired, and a wet nurse for the baby was sent for immediately. Katla refused to give the babe up, asking that she be able to meet the nurse first, which seemed a reasonable request to Brandr.

"Very well," Hilde said. "Walk with me."

The people from the village called out final well-wishes, and the big double doors swung shut behind them.

"How is Arn?" Brandr asked, placing a hand at the small of Katla's back to keep her beside him. May as well let folk know right from the start she was his.

Hilde looked at him sharply, a quick appraising glance. "You know about his sickness."

"Tales travel on the wind." Brandr shrugged. "I have ears. Does he suffer?"

Hilde bit her lip. Her mute response was answer enough.

"He can no longer wield a sword?"

Hilde shook her head.

"You have no son," he surmised.

"Arne gave me five daughters before the sickness struck him," Hilde said, her long-fingered hands clasped tightly over her own belly as if wishing could place a man–child there. "But never a son, and so the chieftains gather." Her pale eyes narrowed. "Now I suppose you will rally them to your side."

"My allegiance is to the man who wears the Iron Crown and sits on the *jarl*'s judgment seat," Brandr said. "As long as he breathes, that man is my brother."

The tension went out of her shoulders, and he read relief in her.

"Leprosy is grounds for divorce," he said softly.

"I am not just your brother's wife," she said with the sting of a whip in her tone. "I am the wife of the *jarl*. It is my duty to care for the people of Jondal." Some of the fight went out of her, and her tone softened. "And for their *jarl*."

Hilde's devotion reminded him of Katla and her determination to provide for the people of her farmstead. When he left for Byzantium, Hilde had been more interested in what baubles the traders might bring for her than in how her people fared. Now she was simply but elegantly dressed. All hint of ostentation had been ground out of her by Arn's illness.

Before they reached the great hall, where stentorian voices were raised in angry debate, Brandr stopped his sister-in-law with a touch on her forearm.

"Hilde, you have been a good wife and a good lady to the people of Jondal. I will do all I can to see that your husband remains the *jarl*. We have come a long, weary way. Will you see to my wife now?"

Katla cleared her throat and tossed him a pointed look.

"And the child as well," he added and was rewarded by her smile. He would have leaned over and kissed his wife's cheek, but no one ever demonstrated affection openly in his father's hall. He suspected Arn would have it the same.

"Of course," Hilde said as she led Katla away. "Please, your chamber is this way, sister."

Brandr would have given a good bit of his portion of the silver he and his friends brought back from Byzantium to follow the women to a cool, dark chamber and a soft bed. But from the sound of things, his brother needed him.

And Arn's need wouldn't wait. He squared his shoulders and marched into the great hall.

Chapter 30

"IF YOU'RE EXPECTING A HERO'S WELCOME, YOU'RE destined for disappointment, brother," Arn said from his place of honor between the twin carved pillars that flanked the judgment seat. "We're a little too busy at present to raise a horn in your honor."

"My welcome can wait." Brandr schooled his face into a bland mask to cover the shock he felt.

Arn's disease had taken a horrible toll on him, destroying the soft tissue of his features so thoroughly, he was forced to wear a silver nose in public. His hands were wrapped with cloths so no one might be able to tell how many digits he had left. All skin that could be covered was shrouded with unbleached muslin. So much of his lips were missing, Brandr wondered that no one had convinced him a full face mask would be in Arn's best interests.

Now he understood why Hilde's impassive face was brittle to the point of breaking.

Silence reigned as Brandr traveled the length of the long hall and dropped to one knee before Arn.

"I ask no welcome save that of a brother," he said.

Arn shifted uncomfortably on the ornate throne. "Everyone else here this day has a claim to press. Am I to believe we'll hear none from you?"

Brandr stood. "My sword and my life are sworn to the *Jarl* of Jondal. So long as you live, you are he." Then he did a slow turn, so he could catch the eye of each of the other chieftains individually. "If anyone disputes that, they will answer to me. Now."

One by one, the other men dropped their gazes. Relief flooded Brandr's body. He didn't relish a fight in his current condition, but he would have done it. Fortunately, his exhaustion must not have been that apparent.

"Very well," Arn said. "I accept your affirmation of allegiance, but I don't need you to fight my battles. If any of you feels man enough to issue a challenge, don't let this nose scare you. Otherwise, I expect and demand that you all honor your oaths."

The chieftains grumbled, but one by one they reaffirmed their allegiance to Arn.

"Now, you all have crops to plant and houses to build while brief summer bides with us," Arn said. "Do not let us keep you from it."

Once they all filed out, Brandr approached closer. "I won't countermand you in public, but I wonder if it was wise to send them away."

"Let them get back to their women and their land. If they're busy doing the will of their wives, they'll forget they wanted my crown." Arn struggled to rise to his feet to privately give Brandr the honor he denied him before others. "Welcome home, brother."

"Sit," Brandr said, taking a place on the edge of the

dais and settling onto it. "Or if you won't, at least let me. I'm fair done in."

"But not too blown to burst in and act the part of the conquering hero," Arn said, a little of the poison-tongued sharpness Brandr remembered so well returning to his brother's speech as he plopped heavily back onto his throne. "I didn't ask for your help, you know."

"No need to thank me," Brandr said with a sardonic half smile. It was as if he and Arn had stepped right back into the same vicious circle of a sparring match they'd left five years ago. Then his smile faded. "That business with the chieftains was but a shower. I fear there may be a real squall on the horizon."

"Truth makes the very air shimmer with the light of its candor. And you have spoken truly, Brandr, son of Ulf," came a quavering feminine voice from across the length of the great gall.

"Dalla." Brandr rose to his feet despite his fatigue.

Known to others as "Dalla the Deep-Minded," the woman who'd been old when he was a boy was ancient now. She walked with deliberation across the hall, leaning heavily on a gnarled cane of ash wood. A ponderous bundle of years rode on her frail shoulders, but if Wisdom had a soul, she would look out at the world through Dalla's calm gray eyes.

Because of the depth of her understanding, the folk of Jondal held her in superstitious awe. But to Brandr, she would always be simply Dalla, the woman who raised him and Arn after their mother died.

Brandr sprinted across the space to meet her, kneeling and pressing one of her fragile hands to his forehead in a gesture of profound respect.

"Stop that," she complained, jerking her hand away. "How can I get a good look at you if you hide behind my bony fingers?"

She grasped his chin and turned his face up to hers, though she was so bent with age he didn't have to lift his eyes very far to meet hers. A smile crackled across her face, leaving her as wrinkled as a winter apple.

"Can't say I like what you've done with your hair, but you've come to terms with what you are since you left us, boy." She nodded approvingly. "I see power hung like a mantle about your shoulders."

"You have always seen more than most." He rose and offered her his arm. She laid a hand on it lightly, and they walked toward the dais where Arn waited.

"Bah, I see more only because I'm not afraid to see." Her white brows drew together, and she cocked her head at him, her gaze as bright as a robin's. "You're home. You're safe and with a new wife and child in tow, I hear."

Brandr started to interrupt, to explain that the child was not his, but Dalla raised a palm to stop him.

"And yet something vexes you," she said with certitude. "What is it?"

"I could never keep anything from you, Dalla," he admitted.

"It is well you should remember that and not try." She stopped walking and turned to him, clearly expecting him to tell her all.

He opened the leather pouch at his waist and drew out the figurine he'd taken from the man who'd abducted Katla. "Have you ever seen anything like this?"

Dalla's eyes bulged, and her lips pulled back to reveal

a perfect set of long teeth. She lifted her cane and batted the object from Brandr's hand. Then she brought the wooden tip down on it hard, shattering the statuette into countless shards. Her jaw worked wordlessly for a moment, and then she spat on the fragments.

"I'll take that as a yes," Brandr said dryly.

"Don't be disrespectful about that which you do not understand," Dalla scolded.

"So you're saying spitting is respectful?"

"Always the quick retort. Some things never change." Her gray eyes narrowed. "What I did bound the spirit of the thing to stop it from bringing harm to any who were foolish enough to keep it near them."

"But what is...I mean, *was* it?"

"Help an old woman sit down first," she said, grasping his arm. "Your brother needs to hear this as well."

Brandr escorted her the rest of the way to the dais and helped her into a chair near Arn's throne.

"Have you ever sailed into a cove and, even though you could see no threat, all the hairs on the back of your neck stood on end?" she asked them.

The brothers nodded in tandem.

"And what did you do?"

"Sailed away to make landfall in another spot," Arn said.

"Why?" Dalla asked.

"Because"—Brandr struggled to find the right words—"there was no welcome in the place. It was obvious that something didn't want us there."

Dalla nodded. "But it wasn't the place itself. It was the spirit who used to live there. They're mostly asleep now, so when you sailed into that quiet cove, you blundered into an ancient, unseen stronghold. You disturbed the spirit's slumber. No wonder it was surly."

Brandr frowned. He didn't want to think his dear Dalla's mind was wandering, but she was making very little sense. "What are you talking about?"

She folded her hands on her lap and leaned forward toward them to spin her tale. "Long before Odin and Thor and the court of Asgard came to the North, there were Others here. Spirits of the land and trees, the water and air. They claimed their place, and the people gave them their due."

"When was this?" Arn demanded.

"Not long after the nine worlds were created, I expect," she said. "What? Did you think it was in my time?"

When he gave a grotesque smirk, she fixed Arn with a defiant scowl, seemingly unaffected by his horrific appearance.

"But then the gods came, and people began to cling to stories of the deeds of Thor and Freya, and learned the secret of runes from the All-Father. Once folk could carve their thoughts on stone and wood so others could think them as well, they couldn't go back to cowering and offering the blood of infants before rocks and trees," Dalla explained. "And without worship, a spirit cannot long survive. So little by little, the spirits of the Old Ones went to sleep."

"The Old Ones," Brandr repeated. Those were the very words Tryggr had used. "So that figurine you destroyed means someone is trying to wake them now?"

"You always did have a weather eye for a storm, boy," Dalla said, pleased with his quick grasp of things. Then her smile inverted. "And with the return of the Old Ones comes a return to a brutish time."

"Does the name Bloodaxe mean anything to you?" Brandr said.

"*Ja*, and it should to you as well, but you two muttonheads never listened when I tried to teach you history," Dalla said testily. "The first King of the Norse was Harald Fairhair. He loved many women and sired far more sons than he could provide kingdoms for. When he died, his oldest son, Eric, decided to solve the problem by killing all his brothers."

"An elegant solution," Arn said with a sly glance in Brandr's direction. "There are those who wouldn't fault him for it."

"Hush." Dalla frowned at the *jarl* as if he were still the ornery boy she'd raised. "Eric's misdeeds earned him the name Bloodaxe, and he woke the gore-hungry spirits of that older time wherever he bided."

"He's not still alive, is he?" Brandr asked.

"No, he didn't even reign long, there's a mercy. He was banished, and I think he died somewhere on the Isle of the Angles."

"Then why would someone say he was coming?"

"Who said that?" Dalla looked at him with alarm. "Tell me all."

Brandr recounted Katla's abduction and everything he could remember Tryggr and his cohorts had said and done. "'Once the Bloodaxe comes,' one said before his friend could quiet him. Do you think it means someone has taken up the name?"

"I think it means someone was born to it," Dalla said. "Harald Fairhair wasn't the only man to lie with more women than he ought. An heir of Eric Bloodaxe has set his eye on Hardanger Fjord." She turned to look at the shattered remains of the figurine. "And it seems he means to wake the Old Ones as he comes."

"Then we need to be ready when he gets here," Brandr said. "I noticed on the way up from the wharf that the fortifications are lax here. We need to rebuild the curtain wall around the village and see that the signal fires are manned and ready to light should we need to summon aid."

"Summon aid?" Arn curled what was left of his lip. "In case it's escaped your notice, brother, you do not wear the Iron Crown here. I say what needs doing in Jondal, not you. I won't have you and an old woman spreading fear among people who should be spreading seeds and working their land."

Arn rose to his feet, swaying with effort.

"You have a new wife to bed, brother. And I have a *jarldom* to rule," he said. "Let us both turn to the occupation we're best fitted for."

Arn waved them both away.

Brandr escorted Dalla from the massive audience hall. Once they cleared the carved doors, Dalla stopped him.

"It was well done not to argue with him," she said. "Arn is tired and wouldn't respond favorably to more pressure."

"He's not the only one," Brandr said, rubbing the bridge of his nose to massage away the fatigue headache building there.

"And besides, Arn's right. You do have a lovely new wife to bed, but judging from the looks of you, I advise only sleep for now," Dalla said. "But when you wake, start building the fortifications and send emissaries to the other *jarls* in the fjord to warn them of the coming threat. 'Tis time to solidify our alliances."

"Then you believe a battle is coming."

"Not a battle," she said, "a war. I have seen it. Your tale only confirms my vision."

"Arn will be angry if I act in his stead."

A dark shadow passed over her features. "Arn will not know. In less than a month, the disease will claim his mind. He will not be able to recall his own name."

Her eyes glittered with unshed tears. Though Arn had been cantankerous, even when he was healthy, and probably hadn't been improved by his suffering, Dalla loved him with the fierceness of a she wolf.

"There will be a new *jarl* in Jondal before the season turns." She patted Brandr's shoulder and forced a smile. "Just when his people need him most."

Chapter 31

THE *JARLHOF* WAS THE LARGEST DWELLING KATLA HAD ever seen. From the outside, the basic structure seemed like a gigantic version of her longhouse, a solid rectangle forming the main portion, but within those outer walls, the great hall occupied the center of the building. It was encompassed by a wide corridor all around, anchored at intervals with massive tree trunks that soared to the thatched roof high overhead. From this torchlit hallway, countless private chambers, all of them spotlessly clean, jutted out to the sides, including, to Katla's amazement, an indoor latrine with a system of tiled trenches to flush the waste out with water from the adjoining well used exclusively for that purpose.

"There's so much to tend," Katla said, amazed at Hilde's organization and industry. Many women with a sick husband would let other matters slide. Perhaps cleaning had been Hilde's way of dealing with Arn's illness. "You must have an army of servants."

"Less than you might think. Of course, we have fewer courtiers and guests in residence, so there's not so much work to keeping empty rooms tidy. Now that Arn's sickness has…" Hilde gave herself a little shake. "It will be good to see these rooms in use. And good to have a bairn under this roof again. It's been too long since there was life in this hall. You are most welcome, sister."

"I thank you." Katla gave her a quick hug, which seemed to surprise her. As Hilde withdrew, the wet nurse she'd summoned to the *jarlhof* arrived for duty.

Una was a clean, healthy-looking woman who'd birthed twins a month past, but the smallest of the babes had died. Fortunately, the young mother still had milk enough for two.

It was a perfect situation as far as Katla was concerned, because as soon as Linnea finished nursing, Una was happy to relinquish her to Katla and return to her own child. Hilde installed Una in the small chamber adjoining Katla and Brandr's and the woman seemed more than pleased by the promise of silver for such light duties. She was especially happy about moving into the *jarlhof*, since her husband had set off on a voyage two months ago and hadn't been heard from since.

The chamber Hilde assigned to Brandr and Katla was dazzling. Each of the massive pine bed frame's tall posts was carved with writhing beasts, gripping one another in such a tangle, Katla's eye couldn't follow all the curves to their end without getting lost in endless twists and turns. The bed was piled with linens and furs and a rich silk covering. Katla felt the sumptuous layers tugging her toward them the moment she stepped into the room, but if Brandr had no rest, in good conscience, how could she?

A large, empty trunk waited to receive their clothes. Hilde had dispatched a pair of burly servants to fetch their baggage from the coracle, but it would take time for them to haul everything up the steep path. In the meantime, she arranged the old baby clothes and swaddling cloths Hilde had lent her in one corner of the trunk.

It pleased her Hilde didn't ask any questions about the babe. She wasn't inquisitive about why they'd arrived with none of the usual provisions one needed to care for a child or why Katla was unable to nurse the child herself. Perhaps Hilde was so bowed down by her own secrets and problems, she had little interest in the details of other's lives. Despite Hilde's cool detachment, Katla decided she liked her tall, grave sister-in-law very much.

Katla was playing a silly game of peek-eye with Linnea that had the bairn giggling uncontrollably when Brandr finally joined them in the well-appointed chamber.

"Is all well?" she asked, distressed by the deep marks of exhaustion under his eyes. He seemed to have aged years since she last saw him.

"My brother is dying," he said, stripping out of his travel-stained clothes. "The chieftains are restive, and to make matters worse, war is on the wind. And Arn wants to do nothing about it." Naked, he plopped across the bed lengthwise and spoke into the thick bedding. "No, all is not well."

Katla put the baby down in the cradle Hilde had set up in the corner and knelt beside the bed to stroke Brandr's head. His hair had grown long enough to lie down now instead of sticking out all over his head like a cankerwort seed. She trailed a fingertip across the back of his neck along his hairline. A lump of tenderness formed in her throat for this good man.

"What will you do?" she asked softly.

He turned his head and drew a deep breath. "Whatever I must."

Before Katla could ask what that meant, Linnea began fussing from her corner. Brandr made a low growl in the back of his throat and covered his head with a pillow.

This was no time for the babe to make a problem of herself. Not until Katla had a chance to convince Brandr they should raise her as their own. She scooped her up and headed for the door.

She paused for a moment, thinking to snuff out the lamp, but it flared briefly and then puffed out before she put her hand to it. In the darkness, she heard a soft snore.

Brandr had put out the lamp before he winked out himself.

Being a fire mage does have its uses. She pushed past the heavy door and closed it softly behind her. Linnea still fussed as Katla walked along the corridor, dodging servants with trays piled with meat or planks to set up as tables in the great hall. She'd seen so few servants earlier she could only surmise that Hilde had recruited some of the villagers. Judging from snippets of overheard conversation, the night meal was going to be a celebratory dinner welcoming the *jarl's* brother.

She was glad Brandr was receiving his due.

But no one gives a plum for the jarl's *brother's wife and child*. She pressed up against the wall while the servants hurried by, oblivious that Katla jiggled a crying babe and could use some assistance. She tried patting Linnea's back and rocking her while she hummed a tuneless little ditty.

Nothing helped.

"The child is hungry," came a wobbly voice from behind her. The thump of a cane on the slate floor punctuated her words.

Katla turned to see an old woman weaving toward her. She patted Linnea's bottom, trying to shush her, but the babe launched into a full-blown wail. "How can you tell?"

"Lots and lots of practice," the old woman said, stopping before them.

The woman peeled back enough of the swaddling to peer down at Linnea, making a soft noise like a dove settling on her eggs. The babe quieted, looking intently at the new face for a moment before she seemed to remember her empty belly. Her lower lip started to quiver, and she cried afresh.

"Well, aren't you going to take the babe to her nurse?" the woman asked. "Naught else will satisfy her."

It irritated Katla that this stranger should be so presumptuous. "I think I know what's best for my own child."

"Mayhap that would be true if she were your own."

Katla's gaze jerked to the woman's face. She didn't have the sly, calculating air of a *seid*-woman who looks to make her living selling potions and runic charms, but she spoke with such conviction, Katla couldn't help asking, "Why do you think she's not mine?"

"Prove me wrong. Fetch out your breast and give her suck then."

"Women sometimes lose their milk, you know," she said defensively.

"*Ja*, but that's not the case here, is it?" The old woman made a clicking noise with her tongue and teeth that distracted the babe long enough for her to stop fussing. "There's not a thing of either you or Brandr in the babe, though I have great hopes for her in your care."

"Thank you," she said with a doubtful tone. Slightly mollified, Katla took Linnea to Una's door and left her with the wet nurse.

"Do not fret that you cannot meet the child's every need," the old woman said, following behind them with her rhythmic, shuffle-clump gait. "No one can ever satisfy all of another person's needs."

Katla raised a wry brow. Obviously she couldn't satisfy Osvald's, or he'd never have taken a thrall to his bed. As soon as it appeared in her mind, she swatted away the notion, as if it were a pesky fly. Where had the thought even come from? She was married to Brandr now. Her life with Osvald was done, and there was no need to give it another thought.

The old woman pressed closer, so Katla was forced to take a step back. "No one will think the less of you for admitting you're not the child's natural mother."

"'Tis not something I need to noise about."

"And not something to be ashamed of either. There are children of the body and children of the heart. I was blessed with both. And both were a mix of joy and disappointment to me, but I loved them all."

When the woman smiled, Katla was drawn to her, despite her interfering bossiness. "I am Dalla. Your husband is one of my heart sons."

"Not the one who disappointed you, I hope."

"Not yet," Dalla said with a quick grin that deepened her wrinkles so, her pale eyes nearly disappeared. "And you must be his bride, Katla the Black. Hush, child, 'tis no *seid* craft. I have ears, and all of Jondal is abuzz with your arrival. May I take your hand?"

Katla thought she needed assistance and offered her arm, but the woman snaked out a bony fist and grasped Katla's hand in hers tightly. Dalla closed her eyes and made a low humming noise in the back of her throat. The old woman's hand warmed in Katla's like a glowing coal, but she couldn't pull free. Dalla's eyelids twitched for several heartbeats. Then they opened, and she smiled.

"I stand corrected," Dalla said. "You are the child's mother. In all the ways that matter, at any rate. I sense a heart connection between you and the child, a strong one." Her eyelids fluttered closed again and then reopened. "Forged in…fire, it was. How appropriate, given the nature of your husband."

"You know about Brandr's…gift?"

"Know about it? Who do you think kept him from burning this place to the ground when he was a child?"

Katla shared a laugh with Dalla and linked elbows with her as she made her way down the corridor to the *jarlhof* doors.

"Open the door, dearie. These old arms aren't as strong as they used to be."

"Where are we going?" she asked after she did as Dalla requested.

"Someplace where the walls aren't listening." Dalla stomped determinedly toward a cleared space not too far removed from the torchlight surrounding the *jarlhof*, where the rocky bones of the mountain pierced its thin skin of dirt. Dalla chose one of the granite seats and settled onto it.

Katla didn't sit. She was too busy trying to take it all in. The fjord spread out below them, a ribbon of black sprinkled with the reflection of stars. The vault of heaven above her sparked with the fire of Freya's Brisingamen necklace.

For years, Katla's whole world had been her small steading on Tysnes. Now she was reminded that the world was a much wider place than she supposed. Sheltering in a tiny corner of it was no true safety from the dangers that might lurk beyond her narrow confines.

"Brandr thinks war is coming," Katla said. Dalla had moved them out of the *jarlhof* so they wouldn't be overheard. May as well say what was on her mind. "His brother doesn't want to prepare."

"All true," Dalla said.

"Whatever Brandr needs to do to protect the people of Hardanger Fjord, I will support him in it."

"Support is not the same as love."

How had they somersaulted so quickly from war to love? "What do you know of love, Dalla?"

The old woman cackled. "Oh, you youngsters! Always thinking love is your own invention and it's never been done before. No cock's ever been harder. No ache was ever so fierce. And the sun rises and sets on your lover's arse!" Dalla swiped away tears of mirth from her creased cheeks and then settled to eye Katla with all seriousness. "In truth, then. For nearly three score of years, my man and I knew the joy of *inn matki munr*. Do I know enough of love for you?"

Katla hurried over to sit beside her. "How did you know it was the mighty passion?"

"How did I know I breathed?"

Katla frowned. "That's not very helpful."

"Mayhap not, but it's true," Dalla said. "Love isn't something you have to wonder about. It simply is, and when it is, you know it clear to your bones."

"Then you and your husband were able to…"

"Speak to each other without words, oh *ja*. Though to be honest, there were times in the beginning when we wished we could not. Truly, are there not some times when you are glad to be able to keep your own counsel lest your thoughts wound someone else?"

"*Ja*, I suppose there are," Katla allowed. "Could you divine everything he thought?"

"No, thank the gods. Or all we'd have accomplished that first year was fighting and making up, which I'll admit has its charms," Dalla said. "With time, we learned how to open our minds only when we wished and how to draw the curtain and have a spot of privacy by common consent. It took practice. But in extreme circumstances, no amount of shielding will work. Our minds were completely bare to each other."

Dalla's face darkened for a moment. "Some things, like the moment of birth and death, are not meant to be shared. Do not think the mighty passion is all maidensongs and bellflowers. Knowing someone that deeply and still loving them, is not for the faint of heart. Why are you so interested in *inn matki munr*?"

"Well, I think Brandr and I have something like that." She stood, not sure she was ready to share her experience with Dalla but wanting her advice about it desperately, since she seemed to know so much.

"You can hear his thoughts?"

"Only sometimes," she admitted. "They come unbidden. Never when I wish them to."

"And he can hear yours?"

Katla shook her head.

"Not once?"

"No."

"Hmph." Dalla's face screwed into a puzzled frown.

"What?"

"Well, offhand, I'd say it means my boy loves you, but you haven't quite made up your mind to love him back yet."

"No, that can't be right," Katla said. Against all expectation, she did love her husband. Her chest ached with love for Brandr.

But she hadn't told him how she felt.

Dalla took her hand and closed her eyes. "Keep still now."

Soft as the flutter of a butterfly wing, the old woman's mind brush hers, probing gently.

Katla stiffened.

"Tight as a pig's arse. You're very young to be this closed off," Dalla said. "I'm thinking, mayhap, sometime past, someone who should have loved you hurt you."

Katla pulled her hand away. "Ridiculous."

"Is it?"

Katla's shoulders sagged a bit. Dalla skewered her soul with a piercing gaze.

"I was married before. The first time my woman's moon came, my husband took a bed slave. Our honeymoon wasn't even up yet. And every month after that, Osvald brought his concubine into our bed, and I was forced to sleep elsewhere."

The shame of rejection made her insides shake. She balled her fingers into fists without being aware she did so.

"I kept thinking, if only I would quicken with child, he'd have no cause to leave me."

"But he never got you with child?"

"No."

"So now you hold back a portion of yourself, tucked away so deep no one can reach it. No one can ever hurt you, unless you reveal that deep part," Dalla said, leaning toward her. "Brandr can't hurt you."

"I don't think he intends to," Katla said.

"Mayhap your first husband didn't mean to either," Dalla suggested. "Did you tell him you didn't want him to take a bed slave?"

She started to broach the subject once, but Osvald had flown into such a rage, she never tried to talk to him about it again. "He said it was not my business. It had nothing to do with us."

But it did.

She realized how she'd hardened into the perfect Norse matron after that. She'd become someone so ruthlessly efficient, had run her household with such tight control, she couldn't be bothered by a little thing like her husband's bed slave. She couldn't be touched by anything at all.

"Do you think Brandr will take a bed slave?" Dalla asked.

Panic knotted her belly. "I haven't had my first moon since our wedding. I don't know."

"Brandr already loves you so much that his mind is open to you. I'll warrant you never heard your first husband's voice inside your head."

"No, I didn't." But she could guess Osvald's thoughts right enough every time she caught him glancing Inga's way.

Katla stood abruptly. "I need to return. Linnea is surely finished nursing by now."

"You brandish that child like a shield to keep from feeling your own need. Will you use her as a buffer between you and Brandr as well?" Katla started to protest, but Dalla waved her off and went on. "A babe is helpless and needy. If you devote yourself to the child, you think it will love you back with the same unconditional fervor." The old woman shook her head. "If you love her, you won't use her so. No bairn needs that sort of weight on it."

"I'm not using her. I saved Linnea's life. Brandr and I did," she hastily amended.

"I'm sure. And now you expect that little one to return the favor."

Katla flinched as though Dalla had slapped her.

"Man." Dalla drew a curved line in the dirt with the tip of her cane. "Woman." She etched a reflective curve next to the first, making them connected top and bottom in a perfect disc. "A child cannot complete the circle. A child's place is in the center of the circle." She made a small dot in the middle of the dirt drawing. "Sheltered equally by both adults."

"That's part of the problem." Katla sank back down. "I don't know if Brandr is willing to put Linnea in our circle. I half-expect him to send her away if she so much as cries too loudly."

"That doesn't sound like my Brandr. Still, the circle of two is complete whether or not a child rests inside it," Dalla said. "But you're avoiding the main problem. Do you wish to have *inn matki munr*?"

Yes, with her whole heart. She longed for that deep connection with Brandr, to feel his voice echo in her soul and send hers to mingle with his. To breathe one breath, share one heartbeat. To know and be known. She ached for that close bond.

"I do."

"Then you must stop holding back. You must risk letting him hurt you," Dalla said, rising when the bell tolled to call them to night meal. "You can never truly love my Brandr or let him love you until you do."

Chapter 32

BRANDR SLEPT THROUGH HIS WELCOME-HOME NIGHT meal. Katla tried to wake him, but it was rather like poking a bear, so she let him sleep. He needed rest more than food and drink. Even his friends were forced to drink to his health roundly without him till the wee hours of the morning.

Brandr slept past the cockcrow. He slept past the sun peeking through the overhead smoke hole. He kept sleeping when Katla wiggled out from under the bedding, dressed, and took Linnea to Una for her breakfast. Then Katla made her way to the latrine.

And discovered her woman's moon had arrived a full two weeks early.

All the horrible memories of that first time with Osvald rushed back into her. He'd been dismissive when she told him she couldn't welcome him to their bed. It was a small matter, he'd said, and ordered Inga to join him in their chamber. Katla was welcome to stay if she wished. She could watch. It might be instructive.

A piece of her soul had crumpled and died that day.

She slipped back into the chamber she shared with Brandr and stealthily found the cloths and lint she needed to keep from soiling her clothes. She was just smoothing down her underdress again when Brandr rolled over and smiled lazily at her.

"Come back to bed."

"I can't," she said quickly. "Linnea is probably done nursing."

"Una will bring her back when she's done," Brandr said, lifting the bed covering in invitation. His beautiful cock was fully engorged and ready, and the sight of it alone made Katla's belly clench. "A morning swive never takes long, and I can't think of a better way to start the day."

"I can't give you a morning swive."

"Don't want it quick? If you want a longer loving, that's fine too. I expect we've already missed breakfast."

"No, I mean, I want to, but I…can't."

Gradual understanding shaped his mouth into a silent oh. "No matter, then. But come back to bed, in any case. Once this day starts in earnest, it's like to be a long one, and I've a mind to hold my wife for a bit before the world rushes in on us."

A knot of caring surged in her chest, and she hurried to his side. He lay back and snugged her close so her head rested on his shoulder and her leg twined over his.

"I expect you're hungrier than I," she said. "You missed a fine welcome meal last night. Your brother clearly meant to do you honor."

"No doubt Arn will have something to say about my missing it," Brandr said, running his hand up and down her spine in a slow caress. "And the meal was Hilde's doing, not his. Even so, my brother will undoubtedly take offense."

"I don't think so." She snuggled deeper into his embrace. "Once I explained that you'd been awake for two days, and during that time you'd abducted your bride, lost your bride, tracked and fought three men, acquired a daughter, and still managed to find your way home—well, after all that, your attachment to your bed was easily understood. Your friend Harald seemed to think the adventure was as good as any skald's tale."

"That's because the one who told it is far prettier than most skalds." He dropped a casual kiss on her forehead. "Actually, it was more like three days awake if you consider that I didn't get much sleep on our wedding night either."

"Is that a complaint?"

"Never." He tipped her face up to his and kissed her, slow and tender.

When he released her, she looked up at him, wishing with all her heart this was a time when she was privy to his thoughts.

"Did you hear what I said?" she asked.

"Is this about trying to get me to hear you inside my head again?" he asked with a slight frown. "Because you were under duress when you thought you heard my voice, and I'm willing to bet that it was just your imagination and—"

She stopped him with a finger to his lips. "No, I mean just now. Did you hear me say you acquired a daughter?"

"*Ja*. And?"

She swallowed hard, hope tightening her throat. "You agree that we should keep Linnea?"

He chuckled. "Katla, I knew it would be so from the first time I saw you holding her. I could separate a bear cub from its mother with less risk than I could part that little girl from you."

She breathed a sigh of relief. Linnea would rest secure within the circle of two she and Brandr made together. "Thank you."

"No need to thank me. Thank the god who dropped her in your lap," he said. "I know you want children, Katla. I've seen the wanting in you, sharper than any hunger." His mouth twitched in a smile. "And it'll be my pleasure to try to give them to you." Then he rose on one elbow and looked down at her in all seriousness. "But if I can't, at least we'll have a daughter together."

Her chest swelled with tenderness. She palmed his cheek. "Have I told you that I love you, Brandr Ulfson?"

He shook his head and then turned it to press a soft kiss on the center of her palm.

"Well, I do."

"I'd love to give you opportunity to prove it, but I guess we'll have to wait a few days for that." He lay back down and hugged her tight.

This time she raised herself on an elbow to look down at him. Before her wedding, the women of her steading had been more than free with advice on how to satisfy a man. "Think you I cannot please you, even now, and without removing a stitch of my clothing?"

His jaw sagged open, and she cupped his chin to close it.

"Watch and learn."

Brandr's arms were outstretched as she'd instructed, and he lay spread-eagle in the middle of the sumptuous bed. Katla had suggested binding him at the wrists and ankles, since the bed was equipped with such lovely stout posts, but he'd given her his word he wouldn't move unless she gave him leave. So she'd let him remain unbound.

He was beginning to regret his promise. He'd never wanted to move more in his life.

"Close your eyes," she whispered.

He obeyed.

Her kid-soled slippers scuffed across the floor. Once she was beside the bed, she leaned to whisper directly into his ear, her lips and tongue moist on his lobe.

"Do not come till I tell you."

He peered from under his lashes. It wasn't exactly a violation of his oath. He still hadn't moved. Much.

As she bent over him, her gown hung slack, giving him a glimpse of her alabaster breasts. The soft hollow between them beckoned him into its soft shadow, but he'd promised to lie still. So his hands only ached to hold her while his cock throbbed.

"Why don't you want me to move?" he asked, still keeping his eyes closed.

"We ever want what we can't have." A soft palm rested on his knee, and his thigh muscles tightened. "I tell you not to move, so you'll want to all the more."

The hand moved over his thigh, skimming lightly. He nearly groaned aloud when she skipped over his groin and splayed her fingers on his chest instead. She leaned down, licked one of his brown nipples, and then blew across it, setting all the wiry hairs whorled around it on end.

"Keep your eyes closed," she cautioned.

"Why? I love to look at you."

"If your eyes are blind, your other senses are stronger," she explained, sliding her hand across his belly to circle his groin with maddening nearness.

Along with heightened awareness of her touch, Brandr wallowed in her unique scent, all cedar and fresh linen and woman. His Katla.

Her fingertips teased the small hairs on his scrotum. "Careful, Brandr. You'll use up all the oil in the lamp if you don't turn down the fire."

His eyes popped open and, sure enough, the lamp was flaring so hot it was a wonder it didn't erupt in an explosion of boiling oil. With effort, he ordered the flame down in his mind, and it obeyed.

"I need to keep my eyes open, unless you want that to happen again."

"As you wish." She unbraided her dark hair and shook it out till it fell like dark rain over her shoulders and down her back.

"I love your hair," he said.

"I know," she said with a feline smile.

She kneaded his balls, gently rolling his testes between her thumbs and forefingers. His cock arched upward in pleasurable agony.

"What else do you love?"

You. He couldn't seem to make his mouth work, so he only thought it.

She laughed. "I love you too."

Then she bent over him, and her hair cascaded around his cock, softer than selkie fur on his skin. Her warm breath streamed across him, curling around his aching loins.

Oh gods, is she going to…?

He fisted the linens, desperate to keep his promise not to move. Every muscle in his body went as hard as iron. Bound by his oath, he was helpless.

She ran the tip of her tongue along his length from base to swollen head. His eyes rolled back, rendering him passion-blind.

Take me in.

Then to his utter amazement, she did.

His whole world was suddenly warm and wet and velvety soft. She engulfed him, drenched him, rained kisses on him. She sucked. Her tongue massaged him.

Here's a tongue-lashing I'll never mind.

She giggled.

"What's so funny?"

She tucked her hair behind her ear and licked him while she met his gaze. "Not a thing."

He warred against the downward pull of his groin.

The sight of his beautiful wife bent over him with his cock slipping in and out of her lips was almost more than he could bear. Pressure rose in his shaft. He fought to keep from spewing his seed in her mouth.

"Do not come until I tell you," she'd said.

Why did she think it was that easy?

She took in as much of him as she could and began fondling his balls again. In. Out. Her wet lips brushed the sensitive spot near the head with each pass with just the right amount of pressure to send him into ecstatic torment.

Was this the vengeance she meant to wreak on him from the beginning? To make him want her beyond bearing while she denied him release?

A pinprick of pain stabbed the base of his skull.

"Brandr."

Her mouth never left his cock. How had she said his name?

"Brandr, my love."

There it was again, echoing sure and sweet in his head.

"Katla?"

He heard her laughter, giddy, ecstatic laughter, but not with his ears. The sound danced through his mind. Joyful. Triumphant.

So she wasn't imagining it when she said she could hear his thoughts, because now he was hearing hers. If they were mad, at least they'd tumbled into lunacy together.

"Beloved." Her soul's voice caressed his. *"Come."*

Chapter 33

DAYS PASSED IN A PEACEFUL PROCESSION. WITHOUT THE burden of an entire farmstead on her shoulders, Katla's world constricted to the pleasant little domestic circle of two she and Brandr shared. Linnea flourished in its center, squealing with delight when Brandr dandled her on his knee. Once Katla's moon subsided, she and Brandr loved each other to exhaustion each night.

Every day they learned more of what it meant to share *inn matki munr*. With Dalla's help, they practiced sending their thoughts to each other and, just as importantly, according to the old woman, learned to erect a wall in their minds when one was warranted.

"Everyone needs a private center for their soul that's all their own," she told them.

Katla was happy, happy as she'd never been in her entire life. Yet in quiet moments, she feared this happiness. It was too much. Too glorious.

Too fragile.

Like Frankish glass, it could all shatter in a moment. After having so much, the loss of it would be crueler than never having had such joy at all.

❦

Brandr sat in council with his friends after Arn retired to his chamber, spent from the exertion of walking from his bed to his throne and back. So long as Brandr confined the attendance in his secret meetings to just his friends, Arn would have no idea his brother was acting in his stead on behalf of the *jarldom*.

"We could wait for the return of the king," Harald suggested.

"Olav is in Ireland," Brandr said. "He's so busy expanding his boundaries, who knows when he'll return to the main bulk of his kingdom? The defense of Hardanger Fjord is up to us."

In the end, it was decided that Harald, Ragnar, Torvald, and Torsten would visit nearby *jarls* in the fjord with warnings about the return of Bloodaxe. Brandr insisted on sending a generous gift of silver to his potential allies from his portion of the cache the men brought back from Byzantium.

"Wealth makes itself friends," he said. "And I fear we'll need them."

The emissaries from Jondal would shore up alliances and make sure the signal-fire system was in place and manned at all hours. Then in a week, they were to meet back in Jondal to report their progress.

"What are you and Orlin going to do?" Harald wanted to know.

"When we were in Miklagaard, you know I served aboard the emperor's *dromond* for a few months," Brandr said. "What I didn't tell you is that while I was there, I learned the secret of Greek fire."

Ragnar's eyes went wide, and he made the sign

against evil with one hand, close along his side where he must have thought Brandr wouldn't see. "A chancy weapon."

"It can be," Brandr admitted. "Without a fire mage to control the flames, it's not unusual for the blaze to turn back on the ship that first releases it."

Fire at sea was a sailor's worst nightmare. The horror of it was part of what made the Byzantine weapon so universally feared.

"We've never used such a thing here in the North," Harald said doubtfully. "Give me a double-headed axe and let me take my chances with the Choosers of the Slain."

"That supposes a battle with dirt beneath your feet," Brandr said. "Wouldn't you rather stop invaders before they reach our land, far from our women and children?"

"So far you're the only one among us who's shackled with a woman and child." Harald crossed his arms over his chest and frowned with fierceness. Then his frown faded. "Oh, I might as well admit it. I hate it when you're right all the time. But are you sure you're right this time? All you're going on is the word of a few sheep molesters."

"And the word of Dalla the Deep-Minded," Brandr said. "Don't forget that. She recognized the figure of the goddess Tryggr carried, and said it was the embodiment of a spirit from ancient times, brutal times. Dalla says the Bloodaxe is bringing the Old Ones with him. And worship of those spirits calls to the worst of men. We can expect no quarter."

Brandr looked around the circle of faces and saw

grim acceptance on each one. "So Orlin and I will find the material necessary to make Greek fire. I've already given the smith the design needed to fashion the drums that will store the ingredients separately until we wish to combine them and funnel the flames out a nozzle. We need a weapon as fierce as our foes. It's our best chance to keep this hate from the past away from our shores."

❧

Katla followed Brandr to the wharf the next morning. "You're sure you must go? You're *jarl* in all but name here. You could dispatch someone else to gather what you need. There's no question you'd be obeyed."

"Whom would I send?" Brandr asked. "It would mean giving the secret of our weapon to another soul, and you know as well as I that a secret between two can be kept only if one of them is dead."

"Yet you and I hold all each other's secrets," she Sent to him.

He swung her into his arms for a deep kiss. *"And I'd have it no other way, love."*

A thrill shivered over her whole body, as though he'd stroked her most sensitive spot. Katla reveled in the way Brandr could hear her thoughts now. It was still a struggle to keep her mind open to him. Being closed off was a long-standing habit for her, but the joy of hearing his deep bass reverberate inside her was worth the effort of opening herself to him.

She gave him another kiss and wrapped her cloak tightly about her form against the stiff breeze coming off the water. Brandr joined Orlin in the waiting *knorr*, along with six sturdy oarsmen should the wind prove unfavorable. Brandr took his place at the tiller and ordered the sail set.

"At least we'll have a chance to see how far we can Send our thoughts." His rumbling timbre lifted her lips in a smile as the vessel eased away from the dock.

"I must hear from you every day," she Sent back.

"Without fail. I'll never hear the end of it otherwise." His silent internal laughter made her chest vibrate pleasantly.

"If I'm not back in a week—" he began.

"You'll be back," she interrupted with more optimism than she felt.

He lifted a hand in farewell.

Her heart swelled. *Inn matki munr* was more than she'd ever dreamed it could be. They'd been given so much. Mortals who revel in this much joy were right to worry that the gods might take offense. Even though she ached to hear more from Brandr, she erected a small wall in her mind, and behind it, she tucked her fear.

She had much to lose.

Katla watched from the end of the wharf until the square sail of Brandr's vessel disappeared completely from her sight.

⤚⤙

Four days later, Katla and Hilde were seated at the large looms by the open *jarlhof* door. Drawing the weft through the warp of the growing length of cloth was a soothing, mind-numbing occupation. Linnea was swaddled in a small cradle beside Katla's loom. The babe seemed fascinated by the dangling loom stones along the bottom. Hilde's quiet companionship was a balm for Katla's worry for Brandr.

If only he was home safe, Katla would be perfectly at peace. According to the thoughts he'd Sent her, she knew he lacked only one element for fashioning his strange southern weapon.

"Oh, my lady!" With her child strapped to her chest in a sling, Una came running up the hill toward the *jarlhof*.

"What is it?" Katla rose.

"'Tis your brother. He's come."

Guilt prickling her soul, Katla left Linnea in Hilde's care and ran down the long hill toward the wharf. She had been so wrapped up in Brandr and her new daughter, she'd barely spared a thought for the folk on Tysnes Island. Halfway down the slope, she found Finn struggling up it, supporting Inga, who leaned heavily on him. Their clothes were covered with soot and filth, and Inga's face was pale and haggard.

"Finn. What's happened?"

"Water first, Katla. We've been two days without." Finn's voice was a rasping shadow of its usual boom.

"Of course." She came along the other side of Inga and lifted the woman's arm over her shoulder. Inga was barefoot, and her toenails were cracked and bleeding.

To conserve Finn's energy, they climbed the rest of the way to the *jarlhof* without another word. As they drew near, Katla shouted out for assistance. One of Arn's sturdy retainers met them. He scooped Inga into his arms and carried her the rest of the way.

"Hilde, rouse Arn," Katla said. "Prepare him to

meet with my brother after I've seen to his food and drink. I suspect his is a tale that will bear only one telling."

Finn tossed her a weary, grateful look and nodded.

Katla served them draughts of cool spring water and fresh milk while she warmed portions of last night's stew. She sliced a couple loaves of barley bread and slathered the pieces with butter and honey. Inga ate sparingly, and when her head began nodding, Katla arranged for her to be shown to one of the empty quarters and put to bed.

Questions tramped on her tongue, but Katla bit them back until Finn pushed back his trencher and swiped his mouth on his sleeve.

"What's happened, Finn?"

"Better I should tell Brandr."

"He's not here, and his brother is gravely ill." She almost warned Finn not to be shocked at Arn's appearance, but something in her brother's eyes told her he'd seen worse than a leper in the past few days. "Come. Let me take you to the *jarl*."

Katla hadn't seen Arn since the night of Brandr's welcome-home night meal. His disease had progressed with devastating swiftness, and his entire face was now hidden by a mask. Only the glittering eyes behind the slits showed there was a living soul within the mass of bandages on the *jarl*'s carved judgment seat.

Dalla and Hilde flanked him on the dais.

"Speak, brother of our sister," Hilde said. "And the *jarl* of Jondal will give you ear."

Finn straightened his spine. "Four days ago, our steading on Tysnes was set upon by a fleet of five dragonships, and we were overrun. The force was led by Albrikt Gormson." Finn cast a grim, apologetic glance at Katla. "I give you my word I had no idea what he was planning when he came to us, asking for your hand."

"Never mind, Finn," Katla said quietly. "What's done is done."

"The next day, another twenty ships joined his in our sheltered cove. These ships and crews owe allegiance to Malvar Bloodaxe of Hebrides, heir of Eric Bloodaxe and pretender to the throne. He ordered the taking of Tysnes as a staging ground for his assault on Hardanger Fjord."

"Where is this Bloodaxe now?" Arn's voice was muffled but understandable.

"On Tysnes, waiting for more of his pledgemen."

Twenty-five ships with more on the way. All the air whooshed out of Katla's lungs. "What happened to the people of Tysnes?"

"Those who resisted were killed. Those who didn't were enthralled," Finn said with bitterness. He turned to Katla. "Einar is dead."

She covered her mouth to stifle a sob. She and Einar had never gotten on well. He never listened to a thing she said, and she never gave him credit for things he tried to accomplish, but now any chance of reconciliation was gone forever.

"If everyone was killed or enthralled, how is it I see you before me this day?" Arn asked. "And where is the woman who came with you?"

"She was exhausted from her travels, my lord," Katla said. "I sent her to bed."

"My question stands, Tysnesman," Arn said.

"I had spent the night in the forest. With the woman. We were not in the longhouse when it was attacked."

Katla raised a brow. She'd never suspected Finn harbored tender feelings for Inga. Now that she thought about it, she remembered he'd always sat at rapt attention whenever she played her flute. In better days, she'd be happy for them both.

"I wanted to join in the defense," Finn said, "but the woman with me convinced me we could do more for the people by staying clear of the fight and learning what we could before going for help."

"A wise course," Dalla said with an approving nod.

"Why didn't you light the signal fire?" Katla asked. "Our allies would have come."

"I'm not so sure of that, but that's the first place I went. The signal fire was already heavily guarded by Bloodaxe's men," Finn said.

"You wouldn't have needed to get close," the *jarl* of Jondal said. "A well-placed fire arrow would have done the job. Or is the arm of Tysnes too weak to draw a bow?"

"I would have done," Finn said, his voice breaking with emotion, "but Bloodaxe had strapped my only living brother to the top of the woodpile, to discourage just such a thing."

"Haukon," Katla whimpered.

"Then Inga and I stole a *faering*, and we've been rowing and sailing to your threshold ever since," Finn said. "Will you help us, my lord?"

In the silence that followed, Katla heard her heart pounding in her ears.

"We are not unmoved by your plea," Arn said. "But we must look to our own. If Bloodaxe is preparing to invade the fjord, we cannot spare men or time to mount an assault on the force that holds faraway Tysnes." He lifted a hand to his guard. "Summon my council in chambers. We must plan for the defense of Jondal and—"

He stopped and looked around the great hall. "Where is Brandr? And the rest of his band of travelers?"

"They set sail a few days ago," Hilde said quietly.

Arn made a disgusted snort. "Just when they might have been useful. Still, we must build earthworks. Barricades. Set the smiths and fletchers to work immediately. Every man must have a sword and a full quiver of arrows." Then he turned his masked face back to Finn. "You and your woman may stay and aid in the defense of Jondal. We welcome your sword arm, Tysnesman."

Finn didn't answer, but Katla saw the muscles in his shoulders bunch beneath his ragged tunic. Arn raised himself to stand and shuffle out without waiting for Finn's reply. The *jarl* leaned heavily on his guard's arm.

"I can't stay here while Haukon is tied to a stake," Finn said wearily.

"You won't go alone," Katla said.

"I will if I have to."

"You can't make the trip back to Tysnes in a *faering* without another rower. Even if you somehow caught fair winds and won home, you'd be too exhausted to be of any use once you got there." Katla grasped his arm.

Finn shook her off. "Just once, woman, would you stop being so blasted practical?"

"Please, Finn. I can't lose another brother."

That stopped him in his tracks, and he turned back to face her. "Then help me. This is something I'm bound to do. And we haven't lost Haukon yet. I want Inga to stay here. She'll bide safe with you, but I'll leave with the morning tide." He rubbed his brow. "Katla, will you do me a favor and provision the *faering* so I can get some rest?"

She nodded mutely and showed him to the room where Inga was already resting. "I assume you mean to marry her, Finn."

"Of course. I always did," he said softly. "I just hope I haven't left it too late."

Once Finn slipped into the small chamber, Katla's spine seemed to collapse. She slid down the wall and sat in the corridor, knees to her chest, and wept.

She mourned for her brother Einar. She keened softly for the people of Tysnes and cursed herself for showing Albrikt Gormson everything he needed to know to overcome their defenses.

"What is it, love?" Brandr's thought curled around her mind.

Katla drew a shuddering breath and swiped her cheeks. *"Nothing. Finn has come, and I'm happy to see him."*

"You don't seem happy."

"How little you know of women." She forced herself to Send the thought to him brightly. *"We often laugh when we're sad and weep when we're happy."*

She heard the echo of his chuckle.

"I have everything we need now. We can't try the weapon till we're home. I'll see your lovely face in two days."

"Safe travels, beloved." Then she closed the door to her mind, oh, so softly.

It wouldn't do for Brandr to know what she planned. He'd only try to talk her out of it.

Chapter 34

JONDAL WAS A BEEHIVE OF INDUSTRY WHEN BRANDR'S small craft sidled up to the wharf. Earthworks and barricades, the very defensive measures he'd suggested and Arn had dismissed when he first returned home, were now being realized. He wasn't surprised Katla wasn't on the wharf to greet him, since he'd heard nothing from her for a couple days, and so hadn't been able to warn her of his arrival. She was no doubt in the hub of all this busyness.

There was a prickle between his shoulder blades as he climbed the hill to the *jarlhof*. It usually boded no good tidings, but he'd learned to trust that prickle.

The prickle became a serrated edge between his teeth when Brandr stopped by the smith's shed and realized the man had halted work on his design for the Greek fire machine.

"What was I to do, my lord?" the smith asked. "The *jarl* ordered me to turn out swords."

"Arn will be worm food before the season turns," Brandr said coldly. The truth of it made his gut churn, but he needed to startle the smith to attention. "Your *future jarl* orders you to return to the commission he gave you and have it ready and loaded onto Arn's dragonship before the next tide."

"You will sail the *jarl*'s vessel?"

Brandr silenced the man with a glare. Arn's ship was swift, shallow on the draft, and answered to the steering oar more faithfully than a blooded hound obeying her master's commands. Arn was in no shape to sail her. It was folly to let her sway idle at the wharf.

"Finish my design," he ordered. "Then you may make all the swords you wish, much good may they do you."

His foul mood didn't improve when Hilde greeted him at the *jarlhof* door with the news that Katla was gone.

"What do you mean she's not here?" Brandr demanded. When Katla refused to answer his Sendings over the last two days, he'd been worried. Now he was livid.

"She left with her brother Finn for Tysnes the day before yesterday," Hilde said.

He listened with growing agitation as Hilde recounted Finn's tale of the invasion of Tysnes Island and Katla's determined response to it. No wonder she'd closed her mind to him. If she lived through this ill-conceived venture, he was of half a mind to take her over his knee and paddle her arse soundly for it.

"What of the child? Did she take Linnea?"

"No, though it pained her sore to leave her," Hilde said. "She knew the babe would be safer here in the care of her nurse."

"If Bloodaxe is coming, there is no safety anywhere in Hardanger," Brandr said bluntly.

Hilde's pale eyes told him she already knew that, but for the sake of the people busily scurrying around her, she was keeping up a brave face. "Will you see the *jarl* before you go?"

"I haven't time," Brandr said, turning on his heel and starting back down the hill. "We need to provision the ships and—"

"If you don't see him now, you won't see him again."

That stopped him. He couldn't sail till the next tide, in any case. "I'll see my brother."

He followed Hilde to the *jarl*'s private chamber. Though Hilde was the finest of housekeepers, the miasma of a sickroom assaulted his nostrils when he entered. His brother rotted while he was yet alive. Brandr wouldn't wish such a death on anyone—not even the heir of Bloodaxe. He sent up a silent prayer for a quick, clean battle death.

At least that's a prayer likely to be answered soon, he thought with grimness.

"Brother." Arn's whisper was wraithlike.

"I'm here, Arn."

"Lead the defense of Jondal for me," he said, every word expelled with effort. He lifted his nubbed hands. "I cannot hold a sword."

"Arn, the time for burrowing in holes is past," Brandr said. "If we wait for Bloodaxe and his horde to come to us, we'll be overrun. We must sail out to meet the foe. Give me your blessing before I go."

"No. Bloodaxe sails with twenty-five ships. We cannot meet him by sea. We must make our stand here."

"We can defeat him on the water if we use the weapon I've brought from the South—Greek fire."

Arn's breath hissed over his teeth. "*Seid*-craft," he said with disgust. "I always suspected you of it."

"'Tis no magick." Brandr had never confided in Arn about his gift of controlling the flame. Now didn't seem an opportune time to reveal his unusual ability. "We must use what we've been given and fight them before they reach our land."

"Then you'll sail alone. Hear me. On pain of banishment, none of the men of Jondal will go with you."

One ship against twenty-five. "I must still go."

Beneath his face mask, Arn growled like a wounded bear. "Even now, you cannot honor your pledge to obey me. Even now."

Hilde sobbed softly in the corner.

"Shut up, woman. I'm not dead yet," Arn said, gasping between each word. "At least I die with honor, while my brother lives an oath-breaker."

"Arn, I respect you as my *jarl* and brother of my blood, but if I do what you ask, I embrace defeat," Brandr said softly. "If that means the lives of the people of this fjord are worth more than my honor, so be it."

Arn turned his face to the wall. "Take none of my men with you. At least obey me in that. Now leave me."

"Good-bye, Arn," Brandr said, fully expecting to see his brother in *Hel* when next they met. Their whole life together had been one long argument. Why wouldn't they expect to continue this one in that cold hall?

"Brandr." As his hand lifted the door latch, Arn's ghostly voice stopped him. "Luck in battle, little brother."

Emotion choked Brandr's throat. He slipped out of his brother's death chamber without speaking again. Finally, he was giving Arn the last word.

❧

Malvar Bloodaxe stood on the highest point of Tysnes Isle and surveyed the mouth of Hardanger Fjord spread wide before him. The moon scattered a line of silver coins across the dark water, marking the path to glory, to riches, to power.

Weeks ago, he'd sent his minions into the fjord to seek out and dismantle the signal fires at strategic points along the waterway. He hoped they'd completed their task, since he was already firmly secure in his base here on Tysnes. He also expected some of them would act on his advice and use a human shield to keep the fires from being lit, as he had here at his staging camp.

The horror of having to burn someone they knew to summon aid would only add to the fear and hopelessness he and his forces counted on.

Malvar had always been cat-eyed in the dark. He turned now to look at the lad they'd strapped to the top of Tysnes's pile of dry wood. The boy sagged against his bonds, but Malvar knew from the shallow movement of his chest he still lived. They gave the youth water but no food. Even so, Malvar judged he'd last as long as he was needed.

He cast a sideways glance at the man standing beside him, Ulf Skallagrimsson, the onetime *Jarl* of Jondal. He was the first of Malvar's converts, the first in a long string of expected capitulations from among the nobility of the fjord. He'd broken the *jarl*, purified him with pain. Ulf was a shadow of the man he'd been when Malvar fished him from the sea.

After Ulf divulged the secret of the signal fires and the complicated arrangements for mutual defense among the farmsteads and *jarldoms* in Hardanger, it was a natural next step for him to renounce the Court of Asgard and embrace worship of the Old Ones.

"I wish I could take you with me when we sail on the morrow," Malvar said, laying a heavy hand on Ulf's shoulder. His mouth twitched in a smile when the muscles under the man's coarse tunic trembled with remembered pain. "You might have convinced your people to give up without bloodshed. In the new order, we will need large numbers of thralls to serve the elite. But the Old Ones demand blood."

Malvar squeezed Ulf's tortured shoulder till he nearly buckled. "So we must give it to them."

"*Ja*, my lord Bloodaxe," Ulf said, slurring his words through broken teeth.

"Stand the watch here with the others while I prepare to place my foot on the neck of my enemies," Malvar ordered. "The fools of Hardanger intended these fires as a means of safety, lit to warn of intruders. Instead, the flames will celebrate my triumph. Once I have subjugated this fjord, I will light the inmost signal fire. It will begin the chain of flame from the inside out instead of the outside in. The fjord will blaze like a shower of stars from the deepest cove to this base on Tysnes, and all will know a new power has arisen in Hardanger."

"*Ja*, my lord," the former *jarl* said woodenly.

"Make that Your Highness," Malvar said. "Even a fool like King Olav will have no choice but to meet me with his own forces, which we will handily defeat. When I am king, I will make a soup bowl of the old fool's skull. And make no mistake. I will be king. You may as well acknowledge it now."

Ulf bent in a stiff bow. "Majesty."

Malvar patted his shoulder again for the pleasure of seeing the man wince. It had been dislocated so badly and so often it would never be right again.

"Carry on, Ulf Skallagrimsson. Guard my victory light well. It will be the last to burn, so it must be the most glorious."

Malvar headed down the path toward the longhouse he'd appropriated for his use. He'd already decided he'd make Ulf his first sacrifice to the Old Ones once the ancient spirits gave him this victory. But he'd miss the *jarl*.

He'd grown to enjoy his screams.

❧

"Ulf Skallagrimsson," Katla repeated in a whisper from their place of concealment, downwind from the group of four guards surrounding the signal fire.

She and Finn had tied up the *faering* on the far side of the island and spent the better part of the day spying on the doings of the men occupying Katla's farmstead. Once night fell, they hiked up to see if they could free Haukon. So far, he was too well guarded, but men had to sleep sometime, and Bloodaxe's men had a well-fed look that leads to nodding heads during the dark watches.

All but the one Bloodaxe called Skallagrimsson. It was difficult to make out the man's features, but when he turned his head, his profile was so similar to Brandr's, Katla's breath caught in her throat. "Do you suppose that really could be—"

"Brandr's father," Finn finished for her. "*Ja*, it must be. And he's betrayed us all by the sounds of it."

Katla's chest constricted. This would wound Brandr more than thinking his father was dead. She felt her husband's mind on the fringes of hers, questioning, angry, but she kept the mental wall between them firmly in place. Whatever Brandr was doing, he didn't need the added burden of knowing the details of the dangers she ran for the sake of her youngest brother.

She and Finn crept closer to the edge of the forest and settled to watch the watchers. Once, Skallagrimsson climbed the woodpile with a dipper of water from the bucket at its base and gave Haukon a drink. The others merely stood or hunkered at their respective corners of the man-high pile.

When Brandr's father clambered back down, he took his place on the fourth corner, on guard despite his bowed back and uneven shoulders.

The next time the breeze set the pines around them whispering, Finn nocked an arrow on the string and drew the fletching back to his ear. But before he could loose the first silent shaft, Ulf Skallagrimsson was on the move again, ambling over to the guard on his right. The *jarl* drew close to the man, grasped the fellow's own dagger, and made a quick, upward stabbing motion. The guard's knees crumpled, but Ulf caught him and let him sink silently to the ground, unseen by the other watchmen, owing to the height of the woodpile and its sharp corners.

Katla put a hand to Finn's bow arm, and he lowered the arrow tip. They watched in stunned silence as Ulf did the job of dispatching the other guards for them, one by one. Then dagger still drawn, Brandr's father started to climb up woodpile toward Haukon.

"Stay your hand, Skallagrimsson," Finn ordered as he stepped into the clearing with bow drawn. "Else I'll split your gizzard."

Chapter 35

"LET ME SPELL YOU AT THE STEERING OAR," HARALD SAID to Brandr, deep into the second watch of the night.

The dragonship's sail billowed out like a pigeon's breast as the vessel sliced cleanly through the smooth water of the fjord. Orlin, Ragnar, and the twins were taking advantage of the favorable sailing weather to snatch a few hours sleep, curled up in *hudfats* in the narrow craft. Later, when the tide changed, they'd have to row, but for now, the *Jarl* of Jondal's ship made fair speed toward Tysnes Island.

"You need rest." Harald insisted.

Brandr sighed. When his friend set his feet, he would not be moved.

"I don't think I can sleep." But he stood in any case and let his friend take the heavy arm of the tiller in his beefy hands.

"You worry for your woman," Harald guessed.

Brandr nodded. *Among other things.*

He feared he'd seen his brother for the last time in this life. He feared the weapon he pinned all his hopes on wouldn't work, since they hadn't been able to test the mixture. He feared the destruction of everything he held dear.

But most of all, he feared for his stubborn, willful wife.

Why did she not Send her thoughts to him? Why did she ignore him when he broadcast his to the four winds? Surely she realized he knew she'd sailed away to Tysnes with Finn on a fool's errand. Hilde had already told him all. Katla's silence wasn't keeping any secrets from him.

The cold, dark possibility she was dead stabbed his heart, but he shoved it away. Surely he'd know if she was. He'd feel her absence in the very air around him. His body would refuse to keep breathing in a world where she did not.

"You sure we shouldn't have strapped more shields to the sides of the ship?" Harald's voice pulled him back into the moment. "Might have made it seem as if there are more of us aboard."

"It wouldn't make that much difference." He hadn't even told Arn he was taking his ship. He couldn't very well add to that misdeed by depleting his brother's armory for the sake of appearances.

"Twenty-five ships we're sailing into, eh?" Harald's voice cut through the wind soughing through the rigging and the steady shush of water against the hull.

"*Ja*," Brandr admitted. "Maybe more."

"Well, that gives us the advantage, then," Harald said.

"How do you figure?"

"When they see us coming, at least half of them will die laughing." Harald smacked his knee and threw back his head in a guffaw that echoed off the rocky sides of the fjord.

Brandr laughed with his friend.

May as well let Death know they were coming to meet Him unafraid.

❧

"Who might you be?" Ulf asked, stopping his ascent of the woodpile but not lowering his dagger.

Katla pushed out of the overgrowth behind Finn. "We're the owners of this farmstead."

"Stay back, Katla," Finn ordered. "We'll ask the questions here, traitor. Step away from our brother."

"I'm trying to help the lad."

"Like you helped your friends?" Katla asked.

Ulf spat on the ground. "They weren't my friends. I know what it is to be bound against your will. I wouldn't suffer them to treat a dog so. This is the first chance I've had to free the lad."

The sound of men tramping through the woods, swearing and breaking off bracken, wafted up to the top of the hill.

Ulf swore. "It's later than I thought. The watch is being relieved. They'll be here in no time. If you want me to free your brother, lower your bow, Tysnesman."

"Do it, Finn," Katla said.

With reluctance, he replaced the arrow in his quiver and slung the bow over his shoulder. Then he ran and climbed the woodpile to help Ulf bring Haukon down.

Katla was right behind him. "Easy," she cautioned. "He may be injured more than we can tell here."

The men's voices were nearer now.

"He'll be injured, all right, if you don't leave now," Ulf said. "Do you have a boat?"

"Hush, Katla," Finn said as he lifted Haukon in his

arms. The lad's head lolled, but Katla heard him catch a snuffling breath. "Don't tell him anything. He can't be trusted."

"If you do have means off this island," Ulf said, ignoring Finn, "I advise you to make for it and don't look back."

"You could come with us," Katla said.

"Are you mad?" Finn hissed and headed for the path in the woods where they'd hidden before.

"But he's Brandr's father."

Ulf's hand snaked out and grabbed her forearm. "How do you know my son?"

"Brandr is my husband," she said.

"You lie. He's in Byzantium."

"He's returned. And he's leading the defense of Hardanger. Something you should have done, old man."

"Enough, Katla," Finn said as he ducked into the thick forest bearing Haukon. "We must go now."

"He's right," Ulf said, releasing her arm. "Go. I'll see about a diversion to cover your escape."

Katla hesitated. Traitor or not, the man was Brandr's father. "Follow that path down to the water," she whispered. "We'll wait for you if we can."

An ugly smile spread across Ulf's tortured face. "I can see why he likes you. Now, get you gone, girl."

The sounds of the approaching guards were nearer now. Fear made her wing-footed. Katla flew across the clearing and disappeared into the thick undergrowth. She started to follow Finn down the path, but angry shouts behind her made her look over her shoulder.

Ulf knelt at a corner of the man-high stack of wood, sparks flying as he tried to ignite the tinder. In a sudden whoosh, the flame caught on the dry wood, spread through the rotten interior of the pile, and blazed out the top to lick at the stars.

Ulf Skallagrimsson dumped all four buckets of water on the ground so there'd be no way to douse the signal fire. Then laboriously, Brandr's father rose and cast a death's-head grin toward the place where Katla and Finn had fled, before he began to limp away from the inferno, heading in a different direction.

He's covering our retreat, Katla realized.

"Who is?" She'd lost her strict discipline, and Brandr's question flooded over her mental wall.

Before she could regain control, she felt her mind's images winging to her husband. She let them fly. She had enough to deal with without trying to shield her thoughts from Brandr any longer.

Four new guards poured into the clearing. One shouted for Ulf to halt, and when he didn't, the man raised his bow and planted a shaft in Ulf's lower back. He plummeted face-first to the dirt and didn't move.

Katla clamped a hand over her mouth to keep from crying out.

The men found their dead comrades and the empty buckets. They beat on the flames with their cloaks, but it was too late. The blaze leaped higher. The fire would burn hot till all the wood was consumed, and then it would smolder for days.

"We have to tell the Bloodaxe," one shouted.

"I'm not going to be the bearer of this news," said another.

"At least we killed the man who did it," growled a third.

"Bloodaxe's temper won't improve with waiting," said the one who'd actually loosed the shaft that dropped Ulf to the ground. He turned to lead the way back toward Katla's longhouse. "Come, you spineless old women. See if you can find where you left your manhood on the way down the hill."

When they'd been gone for the space of ten heart-beats, Katla crept back out of hiding and ran to Ulf. The long shaft of the arrow stuck out of his back.

"Do you yet live?" she asked in a whisper.

With effort, he raised himself to his hands and knees. "*Ja*, girl. Why are you still here? Fly while you can."

"Not without you." She helped him rise to his feet. "Can you walk?"

"Not far." He spat a gob of blood and reached around and broke the shaft of the arrow off close to his skin.

"Why did you do that?" Katla demanded as she propped one of his arms over her shoulders. "It'll be even harder to get out now."

"'Tis not coming out, and we both know it," Ulf said, not bothering to stifle the groan that followed. "I'll not stir a step unless you promise to leave me if they return or if we are followed."

Katla tried to move him, but it was like shoving a boulder. There was no give to the man.

"All right, I promise," she said. "Now come."

"'Tis hopeless."

"No, it's not. Look."

On the dark shadow of the mainland, an answering signal fire burned brightly. As they watched, another farther in the fjord blazed to life. And another.

Pinpoints of promise, they called the folk of Hardanger to honor their oaths to meet a common threat.

Katla looked up at her husband's father. "There is always hope."

❦

"To the ships!" Malvar roared when the guards reported that their captive had been freed and the signal fire had somehow been lit. Even now, the flame on Tysnes Island's high point was being answered by other fires on both steep sides of Hardanger Fjord. "Move!"

He gave one who didn't scramble away fast enough a vicious kick. "Before I order you roasted over that flame."

His men poured out of the longhouse in a near stampede and made for their waiting ships in the cove. They would have to row to clear the narrow mouth of the inlet. And after that, the tide was against them.

Once Malvar's flagship waddled into the main channel of the fjord, he saw the sky to the East was lightened by dozens of signal fires winking on one by one. He gripped the gunwale by the long neck of the prow so hard his nails bled. His advance guard had failed to disable or secure the system of signal flares.

His attack had lost the element of surprise.

No matter. He still had the weight of a superior force behind him. Even the smallest ship in his flotilla bore two-dozen warriors. There were fifty shields affixed to each side of his ship, one hundred strong backs bending in concert to row his *drakkar* into the fjord.

Wind sang in the rigging. Death rode on his shoulder. Malvar was proud to be the one bringing it.

❧

The zing of an arrow in the dark. A man's guttural cry. The figure was shadowy on the far side of a towering fire, but Brandr saw him go down in the images Katla Sent to him. He felt her distress as if it were his own. She crept forward.

"No, girl," he mumbled in his sleep. He drifted up to full consciousness and back down again, unsure whether he was dreaming or waking. He smelled the pitch-soaked pine blaze and recoiled from its heat as she moved around it. He'd never had such a vivid dream, and even as he lay in his *hudfat*, heart pounding and fully awake now, disjointed images continued to scroll across his mind.

Her white hand showed stark against the man's dark shoulder. The fletching on the arrow sticking out of his back was so vivid Brandr could see where the feather's barbules had separated from one another. The man turned his head.

"Father." Brandr sat upright.

Harald still manned the steering oar. His other friends still slept. The wind had lessened, but they were making good progress toward the mouth of the fjord.

And if his dream...or vision—he was unsure what to name it—was true, Ulf Skallagrimsson was still alive.

"Brandr, look." Harald pointed off the starboard bow.

A signal fire was burning. An answering blaze flared to life on the opposite side of the waterway.

"They're all lit," Harald said. "All the way to the sea."

And the people who lit those fires were preparing to join Brandr and his men. If there was enough time, the fighting ships might form up into a force sufficient to make a stand on the narrow waters of Hardanger.

Then between one breath and the next, the sail on Brandr's ship went slack. The wind died, and the waters that had been surging out of the fjord, rushing to join the sea, now pushed the defender's *drakkar* back.

"We've lost the tide," he said. Momentum would swing around to the force heading into Hardanger now. "Wake up, men. It's time to row."

Chapter 36

"HAUKON, ARE YOU INJURED?" KATLA CALLED DOWN to the *faering*.

"No, not so much," his voice rose, thready and weak, from the bottom of the boat. "Just feel like I lost a dozen fights and drank far too much mead."

"Katla, what are you thinking, dragging that traitor along?" Finn demanded when he noticed she had Ulf in tow at the water's edge.

Haukon lay sprawled in the bottom of the boat, but he was conscious and smiled weakly at her as she helped Brandr's father into the bobbing *faering*.

"All the time I was bound, this man was ever kind to me when the others weren't looking," Haukon said. "It's all right, Finn."

"No, it's not all right." He untied the line that moored the craft to land and pushed away from the island with an oar. "He'll lead them right to us."

Katla bristled as she ignored her brother's objections and hustled Ulf into the prow of the *faering*. Finn hadn't seen all Ulf had done at the top of the hill. With a touch on her forearm, Brandr's father stopped her from arguing.

"Rest easy, girl. He's right. I was a traitor, but Bloodaxe has bigger plans than following me," Ulf said with a wheeze. "Look."

Katla peered over Finn's shoulder to where Ulf pointed. Once Finn glanced that way, he settled on the bench to use both oars to keep the *faering* in the deep shadow of the land. Their only safety lay in going unnoticed.

A flotilla of at least thirty ships passed by on their way into the mouth of Hardanger Fjord. By the time the last one sailed by, the tide and prevailing winds had turned, and the invaders oars were shipped. Their square sails billowed out in the fading night.

"*Oh, Brandr, he's coming.*"

"*I know, love. I see the signal fires. Is that your doing?*"

"*No. It was your father's. He's alive.*"

Katla felt Brandr's conflicting waves of joy and wariness tumbling in her chest.

"*But he's wounded.*" Brandr's words were clipped. "*How bad is it?*"

Katla didn't wonder how he knew that. Evidently *inn matki munr* was a deeper bond than she'd ever imagined. It was as if they shared one soul. Everything she knew or experienced or felt, he did too.

Ulf coughed violently, and when he pulled his hand away from his mouth, Katla saw it was black with blood.

"*His wound is bad enough.*" Even if she could transport him to her longhouse and use the herbs she'd gathered for doctoring her people, she doubted she could save him.

"*Keep him alive for me.*"

"I'll try. Keep yourself alive for me."

He chuckled softly. The sound tickled her mind. *"I'll try too."*

Neither of them would be able to deliver on their promises, and they both knew it. Despair roiled in her gut.

"Brandr, I'm sorry I shut you out of my mind. Forgive me."

"That's all right, princess. I may decide to do the same before long."

"No." She scrunched her eyes tight. *"I want to be with you. Whatever happens."*

"And whatever happens, I am always with you, Katla. I want you to remember that. Good-bye, love."

When the link between them was severed, Katla gasped. Even when she held him at bay, she'd always been able to sense his presence, pressing against the mental barrier she'd erected. Now there was nothing.

She buried her face in her hands and wept.

～

Morning dawned with a sky made for weeping. The clouds were the yellowish purple of a week-old bruise. A few ships had joined Brandr's in the night, but not nearly as many or as heavily loaded with warriors as he'd hoped.

As soon as it was light, he ordered Harald to signal them with flags to stay well behind him. Mist rising from the water made it difficult to spot the other vessels. Brandr caught only glimpses of empty masts or the occasional long-necked prows jutting above the carpet of fog. Rowers grunted in concert with each long stroke.

"May as well see if this thing will work," Brandr said and positioned himself before the mast, standing on two metal casks brimming with the volatile elements of Greek fire. He hefted the long metal tube where the two compounds would join and aimed it far off the port bow. "Open the valves."

The twins turned the wheel-shaped fittings, and the tube warmed under Brandr's touch as the two mixtures were joined. But instead of shooting out the open end of the tube in a snaking blaze of unquenchable flame, sludge oozed from the tip, sparking and fizzling till it slipped under the waves with a disappointing sizzle.

"That's not how I remember Greek fire working in the South," Harald said.

"We have all the ingredients," Brandr growled in frustration.

"Must not be the right amounts of each," Orlin observed somberly.

Brandr sank down on his haunches. Orlin was right. It was a touchy concoction at the best of times, and he'd been rushed. The mixture was out of balance somehow, and there hadn't been time to work with it till it was right.

In the distance, the faint squares of a long row of sails began to take shape in the morning haze. Bloodaxe was coming with the wind at his back.

"What do you want to do?" Harald asked.

Brandr hung his head for a moment and thought. "Signal the others to bleed off and wait near land. Use only enough oar to hold our position." Brandr walked as far forward as he could and stared at his approaching foe. "We'll let him come to us. If I tell you to abandon ship, grab an oar to keep you afloat, and go. No argument."

"And then?"

"Then we'll see what a fire mage can actually do."

❧

Malvar stood in the prow of his ship, scanning the horizon for any signs of organized resistance. The mist obscured his vision, but it seemed the signal fires hadn't called down the warriors of Hardanger to meet him. The only thing out of the ordinary was the way the mist piled up in one place, dead center in front of Malvar's ship.

"What's that?" one of his men asked, a superstitious tremor in his voice.

Out of the watery mists, a fierce dragonhead rose, and behind it, as if he were mounted on the great wooden beast, a single man wreathed in clouds lying on the water. Silently, he stood, unmoving and unflinching, as Malvar's flotilla drew nearer.

The mist parted, curling upward like disembodied souls straining skyward, and a blue glow was visible, growing between the man's upraised palms. It bloomed as big as a head of cabbage and then divided into two, so the man held a glowing orb in each hand.

"Sorcery," someone whispered.

"A fire mage," said another. "He holds the flame and isn't burned."

"Who is this that he thinks to dazzle us with cheap tricks and false magick? The Old Ones are the only power we revere," Malvar roared. "Someone put an arrow down his gullet. He'll bleed like the rest of us."

But before anyone could obey him, the man hurled the ball of flame to the base of Malvar's mast. The sail caught in a searing moment. The second ball of blue fire burst on the deck of Bloodaxe's flankship, sending the crew into a panicked rout.

"Archers!" Bloodaxe bellowed. "Bring that man down."

❧

"Shields up," Harald shouted from the tiller.

Brandr's crew let their oars drift in the oar ports while they hunkered beneath their round discs of hardened leather. Brandr flattened himself to the dragon's neck, sheltering under the beast's horny head. He was glad Arn had spared no expense for this figurehead, choosing a design with a flared horizontal crest at the base of its skull that acted as a shield for Brandr now.

From this place of relative safety, he commanded the existing flames on his enemy's ships with a slow wave of his arm. Tongues of fire leaped from one ship to the next, dancing along the rigging and dropping burning ash on the panicked crews beneath. The long line of attackers broke as the outer ships sheared off, trying to distance themselves from their burning cohorts. Brandr arced fire from his palms to their retreating sterns.

The air was filled with screams and the hollow song fire always sang when it fed, licking at the pitch-soaked hulls with relish. The fjord around the attacker's ships boiled with the flailing of drowning men as they fled the flames for a watery grave. Brandr recognized one of them as Albrikt Gormson.

But Bloodaxe's burning flagship continued to

advance on Brandr's. While panic reigned on the other ships, a bucket brigade had formed on this one and was dousing the flames with methodical efficiency. Growling curses carried across the water as Bloodaxe drove his men to keep rowing.

Brandr glanced back at his friends. "He means to ram us. Time to abandon ship."

Without a word of dissent, Ragnar, Orlin, Torvald, and Torsten grasped their oars with both hands and leaped into the water.

"You too, Harald." Brandr clambered back to the stern where his friend still sat.

"Can't swim."

"You'll never learn any younger," Brandr said as he broke off the steering arm of the tiller, shoved it into his friend's hands, and pushed Harald over the gunwale into the frothing water.

Harald surfaced, sputtering and complaining, but he was afloat.

Brandr turned to face Bloodaxe's dragonship bearing down on him. His Greek fire mixture didn't work as he'd planned, but he was certain it would burn. He gathered all his concentration and drew a deep breath. The shouts and chaos faded around him. Flame grew between his palms, beautiful in its purity, terrible in its destructive power.

He focused all his strength, and as the neck of Bloodaxe's *drakkar* smashed Brandr's dragonhead to kindling, he hurled the hottest ball of fire he could produce into the prow of his own ship.

The Greek fire machine erupted into a blazing inferno that scorched the sky.

After Bloodaxe's horde left her steading, Katla and Finn sailed around the island and cautiously nosed into the sheltered cove. Her people who'd survived the invasion were overjoyed to see her. She ordered all their thrall collars struck, because she wanted to convince them Bloodaxe wouldn't be returning. He was going to meet her husband in battle, and Brandr Ulfson was more than his match.

Even if she wasn't entirely convinced herself—after seeing Bloodaxe's massive flotilla of ships—she had to present a brave face. But that didn't stop her from having Finn organize a party of archers to guard the cove against returning enemies.

Then she asked for help moving Ulf Skallagrimsson into her old chamber. At first her people balked, since they'd seen him with Bloodaxe, but when she told them he'd been responsible for lighting the signal fire, and the defense of the fjord was underway because of it, they grudgingly accepted him.

It was a small matter. He was dying, at any rate.

When Ulf refused to let her try to remove the arrowhead, she was relieved. The shaft had sunk beneath his skin, and going after it was beyond her doctoring skills. So she cleaned and dressed his wound and made him lie down in her own bed. She gave him willow bark tea for pain until he demanded mead instead.

She was delivering his fourth horn of sweet oblivion when the flashes of a vision came. Katla's knees gave way, and she sank to the flagstone floor of her chamber on Tysnes.

Fire scorched through her mind. Ships aflame. Men leaping into the sea, their clothing alight with blazing tongues. Smoke obscured her sight.

A blazing orange tunnel encompassed her, held at bay by a pair of outstretched hands.

Brandr's hands.

As he passed through the conflagration, Katla cowered on the cold flagstones, seared by the heat in his Sending. The acrid scent of burning wood, flesh, and pitch made her belly heave.

A man whose beard and hair were aflame hurled himself toward her, and she was plunged into the frigid water of the fjord. The link between her and Brandr was sliced in two as completely as if someone had taken an axe to it.

Shaken and gasping, Katla came to herself in her bedchamber, spilled mead soaking her hem and filling in the cracks between the flagstones.

Old Gerte's grandmother had been linked with her grandfather by the chains of *inn matki munr* while he drowned. If Brandr was underwater, he must have been unaware of it, for she received nothing more from him.

She wept in silence. She couldn't keen and wail. She was too empty to do anything but let her soul seep from her eyes.

‿◈⁀

Brandr tumbled into the sea, tangled up with Bloodaxe, each of them grappling for the other's throat. Water doused the man's flaming head, but Brandr saw Bloodaxe's lips were gone, his flesh pulled back to reveal his teeth clenched in a death's-head grin.

Bloodaxe was a dead man, but he wasn't satisfied to travel to *Hel*'s cold hall without the man who'd sent him there in tow. A thumb pressed against Brandr's throat. He wrapped his arms around Bloodaxe and squeezed for all he was worth. Dark spots bloomed before his eyes, but Brandr held on. Finally, Bloodaxe released his last pent-up breath in an explosion of bubbles.

Brandr brought his feet up and kicked himself away from his drowning enemy. Bloodaxe struggled feebly for another few heartbeats and then floated away in the relaxation of death.

A single bubble of air escaped Brandr's nostril and tickled his cheek. Overhead, the surface of the water blazed with his Greek fire. Beneath him, the broken back of Arn's dragonship sank into the blue depths. Lungs burning for a breath, he kicked toward the surface.

Even a fire mage couldn't put out the Greek fire till it had exhausted all its fuel, but he could move it if he could summon the concentration. He splayed his fingers toward the roof of flame and willed it to part above him.

A small oval of open water appeared and then shrank back. Brandr continued to kick toward the surface, trying to marshal his remaining power. Death by fire or death by drowning was still death. If he couldn't open and maintain a space in the oily surface, he was going to die either way.

Chapter 37

KATLA SAT BY ULF SKALLAGRIMSSON'S BEDSIDE through the dark watches of the night as his life wheezed out of him. He'd drunk enough mead to send him into a stupor so deep he should have been insensible, but Ulf balanced on the cusp between life and death, fighting for each breath.

"Be at peace," she told him. If he must suffer a straw death, she wished it would at least be an easy one.

"No, I must wait for Brandr," he said, his voice a wisp of sound.

Katla turned her face away. She couldn't let his father see her hopelessness.

"He's coming, girl. I feel it."

Katla wished she did. She hadn't felt anything since that horrific vision. It was as if her heart had gone numb. Like a limb that had gone to sleep, the muscle in her chest felt like a heavy void, taking up space inside her but only as dead weight.

Someone was shouting in the distance, and Katla gave herself a small shake.

"I'll be right back," she said to Ulf.

"Hurry."

She pushed into the main long hall and found all her people stirring. The double doors at the far end of the longhouse swung open and let in the dawn. And her brother.

"Brandr Ulfson," Finn shouted, slightly winded from sprinting up the hill from the wharf. "He's returned. Malvar Bloodaxe is dead, and his forces routed!"

Katla's chest was full of prickles, as if the blood only then began rushing back into her numb heart. She ran down the center of the long hall and out into the pearly light. Brandr and his friends were making their way up the winding path. She drank in the sight of his golden head.

Her people spilled out of the longhouse behind her. Finn was shouting out details of the sea battle and the way Bloodaxe's force had dissolved before Brandr's unconventional use of a southern weapon that incinerated the lot of them.

Someone started up the chant: *"Herra af eldur!"*
Lord of Fire.

Brandr topped the last rise and stopped when he saw her. The way her insides sizzled at the sight of him, she could well believe he was the lord of flames.

"My very own ice princess."

The rumbling timber of his voice reverberated in her head, and she heard his smile in the warm sound.

"If I was ice, you have melted me, my love," she Sent back to him and lifted her skirts so she could run unimpeded into his arms.

~∽~

Ulf was still alive when Katla led Brandr back to his bed. Her husband's sadness pressed on her chest, as if it were her own grief.

"Bloodaxe?" Ulf asked between gasps.

"Dead," Brandr affirmed.

Ulf's eyes closed in satisfaction, and he nodded. Then he reopened his eyes to fix Brandr with a steady gaze. "Does your brother yet live?"

"I left him alive, but—"

"But I will probably see him again before you do. Is that long face you're wearing for your brother or for me?"

"Both." Brandr swallowed hard, and Katla gripped his hand tightly to offer her support.

"In my life, I have done many terrible things. But when I look at you, I see one thing that turned out right." Ulf's chest rose in a shuddering gasp. "Despite my best efforts to bend you otherwise." His blood-stained mouth twitched in a half smile. "So you see, I do not mind to die now. I am joined to my people, knowing I leave a worthy *jarl* in Jondal. Rule long, son." He reached out a quavering hand. "Rule well."

❦

Ulf would not have liked to be buried, Brandr knew. So, he was sent to his gods in the old way, in a small soul boat built specially to become his floating pyre. Once the craft cleared the mouth of the inlet, Brandr arced a blue flame to it from the shoreline and watched it burn until the last charred spars sank beneath the waves.

He put an arm around Katla's waist and drew her close. "We need to go home, I'm thinking."

"I'm already packed."

"What? I won't have to abduct you this time?"

"No. I can't wait to see Linnea again. I'm sure she'll have grown so while we've been gone, we'll scarcely know her," Katla said. "Besides, Finn has things well in hand here. The people are rebuilding. Everyone knows what they need to do without me goading them along."

Brandr kissed her temple. "Don't fret, woman. You still have me to goad."

"And don't you forget it." She smacked his chest playfully. He caught up her hand and pressed a kiss in her palm. Heat bloomed between them.

"But Finn will want to come with us for this trip. He left Inga at Jondal, and I'm thinking we'll have a wedding before they sail back to Tysnes."

Brandr nodded. "A good beginning."

She stood on tiptoe and kissed him, reveling in the contentment she felt rolling off him. It was like the smell of fresh, warm bread, or the comfortable texture of well-worn linen on her skin.

"*Ja.* Finn and Inga had a rough beginning. I only hope they find the mighty passion as we did," she said. "Then whatever befalls them, they'll have a good ending too."

Here's a sneak peek at

SINS OF THE HIGHLANDER

by Connie Mason with Mia Marlowe

THE PEAT FIRE HAD BURNED OUT AND THE ASH GONE gray, but Rob MacLaren didn't feel the least bit cold. Not while his hot-blooded woman writhed under him. Their breaths mingled in the frosty air of the bedchamber. Fiona tilted her hips, welcoming him deeper, and he bit the inside of his cheek to keep from emptying himself into her.

It was too soon.

He never wanted it to end, this joining, this loss of himself in the woman he adored.

Rob raised himself up on his arms and gazed down at her. The candles had burned down to nubs but still flickered enough to cast her in soft light. He could see his wife clearly. Her strawberry nipples peaked, with cold or arousal he couldn't be sure, but he loved looking at them just the same.

"What are ye doing, daftie man? 'Tis too cold!" Fiona raised herself up and clung to him for warmth.

"That's what ye get when ye marry a man on Christmas Day—a cold bridal night." He gently pushed her back down, and she sank into the feather tick.

"It doesna have to be cold." Her skin rippled with goose-flesh. "Come back under the covers, love."

"I canna. I need to see the lass I wed," he said. "I want to watch ye melt for me, to see your face when ye make that wee kitten noise just afore ye come."

"Wee kitten noise, is it?" She shook with laughter. "Have a care, husband, lest I bare my claws."

She raked her nails across his chest, and the sensation made his balls clench.

He lowered himself and kissed her, devouring her lips and chasing her tongue. He withdrew for a heartbeat for the sheer joy of sliding slowly back into her slick wetness. Then he raised himself again and reached between them to stroke her over the edge.

"Oh, Rob." Her inner walls clenched around him, and he felt the soft tremor that signaled the start of her release. "When ye do that, I don't care a fig if it's so cold I catch my death…my death…my death…"

Her voice echoed round the chamber and faded into the distant thatch overhead.

Rob jerked awake.

He wasn't in his bridal bedchamber. He was lying on stone-hard ground with a stone-hard cock still primed to make love to the woman in his dream. Stars wheeled above him in a frigid sky. His band of men snored nearby.

And the fact that Fiona was dead slammed into him afresh.

He'd married her two years ago at Christmas, and she'd been gone by Epiphany. Twelve days, he'd been a husband. Only twelve.

And now a night didn't pass without his wife visiting him as some phantom, sometimes tender, sometimes terrifying. She lived in his dreams, but always he was powerless to hold her to earth.

She was so vibrant, so real by night, he suffered all the more in the waking world with the knowledge that he'd not find her there.

One of the men in the clearing let out a loud snore and mumbled in his sleep. It was hours till dawn, and even more till Rob could accomplish what he intended in the coming day. But he would not seek sleep.

He couldn't bear to lose Fiona again so soon.

～✦～

Rob narrowed his gaze at the stone kirk across the glen. The bagpipes' celebratory tune ended with an off-key wheeze. He and his men, concealed on the edge of the forest, had watched the bridal procession and the arrival of the groom's party. Now he heard nothing from the kirk. The only sound was the harsh cry of a jay from the branches above him.

The ceremony must have been beginning in earnest. Rob snorted, his breath like a curl of dragon smoke in the chilly air.

"'Tis time, Hamish."

"I wish ye'd reconsider." His friend shook his head, his scruff of red beard making him look like an alarmed hedgehog. Hamish never let his beard grow beyond the stubble stage. A metal worker couldn't chance much facial hair. Even his eyebrows were habitually singed off. "If ye go through with this, folk will say ye're...that ye're—"

"Mad? They say that already." Rob mounted his

black stallion. The beast sensed his agitation and pawed the dirt, restive and spoiling for action. "I see no other path before me. Now will ye help me or no?"

"Aye, Rob, ye've no need to ask, but—"

"Then get the men ready to ride. I hope to be in a wee bit of a hurry when next ye see me." He shot his friend a mirthless grin and spurred his mount into a gallop across the glen.

It was possible the next time Hamish saw him, Rob might be in no hurry at all.

He could very well be dead.

❧

The smell of incense was so cloying, Elspeth Stewart feared she might faint dead away. But a bride must stand before the altar.

She drew a shallow breath and swallowed hard. That was better. As the priest droned on, she sneaked a glance from under her lashes at the man who would be her husband.

Lachlan Drummond.

Tall and commanding in his dress plaid, he wasn't altogether unpleasing. His face was tanned, and the lines at the corners of his eyes suggested he'd squinted into countless northern suns. Those lines didn't trouble her. They proved the laird was a man of action, not like the dainty fops who visited from the English court from time to time.

No, it was the deep grooves between his brows and the hard set of his mouth that gave her pause.

"Dinna fret yerself," her mother had assured her

when she complained that she didn't know her betrothed well enough to even speak to him if she met him in Queen Mary's court. "An arranged match is a safe match. Yer father has chosen the Drummond for ye, and ye'll do well to bide by his wishes."

The queen had approved too. She'd angered so many of the nobles with her other policies, she didn't dare gainsay two of them on something as inconsequential as the marriage of one of her ladies-in-waiting.

Inconsequential to everyone but me, Elspeth fumed.

An exchange of breeding cattle, a grant of grazing rights, a promise of fealty between their clans; that was really all that was being solemnized now. It was certainly no marriage as she'd ever imagined it.

Or Seen it. Elspeth was gifted with a bit of the Sight, and never in all her prescient dreams had she seen this match on her horizon.

This loveless ceremony was as far removed from the tales of courtly devotion in her precious little book of sonnets as the distant moon.

Yet when the priest asked Lachlan Drummond to pledge his faith to her, his voice was strong, the tone pleasing. He even sent her a quick private smile.

Elspeth jerked her gaze back to her folded hands. Her cheeks burned as if she had a fever.

She wondered if her mother was right.

"Passion," Morag Stewart had said, "is a dish that flares hot, but then goes cold as a tomb often as not. An arranged match is like a cauldron set to simmer over a low fire. A nourishing broth heated evenly warms a body from the inside out."

Elspeth wasn't sure how she could do the things

her mother said her husband would expect of her. Bizarrely intimate things. Of course, she'd seen horses mate, and dogs too, but she never suspected people did something as…primitive as the mere beasts.

And now she'd have to do it with a man she barely knew.

Silence jerked her back from her musings. The priest had asked her a question and was waiting for a reply. She blinked stupidly at him. What had he said?

Suddenly the double doors of the nave shattered. A man on a large black horse was silhouetted in the opening for a heartbeat. Then he urged the stallion into the kirk and charged up the center aisle.

"Mad Rob!" she heard someone call out.

Half the horseman's face was painted with woad, and his cobalt eyes burned as brightly blue. With his dark hair flying and the fierce expression of a berserker on his features, he certainly looked mad.

"The MacLaren," shouted another.

Her bridegroom was silent, but a muscle worked furiously in his cheek.

Her father reached for the horse's bridle, but the MacLaren shouted a command, and the stallion reared, pawing the air. Then it lashed out with its hind hooves, and everyone scrambled out of reach of the slashing kicks.

Elspeth watched in disbelief as the man drew a long claymore from the shoulder baldric strapped to his back and laid the flat of the blade across Lachlan Drummond's chest. Riding a horse into the kirk was bad enough. Mad Rob had broken the sanctity of holy ground by drawing his weapon.

All the other men had laid their swords and dirks outside the doors, which now hung drunkenly from the hinges.

Elspeth half expected the Almighty to strike the blasphemer down with thunderbolts from the altar.

"Twitch so much as an eyelash, wee Lachlan, and I'll take yer head," Mad Rob said as pleasantly as if he'd offered Drummond a plate of warm scones.

Then he leaned down and scooped Elspeth up with his other arm and dropped her belly-first across his kilted lap.

She was too astonished to be afraid. All the air fled from her lungs with a whoosh. Her head and arms dangled on one side of the restive stallion, and her legs kicked on the other. She couldn't rail at the man, since she was busy fighting for breath, but she struggled to free herself from such an undignified position.

"Hold still, lass, lest my hand slips and I lop off a bit of your groom."

Now fear sliced into her. She froze and looked at Lachlan. The madman's blade had slid up to his chin. Her bridegroom hadn't taken his black-eyed gaze from Mad Rob's face.

"I'll be going now, Drummond," Rob said in the same reasonable tone a man might use to discuss cattle or the weather. "If ye've the stones for a fight, ye may collect yer bride at *Caisteal Dubh*. But dinna show your face till month's end. Come for her sooner or try to follow us now, and I might have to kill her."

Elspeth couldn't look up at her captor's face, but she heard a wicked smile in his voice.

Kill her reverberated in her mind.

And all she'd thought she'd lose when she woke this day was her maidenhead.

The madman wheeled the stallion around, and Elspeth hooked an elbow around his knee lest she fall as the kirk and the people in it ran together in a blur of colors. Her mother keened like a lost soul over the din of shouts. The stallion clattered back down the aisle and shot out into the crisp November air, making a beeline for the distant forest.

With every jarring stride, Elspeth's ribs took a pounding. Then she felt both the MacLaren's hands at her waist. He lifted her without slowing the stallion one jot, controlling the beast with his knees and will alone.

"Can ye ride astride?" he shouted.

"Aye." She threw one leg over the horse's neck and settled herself before him, matching his rocking movement to keep her seat. She dug her fingers into the horse's mane. Trying to leap off at this speed would mean a broken neck. There'd be another chance to escape later.

For she must escape. A month, even a night, with this madman would mean ruin.

Lachlan Drummond would surely come for her. He'd be obliged to, according to the contract between him and the House of Stewart. And her father and his men with him.

She twisted and glanced under MacLaren's arm. Men were milling before the church, not giving pursuit, clearly taking Mad Rob's threat to kill her seriously.

Once they reached the trees, a shout went up

behind them. Rob pulled the stallion to a stop. Elspeth gasped a shuddering breath as his arm around her waist tightened. They turned to see her bridegroom and her father mounting up to follow.

"Apparently, they hold your life less precious than your honor, lass," the MacLaren muttered. "Hamish! Tell the lads to lay the trails. Now ride."

A half-dozen other horsemen appeared from their places of concealment in the trees. They circled the small clearing, obliterating any betraying tracks, and then they all hied off in different directions to confuse Drummond's men and cover Mad Rob's escape.

Elspeth and her captor rode wildly over hill and down dale, eeling through copses of spindly trees. The MacLaren's horse was hill bred. Not as showy as the palfrey Elspeth had ridden to her wedding, but hardy and deep chested and apparently willing to run till it dropped if the man on its back demanded.

Shouts of discovery rose behind them. The men in pursuit must have split up, and someone followed their trail. Elspeth's heart nearly burst from her chest with hope.

"Hi-up!" Mad Rob bellowed at the stallion, and it leaped into a burst of speed as if being chased by a thousand demons but feared the man on its back even more.

The MacLaren leaned forward. Elspeth bent over the horse's neck, Mad Rob's hot breath searing her nape, and held on for her life. They dodged trees, leaped over fallen trunks, and splashed through a burn in full spate. The world ripped by her in a green blur.

Her pearl-studded snood peeled off as the wind

whipped past them. Her long brown hair uncoiled and fluttered behind her. She hoped it was flying in the MacLaren's face, but a quick glance back showed it waving over his shoulder like a banner.

When they reached a rise, Mad Rob paused long enough to look back. A dozen horsemen were in pursuit.

"Drummond is a better tracker than I credited him," he muttered.

Elspeth drew several gasping breaths, trying to still her pounding heart after their mad dash. She squinted at their followers but didn't see her father's dun mare in the pack.

"Your horse carries two," she said. "Surrender, and I'll convince them to spare you."

"Drummond wouldna know mercy if it bit him on the arse."

"Ye'll never outrun them."

"Then we'll go to ground."

An angry swarm of crossbow bolts buzzed around them. Mad Rob whipped the stallion's head around, and they plunged down the far side of the hill.

When they reached the bottom, he reined the horse to a slow trot along the base of the hillside.

Elspeth tried to wiggle free as soon as they slowed their pace.

"Hold still," he snarled. "Dinna try me, wench. I've nothing to lose."

She settled then, taking hope from shouts of the men following them. Their voices echoed from one rise to the next. The horses' hoofbeats on the far side of the hill sounded like approaching thunder.

Mad Rob seemed not to hear them. He just kept scanning the craggy slope. Then he turned the stallion's head back up the incline, making for an outcropping of dark granite.

"They're almost upon us!" Elspeth shouted. "Surrender and live."

He didn't slow his determined flight toward the rocks. Then when they almost dashed into them, Rob brought the stallion up so short it nearly sat on its haunches.

"Get ye behind the rock." He nearly threw her off the horse and leaped down behind her. He pushed her between a pair of cottage-sized boulders, leading the stallion behind him. "To the right."

There was a yawning hole in the hillside, a cave whose entrance was hidden by the rocks. Elspeth staggered into the darkness as the MacLaren and his mount followed. The ground was uneven beneath her feet.

The cave was cool and dark and ripe with must. She extended her hands before her lest she walk into a wall.

"How did ye know—?"

Mad Rob clamped a hand over her mouth and pulled her back against his chest. "Not a word if ye wish to keep breathing." His whisper tickled her ear.

She stood perfectly still, inhaling the scent of leather from his gloved hand. She heard his soft breathing and the stallion's trappings creaking as the horse shifted its weight. Then in the distance, she made out the tattoo of hoofbeats and muffled shouts as the men who were pursuing them overran their hiding place.

Then those sounds faded, and all she could hear was the pounding of her blood coursing through her veins. The heartbeat of the man standing behind her thudded against her spine. He relaxed his hold and removed his hand from her mouth.

She turned to face him and shouted out: "I'm here! Hel—"

His mouth descended upon hers and swallowed up her cry.

She'd been kissed sweetly before, stylized expressions of courtship during some of the dances favored by Queen Mary's court.

This kiss bore no resemblance to those. This was a ravishment, a demanding plunder of her mouth.

He stole her breath, but she was so surprised by the sudden invasion, she didn't think to pull away. She froze like a coney confronted by a fox.

He filled her with breath from his own body, warming her to her toes.

I should be revolted. I should be screaming to get away.

But then his mouth went suddenly soft and beguiling on hers. Elspeth had never imagined the like.

How strange, this shared breath, this mingling of souls.

Without conscious thought, her fingers curled around his collar. She received a flash of Sight. Not exactly a vision. More like a deep Knowing.

Rob MacLaren had a hole in his heart, a void nothing could fill.

He no longer seemed mad to her. Just empty. Her chest constricted in empathy.

An image forced itself into Elspeth's consciousness, creeping in softly but with determination. The willowy form of a woman with long coppery hair took shape in her mind, distant and hazy. Elspeth couldn't see her face. The woman turned and fled into the mist.

She sensed deep sadness in MacLaren, an ache that wouldn't be stilled. A loss for which there was no comfort.

He'd abducted her from the altar, but she couldn't feel anything for him but pity.

As the Sight faded, pain seared through her brain. It always did when she was touched by her gift, but it paled in comparison to the nameless hurt he bore. Elspeth reached up a tentative hand to comfort him, palming the cheek that wasn't covered with woad.

He wrapped an arm around her waist and tugged her closer. Her lips parted. His tongue swept in. Her belly clenched, and a warm glow settled between her legs.

He left her lips and began kissing her chin, her cheeks, her neck. "Ach! Ye're sweet, lass."

Pity dissipated like morning mist. Instead, little wisps of pleasure followed his mouth's path. The stubble of his beard grazed the tops of her breasts, and her nipples tightened almost painfully. She sucked her breath over her teeth to keep from crying out in pleasure and surprise when his palm covered her breast, the pressure sweet even through the stiff boning of her pink silk bodice.

She'd been sickened by the thought of submitting to Lachlan Drummond's intimate caress. Now her whole body thrummed with life. She tingled with awareness as Rob touched her.

She'd never understood how a maiden could allow herself to be ruined before. Unruly, unwelcome urges seared through her. The sensations were so unlike her, she wondered if they were somehow part of what she'd Seen of the copper-haired woman.

To her amazement, she ached to lie down beside this man. To feel his body cover hers. To give to him what Lachlan would have taken.

This was madness, but she couldn't bring herself to end it. With each kiss, his sadness lessened and her pleasure increased. She'd never dreamed she'd experience such astonishing delight.

Only a little longer, she told herself as bliss sparked across her skin. His kiss was like a draught of heady wine. The discomfort that usually accompanied the Sight was leaving, but her head still felt fuzzy. Was it clouding her judgment?

One kiss more. Then I'll stop.

She splayed her fingers across his chest. His muscles were like a brazen shield beneath his shirt and plaid. He growled with satisfaction. She smoothed her palms up to his shoulders and down his arms.

And encountered sticky wetness on the left side.

"You're bleeding," she whispered. One of the crossbow bolts must have found its mark.

He dipped his head and mumbled into the well between her breasts. "'Tis nothing."

It was enough to recall her to sanity. To serve Queen Mary, she must be either a pure maid or the wife of a nobleman. If she couldn't remain the first, she'd never be the last. She pulled away from him.

"Truly, 'tis naught but a scratch. Come, lass."

He folded her into his arms again and delivered a string of kisses along the curve of her jaw.

"No!" she said

When he tried to kiss her again, she delivered a ringing slap to his cheek. Reason flooded her mind again. Perhaps he was called "Mad Rob" because he could entice others to insanity. She jerked herself out of his arms.

"Now keep away from me," she ordered.

He chuckled mirthlessly. "Lass, I've killed dozens of men. Do ye really think ye can stop me from whatever I may decide to do with you?"

He took a step toward her, his eyes glittering fiercely in the dark.

Lord of the Black Isle

by Elaine Coffman

———— ❧ ————

A Warrior's Life…

Laird David Murray would give his life to pull his clan through this time of strife and conflict. With enemies both inside and outside his keep, he has never felt so alone and desperate. Until he meets a beautiful healer with uncanny knowledge from another time…

Meets a Healer's Heart…

Elisabeth Douglas was a doctor in her own time. Now she's the only one with the knowledge and skill to help Laird David save the lives of his family…

———— ❧ ————

"Coffman's writing is deft, capable, and evocative."—Publishers Weekly

"Full of action, danger, passion, and drama…A must-read for medieval and time-travel fans alike"—RT Book Reviews, ★★★★

"Delightfully infused with suspense, humor, heartache, an entertaining plot, well-drawn characters, and a wily ghost, this story is a keeper."—Romance Junkies

For more Elaine Coffman, visit:

www.sourcebooks.com

The Highlander's Prize
by Mary Wine

---- ❧ ----

Clarrisa of York has never needed a miracle more. Sent to Scotland's king to be his mistress, her deliverance arrives in the form of being kidnapped by a brusque Highland laird who's a bit too rough to be considered divine intervention. Except his rugged handsomeness and undeniable magnetism surely are magnificent...

Laird Broen MacNichols has accepted the challenge of capturing Clarrisa to make sure the king doesn't get the heir he needs to hold the throne. Broen knows more about royalty than he ever cared to, but Clarrisa, beautiful and intelligent, turns out to be much more of a challenge than he bargained for...

With rival lairds determined to steal Clarrisa from him and royal henchmen searching for her all over the Highlands, Broen is going to have to prove to this independent-minded lady that a Highlander always claims his prize...

---- ❧ ----

"[The characters] fight just as passionately as they love while intrigue abounds and readers turn the pages faster and faster!"—RT Book Reviews, ★★★★

For more Mary Wine books, visit:

True Highland Spirit

by Amanda Forester

— ❧ —

Seduction is a powerful weapon...

Morrigan McNab is a Highland lady, robbed of her birthright and with no choice but to fight alongside her brothers to protect their impoverished clan. When she encounters Sir Jacques Dragonet, she discovers her fiercest opponent...

Sir Jacques Dragonet is a Noble Knight of the Hospitaller Order, willing to give his life to defend Scotland from the English. He can't stop himself from admiring the beautiful Highland lass who wields her weapons as well as he can and endangers his heart even more than his life...

Now they're racing each other to find a priceless relic. No matter who wins this heated rivalry, both will lose unless they can find a way to share the spoils.

— ❧ —

"A masterful storyteller, Amanda Forester brings new excitement to Scottish medieval romance!"—Gerri Russell, award-winning author of *To Tempt a Knight*

For more Amanda Forester books, visit:

www.sourcebooks.com